Midnight Sun

Midnight Sun

LAWRENCE OSGOOD

GOOSE LANE

Edited by Laurel Boone.
Cover illustration by Gary Braasch/CORBIS; *Sunset over Pond*.
Cover design by Julie Scriver and Lisa Rousseau.
Book design by Lisa Rousseau.
Printed in Canada by Transcontinental.
10   9   8   7   6   5   4   3   2   1

Library and Archives Canada Cataloguing in Publication

Osgood, Lawrence
Midnight sun / Lawrence Osgood.

ISBN 0-86492-434-8
1. Inuit — Fiction. I. Title.

PS8629.S44M53 2005   C813'.6   C2005-903503-X

Published with the financial support of the Canada Council for the Arts, the Government of Canada through the Book Publishing Industry Development Program, and the New Brunswick Culture and Sports Secretariat.

Goose Lane Editions
469 King Street
Fredericton, New Brunswick
CANADA E3B 1E5
www.gooselane.com

These Siberian tribespeople knew they were not alone and their lives had changed already although, at this point in time, it still seemed possible their flexible and resilient mythology would be able to incorporate the future into itself and so prevent its believers from disappearing into the past.

— Angela Carter, *Nights at the Circus*

We Eskimos do not concern ourselves with solving all riddles. We repeat the old stories in the way they were told to us and with the words we ourselves remember. And if there then should seem to be a lack of reason in the story as a whole, there is yet enough remaining in the way of incomprehensible happenings. If it were but everyday ordinary things, there would be nothing to believe in. You always want these supernatural things to make sense, but we do not bother about that.

— Orulo, an Iglulingmiut informant, in Knud Rasmussen, *Intellectual Culture of the Iglulik Eskimos* (1929)

CONTENTS

9   One
       Sea, Village, Moon

63   Two
       The Barrens

121   Three
       Visitations

199   Four
       The Meeting

253   Five
       Village, Moon, Sea

ACKNOWLEDGEMENTS

I would like to thank the Canada Council for the Arts for two generous grants during the research and writing of this book and especially Megan Williams, then Explorations Program Officer for the Northwest Territories, for her enthusiasm and support. I am also grateful to the late Candida Donadio for early encouragement that helped shape the book and to my friend Helene Golay for her close readings and many insightful suggestions. I thank my agent, Robert Lecker, for placing *Midnight Sun* with as wonderful a publisher as Goose Lane Editions, and, to my editor there, Laurel Boone, I give thanks for the great pleasure of working with her and acknowledge her superb and sympathetic readings that have made of my manuscript a truly better book.

A short version of the first chapter of *Midnight Sun* appeared in *Pleiades* magazine and subsequently in *The Year's Best Fantasy and Horror*, St. Martin's Press, 1999. An early version of the third chapter appeared in the *Canadian Fiction Magazine,* as did a long short story, entitled "Dog Children," that became the core narrative of "The Barrens," the novel's second section.

Finally, and in many ways most importantly, I'd like to thank my Inuit friends for enriching my life over so many years.

ONE

Sea, Village, Moon

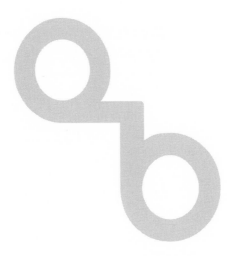

Deep below the frozen surface of the Polar Sea, Sedna stirred. A seal had entered her roofless stone house and pushed its nose into the black hair hanging like a curtain of seaweed around her naked seated body. With practiced nudgings of its soft snout, it lifted and divided tangled strands from her sleeping face until they floated above her arms and breasts. Then it left her. The wake of its flippers gently rocked the emaciated body of Sedna's father Isarrat-aitsuq on his stone bed along one wall of the room. Rising through the mass of other seals, walruses, fish in schools, and solitary whales floating motionless or circling lazily above the house, the seal swam away across the sandy basin set like a crater in the ocean floor with the house at its centre and Sedna at the centre of the house. Reaching the basin's rim, the seal disappeared beyond it into the murky reaches of the Arctic seabed.

Half waking, Sedna raised her right hand to her head. The hand had no fingers. Dreamily she shoved its blunt stump into the curtain of hair now falling once more around her shoulders. A memory of fingers ran down her arm.

On a pebbled beach at a place called Pangnittuuq, a young girl sat on a rock, her head tipped to one side as she combed the hair that hung down into her lap. The black strands glistened in the sunlight that also danced on the waves in the bay before her. As she ran her comb through the hair, it crackled like a fire of twigs. She held the comb as her mother had taught her. Carved from bone, its prongs smoothed by thousands of strokes through other women's hair, it was the only thing she had of her mother, who had died when she was a child. On the back of the comb, where her fingers gripped it, a face between animal and human was incised in the bone and outlined in lamp black. Her mother had told her it was magic.

Behind the girl her father sat in front of a tent of caribou skin chipping at a stone point. Two young men, her brothers, squatted watching him. Her back to them all, the girl combed her hair and looked out over the water. She was dreaming of a lover.

A sleepy giggle rose from Sedna's belly and broke from her lips in a string of bubbles.

All that summer, kayaks had appeared around the headlands of the bay and approached the beach. Coming from other camps along the coast, they were paddled by resolute young men of marriageable age wearing their best sealskin anoraks. Holding their heads high, they dug the blades of their paddles into the water first on one side, then the other. Turning away but watching sideways through her hair, the girl pretended to pay no attention to them. But a smile would play around her lips when a kayak got close enough for its paddler to see the full glory of the glossy curtain that hid her face. The young men's eyes would widen and their tongues dart into the corners of their mouths.

But when a kayak ground against the pebbles on the beach and a young man leaped to shore, she'd swing around. Throwing her hair back over her shoulder and arching her spine so her small breasts thrust against her caribou-skin dress, she'd give the young man a hard look. Many of them were ugly, but even the handsome ones were startled by that stare. They all dropped their eyes under it before straightening their shoulders and, raising their heads again, went up to her father's tent. Listening to their voices, she never failed to hear in their mumbled recitals of family connections or high-pitched boasting about hunting skills the effects of her challenging look and of the jittery lust the combing of her hair had caused in them. That too made her smile. None of them was anything like the lover she was waiting for.

And when they strutted back to their kayaks, not daring to meet her eyes again, and paddled away, sitting straight as stalks of grass and taking tremendous strokes in a last effort to impress her and her father, she often laughed out loud.

That made her father angry.

"How come you do that?" he'd shout at her. "How come you're so bad? You laugh at that young man like that, he never come back. You never want to marry? You think I'm going to hunt for you all your life? Useless girl!"

Then one windy day yet another kayak appeared around the point. Even at a distance the paddler looked different from the others. Sitting high in his kayak, he took strokes through the choppy water that were smooth and powerful, and as he drew nearer, she saw that his anorak must be made of bird skins. Fluttering in the wind, thousands of feathers made his whole upper body seem to quiver. And there was something strange about his eyes.

Keeping the curtain of her hair parted with the fingers of one hand while she combed it with the other, the girl watched him approach, arrogance and mastery in the long, strong sweeps of his paddle.

The girl felt a flush of warmth in her loins. She realized she was sweeping the comb through her hair in time with his paddling. She stopped, then after a moment resumed with slower, more deliberate strokes.

A short distance from shore, the stranger rested his hands on

his paddle and, letting the kayak drift, turned his head toward
her. And she saw what was strange about his eyes. They were
covered by a strip of ivory with two slits in it. Why was he
wearing sun-glare goggles? They were for protecting eyes against
snow blindness in the spring and fall. No one wore them in the
summer. A leather thong held the white strip tightly on his head,
and around the narrow openings in its polished surface she could
see lines scratched with soot like the ones on her comb. Above
the goggles his forehead was long and sloping, and below them
his cheekbones were high and far apart. His nose was sharp, his
chin small, and the lips were as thin as knife blades. The girl had
never seen such a man. When she dropped her eyes from his face,
she saw that the fingers that lay on his paddle were long and bony
and taut with sinews. Her own hands now lay in her lap.

The stranger began to sing. His rasping voice cut harshly
through the soft summer air.

> My house has food,
> My bed is warm,
> My arms are strong,
> My reach is long.
> Girl who will not marry,
> Come with me.

She was on her feet before she knew it, the comb falling from her
lap. (Later, her father would pick it up.) She ran to the water's
edge. The man grounded the bow of his kayak on the beach,
released the watertight skirt around his waist, reached for her
hand, and pulled her onto the deck. Though his eyes remained
hidden behind the ivory goggles, she felt them on her as she knelt
there. Then, obeying a motion from one of his sinewy hands, she
crawled between his legs and curled up under the translucent skin
of the kayak's deck. The smell of his animal clothing, strong in
the stuffy air, was mixed with another, unfamiliar smell. She felt
the kayak slide backwards, turn, and pull ahead.

Through the pounding of the blood in her ears she heard her father's voice calling her name. It grew fainter. She closed her eyes and waited for the time to pass until she came to her husband's home.

In her half sleep, a sigh slid from Sedna's lips and rose above her head in bubbles. Languidly, she opened and closed her thighs. Water slapped and caressed her skin. The girl had been happy with that husband. His tent was indeed always full of food and the bed in it warm and soft with animal furs. And he was a passionate lover.

When the man made love to her the first time, carrying her up to his tent from a rocky shore, her legs paralyzed by the long crouch in his kayak, she thought it was only haste that made him forget the ivory mask. She reached to pull it off, but he seized her wrist and, releasing it only when she cried out in pain, shook his head. Then he started moving inside her.

After that she never tried to remove the mask. He wore it all the time. She even made a fetish of the smooth ivory that hid his eyes, studying the lines and circles scratched there and making up meanings for them. Sometimes, while he was inside her, she pulled his head down and licked the ivory with her tongue. It tasted of sea salt.

There were other tents along the rocky shore, where a breeze was always blowing, and the families in them visited and welcomed her and gave her what she needed in the way of domestic utensils — bone needles and a needle case, a stone pot, a wooden stirrer, a new comb. It didn't seem to matter that she'd brought no possessions with her.

In the water over Sedna's house, a school of fish flashed by among the sea mammals hovering there. A bowhead whale spun ponderously on the axis of its own body, as if taking sympathetic pleasure in the picture that floated

before Sedna's closed eyes: busy tents, stone beach,
calm ocean, endless sky, passionate husband. Two
seals watched her attentively.

The picture changed and Sedna whimpered. The seals
dropped into the house and circled her. The bowhead
swam away.

One afternoon as he reached the climax of his lovemaking, her husband threw back his head — and the ivory mask slipped off. The girl found herself staring into the red eyes of a giant seabird. She screamed, and in that instant everything changed. Their tent was not a tent but a nest, the rocky shore not a shore but a cliff, and the site of their home not a beach but a ledge. The furs beneath her were not furs but fish skins, and the utensils scattered around her were not utensils but scraps of bone. The smell of rotten food clung to everything, and the nest of sticks was streaked with excrement. She screamed again, and as she did, her husband screamed too, his hooked beak opening wide to show a knifelike tongue, his hot breath stinking, his fiery unhooded eyes staring at her without expression. Then his talons released her, and he rose away from the nest with a steady, indifferent beat of his long wings.

At the base of the cliff, a wave broke against the rocks, and a gust of wind threw a spatter of salt spray into the girl's face.

The bird returned as the sun was setting. It dropped a fish into the nest and began to tear it with its beak. It tossed some pieces toward the girl. She shrank away, watching the bird savage the fish. That day she stopped eating.

The women from other families who'd welcomed her and given her some of their possessions were not women at all but other giant birds in the colony of nests built all around her on other ledges. The comb one had given her was not a comb like her mother's but the backbone of a fish. The girl stopped combing her hair. Soon it lost its lustre and became matted, tangled, and sticky with ooze from the nest's litter.

As the girl grew weaker and thinner, her bird husband, its talons holding her down on the rotting fish skins, seized and penetrated her less often. It spent more and more time away. But when cramps doubled her over one morning, she was terrified they meant she was with child. When the bird had made love to her while she still believed him human, she'd often imagined the children they'd have, strong handsome boys and pretty girls. Now the thought of offspring appalled her. Curled in pain in a corner of the nest, she imagined monsters forming in her womb. It was only when the cramps became constant that she understood they were caused by hunger. She hoped they would kill her.

The bird's ivory mask, lying where it had fallen when it slipped from his eyes, gradually disappeared under a thickening layer of fish bones, fish heads, fish skins, and the bird's excrement.

When the cramps in her stomach finally subsided and she was still alive, visions began to appear to the girl and float before her eyes in the wide blue sky bright with the summer sun. She saw the pebbled beach at her father's camp, saw his tent of caribou skins above the beach, saw her brothers braiding strips of walrus hide for rope, saw her father's dogs on their summer island leaping for meat scraps thrown from her father's boat, saw her father looking out to sea from the shore where she used to sit combing her hair, saw him holding the comb she'd dropped when she ran to the stranger's kayak.

Then one day, looking down from the nest, she saw her father's boat bobbing in the waves at the base of the cliff. He and her two brothers were waving at her. They called her name. With no hesitation at all, not caring if what she saw was real or only another vision, the girl rolled over the edge of the nest and fell into the sea.

Sedna's sleepy eyes saw the girl falling, a mass of foul hair streaming above her head. When she landed in the water and rose again to its surface, Sedna felt again on her arms the grip of her brothers' hands lifting her into the boat.

Now lying on real furs, the girl snuggled into them. Her father gave her one quick look, and then all three men picked up their paddles. Bending toward the water, each on his side of the boat, her brothers bowed their heads to their work while her father sculled vigorously in the stern. They ignored her, but she felt their indifference as a warrant of her safety. She let the rhythm of their steady, surging strokes rock her to sleep.

In the half sleep of Sedna's memory of sleeping, the sound of the seabird's first cry came to her like a scratch on the surface of the sky. But its second cry woke her up, and as she stared blindly at the wall of black stone across from her platform in the house at the bottom of the sea, wide-awake images rushed into her mind.

The great bird swooped over her father's boat, cried as it rose to turn, swooped back, hovered with talons spread, cried again, and lifted away. Her father and brothers glanced at it, then at each other, and went quickly back to their paddles. The girl stared wide-eyed at the sky. She saw a dark cloud like a spiral of smoke rising from the distant cliffs. The cloud spread, and the whole colony of giant seabirds raced toward her through the sky and with the whirring of hundreds of wings swept over the boat, banked like one bird, turned, and swooped again. The sound of their cries as they passed was deafening. As more great birds of every kind — gulls, guillemots, terns, petrels, murres — joined them with each pass over the boat, their mass filled the sky, its shadow darkened the water. The boat bucked in waves whipped up by the beating of their huge wings.

Gusts of wind seized her brothers' hair and flattened their anoraks against their chests. Soon the waves were so big that no matter how far down the sides of the boat they reached, their paddles caught air as often as water. Her father tottered as his own paddle struck the empty troughs of waves whose frothy crests now broke regularly over the gunwales. The skins around the girl grew wet and cold, but she hugged them close. The din of the birds' mixed cries, the heat of their passing breath, and the musty smell of their feathers swept over the boat again and again.

Suddenly her brothers dropped their paddles and, gripping the sides of the wallowing boat, looked at her father. His own hair blowing wildly about his head, he nodded. With one swift movement, the young men seized their sister and threw her overboard.

A shudder ran through Sedna's body as the girl's body struck the water.

The girl struggled up, and just as her bird husband dropped from the rushing cloud, its talons stretched to sink into her shoulders, she grabbed the boat. The bird veered away. She looked at her father. He met her gaze for one long moment, then reached between his legs, and his hand came up holding a long knife. He brought it down on her fingers.

The girl fell back into the sea, and the first joints of her fingers fell with her.

As she came up again and the birds screamed overhead, she reached for the lurching boat and gripped its gunwale with her mutilated hands. But again her father brought down his knife. The boat rocked, and again the girl fell into the sea. And the second joints of her fingers fell with her. She reached out once more and lay her bleeding stumps across the gunwale. The knife came down again. And for the third time the girl fell back into the sea, and the third and last joints of her fingers fell with her.

But her father's work was not yet finished. When she hooked her thumbs over the side of the boat, he chopped them off too. Then, as the birds rushed by once more, releasing a long cacophonous scream, the girl sank slowly into the dark waters of the Polar Sea.

When she was gone, the cloud of birds swept over the foundering boat a final time, rose silently into the sky, and dispersed.

One bird still circled far overhead, shrilling and crying. Then it too flew away.

Sunlight once more struck the boat and glittered on the heaving sea. Slowly the waves subsided, and in the boat the father and his sons turned their backs on one another and bailed. When the boat was dry and the sea more calm again, they started on the long paddle back to the place called Pangnittuuq.

The girl fell through the sea. But as she drifted down, her tangled hair floating above her head like a banner, the water around her began to churn and boil as first the tips of her eight fingers and then the sixteen other severed joints and finally her thumbs, falling through the water beside her, changed as they fell into ringed seals and bearded seals and walruses and narwhals and, last, whales. By the time she reached the ocean floor, landing at the centre of a roofless house of stone that was waiting for her there, the drowning girl had become Great Sedna, and the children of her two hands were massed in schools and pods around her.

The memory fading, Sedna looked down at the stumps in her lap. Their wounds had long since healed. But her thighs and forearms were now smeared with sea-mammal excrement that she had no fingernails to scrape away. And as for her hair, how could hands without fingers hold a comb, even if she had one?

Sedna raised her head to the sea creatures swimming above her. They were independent now. But as if they also still lived in her fingers, she could summon or send them away as she wished just by thinking about them. Some always hung in attendance like those overhead, but some-times in the past she'd call to all the living creatures in the ocean. Coming by the thousands, they'd arrive from the farthest reaches of the Polar Sea and slowly fill the great basin surrounding her house. Seals, walruses, narwhals, whales without number. On those occasions she'd known she was truly Great Sedna.

But her power to control the ocean's animals had also given her power over the Inuit she'd once lived among. For when the sea creatures left their usual waters to gather in the basin, the Inuit starved. On those occasions an angakuq, a shaman able to make spirit journeys, would soon come swimming down to beg her to release the creatures. The first time this happened, she sent him back to get a comb. After that, the procedure was always the same. An angakuq would carefully untangle her long hair, comb it out, and plait it into a thick braid. This done, he'd use the edge of the comb to scrape the rest of her body clean. When restored to cleanliness and satisfied with the weave of the braid — she sometimes made him do it more than once — she'd release the sea animals and send them back with him for her people once more to kill.

But she also began to send back messages. Using her power to starve or feed the Inuit, she began to impose on them, often with a capricious cruelty, duties and taboos. Then she'd wait for an angakuq to swim down to ask what someone had to do to be relieved of suffering or misfortune. For, to her delight, people began to believe that accidents and illnesses and hunting failures were punishments she'd sent for failing to pay attention to her rules. She readily accepted their belief and made up more rules. Her sense of power grew.

Now Sedna sighed. It was a long time since an angakuq had arrived at her house beneath the sea. When she first realized that too much time had passed without a visit, she called in some sea animals and waited for an angakuq to come down and beg her to release them on performance of an atonement.

None came.

Bewildered, then angry, she called in more animals and then still more until they filled the basin and beyond it far out over the Arctic seabed. But still no angakuq came swimming through the assembled children of her fingers

*— every finned and flippered creature in the Polar Sea —
who circled slowly overhead like a massive whirlpool with
her house at its centre.*

No angakuq ever came again.

*Hair filthy and unbraided, body soiled, she'd lived
since then in a world of loss, boredom, loneliness, and
long sleeps with only Isarrataitsuq for company, lying
with his back to her on his own stone platform.*

*Sedna sighed again and looked across the watery room
at her father. When he'd grown old, remorse had led him
one summer evening, or so he'd told her, to lie down on
the pebbled beach by the boulder where she'd sat to comb
her hair and, rolling himself into the sea, let it take him
and drown him. When he'd suddenly appeared in her
underwater home, she'd felt no hatred or rancour for
what he'd done to her that bright summer day below
the cliff. It had happened, after all, when she was only
human.*

Only human.

*The thought was so remote that Sedna's mind could
hold it only briefly. Then sleep flooded her.*

The dogs howled. Starting with one, quickly joined by others till
dozens of canine voices were crooning to the April moon, the
sound climbed in a jagged chorus into the Arctic night and then
suddenly collapsed, falling back out of the sky in disconsolate yaps
and weak barks. Then silence.

The full moon kept shining.

Except where it cast straight-edged shadows from roofs in the
small, isolated Inuit village of Poniktuk, the moonlight fell on
nothing but natural outlines in a vast frozen landscape where

ocean could be told from land only by its flatness. Even that was sometimes broken by pressure ridges of upthrust ice that zig-zagged across the level surface like trails of giant burrowing worms. Landward from Poniktuk for hundreds of kilometres the bucklings of the earth's crust, the hollows of valleys, the expanses of lakes all reflected the moon's light with a uniform whiteness. Nowhere in the land was there a hint of colour. Shaped and hardened by wind and cold, the snow sometimes rose into towering drifts and sometimes rippled into row after row of tiny ridges like ribs of sand on the ocean floor seen through clear summer water. But release to summer of this white emptiness under the icy moon was now unimaginable. Set on the edge of a frozen bay, the twenty houses in the village huddled together like hunched victims of the winter's storms.

The dogs howled again.

In his bed, Simon Umingmak, chairman of Poniktuk's settlement council and uncle, brother, grandparent, or in-law to nearly everyone in the village, groaned in his sleep and rolled his large body toward his young wife's warm plumpness. Even in sleep it would have been beneath his dignity to do anything like snuggle, but as a heavy arm fell across her belly and a bent knee overlay her thigh, he sighed. And the bad dream went away.

By day the shrewd manipulator of all the power in Poniktuk, Simon was often troubled at night by furtive anxieties that crowded his mind with frightening images. But embracing Ruby, his recent bride and his dead first wife's niece ("That *Simon!*" female relatives had said when they married, and the men his own age had snickered), usually made the disturbing pictures go away. As it just had. Tonight the half-heard howling of the dogs may have helped. It was a sound from a happy childhood long before the creation of settlement councils or even settlements, when he'd spent winter nights in a warm igloo with his father on his trapline, their dog team tied up outside.

Simon nuzzled Ruby's soft upper arm. The warm, pungent flesh bore a greenish bruise where he'd hit her when he was drunk two nights ago. Ruby lifted the arm and cradled his head against a dark-nippled breast. Simon sighed again and licked the nipple.

In another part of town, another body turned on its side. Simon's nephew Nate, asleep in his parents' house, pulled the eiderdown tighter around his shoulders and drew up his knees. His young nights were untroubled by anxieties or his days by village politics. The year was nineteen hundred and eighty-two, and even more than most Inuit villages, Poniktuk (pop. 156) existed by and for itself, virtually undisturbed by intrusions from the outside world. Telephones connected the Poniktungmiut to each other and sometimes to other villages, the closest hundreds of kilometres distant, but the slightest quirk of atmosphere or weather could break that connection. Television was unknown and only confusedly imagined. Radios were useless; the land forms between Poniktuk and Inuvik, five hundred kilometres away, interrupted and broke up signals broadcast by CBC Inuvik, the only station in the region. By a freak of those same land forms and others across many more thousands of kilometres, an atmospheric skip did sometimes bring a radio program to Poniktuk — in Russian. The only certain communications from the outside world came as mail delivered by the "sched," the weekly scheduled flight that originated in Inuvik and touched down at several other villages on its way to Poniktuk. (Gossip also travelled that route.) But bad weather often delayed or cancelled the sched. While the rest of the world moved rapidly into the telecommunications age, Poniktuk remained solitary, content to be ignorant of outside developments, technological or otherwise, and happy in its immunity to outside influences, social or political, that it could not, did not — and did not even want to — understand.

But there were tape recorders in town, and Nate and his friends listened to mail-ordered tapes with awe and fascination. They spent many hours sprawled on couches and chairs listening to KISS and Tiny Tim and Jefferson Airplane. If the urge to action seized him, Nate would try to persuade his father to lend him his snowmobile so he could zip around the frozen inland hills, rifle slung on his back, hoping to see a wolf to shoot for his mother for parka trim but mostly just wanting to race across the hard snow with his friends. There wasn't much else for a young man to do in Poniktuk in the winter. He slept alone.

Two years ago, Nate had dropped out of the high school in Inuvik — the Poniktuk school went only to grade eight. A promising student urged by the teaching couple at least to try to continue his education and the only member of his small class to accept their challenge, he'd flown off in the Department of Education charter, full of a spirit of adventure and looking forward to learning the ways of the larger world. But separated for the first time from his family and friends and subjected to incomprehensible disciplines in a boys' residence run by the Anglican Church, he'd become instantly homesick. Demoralized and ashamed of these unmanly feelings but unable to master them, he'd sought escape from them in sports, especially hockey, which he played with a mixture of instinct, cunning, and ferocity that earned him some extracurricular fame. But these hours of happiness were short, and the hours of schoolwork and confinement to the Anglican residence were long. The unmanly feelings persisted, he became surly in class, didn't listen, moped idly through the evenings instead of doing homework, and began to get in trouble, organizing pranks against the dormitory supervisor, a lay brother, breaking rules against carrying food out of the dining room or wearing shorts to chapel. In more daring escapes, he sometimes slipped out of the dormitory alone on weekend nights when the Inuvik bars were closing and wandered around town till he found a party. Too young to drink in the bars, he felt like a man when he got drunk at a party.

Haunted by longings for fresh caribou meat and raw frozen fish, his mother's bannock and the company of his lifelong friends, and failing all his courses, Nate quit at the end of the first half of the first year of high school, just a step ahead of expulsion from both residence and school. He returned to the comfortable familiarities of Poniktuk.

But he'd seen something of the outside world. With three thousand inhabitants, Inuvik was hardly a metropolis. But it had television, it had movies, it had bars, it had parties, and it had a huge Hudson's Bay store. Poniktuk, of course, had none of these. On many days after or even during school, Nate had walked up and down the aisles of the Bay, gazing at things to buy so abundant — games, toys, clothing, rifles, fishing gear, radios, cassette players, TVs, bicycles, snowmobiles, tapes, magazines, candy — that he couldn't resist shoplifting something. He had no money, but he *wanted.* He took only small things that fit into pockets and was never caught.

The trove he brought home with him to Poniktuk and the stories he told of how he'd stolen each treasure made him a hero among his peers. His were the tapes of KISS and Tiny Tim and Jefferson Airplane. In their parents' living rooms, they listened over and over to these tapes in a trance of envy of the life of extravagance and orgy they heard celebrated in the music. Memories of his own confused sexual experiences at two drunken parties in Inuvik that had been anything but extravagant or glorious, Nate kept to himself or had, by now, suppressed. But memories of other possibilities and goods that enlivened life in the outside world stayed with him.

Nate turned on his stomach and hugged his pillow.

At eighteen years of age, in a world of indulgent elders, peer admiration, and welfare cheques, he'd allowed the cunning and ferocity of his hockey days to slip into disuse and his desire for adventure to wither. He'd given his life over to indolent longings to be and to have what he had no hope or means of being or possessing. It was a life of sudden activity and chronic boredom. On the whole he didn't mind it.

The sun was rising.

The Arctic night gave up its stars reluctantly as the eastern sky turned grey and the moon set in the west. At the end of their tie-lines, the dogs curled into hollows their bodies had long ago melted in the snow and, noses tucked under their tails, went to sleep.

Daylight increased, the eastern sky turned from grey to pink to violet, and when the sun at last broke the horizon, its rays crept across the frozen land and, reaching Poniktuk, picked out the colours of its houses. Blue, purple, lavender, aqua, lime green, lemon yellow, fuchsia, orange, and pink siding came to light alongside roof-high snowdrifts that blizzards had wrapped around the houses' corners. Touched by sunlight, the village homes, among the larger shapes of school, fire hall, generator plant, mechanics' shop, church, and mission building, now looked less like hunched victims and more like cheerful hunkered-down survivors.

The sky turned blue, and the Poniktungmiut began to wake up.

Nate's dwarf Auntie Akpa yawned and stretched her lumpy arms above her head, careful to not disturb the slender shape beside her, her thirteen-year-old niece Della, who'd slept over. In a moment she'd have to wake the girl and get her off to school, but for now she could let her mind wander into the day ahead. It was the day the sched arrived from Inuvik, bringing mail and who knew what Sears catalogue surprises for individuals and dry goods and groceries for the store. Her older brother Simon would, as usual, empty the mailbags on the store floor after the plane had left and hand out letters and packages as if they were presents from himself, calling the recipients to step forward and often making jokes about what their letters and packages might contain. It was one of the few occasions when almost everyone in the village was together because, while mailing letters might go unobserved, this public receiving of mail allowed those present a glimpse of each others' private lives. And who would want to miss a chance like that? Although she rarely received anything, Akpa was always there, on the lookout from the top of a stack of soft-drink flats and sometimes adding a bawdy speculation of her own to her brother's jokes.

Beside her, Della dozed, prolonging in her mind a dream that some of the older boys had invited her to listen to tapes and that her cousin Nate, the undisputed hero among them, had smiled at her in a way that made parts of her body she'd only recently become aware of feel good. In real life, to her heartbreak, he never paid her any attention.

One surprise the plane wouldn't bring, Akpa reflected, was Father Evans. The Anglican priest who'd spent years in Poniktuk and guided her through many uncertainties, both religious and practical, would never come back. Over the last two years, she'd watched him sicken and grow frail until a plane from the diocese had finally come and taken him far away south to a hospital. Word had reached Poniktuk a month ago that he was dead.

Akpa heaved a sigh and dug an elbow into Della's ribs.

"Up, girl! Time you stop dreaming and start thinking to get smart. Della! Up! Go to school!"

Della flinched and opened her eyes on yet another day of unrequited love.

In other homes other children were shaken out of bed, told to dress, given a piece of bannock, bundled into boots, jackets, mitts, tuques, and windpants, and sent off to school with stern urgings to learn. The young teaching couple — who, after the departure of Father Evans, were now, with the town mechanic and the nurse, the only white persons in Poniktuk — were already at the school. In the grades six, seven, and eight classroom, they were studying the calendar and counting the weeks till the school year ended in June.

The mid-April sun had risen above the horizon into a cloudless sky.

At his kitchen table, Nate's father Eli sat smoking his first cigarette of the day. He was the only one awake in the house and had already made himself coffee. He stared out the kitchen window at the frozen bay and remembered other April mornings when by now he'd have been out on the sea ice for several hours in sealskin boots and caribou clothing, a young man hunting basking seals and wondering if he'd meet a polar bear. It wasn't so long ago, and nobody had a house to live in then. They lived in tents and igloos. His youngest son Iku, given the birth name of his great-grandfather but usually called Nate, his baptismal name, would never, Eli reflected, do anything like that. Maybe it didn't matter, but he couldn't help sometimes thinking it did.

At the nursing station, Ethel McGarr rolled onto her other side and told herself for the third time that she really should get up. But there were no patients in her two-bed ward. Another few minutes of snoozing wouldn't hurt; she needed all the sleep she could get between now and her annual holiday, still three long months away. She dozed off. And at the garage, the mechanic, nursing a hangover and twenty minutes late to work himself, wondered sourly where his helpers were and if any would show up for work at all today.

Simon reached orgasm inside Ruby's plump body — no need for a pillow under *her* buttocks — rolled away, and fell asleep again wondering if his contact in Local Government in Inuvik would manage to slip to the pilot of today's sched his usual forty-ouncer of Canadian Club in a disguised container.

Nate yawned and slept through the morning that promised a perfect day of Arctic spring, cloudless, crisp, and sunlit.

When the sched arrived that afternoon, almost everyone went out to the airstrip to meet it, some walking but most on snowmobiles, young men at high speed standing up, hot-dogging it, older people going more slowly, knowing the plane would be there a while. Simon drove the town truck out and backed it up to the Twin Otter.

But before the plane's freight could be unloaded, two passengers got off. The first was seen to be a relative of Simon's and of many others in Poniktuk, Andy Kublu from Seal Harbour, another village along the plane's route. When he'd backed down the ladder hooked to the Otter's floor, he turned around and smiled at the crowd and then moved through it shaking hands with everyone, starting with Simon.

The other passenger was a white man, a stranger. He too smiled when he got off, but he didn't go around shaking hands.

A tall, rangy man with a prominent nose and a full-lipped mouth framed by a trimmed black beard, he wore handmade caribou-skin boots and a big store-bought down parka, its hood trimmed in some kind of fur nobody recognized. ("Whiteman fur," Akpa decided. "Cat?" Ruby wondered, having heard of cats but never having seen one.) While men unloaded the plane, the stranger walked to the edge of the airstrip and stood looking at Poniktuk and at the land around it. If his smile meant anything, he liked what he saw.

When the mailbags and flats of soft drinks and other groceries and packages had been transferred to the truck, the pilot handed Simon a large cardboard box labelled Aeromint. Simon climbed into the cab and set the box next to him on the seat.

"Come for coffee," he said to Andy Kublu before he drove off.

As the Poniktungmiut started back to town, Andy looked around to see where the stranger was, and the man, as if he'd been waiting for this signal, joined him without a word and walked beside him into the village. Nate, who'd ridden out on the back of his brother Wayne's snowmobile, walked behind them. The stranger came from the outside world he'd briefly lived in. If he followed the man and Andy Kublu to his uncle Simon's house, he might hear something interesting.

The plane taxied the length of the airstrip and took off for its next stop.

When Simon drove the truck past the store and parked it in front of his house, everyone knew it would be a while before mail was handed out, maybe even tomorrow. Because everyone also knew it wasn't chocolate bars in that box labelled Aeromint. They went back to what they were doing before the sched arrived, disappointed about the mail but not resentful. In a village like Poniktuk, you got used to disappointment. And Simon was the village boss.

Several hours later, the drone of the Twin Otter was again heard overhead, and as the plane circled Poniktuk before landing, Simon and his two guests emerged from his house and climbed into the truck. This time people stayed at home and watched the truck make a slow, concentrated progress through the village, Simon driving. Andy Kublu sat beside him, and the white stranger sat at the passenger window. He wasn't smiling anymore.

After several failed attempts to climb the ladder, Andy had to be pushed from below and pulled from above onto the plane, but the stranger made it up on his own. The plane took off without his having said goodbye to Simon. Simon drove slowly home.

An hour later Ruby was talking on the phone to Akpa's sister Big Helen. Simon had passed out in the bedroom.

"He doing some kind of business with Andy Kublu and them others in Inuvik," she said about the white man.

"Which ones them others?"

"You know, them others like Luke Talimak from Uugaaqtuk came in here a while ago and talked to peoples?"

"About what?"

"I dunno. I never understood too good."

"So what they talk about today?"

"That white man keep saying something like . . . land rights?"

"Oh? What he mean by it?"

"You better ask Simon when he wake up. Or maybe not. I think he don't like it too much."

"What else they say?"

"I never listen too careful. White man and Andy keep trying to talk Simon into something. I think they maybe want someone in Poniktuk should work for them. Simon get real pissed off at that, say he could do anything needs to be done around here and don't want to hear no more. So then they talk about hunting caribou and drink up that bottle of CC. But maybe ask Nate. He was there."

When this version of the visit to Poniktuk by the fieldwork coordinator for the Aboriginal Rights Alliance, or ABRA, a regional Inuit land-claims negotiating group of which Andy Kublu was president, reached Eli's house, he and his wife Ruth wondered what it meant. Nate had come home by then. He'd listened to the men talking, but he couldn't help his parents out because everything he'd heard in his uncle's house was spinning around in his head in a muddle. Some isolated phrases were clear — "the peoples' rights" and "game management" — but they had no meaning he could articulate because he couldn't fit them together with other words and phrases he hadn't understood in the first place and now could only half-remember. His uncle had poured him a couple of rounds of CC.

Late afternoon light lingered on the snow-covered rooftops of Poniktuk, casting shadows that now lengthened slowly away from the buildings in the opposite direction from the shadows in the morning. But as the sun fell, the moon rose. At first it was only a pale pock-marked disc in the eastern sky. But when daylight finally drained away below the western horizon, the moon grew brighter. Rising high into the sky, it took charge once more of the Arctic night.

Kneeling on the floor of the double house he shared with his sister Siqiniq in the sky, Aningan put a hand on the bleached caribou shoulderbone that lay in front of him. It covered an opening through which he could look down at the world. Because Siqiniq was asleep in her half of the house, it was night down there. And in their sky country of hills and valleys rich with caribou and small animals and rivers and lakes always filled with fish and waterfowl, it was also night. There was silence in the many houses of the Inuit dead. Hunters were back from hunting, children had finished their games, food had been cooked and eaten, and lamps put out. Everyone in the land of the sky was asleep except Aningan.

To people looking up from the world below, he was the full moon.

His hand on the bone, Aningan hesitated. How many

*times since he and Siqiniq had left it had he knelt, as he
did now, to gaze down at their abandoned world? Many,
many times. And how often had he wished to be down
there again and human? Often. But for how long had he
felt reluctant, as he did now, to push aside the bone and
look through the opening? Too long. Yet this brief night
would be one of the last for a while that he'd be able to
observe the world. For his powerful sister was beginning
to stay awake more and more now, filling the sky with
her heat and light, which meant he would sleep more
and more until she took to her bed again in her half of
their house, at first only for naps but then for longer, and
he could be awake for longer and busy himself again with
the Inuit dead in the land in the sky.*

Still he hesitated.

*Since becoming the moon spirit, he'd helped settle
the dead into their new homes when they arrived, often
unhappy and confused. He'd also helped the living Inuit,
guiding hunters toward game, teaching angakut healing
songs and sending them future-telling dreams. He'd made
barren women fertile with shafts of his moonlight, saved
children from accidents, given old people easy deaths. So
why was he now afraid of what he'd see if he moved the
shoulderbone and looked down at their living world?*

*Aningan grunted. He lifted the shoulderbone and
leaned forward. Night winds whispered through the
opening.*

*In the light he was sending there, the land looked
pale but alive. Snow still covered most of it, but brown-
ish patches showed, and reflections of himself shimmered
and glinted in leads of open water along the seacoast.*

He felt better.

*He knew by heart every contour of that landscape
and had seen the seasons wash across it so many times
that their repetitions were like mere blinkings of his eyes.
Whenever he lifted the shoulderbone and looked down,*

he recognized the places where he and Siqiniq had lived in
skin tents and snow houses, moving from one to the other
as the seasons dictated their hunting and fishing. But for
some time now he'd also seen along the coast clusters of
strange sharp-cornered structures that never moved. And
for a long time now no Inuit dead had come to live with
him in the sky.

As Aningan took in the familiar view — and its un-
familiar elements — his uneasiness returned. He was
accustomed to thinking himself as much the master
of that world as he was of the afterworld in the sky.
But tonight, as too often before, the landscape failed
to offer him any sign that it or its people acknowledged
either his wishes or his rule. It lay below him like a great
sleeping animal, calm, self-contained, indifferent.

Aningan sat back on his heels. This was what he'd
feared.

What was the matter with him? What was the matter
with them? Why didn't the living Inuit respect him or
their dead come to live with him? Why couldn't he see
what the matter was?

Then he remembered the loon.

Orphans, they lived with their grandmother. One day a relative
gave them a walrus skin. His grandmother wanted it for her
sleeping platform, but he took it from her to make a rope for his
harpoon. She put a spell on the skin, and when he was stretching
it to braid, it snapped back in his face and blinded him. He knew
right away his grandmother was to blame, and from that day on,
she treated him badly all the time, feeding him only scraps of food
while she and his young sister ate good meat and fish. But Siqiniq
hid food in her sleeves for him and fed him when their grandmother wasn't looking.

When summer came and he felt the warmth of the sun on his
face, he longed to go hunting but could not. Then one day he heard
a loon calling from the lake behind their campsite and recognized

its voice. It was the same loon he'd thrown fish to the summer before while it recovered from an injured wing. He asked Siqiniq to lead him to the lake and leave him there. He called to the loon and, choking back childish tears of misery and frustration, told it what his grandmother had done to him.

"Come into the water and I'll do something for you," the loon said.

Astonished to hear a loon talk, he waded in.

"A little farther."

Hands in front of him, he took another step and felt feathers. But when he moved his hands forward, he had to stretch his arms as far as he could before he touched water again on the other side of the bird. This loon was huge.

"Climb on my back," it said.

He climbed on.

"I'm going to dive. Hold tight and keep your eyes open. When you can't hold your breath any longer, squeeze my neck."

They dove.

"What can you see?" the loon asked when they surfaced.

"I can see the back of your head! I can see water around us!"

"Hold on tight. I'll dive again."

Four more times they went under the surface of the lake. Each time they came up, he could see more. First he saw the shores of the lake, then he saw the hills beyond them, then he saw caribou grazing on the hills, and finally he saw individual hairs on the backs of the grazing caribou.

After the last dive, he asked the loon to dive once more.

"I think you see well enough already," said the loon.

"No, I can only just make out some hills beyond the lake," the boy lied. "Dive again. Remember how I fed you all last summer."

"All right," said the loon.

But when they surfaced and he blinked the water out of his eyes, the boy could no longer see the hairs on the backs of the caribou, only the animals themselves.

"You could have had better sight than any man has ever had," said the loon. "But you lied to me to get even more. So now you will see like other men. But one day you will cease to be a man, and then you'll get back the sight I just now let you have."

With that the loon returned him to the shore. When the boy had climbed off its back and stepped onto dry land, he turned back to the lake and was surprised to see an ordinary loon in the water. Angry with himself for spoiling his chance to see better than anyone had ever seen before and puzzled by the loon's prediction about ceasing one day to be a man, he nonetheless thanked the bird for restoring his sight. It stared at him for a moment with small red eyes and flew away.

Back at the camp, his sister could hardly contain her happiness when she saw he could see again. He didn't tell her about the loon; he just said his sight had suddenly come back. His grandmother pretended to be happy too. And now the boy went hunting every day and, getting better and better at it, always came home with something to eat. And he was careful to share what he killed. More families had joined their camp, and following traditional rules of distribution, he took food to many of them. To his grandmother also he was generous, but he was thinking of revenge. He finished making the rope for his harpoon.

Soon it was time for white whales to come into the warm shallow water along the ocean shore with their newborn young. The boy and his sister and grandmother moved camp away from the lake to the seacoast along with everyone else. One hot day a pod of whales swam into sight. Everyone ran to the beach.

"Get me a nice little juicy one!" his grandmother cried. "Here! Tie the harpoon line around me, and when you've struck a whale, we'll pull it in together."

The boy knotted his braided walrus rope around her waist. But when the whales came close to shore, he threw his harpoon not at a young one but at the largest whale he could see. The harpoon struck, and, before she knew what was happening, his grandmother went flying off the beach like the tassel on the end of a whip. At first she seemed to run along the water behind the whale, but then the whale sounded and she disappeared.

When the whale surfaced and she came up sputtering, she screamed at the boy.

"Why are you doing this to me? I who wiped the shit off your little ass when —"

With a gulp of salt water, she was gone again.

Everyone on shore watched silently while the whale dragged her farther and farther out to sea until, with a final dive, she was lost to sight. The other whales had already swum away. People went back to their tents.

When that summer ended, everyone moved inland to an autumn camp. The brother and sister continued living together, and because he still brought food to others in the camp, they thanked him for it but otherwise never spoke to him.

As fall became winter, the boy reached the age when he knew what it was to be a man. Now he wanted a wife. But no parents in the camp would accept as a suitor for their daughter a boy who'd killed his grandmother. As family after family turned him away, he became more and more angry. Didn't he bring them all food? Wasn't he the best young hunter in the camp? But anger only made his sexual appetite hotter and stronger.

When the great darkness of midwinter arrived, men in the camp always built a large igloo for singing and dancing to keep evil spirits away till the sun returned. Night after night a frenzy gripped people, and men and women, naked to the waist, danced and sang and drummed in the qaggiq in the flickering light of seal-oil torches. And night after night Aningan slipped away from it to their igloo, where his sister Siqiniq, tired from dancing, had gone to sleep. Hot from his own dancing, he stripped off his clothes, blew out the seal-oil lamp, climbed onto their sleeping platform, embraced her, and in the darkness took the nipples of her small young breasts between his teeth. And from there he went on, grunting and guzzling, to satisfy his lust in every way he could imagine on his sister's body. When he was done, he let her go and, dressing quickly, ran back to the qaggiq.

Siqiniq didn't know who her brutal lover was. Every night she tried to stay awake with her lamp lit to see him if he came, but she always fell asleep. When she woke, he was upon her and it was dark. But one night she smeared lamp black on her breasts before she fell asleep. And when the man had finished with her and had left, she lay awake and listened. Soon she heard loud laughter coming from the qaggiq. She dressed and ran there. Everyone was pointing and laughing at a young man with lamp black all over his face. It was her brother. Siqiniq spun around and ran back to their igloo. In the dark she picked up her grandmother's ulu from beside the extinguished lamp and, with a single swipe of its curved blade, sliced off her left breast. She ran back to the qaggiq.

"Here," she said, holding out the breast to Aningan while everyone fell silent. "Since you like my nipples so much, here's a whole breast for you."

Then Siqiniq threw it at him, snatched a torch from the wall, and ran out into the night. Aningan reached for another torch and ran after her.

Around and around the qaggiq they raced until suddenly they began to rise into the air. Aningan's torch blew out, but Siqiniq's blazed brighter and brighter as blood streamed down her torso. Faster and faster they rose into the sky, she leading him, he chasing her, still possessed by lust but then beginning to feel himself change, frightened at first when he felt the change, felt his desire stream from him like water, felt his body empty of lust like a sucked marrow bone, until at last they arrived at the land in the sky, a land that neither had ever suspected was there, and looked at each other without a trace of anger or lust, feeling only a cold joy knowing they'd become spirits.

Aningan sighed.

The first thing he'd done in their sky land was build, at Siqiniq's direction, their double house. When it was finished, she moved into her half, telling him he'd never see her again because from then on their waking and sleeping times would be perfectly opposed. And now the moment in that cycle when he would once again be helplessly overcome by long, unbreakable sleeps was fast approaching. And his last look at the world below had once again disappointed and humiliated him. The loon's gift of sight now mocked him.

"*Suuq!*" Aningan muttered, and clenched his teeth.

Anger began to rise in him — anger at his sister. It was she, he thought, who'd betrayed and humiliated him in the qaggiq, she who'd led him into the sky, where, more powerful than he, she controlled his waking and his sleeping and so dictated when he could and could not travel through their land in the sky, hunting and fishing and visiting the dead who'd come to live there. From the moment they were spirits, she had refused him anything but a pale reflection of her own great radiance. Had she also, he suddenly wondered, used that power to warm the world in order to woo the Inuit away from him, persuading them to close their minds to him and even go somewhere else when they died? Was this her revenge for what he'd done to her in the winter darkness of their igloo so long ago? Yes, Aningan thought, and his anger increased. Ending his sexual pleasures on earth, she'd spoiled his human life when he had it. Drawing him into life as a spirit, she'd ruined that too.

With a sweep of his hand, Aningan slid the caribou shoulderbone back over the opening. As he knelt over it, a wave of self-pity for all he'd lost and a longing for all that was human seized him. What his sister had done was too much to bear. He jumped to his feet and ran out of the house.

A faint golden glow coloured the crests of low dry hills in the distance. In her half of the house, Siqiniq must be stirring. He'd have to hurry.

Aningan ran to where his dogs were tied. When they saw him coming, they leaped and howled. He quickly harnessed them and one by one attached their harnesses

*to the towline of his komatik. An anchor of caribou antler,
sunk into the ground behind the sled, held the straining
dogs in check.*

*He jumped on the back of the komatik and, gripping
its upright panel with one hand, gave a wild cry. With
the other hand, he pulled the anchor free and tossed it
into the sled. The dogs dashed forward.*

*In no time at all they'd crossed to the edge of the upper
world and were racing down the sky. On this cloudless
night, they would make the whole journey to earth on the
sky's clear ice. As the dogs settled into a trot, the click and
scrape of their claws echoed through the atmosphere. Inuit
out early looked up and wondered where the noise was
coming from and what it was. If they saw anything at all,
they saw a wisp of cloud or a flicker of northern lights.*

*With a landing as soft as moonlight, Aningan and his
dogs touched down on the top of a hill above the village
of Poniktuk beside a small bay of the Arctic Ocean. Leaving
his body behind, the moon spirit flew toward
the rows of houses. Hovering above them, swooping
from one to another, darting in and out, he searched for
a suitable human shape to enter. He found one. And now
his lead dog on the hilltop leaped into the air, and the whole
team lifted away through the lightening sky toward the
white-faced moon. In the komatik, Aningan's empty body
sat pale as a stone.*

*By earth time it was a little after five o'clock on
a cold April morning.*

Starting from sleep, Nate wondered what had awakened him. It
wasn't a dream; no lingering images flickered in his mind. It
wasn't a noise from inside the house, although now he could hear
his sister Helen in the next room murmuring to her daughter

Sarah. It wasn't a noise from outdoors either; he was sure of that. But he was wide awake, his senses tingling.

Raising himself on an elbow and reaching out a bare arm, Nate lifted a corner of the blanket hanging over the bedroom window. Snow still covered the ground outside, and he stared for a moment at the drift sweeping to the roof of the house next door. In the April dawn, it had a ghostly look. All winter, when he woke up, he'd lifted the blanket and checked the drift, watching it build from the first snowfall in September and noting how the winds of every winter storm changed its shape.

One more month now, he thought, and that drift is gone. And then the geese will be here.

He dropped the blanket and rolled onto his back.

Every spring that he could remember, while the days grew rapidly longer and the sun brighter and the temperature warmer, expectation enlivened the whole village. Whenever people stepped outdoors to walk from house to house or stopped for a smoke or a piss while out on the land, they'd look up at the sky and ask themselves or each other when the geese would come. As a boy he'd developed a stiff neck craning day after day to be the first to spot a string of birds flying overhead. He never was first, but his father Eli often was.

When the geese did finally arrive at the end of their long migration and began choosing sites for breeding and nesting, every family in Poniktuk hustled to get tents and camping gear together. The geese would provide the first fresh meat since the fall caribou hunt. The store quickly sold out of shotgun shells, the school closed for three weeks, and the whole village took off for geese-hunting camps, by dogsled when he was a child but now by snowmobile, travelling for hours over frozen lakes and streams and gradually thawing land. For the rest of the year, there was never any excitement like the geese hunt.

Nate longed for it to begin.

Then, staring at the ceiling, he was suddenly rising out of his bed. He zoomed toward the ceiling, then through it and through the roof too into the outside air of a brilliant day that, as he floated above the house and looked around, he realized was not the day he'd just seen through his window — the snowdrift next door was almost gone. Rising higher, he watched the rooftops of Poniktuk grow small below him. Nothing of himself interrupted his view — no feet, legs, belly, arms, nothing. At last he stopped rising. Now he could see far in every direction — out to sea across ice divided into fields by leads of open water and inland across folds of hills and valleys still white with snow or brown with thaw. Suspended in the air, feeling no cold, marvelling at hanging there without a body, he surveyed the world below him until he saw a flicker of movement in the cloudless sky far away to the south. His vision sharpened, and he saw a skein of geese. They were flying high above a small valley where clumps of willows edged a stream that ran from a frozen lake at the head of the valley to a melt pond with a narrow sandy beach at its middle and then disappeared into the ground. As the geese flew steadily forward in a stepped V-formation, he could see individual feathers fluttering at the tips of their wings. And now his hearing picked up wind-borne snatches of their garrulous two-note honking as the sound rippled back and forth through the skein like squawks of challenge and encouragement.

Although he was still in the sky, he also saw himself crouched in a blind made of willow sticks near the sandy beach of the melt pond, and he heard his own voice raised in the cracked cry he'd known how to make since childhood to call geese down. The geese kept flying. His crouched self called again, and a dozen birds dropped from the formation, plummeting at first straight down, flapping their wings crazily as if already wounded but at the last minute opening their wings to glide serenely toward the beach. He saw himself raise his shotgun and hit three birds in quick succession before the rest veered up again out of range.

From his airy suspension in the sky, he watched the dead birds fall.

Then, as if he'd fallen from the sky as swiftly as the birds, valley, stream, melt pond, cloudless sky, and geese all vanished, and Nate found himself staring again at the ceiling of his bedroom.

Holy! he said under his breath. What the fuck was that?

But his heart thumped. He knew that what he'd seen was a promise. He also knew that he'd know when the day came to ride out to that small valley on his brother Wayne's threewheeler and bring home the first three geese of the year.

Nate lay in his bed astonished by the certainty of his vision and relishing the pride he would feel riding back into town with a bulging blue postal bag tied to the threewheeler's rack for all to see. Then he turned on his side, drew up his knees, tucked his penis between smooth thighs, and went back to sleep. In the dream that presently came to him, he held the nipple of a small, round breast between his lips while his teeth nibbled it. Nate's right hand groped between his thighs and began to move foreskin pleasurably back and forth over a swelling glans. He opened his legs and shortly, with a gasp, ejaculated.

In the next room his sister, known in the village as Young Helen to distinguish her from their aunt Big Helen, had also gone back to sleep. But beside her in the bed, her three-year-old daughter Sarah lay awake with eyes wide open: she knew something scary had just happened.

When sunlight reached the drift sweeping up to the roof next door, tiny prisms in its crust, refrozen during the night after melting in yesterday's sun, sparkled before melting again.

Simon was at the settlement office talking on the phone to a wholesaler in Winnipeg who wanted to sell him three dozen cases of thousand-watt light bulbs. He was trying to explain that the streetlamps in Poniktuk did not take thousand-watt bulbs, and besides, this far north there would soon be no real darkness at night anyway, but the guy kept interrupting with a pitch about a lifetime guarantee (whose life? Simon wondered) and prepaid shipping costs and how about a dozen cases then? It wasn't the first time a salesman from the south had somehow got the settlement office number and tried to con him into spending money on something completely worthless. Another time it had been swimming pool supplies.

This son of a bitch must think I'm an idiot, Simon thought, and slammed the phone down.

But the movement caused a stab of pain in his forehead, and that in turn reminded him of yesterday afternoon's meeting with Andy Kublu and the white guy. He'd finished off the forty-ouncer of CC on his own after they'd left. Now he had a hangover.

Simon swung his chair away from his desk and looked out the window.

His office occupied a corner of the second storey of the fire hall, one of only two two-storey buildings in Poniktuk. He'd come to enjoy his elevated view of the village without ever claiming, to himself or anyone else, that as long-time chairman of the village's settlement council this superior view of Poniktuk was his acquired right. But as it had in the past, the prospect soothed him.

There was only one thoroughfare in the village, a dirt road now covered with snow and lined with plowed drifts. Tall goose-necked streetlamps marched in long strides down one side of it. The road divided the village's two rows of houses, one that followed the curve of the bay and the other falling in with the curve on the other side of the road. The houses were staggered so that those away from the bay still had a view of it. The fire hall-office building stood at the north end of the village at a point where other roads led in various directions to the school, the airstrip, the generator building, the fuel-storage tanks, the lake that supplied the town's water, and the dump. The abandoned Anglican mission stood nearby. The only building not in sight from Simon's window was the town's other two-storey building, the nursing station. As the most recent addition to the community, it had been built at the edge of town behind the fire hall.

The glare bouncing off the snow on the village rooftops hurt Simon's eyes. He looked beyond the village to the airstrip and then beyond the strip across the mile or two of frozen marshy flatland that led to the first of two ranges of hills that defined the horizon. This too was a familiar sight. But now the sun, staying longer in the sky each day, would soon turn all that land from white to brown and then, in a burst of extravagant summer daylight, to green. Spring had already arrived, and Simon allowed himself a moment of self-congratulation for having guided his village safely through yet another winter.

But now the snow glare made his head throb, and he swung his chair back to his desk.

Yesterday, in his kitchen, Andy Kublu and that white guy — Tom? Don? Don something — had been eager to get him involved in — what did they call it? SABRA? BABRA? ABRADABRA? Just ABRA? Yes, that was it. ABRA. And what the hell did it stand for? He couldn't remember. He did remember they'd said joining it would lead to some new kind of bigger government that included other villages and would give new powers to Inuit people called "native rights" so they could "run their own lives."

But what were these guys really up to?

Simon hadn't run Poniktuk for nearly twenty years without learning something about exercising power. And a power grab was what that ABRA deal had sounded like to him even before he cut off talk about it. Details of their strategies and plans refused to emerge this morning from the haze of his hangover, but the conclusion he'd reached yesterday, especially when alone with the bottle of CC after Andy and Don had left, was still the same: they wanted to take running Poniktuk away from him. And that pissed him off. What else did they mean by a bigger government? And who'd run that? Andy and his buddies, with that white guy sucking up behind them, you could bet on it.

Since he'd become settlement council chairman, everything had worked just fine in Poniktuk. He rarely had to deal with people in the Federal government, far away in southern Canada, and as for people in the Territorial government, he'd long ago figured out how to deal with them. They gave him the money to run the town, and he ran a trouble-free town for them. Period. Nobody rocked the boat; his authority in Poniktuk was unchallenged.

But Simon knew his authority had long been the envy of other Inuit leaders in the region, including Andy Kublu. And now Andy and his buddies wanted him to join this ABRA so they could screw him out of it.

Simon pressed his fingers to his temples, and a queasiness not solely caused by hangover indigestion squeezed his bowels. Maybe he hadn't handled that visit with those guys too well yesterday. Maybe he shouldn't have got pissed off. If he'd let them think he was going along with them — and maybe had a few less drinks — he'd be able to remember better today exactly what they were up to. Was it too late to fix that?

No, it wasn't, he decided. He could call up Andy Kublu in Seal Harbour and say he'd thought it over and wanted to know more about ABRA.

Simon lowered his hands. His hangover headache hung on, but the queasiness in his bowels subsided. Just as he reached for the phone to call Andy, it rang.

"Simon?"

"Hello, Jim."

Jim Fraser, deputy assistant supervisor of Local Government in Inuvik, stopped to wonder, as he did every time it happened, what made the Inuit so good at voice recognition. They were never wrong.

Simon waited, pleased by the silence at the other end of the line.

"So how's everything in Poniktuk?" Fraser, recovering, said.

"Good."

Fraser paused again. Poniktuk was the most reliable settlement he supervised. He'd heard that some of the younger generation there called Simon Idi Amin, but that was their problem, not his. His problem, no, his advantage was that he could rely on Simon to handle all local difficulties at their source. In return he threw him favours from time to time — a lump of discretionary cash from a budget surplus, for instance. They were old hands at working together.

So why did he get the feeling, talking on the phone to him,

that Simon always knew something he didn't and was using it to manipulate him? He was a secretive bastard. But that was the trade-off, Fraser supposed: administrative comfort at the cost of personal insecurity. No, that was putting it too strongly. He did hold the purse strings after all, and that, in the end, gave him the upper hand. And he had a surprise up his sleeve for Simon this morning. A couple of them.

He cleared his throat.

"Reason I'm calling, Simon, we've got a new area officer for Poniktuk. Just came on staff. Young guy named Bill Tremonte. That's M-O-N-T-E, pronounced 'monty.' Recent university graduate."

"Oh?"

"I thought we'd come in there this afternoon. There's a DPW crew going in to check your generating plant, and I thought we'd hop on their charter. Let you get acquainted with Tremonte and vice versa."

"Sounds okay to me, Jim."

"You think you could get a community meeting together for this evening? So your people can get to know him too?"

"Kind of short notice," Simon said.

"I know. But I only just heard about the charter."

"I'll do what I can, Jim. What time you figger to get here?"

"Around five."

"I'll meet the plane. And maybe you could bring me a little something with you."

"Huh? Oh. Yeah, sure." A bottle of Canadian Club, Simon's little weakness. "I'll do that."

And now for the second surprise.

"I understand you had a couple of visitors yesterday."

"Oh?"

"Couple of guys from that aboriginal rights group, am I right? Andy Kublu and Don Thornton?"

"Could be."

"You going to join them?"

"Dunno."

"Ah."

Fraser grimaced. In his eagerness to find out Simon's intentions, he'd forgotten that frank declarations of intention were not Simon's way. In his own bureaucratic world, you asked a direct question and got a direct answer. But with someone like Simon, you had to skirt a subject without even mentioning it until you finally found out something by piecing together hints and allusions while you still talked about something else. (Hunting and the weather were favourite subjects.) But no matter how long civil servants like himself stayed around, Fraser reflected, they seldom became good at this game. And Simon was a master at it. He sighed, resigning himself to a future circuitous exploration of Poniktuk's participation in ABRA.

"Well, see you later then, Simon," he said.

"Okay, Jim."

And they hung up.

Simon frowned. How the hell did Fraser know about Andy and Don Thornton? Was he working with them?

The queasiness gave his bowels another squeeze.

At first contact, he and Fraser had been wary of each other, probing each other's official standings for weaknesses. But early on Simon had decided he had the upper hand because he could make things happen in Poniktuk that made Fraser look good or bad. Projects not completed, settlement accounts screwed up, things like that were bad. If he let things get really bad, Fraser could lose his job or at the very least lose face in his department. But *he* could never lose *his* job. As long as the Poniktungmiut voted for him — and he always made sure they did — he'd be settlement council chairman until he decided to quit. Still, it was useful to keep his government contact friendly, and he usually did what he could to make Fraser look good.

But if that son of a bitch was buddying up with ABRA . . .

Attack on his authority from two directions at once might be more than he could handle.

But then Simon grunted, and his face broke into a grin. What was he thinking? That was his hangover talking. He wasn't feeling too good this morning, but he wasn't called Idi Amin by the boys in town for nothing. If ABRA and Local Government were both lined up against him, he'd take all the more pleasure in beating the shit out of both of them. But first he had to know more about ABRA.

A hum sounded in Simon's throat. He'd follow through with his idea to call Kublu and tell him he'd changed his mind. But now he'd do something else too. He remembered they'd asked him to appoint a fieldworker in Poniktuk. So he'd agree to that. Then, as settlement council chairman, he'd make the worker report to him everything ABRA did. He'd have a right to those reports. The hum in his throat turned into a chuckle: seemed like he had some native rights of his own.

Simon swung back to his window, and as he studied the houses below him, he ran through their occupants in his mind to find the perfect candidate to do fieldwork for ABRA. His headache persisted, but the queasiness was gone.

In Inuvik, Jim Fraser steepled his fingers and tipped back his chair. His too was a second-storey office with a window, but his view was not like Simon's. He could see a corner chunk of the Igloo Inn, Inuvik's one hotel, a tangle of wires on utility poles where ravens gathered and squawked — he could see their beaks opening and closing but couldn't hear them (the building was climate controlled) — and a piece of sky. It was not a commanding view, but Fraser was not a commanding assistant deputy superintendent: a slight man with sandy hair, now thinning, bony cheeks, and a raw complexion that revealed his Scottish ancestry. Behind his back, junior members of his staff called him the Pink Rabbit.

Like most of the Territorial bureaucracy, he considered ABRA a threat. If ABRA got everything it was rumoured to be negotiating with the Feds — land ownership, self-government, economic preferences, and a ton of other benefits — officials like him would be out of a job. Granted that the present set-up was complicated: the Feds made annual grants in the millions to the Territorial government to run programs and departments whose jurisdictions were often the same as the Feds' own. But the very intricacy of relations between the two governments and the complexity of their overlapping services were the bread and butter — and jam — of both bureaucracies. Turn over those functions to the Inuit, and not only would there be a horrendous fuck-up, in his opinion, but the knowledge — you could say wisdom — of people like himself accumulated over years of experience in the north would be lost. Even he sometimes had lapses, like just now when he asked Simon that direct question. But that was not the point. The point was good government. Fraser saw it as his duty to oppose ABRA — not just to save his job, of course, but to save the native people from themselves.

And there was a glimmer of hope.

Just because of all the overlaps, ABRA had to negotiate with the Territorials as well as the Feds, and, understandably, the Territorial negotiators, of which he unfortunately was not one, were dragging their feet on the way to the table. But in the end the Feds could force the Territorials to comply because, just as he held Poniktuk's purse strings, the Feds held the Territories'. Why the Feds wanted to surrender responsibilities in so many areas was a mystery to him, but now that he thought about it, maybe they just wanted out. Certainly in his experience the Feds were often clueless. But the catch was, their willingness to surrender responsibilities made the response of the Inuit communities coming under ABRA of paramount importance. Because if they weren't willing to *assume* responsibilities, the whole thing fell apart.

From what he'd heard, most of the communities in the region were leaning toward joining. But Poniktuk, the most isolated, wasn't yet in the loop, and there was the glimmer of hope. By its mandate from the Feds, ABRA had to have all the communities in the region on board. So if they didn't get Poniktuk, they were fucked. Which was why so much depended on which way Simon jumped.

Fraser acknowledged that, talking just now to Simon, he'd

blundered. But arriving this evening with a twenty-sixer — no, make that a forty-ouncer — of CC, he knew Simon would take him and Tremonte home for a few drinks at his kitchen table before the meeting. He'd have to play the skirting-around-the-subject game, but, this time prepared, he was confident he'd be successful. In the meantime, maybe he could find something in his files to offer Simon that would counter the offers Andy Kublu and Thornton must have made him yesterday. Fraser suddenly smiled.

He picked up his phone and called Bill Tremonte into his office.

"We're going into Poniktuk later this afternoon," he told the gangly young man standing at attention on the other side of his desk. "DPW's going in too. Call and tell them we'll share their charter. Then dig out the file on the Territorial government's devolution policy. It's a couple of years old. Have a look at it. I want you to make a short presentation on it at a community meeting this evening. It's time you got your feet wet."

People in Poniktuk walked toward the school. The sun had just set, but the sky was still light and the air full of vigour. Reluctant to go indoors on such a promising evening, groups stood on the school steps smoking cigarettes, looking across the bay, talking about the coming geese hunt. Eventually they went in.

Simon had sent word the meeting was at eight o'clock. By half-past more than a dozen adults were squeezed into children's desks in the grades six, seven, and eight room, largest of the school's three classrooms. Having left their boots in the vestibule, some parents had considered looking into the desks where they sat while they waited for the meeting to begin to see what their children might be studying. But most had decided against it. Few of them had gone to school themselves, and although their belief in education was all the fiercer for that, there existed the embarrassing possibility of discovering they couldn't understand their children's studies. So most parents' hands remained in their laps. The two or three who lifted a desk lid and reached inside could be seen regarding a workbook or a text with grave attention.

Time passed.

Attendance at government meetings was rarely large anymore in Poniktuk. The novelty of crowding into a classroom to see which government officials had come this time and listen to them say what they'd come to say had worn off long ago when people realized that what government officials had to say was often incomprehensible and, when it could be understood, seldom made sense. Some people still came to most meetings, though less now in the hope of entertainment than from a sense of duty. Among the faithful were Nate's parents Eli and Ruth, his aunt Akpa, her sister Big Helen, Obie, chairman of the housing committee, and Zebediah, chairman of the Hunters and Trappers Association. They were in the classroom now, making small adjustments from time to time to their cramped limbs. Nate's older brother Wayne was also present with his hunting partner Harry Ingasuk, but not Nate.

At a little before nine, Simon came in with the government men. They went to the front of the room. The older government man sat down in the teacher's chair and the younger one settled a thigh on the edge of the teacher's desk. Behind them Simon leaned against the blackboard. The older man nodded at the assembly and then looked down at his clasped hands. The younger one looked away.

And more time passed.

Fraser knew the protocol was for Simon to start the meeting. It always took a while, and tonight, he noted grimly, it might take longer than usual. Their pre-meeting meeting had not gone well.

Simon had been jocular at his kitchen table, urging him to match him drink for drink and teasing him when he declined. He could handle that. But Tremonte hadn't handled anything. On his very first sip of rye, Bill had choked and his eyes had watered, and

Simon had burst out laughing and taken off on a virtual aria of jolly sarcasms about how lucky Bill was not to be able to swallow hard liquor. His contempt for the new area officer was obvious. Then the stupid boy had tried to redeem himself by launching into an earnest and highly technical explanation of the Territorial government's policy of devolving of administrative responsibilities to local communities, until Simon laughed again and said he was just a dumb Eskimo and Bill would have to say it all in little words if he wanted anyone in Poniktuk to understand. Where did they find these whiz kids, Fraser had wondered.

After these pleasantries, he'd patiently begun to invent conversation about anything except the aboriginal-rights movement so he might in time begin oblique approaches to the subject in the hope of getting Simon to reveal himself. But at his very first glancing reference, Simon had taken off on a long spiel about spring geese hunting that wound its way at a leisurely pace to a criticism of the International Migrant Wildfowl Treaty, which made it technically illegal for Inuit to hunt geese in the spring. Fraser eventually realized this must be Simon's way of approaching the subject, since spring geese hunting could be considered an aboriginal right threatened by the treaty. He took advantage of the opening to say something about the possibility of re-establishing that hunting right and other compromised aboriginal rights through negotiations with government bodies under proposals like the devolution policy. But that only made Simon narrow his eyes and pour himself another drink. When he broke the silence that had lasted, perhaps intentionally, till it became uncomfortable, Simon started telling stories about his childhood, when he and his family and their relatives still led a nomadic life, following the seasons and the seasons' game from camp to camp, taking the winter's pile of trapped furs to a trader's outpost in the spring in exchange for things like coffee and tea and sugar and flour that had never been part of their diet before and that they began to crave so much they also began to settle down in communities around the outposts and, in doing so, surrendered their way of life.

Every now and then Simon shot him a glance to see how he was reacting to this recital, and it gradually dawned on Fraser that *Simon* might be probing *him* to find out how *he* felt about traditional Inuit customs that in the present political dialogue were being called aboriginal rights. This was an unexpected and alarming turn of the tables, and now Fraser found that he was the one being evasive. He responded to Simon's hints and glances only with bland generalities and, in the meantime, poured himself another drink or two from the forty-ouncer. That had not been prudent.

So here he was, sitting half stewed in a stuffy schoolroom full of attentive Inuit, waiting for Simon to start a meeting whose only excuse had been for him to find out, before the meeting, which way Poniktuk's council chairman was going to jump on ABRA and if he'd bite on the devolution idea, at both of which undertakings he'd utterly failed.

Fraser took a tighter grip on his hands. He closed his eyes. He was getting a headache.

While the assistant deputy supervisor of Local Government sat grimly at the teacher's desk, his junior officer was also having a bad time. Bill Tremonte didn't know where to look. He tried looking at his hands like his boss or at one of his shoes, but his eyes kept being drawn back to the people seated before him like overgrown children, the first group of Inuit he'd ever faced. They were watching him. With dark steady eyes, they were watching him closely. It was unnerving. But the longer they stared at him, the less he was able to look away. Yet the more he met their looks, the less he could bear their impassive study. Soon his own eyes were darting all over the room, and it became a matter of some interest among the members of his audience to guess where his glance would skitter next. Foot, wall, window, hands, Eli, Akpa, Big Helen, back to Akpa. What was making the young man so nervous? In Akpa's eyes at least, he was a nice enough looking young man, tall and kind of stringy and too skinny, but the last area officer had been like that too. Maybe, she thought, all young white men's mothers never fed them good.

After a while, a few teenagers drifted into the room and stood along a wall, Nate among them.

"Might as well get started," Simon said suddenly.

There was an audible sigh and rustle of clothing.

"Right!" said Fraser, and he released his hands from their grip on each other and rose carefully to his feet. He braced his fingertips on the desktop. "I guess you all know me. I'm Jim Fraser with the Department of Local Government. And this . . . this is Bill Tremonte, who's going to be your new area officer. I'm sure you're going to like him. Bill?"

"Hi," said Bill Tremonte.

"We think he's a good man. . . . What we'd like to talk to you about tonight — what we'd like to get your input, your feelings, about — that is, what we've come here for, our purpose in asking Simon to call this meeting" — what the hell did we come in here for? Oh, yes — "Our purpose is to talk to you about something called devolution. But before we get into a discussion about it, I'm going to ask Bill here to take a minute to explain what that word means. To explain it in a way that I hope we'll all be able to understand. Okay?"

No objection was raised.

"Bill?"

Tremonte lifted his leg off the edge of the teacher's desk and planted his feet. Fraser sat down.

At his desk Zebediah leaned forward. Eli tilted his head back and concentrated on opening his mind. Big Helen frowned. Akpa prepared to listen carefully; she'd felt a thrill of alarm as Fraser introduced the new officer. Was the young man really going to explain something about the devil?

"It's kind of like the way you people used to organize your lives when you were still nomadic," Tremonte said. "In extended families. That is, you had your head man, but then every family had its head of the family, and each one of those families within the — within the extended family — basically looked after itself. Although you shared, of course. But the important thing was that while you went from camp to camp following the season's game, each member within the family and the extended family was responsible for himself or herself or themselves."

The sea of polite faces remained attentive, the dark eyes steady. Tremonte drew a shaky breath.

What he know about how we use to live? Eli thought. Boy, these government fellas!

"What I'm saying is, that's kind of what devolution's like. I mean, you still have the big government in Ottawa — you all know about that big government — but that's already 'devolving' some responsibilities to our government in Yellowknife and Inuvik, the Territorial government, which isn't exactly a little government — ha — but you know what I mean. Anyway, that big government has been sort of like the head man in those traditional nomadic extended families. He made a lot of decisions for everybody, and so has that big government in Ottawa. But he didn't make *all* the decisions. Some were still made by the head of each . . . uh, each *family* family. And that's what *our* government is like. The head of a family family. But what we want to do now is pass on a lot more government to you. That's really the whole thing. Devolution means more government to you. In a nutshell."

The silence in the room when he stopped was substantial.

"Any questions?" Bill asked.

What the hell, Big Helen thought, *more* government? We already choking on government!

What he getting into nutshells for? Ruth wondered, and then turned her mind from the odd preoccupations of white people — although this one looked nice enough — and back to what she'd been thinking about while waiting for the meeting to start. Through a window she could see the sky had darkened, and Eddie Qarlik, the school custodian, had just turned on the classroom lights. But there was no mistaking that geese-hunting time was almost here. Between all the men in her family, they might get enough geese this spring for her to pluck enough down for a new hunting parka. For Nate maybe. What a lot of plucking that would be! she thought with relish.

Beside her, Eli had closed his mind. It was like it always was. Maybe somebody else could understand what these guys were saying. He couldn't. And his mind too went to hunting geese. Behind him Zebediah slumped at his desk. He didn't see any way this had anything to do with hunting and trapping. Not his business.

"Thank you, Bill," Fraser said, not looking at him, and rising again to his feet. "Maybe I can add something to that. I know how well Simon here and" — nodding to them in their seats — "Zeb and Obie and the rest of you take care of things in Poniktuk. It's just about the best community in the region. Believe me, I know what I'm talking about. So, anyway, what we're thinking of doing with this new policy we call devolution is just give you a freer hand, give you more power in your own community, let you run things according to your own lights." (Jesus, Fraser thought, I'm sounding like ABRA.) "Still within the framework of the Territorial government, of course. Of course. So maybe we can move on now to a discussion. Let's hear what you think."

But again there was only silence.

Simon sighed and stepped forward. But a voice rose from the audience.

"How come you government guys allus come in here telling us what you gonna do, then you ask us about it?"

Heads swivelled. The voice had come from the teenagers along the wall, and it had just broken a rule: young people don't speak out in public before their elders. To ask a visitor a rude question broke another rule. Eyes scanned the teenagers. Was it Eli's boy who'd spoken? He was staring hard at the government guy.

Eli had recognized Nate's voice and dropped his head. Ruth glanced at him, then looked down at her own hands. Whatever had got into their youngest son to embarrass them like this? She prayed he wouldn't say more.

"Sorry?" said Fraser, trying to locate the speaker. "I didn't quite catch that."

"How come," Nate repeated — and now Ruth closed her eyes

— "you guys keep coming into town to tell us what you gonna do, then you say 'discuss'? Seems to me you wasting our time. You gonna do it anyways."

"Well . . . well, no." Fraser had spotted the young man leaning against the wall with his arms crossed on his chest. He smiled at him. "Of course the government in Yellowknife — your own elected representatives — make laws and pass legislation. But they depend on those of us at the regional level to let them know how you people feel about what they're doing. And believe me, they listen to us. So that's why we have meetings like this one. We want to listen to you so we can advise them."

"What you want to hear?"

"What?"

"What you want to hear from us?"

Now Fraser only stared.

"I think what Nate trying to say is," Simon said, "we allus glad to see you guys and appreciate you coming in here to let us know what figger in the way of new ideas from government. But maybe we need a little more time to think about this . . . this here what-chucallit."

"Devolution," said Tremonte.

"Devolution," said Simon.

"Devolution," Nate said. "How that figger with land rights?"

"With what?" Fraser said.

"Land rights."

Tremonte's ears perked up.

"With land rights?" he said.

"How this devolution thing figger with lands rights," Nate went on. "What I been hearing the other day, we might be getting our own government pretty soon anyways. So why bother with this devolution thing from you guys?"

Chairman of Hunters and Trappers Zebediah looked sharply at his old friend, housing chairman Obediah. What was going on here? Weren't they in charge of things already? Our own government? What did young Nate mean by that? And what was he doing being so outspoken? No one had ever heard him say anything worth listening to before, in or out of meetings. Obie's eyes acknowledged Zeb's perplexity and then shifted to Simon. Zeb followed his thinking: whatever young Nate was doing, Poniktuk's council chairman would have the last word about it.

But for the moment Simon said nothing.

In the silence that continued to possess the room, its cause no longer polite attention but puzzlement and curiosity, Akpa at her school desk frowned. She didn't like what her nephew was doing. She'd always known him to act as a young Inuk should, but all of a sudden here he was acting like she didn't know what, saying things that could only upset people. She didn't like that at all. Nor, she could see, did her sister Helen.

But Big Helen had more scorn for what her nephew was saying than alarm about his saying it. Our own government, Big Helen snorted. Who of us smart enough to be doing all them things? And these Territorial guys been running everything so long, they gonna just give up?

"Maybe Bill here," Simon finally said, "could come back again in a little while when we been having time to think about all this. We really glad to see you, Bill. We been missing regular visits from you guys. But we know how busy Jim is. Tell you what. We got council meeting coming up in a coupla weeks. Maybe we put this . . . this . . ."

"Devolution?" Tremonte offered again, feeling useful at last.

Simon's head bobbed to acknowledge his area officer's help.

"This devolution on the agenda. That way we have a chance to talk it over some. Then maybe Bill come back the week after or week after that for another meeting."

When everybody will be out of town hunting geese, Simon added to himself, as he knew everyone else in the room, except the white men, also knew.

"That okay?"

"Sounds fine by me," said Fraser, who wanted by now only to get on the DPW plane again and go home. This whole trip had been a disaster, and whoever that mouthy young cocksucker was, he was the last straw. His head throbbed.

The meeting was clearly over.

But nobody stirred. Except for an interesting train of thought unspooling in Simon's mind, Fraser's suppressed impatience, and an uneasy feeling now stealing over Bill Tremonte that he hadn't understood anything of what had happened, the occupants of Poniktuk's grades six, seven, and eight classroom seemed held in a spell of immobility cast by Nate. Limbs shifted, but no one moved to get up.

Then Eli swung his legs out from under his desk and, rising, put on his parka. It was a signal. Others now rose and, stretching their cramped muscles, put on their own parkas. But as if the fluorescent-lit schoolroom still held something too fragile or mysterious to be violated by speech, they remained silent as they shuffled into the school's vestibule in stocking feet and put their boots back on.

Leaving the school, Poniktuk's citizens dispersed toward their homes under a clear night sky full of stars into which the moon had not yet risen, still not saying much but minds spinning with words never heard before — "land rights," "our own government," "devolution."

Custodian Eddie Qarlik put out the lights.

Akpa had been the last to leave the classroom. Having climbed down from her chair and pulled Poniktuk's smallest but most perfectly sewn Mother Hubbard parka over her head, she'd rolled out of the building on her short overmuscled legs into the star-filled night. Except for Nate's speaking out about things he should have known were better left to his elders, it had been a meeting like many others — hard to understand. But this one had also produced a disappointment: that young government man hadn't said a word about the devil after all. Only about government. Again.

Simon was keeping Fraser and Tremonte company.

"Come back for a nip?" he asked as their footsteps squeaked on the hard-packed snow.

"No, no thanks," said Fraser. "Shouldn't keep the charter waiting. I'll call you about . . . about . . . I'll call you."

And with that he gave Tremonte a not too friendly shove.

Startled but putting down his boss's roughness to personal urgency, not rebuke, Bill fell in beside him and began a mental review of his initial performance as Poniktuk's area officer. He had to admit it had not been a big success. Choking on the rye had been humiliating. It must've been nerves. And his explanation of devolution, although he'd tried to use some of Simon Umingmak's own examples from traditional Inuit life, had somehow got all balled up. That was probably nerves too, brought on by all those people staring at him. But the meeting had also opened a topic he wanted to pursue. He'd do some research at the office, and when he came back for that next meeting, he'd spend some time with the young man who'd brought the topic up. Land rights.

Simon's thoughts were also on Nate. As he watched the two government men pass in and out of the cones of light shed by the streetlamps along the road to the airstrip, he congratulated himself that another community meeting was over without the government representatives getting anywhere. But this meeting had provided another source of satisfaction. He'd never have thought Nate capable of remembering Andy Kublu and Don Thornton's arguments from yesterday better than he did, let alone reach his own conclusions about them and have the nerve to speak out in public. But Simon was glad he had. Nate had solved a problem: always a manageable boy, he was going to be ABRA's fieldworker in Poniktuk.

Nate and his cousin and best friend Lawrence were walking together toward Lawrence's home.

"How come you speak out like that?" Lawrence asked. "Where you get them ideas from anyways?"

"Dunno," said Nate. "They just come to me. No big deal."

But it was a big deal. Since those words had come bursting out of him, he'd had a feeling like nothing he'd ever known: his mind was flying.

TWO

The Barrens

Standing on the pebbled shore of a large lake without a name at the source of the Blackstone River three hundred kilometres inland from the Arctic Ocean on a bright afternoon in late June, Ralph and Gwen Morrissey watched the single-engine float plane that had brought them there take off. Their wilderness canoe trip had begun. The plane skimmed across the wave-ribbed water, rose into the air, banked to take a bearing to the south, the sun flashing on its wings, and then ascended into the vast sky. Instinctively, Gwen raised her hand and waved. The plane held to its steady climb. They watched till it became a black dot that suddenly vanished.

Flying from Fort Rae, nearly five hundred kilometres away, they'd looked down through the plane's scratched windows at a landscape like nothing they'd ever imagined. Waterways straggled in every direction toward horizons where the haze of distance erased the division between earth and sky, leaving only a moist blur. Directly below them, what land there was looked stretched and torn, its skin rotted by countless lakes and ponds and swamps. Streams meandered between many of these bodies of water but often ended abruptly in one of them or, leaving one, showed at first a glint of water but at last simply petered out as a streak of pale green vegetation. Many of the ponds had no visible source. They lay alone within their ragged shores, rising from nowhere, draining into nothing. In some of these, an aquatic growth the colour of blood ringed the shore.

Jesus Christ, Ralph thought, so this is what the barrens are like! If you got lost down there, you'd never make it out alive.

He glanced across the cramped cabin of the plane at Gwen. But Gwen was looking out her own window.

Nothing she saw made sense. The lakes and ponds seemed flung across the land in anger and left there in contempt. She whispered without much hope a wish that the country of the Blackstone River would not be like this. What had they got themselves into?

But soon the country below had begun to change. More land pushed its way among the lakes, ponds disappeared, streams shrivelled up. The country rose into uneven hills. It also threw off the vegetation that before had coloured its surface varying hues of green. If the land had then looked like rotting skin pocked with watery sores, it now looked like dry skin stretched over badly mended bones. Its colour was dull grey. Can all that be rock? But no, Gwen could see wrinkled scars running down some hillsides, and there were patterns of cracked hardpan on the flats. It was a country that had once held water. What could have dried it out so terribly? Now an isolated lake or pond, with shores of anemic green, looked almost tropical surrounded by these grey humps of dead earth.

Christ, this is worse, Ralph thought. A life could blow away down there like a pinch of dust.

Turning at the same moment from their windows, Gwen and Ralph caught each other's eyes over the gear piled between them. They both quickly grinned. Only shouting could have made their voices heard above the roar of the plane's engine, and neither felt like shouting. But their grins seemed to say, Isn't this something?

Then they looked away again.

Ralph scrunched into his seat, tipped his head back, and settled the brim of his bush hat over his eyes; he'd seen enough. But Gwen stayed at her window.

The plane carried them steadily deeper into the Arctic desert. Somewhere down there was the starting point of their trip.

A large lake at last appeared on the horizon. As it seemed to move toward them, the land below reacquired a tinge of green and other lakes came into view. Then the plane banked and dropped, and in a moment they felt the cushioned bump of pontoons touching water. Then they were moving toward a beach.

They stood there now.

While unloading gear from the plane, unlashing their aluminum canoe from one of the pontoons and floating it to shore, and watching the plane take off, neither Ralph nor Gwen had given the country beyond the beach so much as a glance. Now they could no longer ignore it; they turned their backs on the lake and looked.

At a distance of five or six kilometres, a curving ridge rose from the tundra like a recumbent arm embracing the land below it. Along its crest, pinnacles of red rock jutted up, and the whole ridge showed a reddish colour on its upper slopes — was it scree or some kind of plant? — but the lower slopes, sweeping down to meet the tundra like a sleeve, were silvery green. The land between the ridge and the beach was astonishingly like a meadow: tall grasses bunched together in moist hollows; low bushes snaked along the ground and then suddenly pulled themselves together and shot three or four feet into the air; grass-fringed tussocks shouldered their way out of sedgy wet spots and pushed up dry bald heads; beds of pale green moss followed hidden watercourses; and everywhere they looked they saw wildflowers. Even on the beach among the pebbles, clusters of a five-petalled purple flower bobbed reassuringly in the breeze, and on the verge between beach and tundra, groups of tiny red flowers grew on small, isolated mounds of moss.

A hot sun in a cloudless sky shone down on all this vegetal activity and on Ralph and Gwen. They turned to each other.

"Let's have a look at that ridge," Ralph said.

"Okay," said Gwen.

And they walked out onto the tundra. The ground was springy beneath their feet; the sun warmed their shoulders; they breathed deep lungfuls of keen air. There was nothing to fear from this land after all.

That evening — although it was hard for them to think of evening when sunlight still bounced off the waves of the lake — Ralph and Gwen sat by the fire they'd cooked their supper on. In the uncanny daylight the flames were almost invisible.

After hiking across the tundra to the curving ridge and climbing it high enough to see that the red colour on its upper slopes was in fact scree of the rock that formed the pinnacles, they'd returned to their pile of gear on the beach and made camp. They'd pitched the tent and spent an hour scouring the tundra for dry twigs and sticks for their supper fire. Ralph noticed dead wood was always at the base of the bushes and dwarf trees and guessed that the branches there were winter killed. But winter in this landscape now basking under such an exuberant sun was unimaginable.

Gwen sat cross-legged before the fire while Ralph lay back on his elbows at her side, legs stretched out beside the fireplace he'd built with large stones from along the shore. The familiar small talk of a new campsite — "Where shall we pitch the tent?" "Let's air the sleeping bag." "Which pack is the supper in?" "You want to wash the dishes?" — had petered out when the chores were done, and for a while now they'd both been thinking their own long thoughts as they gazed at the dying fire.

They'd met the year before on a spring canoe trip sponsored by the Ontario Outing Club. Both had recently joined the Ottawa chapter, and the trip leader had paired them in one of the weekend's four canoes. Ralph was an experienced paddler and Gwen a novice, but he was a considerate instructor and she a determined learner. By suppertime on Saturday they'd become a team. All day Sunday, while the thin spring air filled the woods that glided by with a magical transparency, they passed the shore of one small lake after another, making short portages between them. Hardwoods standing among the evergreens showed feathery hints of summer leafage. The temperature was bracing. Spring birds sang. On Sunday evening when the trip was over, they agreed to have dinner together in two days.

More outings, more dinners, more time together followed. Ralph learned that Gwen worked as an editor for a feminist press and Gwen that Ralph had a job in the map division of the Geological Survey. Ralph met her mother, who taught English at the University of Ottawa, and her twin sister Trish, who ran a store called Trisha's Treasures on Bank Street. Gwen's father had died the year before of cancer. Ralph's closest relative was an uncle who lived in Vermont; his parents had been killed in a car crash while he was at university. Soon they were in love, and soon after that, they married. It was Ralph's idea to do without a honeymoon — their wedding was in May — and save their money for a wilderness canoe trip in the summer. Gwen enthusiastically agreed. A friend in the Outing Club directed their attention to the Blackstone River in the Arctic barrens. They would start their lives together with a great adventure.

Staring into the flames, in her mind's eye Gwen was seeing again the landscape they'd flown over earlier that day. To be trapped among those dried-out hills or in the maze of swamps and ponds would be a nightmare. But her whispered wish while looking out the plane's window had come true: the country of the Blackstone River was nothing like that. Their hike that afternoon to the ridge had crossed a tundra meadow lively with wildflowers, grasses, mosses, sedges, lichens, and little bushes, and the view from halfway up the ridge had been breathtaking. The unnamed lake stretched sparkling to the horizon; gentle hills lined its nearby shores like amiable guardians.

Ralph was going over details. Planning the trip had been his job. Now that they were actually at its beginning, at the start of three weeks on an Arctic river, with very little probability of encountering anyone else, he felt impelled to review his preparations and the state of their provisions. Because this was it. The look and feel of the land on their afternoon hike had calmed his fear of the land he'd seen from the float plane's window. But his alarm hadn't gone entirely; he couldn't be sure that something like those nightmare landscapes wasn't waiting for them along the course of the Blackstone River. He'd been warned and must be sure they were prepared. He went over everything in his mind.

Food was packaged in separate plastic bags labelled for day and meal — day 1, day 2, day 3, breakfast, dinner, etc. — and bundled together by week into waterproof sacks. A commissary bag held items used every day for lunch — cheese, hard salami, crackers, lemonade mix, and chocolate — and bulk items like sugar, tea, coffee, rice, flour, seasonings, lard. His fishing gear was handy in a day pack, reel oiled, sectional rod in its own container, lures, sinkers, leaders in a tackle box. Waterproofed Geological Survey maps showed the course of the river from the big unnamed lake all the way down to the river's mouth on the Arctic Ocean and then along a short stretch of coast to the Inuit village of Poniktuk. He'd studied those maps for hours. He had a Swiss Army knife and a fish-filleting knife. He had a compass. He had no firearms. But he did have a bear horn that made a horrendous noise in case they encountered a grizzly. They both had a change of clothing, a pair of running shoes for comfort around campsites, boots for hiking and paddling, and extra silicon waterproofing for the boots.

Was there anything he could think of that he'd forgotten? There wasn't. Even so, he would be very cautious on this trip.

Gwen looked down at the lover who'd become her husband. She realized they didn't yet know each other very deeply — everything had gone so excitingly fast — but she knew they loved each other. And that was enough. Below the brim of Ralph's hat, she could just see the line of his jaw; it already had a dark red stubble on it. It was a well-set, altogether trustworthy jaw, and resisting the impulse to reach down and stroke it, she wondered what it would feel like against her skin as their trip went on. Would his beard grow softer as it grew longer? She felt a sexy stir as she thought of its scratchiness tickling the hollow of her neck. She reached into her ditty bag, took out her hairbrush, and released her blonde hair from its daytime bun. Long strokes in front of one shoulder, then the other, down its full length made the glistening hair crackle. Ralph looked up at her.

Gwen's face amazed him. As he often did when he had a chance, Ralph studied it: blue eyes under lashes and eyebrows so blonde they were nearly invisible, a straight nose a little sharp along its ridge but ending in delicate nostrils, a wide generous mouth above a small, firm chin, lean cheeks whose skin when he kissed or touched it was always smooth and fragrant as a pear. The face of a sensible girl, Gwen had once disparagingly called it. But to him it was so perfectly put together that he never stopped marvelling at his luck; of all the men in the world the face must surely have pleased, it had turned with love only to him. It sometimes seemed odd to him to love the face so much and not be able — not yet at least — to read all the thoughts behind it. He had moments of believing his own love deficient because of that. But then he would tell himself that being surprised by her thoughts when she spoke them was infinitely more rewarding than knowing them in advance, and he'd welcome his ignorance and wait for her to speak with the alert anticipation of a chosen lover.

He turned toward her now and ran a hand along the trouser seam on the inside of her thigh.

"Let's go to bed. Busy day tomorrow."

Gwen nodded and put away her brush.

After pouring a pot of water on the fire (for even if it was laid on pebbles and couldn't spread, they were conscientious campers) and placing the cooking gear under their overturned canoe, they walked to the tent, pitched in a grassy hollow.

When they'd zipped up the mosquito netting and clapped their hands inside a dozen or more times to kill the mosquitoes that had followed them in, they silently undressed each other and made long, slow, meditative love on top of their double sleeping bag. It was the first night of their delayed honeymoon. In the sun-filled tent, the colour of its nylon walls turned their skin pale blue.

When the air began to chill them, Ralph and Gwen wriggled into the sleeping bag. She turned on her side, knees drawn up. He curled himself around her. They fell quickly asleep.

<

In her stone house under the sea, Sedna jerked in her sleep. The sea mammals circling above the house twitched flipper and fluke nervously.

She was dreaming of a great devastation. Storms drowned men in kayaks. Sea creatures nibbled at their flesh. Other men froze to death on pans of sea ice, their eyes turning to hard black pebbles, their tongues to pink stones. On land, huge herds of caribou and muskox ran crazed across the tundra, ran and ran till they fell dead. Women died in bloody childbirth, and children died of starvation. Whole populations of Inuit shrivelled into corpses from disease.

Sedna growled in her sleep. The sea mammals overhead, defecating in spurts, swam away.

She dreamed more. Many angakut, both men and women, swam toward her through storm-darkened waters, combs of all kinds clutched in their hands. Her sleeping self smiled. Down they came like schools of fish with human arms and legs, waving their combs ahead of them to signal urgent wishes to untangle and braid her hair and scrape her body clean. But when they reached the water directly overhead, they veered aside and, turning into a school of real fish, insolently flashed silver bellies at her and sped off.

With a jolt Sedna woke. The dream still vivid, she

glowered upward into the water she'd just seen filled with eager descending angakut. Not even her sea mammals were swimming there. Ill temper roiled her mind.

How long had she been asleep? Had she ever had a dream like that before? She couldn't remember. But its meaning was clear: if the Inuit ever stopped ignoring her, they would only mock her.

Two fat bubbles burst from Sedna's nostrils. Would human beings ever really dare to mock her? In the past, never. But now? They already ignored her.

But had these dreams come to her for a reason?

Sedna tensed her buttocks, first one, then the other, in a sedentary dance of inspiration. Yes, they had! She rocked back and forth, sending ripples through the house. A few curious seals returned to the water overhead.

Now she understood. Her dreams was telling her what to do. But it was a long time since she'd scourged her people, and she'd never done so with such devastation.

Not kill them. No. What would be the use of that? But terrify them, make them know how much she still could harm them, know she still controlled their world. Send them . . . not great plagues and killing storms but . . . a wind. A scouring wind over land and sea so strong they'd know it had to come from her. That would make them think. That would make them send her angakut. And her body would at last be clean again and her hair braided.

With the lick of a fat tongue across lips that widened in a smile, Sedna closed her eyes and concentrated on summoning a wind. It would have to come from Narsuq, a spirit of the upper air who kept all the world's winds wrapped inside his voluminous clothing, which was made of caribou hides he had snatched with little thieving gusts and breezes from the drying racks of hunters. In the past he'd always obeyed her. But now? Sedna bent all her power to commanding Narsuq to shake a ferocious wind from

his parka. In her mind's eye, she saw the clothing flap.
How long was it since she'd done something like this?
She'd been lazy, letting sleep possess her. But no more. It
felt good to be her Great Self again.

When they'd had breakfast, Ralph and Gwen made ready to cross the unnamed lake to the outlet of the Blackstone River, where their run to the Arctic Ocean would begin. Standing on the shore, Ralph consulted his map, folding it, holding it at waist level, and turning it so the squiggly brown line that represented the ridge they'd climbed was behind him. Then he looked up and chose the direction they should take across the lake to the river. He held the stern of the canoe steady while Gwen clambered over their gear and settled in the bow. Then he placed one foot in front of the stern seat and, hands on the gunwales, shoved off with the other and sat down.

They were afloat. They lifted their paddles and dug them briskly into the lake's sunlit surface. The canoe quartered into a light breeze. Small waves lapped at its hull. Behind them, the shoreline gradually disappeared.

"Is the wind coming up some?" Gwen called out after a while.

"Just a bit," Ralph said.

And he looked to his left and right. There was no land in sight, only waves.

Moments later they were paddling into a near gale. Whitecaps hissed toward them, and spray flew into Gwen's face and lap every time the bow spanked down into a trough. But she gave no thought at all to reaching for the rain pants and jacket tucked under her seat. The troughs were deep, and it was all she could do to catch enough water with her paddle to continue stroking. In the stern, Ralph changed course to head the canoe straight into the wind. The waves were too big for quartering. But it was a struggle to keep the boat headed straight, for every time it crested a wave it slewed sideways, threatening to turn broadside. If it did that, they'd flip. Reading each wave an instant before it struck the bow, he used all the strength he could muster to ride it out and grab enough water to make a correcting stroke. Then the next wave came. In the bow, Gwen felt the boat slew and turn straight again on the crest of each wave and understood their danger. She kept paddling. But only Ralph saw how close they came to shipping water every time the canoe splashed into a trough.

Heads down against the wind and eyes grimly fixed on a sliver of land that had come into sight on the horizon, Ralph and Gwen bent hard to their paddles and tried to close their minds to what would happen if the waves got bigger.

The land inched toward them. At last they reached it.

Riding a breaker, the canoe crunched onto the beach. Gwen quickly shipped her paddle and stepped out. She pulled the bow further up and held it steady between her knees as waves broke under the boat while Ralph climbed out. Together they pulled the boat out of the water.

"Some wind," Gwen said.

"Yeah," said Ralph. "We're not going anywhere till it dies down."

Gwen sat and then lay back on the beach. Its pebbles were warm. She closed her eyes. A low hill behind the beach broke the main force of the wind, but enough of it reached her in whispery gusts to begin to dry her clothes. She felt the breeze flutter along her body.

Ralph squatted beside her. He scooped up a handful of stones and, squinting at the lake, flicked them at it one by one like marbles. Presently he dropped the stones still in his hand and, rising, went to the canoe, reached into a side pocket of his knapsack, and took out the topo map and his binoculars. Hanging the binoculars around his neck and walking softly on the pebbles in case Gwen had fallen asleep, he crossed the narrow beach and climbed the small hill behind.

The wind immediately blew his hat off when he reached the top and would have blown it into the lake if the chinstrap hadn't caught it. He let the hat bounce on his back as he leaned into the wind and stared at the countryside before him. Then he looked down at his map, held firmly in both hands at his waist. Checking back and forth between it and the land and turning the map this way and that, he tried to match what he saw with the map's markings.

He couldn't.

Now he turned his back to the wind and, slipping the map inside his shirt, lifted his binoculars and turned to face the wind again. He swept the low-lying country with deliberate slowness, bracing his elbows against his chest to steady his hands. Slowly, slowly, he swung his upper body, moving the small magnified circle across the tundra, waiting with deliberate patience for a glint of water to appear that could be the Blackstone River.

It didn't.

He lowered the binoculars, stood still for a moment, then turned his back to the wind again and let it push him off the hilltop. Except that they had to be roughly opposite their overnight campsite, he had no idea where they were.

"Where are we?" Gwen asked when she heard his footsteps crunch across the pebbles and stop by her head.

"I'm not sure. We had to turn off course out there. Best thing will be to stay along this shore when the wind drops. We'll be sure to catch up with the river sooner or later if we do that."

He stared at the angry surface of the lake. Spume flying off their crests, the waves seemed even bigger than when they were fighting their way through them. A miracle, he thought, that they'd made it to shore. And what was so strange was that the sky was clear. No sign of storm clouds. In fact, not a cloud in sight. Ralph shook his head, dropped to the beach, and stretched out next to Gwen.

"Nap time," he said, and pulled his hat over his eyes.

Gwen nodded, her own eyes still closed. How extraordinary, she thought, to actually feel the wetness leaving her trousers and her shirt, the sun was so strong, the air so dry. Wisps of wind continued to whisper around her head. Through them she heard waves break on the shore and rattle its pebbles as they withdrew, as if sucking on them. It was an oddly comforting sound, and Gwen let herself drift into it until she felt herself floating in the warmth of the sun and gliding slowly away from the tactile world of stony pebbles under her back into some warm, soft, airy other dimension.

An hour later the wind dropped as suddenly as it had come up. The silence woke Gwen. She sat up and looked around. Ralph was stretched out beside her.

"Ralph, the lake's calmed down."

He sat up. There were no more whitecaps.

"You're right. Let's have lunch," he said.

Gwen rooted around in the commissary pack and pulled out a chunk of cheddar cheese, a package of wheat crackers, the hard salami, lemonade crystals, and a bag of dried fruits. Ralph mixed lake water with the crystals in a plastic bottle, and they sat with their legs tucked under them and ate lunch.

"This is the life," Ralph said, smiling.

"That was some beginning, this morning."

Ralph nodded. "No more lakes on the trip, though. This is the only one." He put an arm around her shoulders and kissed her cheek. "You were great out there."

She smiled and shrugged.

Gwen wrapped the leftovers and put them in the pack. They launched the canoe and paddled easily out onto the glassy swells that rose and fell benignly on the surface of the lake.

Until late that evening they paddled along the shore. They didn't find the river. Finally they made camp.

That night in their sleeping bag Gwen rolled toward Ralph and, kissing his stubbled cheek, draped an arm across his chest and fell asleep. Ralph lay on his back with an arm under her neck. It was a while before sleep came to him.

Mid-morning of the next day they approached what Ralph was sure would be the Blackstone River. He had the map in front of him, tucked into a fold of his knapsack, and for some time he'd been keeping his eye on the blue hairline that represented the river and looking back and forth between the lakeshore and the land behind it and that hairline and the topographical markings around it. Everything looked right. This had to be it.

But it wasn't.

When they reached it, a trickle of a stream flowed into the lake, not out of it. From the stern of the canoe, Ralph stared at it as if staring could make it widen and flow the other way.

How could he have been so wrong?

He looked back at the map. But now, by some malicious trick, it hardly even looked like a map any more, or at least a map that meant anything. He'd worked on maps for years and considered himself an expert, but this one now seemed only a piece of coloured paper whose brown lines for elevation, blue lines for watercourses, coded markings for muskeg and esker, green patches for stands of trees, and blue blotches for lakes corresponded to nothing in the real world.

"Keep going?" Gwen asked over her shoulder.

"Yup," Ralph said and, looking away from the map, picked up his paddle.

In his mind's eye he saw the waterlogged land they'd flown over two days ago — was it only two days! — and recalled the thought that had come to him then: if you got lost down there, you'd die.

Were they, he suddenly wondered, even on the right lake?

Paddling again, watching ripples spread arrowlike from the canoe's bow and vanish into the lake's calm surface, Ralph cursed himself for not having followed their flight on the pilot's maps. He should've sat next to the pilot instead of in the cabin. He'd been too trusting. He gripped his paddle tighter and dug it savagely into the water. The canoe jumped forward.

In the bow, Gwen felt the boat surge ahead and matched her paddle strokes to Ralph's. She realized he'd thought that stream would be the Blackstone River and was upset to have been wrong. But it stood to reason that they had only to keep on going along the lakeshore and they'd eventually come to the river. In the meantime, with the lake so calm, there was the strange sunlit landscape to look at, the warmth of the day to feel through her clothing, and the pleasant exercise of dipping her paddle into the water and lifting it out again. She hoped Ralph was over his disappointment and enjoying this bounty too.

A hot sun high in the sky glistened on the water's surface and made a row of hills some distance behind the shoreline shimmer and ripple as if seen through invisible flames. Early in the afternoon, the Morrisseys passed without recognizing it the beach where the plane had landed them.

Toward the end of the following morning, turning the point of a sandspit that hooked around a little bay, Ralph saw what looked like a strip of banked gravel at the head of the bay. All morning he'd closed his mind to everything except reaching ahead with his paddle and drawing it firmly through the water. Making the motion over and over, feeling his muscles flex, he'd concentrated on making his strokes as textbook perfect as he could. Now he laid his paddle across his knees and squinted against the sun's dazzle into the small bay. If that strip of gravel was a cut bank of the kind that moving water scours from a shore, it could mark an outlet. It could mark the beginning of the Blackstone River.

But he said nothing as they started paddling again. Even when he saw it was indeed a cut bank, he kept silent. But when they reached it and discovered a wide stream slipping quietly off into the countryside, he didn't hesitate to guide their canoe straight into it. And when, after a few more strokes, he felt a current grip the boat and begin to speed it by grassy banks that closed in beside them, Ralph took his paddle out of the water again and drew a long breath. Then he twisted in his seat to look back.

Beyond the banks already narrowing his view, the lake lay indolent and glittering, a body of water as indifferent in its present calm as it had been dangerous in the wind that nearly drowned them.

Gwen too was leaning on her paddle.

"This the river?"

"This is it," Ralph said, and assured himself it had to be.

For if the pilot had landed them on the right lake after all and this was its principal outlet, then there could be no doubt they were on the Blackstone River. And from here all they had to do was follow its course until they reached the Arctic Ocean and the Inuit village where at last they'd catch a plane toward home.

And if it wasn't the right lake?

If it wasn't the right lake, they were starting down an unknown stream into a wilderness they'd never come out of.

"Let's go a little farther and then look for a campsite."

"Fine," said Gwen.

As they picked up their paddles, the vast silence of the empty Arctic air swallowed their voices.

Coming from the sea, the wind that forced the Morrisseys' canoe off course on the nameless lake sent dust devils swirling along Poniktuk's main road, raised a cloud of sand over the airstrip, rose through the valleys beyond into the hills that became a plateau, and hovered above the tundra there like a wide invisible banner, flapping savagely.

"Holy!" said Lawrence, caught outside his parents' house. He and Nate were cleaning his father's outboard motor.

Dust flew up his nose and stung his cheeks. Blinking, he turned his back to the wind and gestured to Nate to grab a corner of the tarpaulin under the motor. The two folded the jumping tarp over the disassembled motor and its parts and weighted down the edges with rocks and tools. Then they staggered around a corner of the house to its lee side.

Lawrence ruffled his hair to get some of the dust out. Nate took a pouch of Drum tobacco from a jacket pocket, rolled a cigarette, and passed the pouch and papers to his cousin. Before turning the corner, he thought he'd glimpsed, high in the sky, a caribou-skin parka suspended above caribou pants. He lit his cigarette and looked up.

There they were. Far away in the sky's bright blue, the pants hung loose, but the parka was flapping. No arms or legs or head came out of the clothing.

"Sky's real clear," he said, and watched as Lawrence interrupted his cigarette rolling to look where the pants and parka were. He just nodded and went back to rolling.

Nate sighed. Since he'd waked up early that April morning almost three months ago and had the feeling of rising into the sky to watch himself get the spring's first geese, he'd been seeing quite a few things other people didn't seem to see. From the airstrip one afternoon he'd seen caribou grazing in a valley far away in the hills. And one evening, walking home from floor hockey at the school gym, he'd glanced at his uncle's house and seen right through the wall into a bedroom where Simon and Ruby were fucking. In the same way sometime later, he'd seen his thirteen-year-old cousin Della undressing in a bedroom of his Auntie Akpa's house. He was watching with growing excitement when Akpa herself waddled into the room and started getting undressed too. Before she even got her blouse over her head, he turned away. He could never tell when one of these sights or visions was going to come to him, and he couldn't make them happen. They came and went on their own.

Nate pulled on his cigarette and, inhaling a soothing lungful of tobacco smoke, leaned against the warm siding and considered what the wind was doing to Poniktuk.

A loose shingle on the roof next door — it was Simon's house — struggled in jerks to free itself and, finally succeeding, sailed into the sky doing flips and dives. The shingles next to the vacated spot now also began to jump and flap, and soon a whole patch of them tore loose.

Plenty of repair work from the housing committee after this

blow, Lawrence was thinking. He'd go see Obie, the committee chairman, as soon as the wind died down. He could probably earn enough money for a whole bunch of new tapes from the catalogue.

Now a strip of aluminum siding from some house upwind went rattling past, bounding along the ground in spastic leaps as if trying to rise into the air. It was followed by a cartwheeling caribou hide, more aluminum strips, a pair of jeans, and a bouncing length of stovepipe with a metal hat on it. Shingles flew everywhere like crazed birds.

"Summer wind never come from ocean side like this before," Lawrence said, cupping his cigarette.

Nate grunted and stole another look at the sky. The caribou outfit was still there, flapping.

He turned his attention to the hills inland from Poniktuk. He'd been looking at them all his life. They were where caribou passed in the spring and fall and fish swam in lakes and rivers in the summer, and beyond them on the plateau were stream beds frozen in the winter where his father and brothers and he set out traplines for fur. But he now looked at the hills with new eyes.

Some day all that land belong to us, he thought, and toed out his cigarette.

The wind continued whistling around the house, now carrying fewer personal items or scraps of housing material. Almost everything loose or lying around and light enough had already been scooped up and carried away toward the airstrip and the flatlands beyond. We'll be finding stuff out there for years, Lawrence thought. He wondered if his cousin's mind was working along similar lines but saw in Nate's eyes an expression that, since the night Nate spoke out at the meeting, meant his mind was far away. Lawrence returned his own thoughts to the tapes catalogue.

Nate rolled and lit another cigarette.

The morning after he'd challenged the assistant regional superintendent of Local Government, the telephone had rung in his parents' house, and to everyone's astonishment the call from

Seal Harbour was for him. Andy Kublu said his uncle Simon wanted to talk to him and he should go to his house right away. It seemed odd for Andy Kublu to be giving him a message from his uncle, who lived only a few doors away, but Nate had already guessed that what he said at the meeting couldn't have pleased his uncle, and he could only think he was being summoned to Simon's to be bawled out, or worse.

He knew his uncle sometimes beat the shit out of people who annoyed or disagreed with him. It was one of his ways of staying head man in town. Everyone feared his fists. But Nate surprised himself by deciding without a second thought to obey Andy Kublu's summons. He acknowledged fear of his uncle, but he didn't really feel it.

He left the house.

The morning's next surprise awaited him in Simon's living room: his uncle complimented him for having spoken out at the meeting, said more young people should use their minds like that, and told him he wanted to make him the fieldworker in Poniktuk for the Aboriginal Rights Alliance. Nate couldn't believe his ears. Only two days ago he'd listened to Simon get angry at Andy Kublu and the white stranger when they mentioned that organization. Could what he'd said at the meeting have changed his uncle's mind? It seemed unlikely, but, buoyed by a wave of such intoxicating self-importance that he could hardly keep a straight face, Nate had accepted the job.

During the following days he'd had more phone calls from Andy promising papers to study and future training to prepare him for his work, and in due course a thick envelope of documents arrived. But a glance revealed that they looked very much like schoolwork, at which he'd failed so badly in Inuvik, and his self-importance suddenly collapsed. What had led him to think he could do this kind of work? He shoved the papers back in the envelope, put the envelope in a kitchen drawer, and hung out the rest of the day with Lawrence, listening to tapes and kidding around. After that, he avoided his uncle when he could and, when he couldn't, lied to him about studying the papers in the envelope, which Simon himself had given him when handing out mail in the store.

Then, almost a month later, came a call to attend a land-rights workshop in Inuvik.

"How long you think this wind keep up?" Lawrence asked, having exhausted his recollection of the catalogue and chosen which tapes to order.

Nate glanced up at the sky. The caribou outfit was smaller.

"Not too much maybe."

"You want to come in for coffee?"

"In a minute."

Lawrence dropped to his haunches and leaned against the wire skirting between the floor of his parents' house and the ground. Out of the wind, the sun was warm, but every now and then a gust curled around the corner like a cold tongue and licked him. He hugged himself.

Nate had seen no way to get out of going to the workshop, and standing at the airstrip surrounded by friends who kept telling him how they envied him, he waited for the charter to pick him up with outward nonchalance but inner dread.

The workshop was run by Don Thornton, the same bearded white guy who'd come to Poniktuk with Andy Kublu. It was scheduled to last a week. Sitting the first day at a big table in a stuffy conference room in Inuvik's Federal Research Centre with representatives from other Inuit settlements in the region and listening to Thornton talk about things he'd never heard of — "economic development," "land-use management," "ownership in fee simple absolute," "data-based negotiating strategies" — had reduced Nate by mid-afternoon to a sweaty panic. On the table in front of him was a loose-leaf binder full of papers like those he'd hidden in the kitchen drawer. Thornton promised quizzes about them at the end of the week. The other Inuit representatives seemed to understand everything Thornton was saying, but he understood nothing. By the end of the day he was ready to quit but couldn't figure out how to ask to be sent home without embarrassing himself.

That night he went drinking with some other workshoppers in the Polar Bear Bar and Dance Hall of the Igloo Inn, where they were staying. No one talked about work. Several were in Inuvik for the first time, and as they drank, liberation from the normal scrutiny of family and other members of their home communities fired their imaginations with fantasies about night adventures in Inuvik. Recalling his ability as a schoolboy to find parties after the bars had closed, Nate let it be known he was a veteran of such adventures, and even before the harsh lights of closing time were turned on in the Polar Bear, he was invited to a party. The other men at his table got cold feet, but Nate left with the middle-aged woman who had made eyes at him from the next table and told him, when they danced together, that she knew where to go.

The place turned out to be her apartment, and the party turned out to be a party of two. But she had a bottle of CC, and as Nate had a few more drinks and groggily came to an understanding of what kind of party she had in mind, his own mind cleared in one swift moment, and the feelings of inadequacy and alarm still nagging him from the day's work session vanished. A fierce intention to make love to the woman, not just to fuck her but make love in wildly imaginative ways, possessed him. He acted on it without hesitation, and although the quickness of his undressing her and taking off his own clothes seemed to surprise the woman, it also clearly pleased her. Over the next hour, on her bed and in several other places in the apartment, Nate's inventions astonished them both. Then they entered a world beyond astonishment.

When morning came, they lay side by side on skewed and sodden sheets, mindlessly but rapturously bruised and exhausted, their lips swollen and bloodied and the odour of sweat filling their nostrils like perfume. They napped.

Dressing while she slept, Nate had a quick breakfast at the hotel and reported promptly at nine o'clock to the Research

Centre. Suffering no hangover at all, he felt full of energy and confidence. Quickly he saw that the others in the room who'd nodded their heads and smiled as if understanding everything Don Thornton said the day before did so only out of politeness; they were just as lost as he had been.

But was no longer.

For the night's activities seemed not only to have dispelled forever any shameful memories of schoolboy ineptitude but to have focused his mind on the work before him in the conference room with a sharpness that surprised everyone. For the first time in his life, Nate felt he absolutely knew what he was doing and was absolutely sure he could do it. So he persisted and the others persisted and Thornton persisted, and by the end of the week they all really did understand more than they had at the beginning, even Thornton, who listened carefully whenever one of the elders described Inuit life in the old days.

Nate returned to the woman's apartment early on the evening after their night together, but her door was locked, no one answered his knocking, and when he went looking, she wasn't in the Polar Bear Bar. He never saw her again. He didn't even know her name.

But there were other pleasures to be enjoyed in his spare time. Now instead of a schoolboy sneaking into the Igloo Inn to find a room where there was a party, he was a paid-for guest with his own room. He shared it with an older workshopper from Uugaaqtuk, Luke Talimak, who was a born-again Christian and teetotaller, so there weren't any parties there. But every time he entered the hotel and walked across the lobby to the desk and asked for his key, he did so with a satisfying sense of deserved privilege. Besides paying for the room, ABRA gave him in advance a per diem of forty dollars for meals and incidentals. He'd never had so much money in his pocket, and at first he couldn't manage it. The evening he failed to find the woman he'd made love to the night before, he spent nearly three days' allowance buying drinks in the Polar Bear for his new workshop friends and for strangers who also seemed to have become friends. Pangs of hunger for the next two days taught him to budget. Now, when he strolled up and down the Bay's lavishly stocked aisles, he no longer had envy in his heart and a schoolboy's fingers itching to steal but instead thought about what he might buy at the end of the workshop.

When that time came, Andy Kublu flew in from Seal Harbour and gave a big party in his hotel room for all the newly trained ABRA fieldworkers. They swilled beer and rum and spilled pretzels and potato chips and pizza crusts all over the carpet, and Nate and some of the others got so drunk they nearly missed their charter flights home the next morning. He just had time to run to the Bay and buy some tapes.

And now for several weeks he'd been trying to explain the things he'd learned at the workshop to his parents and grandparents and aunts and uncles and cousins and friends and their brothers and sisters and husbands and wives and children in Poniktuk. But especially to his uncle Simon, who was making him tell him everything he knew about ABRA and its future. Nate saw no reason not to.

He looked up at the sky. The caribou clothing was a tiny dot.

"How about that coffee?"

"You got it," Lawrence said.

Hunching their shoulders against the wind's anticipated hit, they stepped around the corner of the house. The wind was weaker, but it still grabbed their hair and flattened their clothing against their legs and chests. Heads down, they moved toward the back porch stairs. As they went up, a strong gust suddenly caught them from behind and, boosting them swiftly to the top of the stairs, nearly blew them across the porch and over the railing on the other side. Lawrence grabbed the doorknob and pulled the door open. Seated at the kitchen table a few minutes later with coffee mugs before them and Lawrence's mother Irene in the living room, listening but pretending not to, Nate began to explain land ownership in fee simple absolute to his cousin.

"So you guys telling the Feds what lands we allus been using,"

Lawrence summed up a little later, "and then the Feds gonna say 'Okay, now you own it,' and then we get money from that land if someone else want to use it?"

"Something like that."

Lawrence thought a moment.

"That some powerful thing, that fee simple absolute."

Considering the words, he saw a stereo set filling a large part of one wall in his bedroom.

"Sure is," Nate said.

He glanced at his cousin and decided he'd done enough explaining. He looked out the kitchen window.

Akpa's house was across the road. Dust settled around it like snow at the end of a winter storm. He wished for one of those moments that would allow him to look inside the house for Della, but nothing happened. But if his penetrating vision had failed him, his imagination suffered no such weakness. In his mind's eye, Nate began undressing his thirteen-year-old cousin. When her small round breasts came into view, he cupped them in his hands. Memories of his first night in Inuvik supplied the images that followed. He got a hard-on under the table.

The wind died down in Poniktuk. An occasional shingle still flew from a roof and a clothespin sometimes lost its grip on another article of clothing, but most of the time only dust now whirled through the air and, down by the bay, salt spray. A corner of the tarpaulin covering the outboard motor belonging to Lawrence's father had long since worked loose. Dust coated all its parts.

While the wind lasted, the people of Poniktuk stayed indoors. Those whose husbands or brothers or fathers had gone in boats to the mouth of the Blackstone River to check their nets for fish worried about them getting caught coming home in the blow. Fortunately none were. But, like Lawrence, many remarked on the strangeness of such a wind coming off the sea at this time of year.

When the wind finally dropped altogether, Nate thanked his Aunt Irene for coffee, crossed the kitchen, and, stepping onto the back porch, looked up into the cloudless sky. The caribou clothing was gone.

The Morrisseys' stream widened and became a swift but docile river. No rapids interrupted its course, and its water was so clear they could see every detail of the bottom, sometimes two or three metres beneath the canoe. Beds of pebbles sped by, and cobblestones of many colours, large black boulders, streaks of white sand, and patches of grass that waved in the current like green hair. Gwen spent rapt moments gazing down at these grasses, notions of river nymphs stirring in her mind.

Ralph took note of the bottom only to gauge its distance from the hull of the canoe. Although it sometimes rose close, it always fell away again, leaving plenty of room for their passage. As they were carried ever deeper into the sunlit tundra, where only the splash of their paddles and an occasional bird call broke the silence, Ralph took comfort in the knowledge that this seemed at least to be a real river. It grew larger not smaller, and its current rarely slackened. It was going someplace. Exactly where was a question he tried not to let himself ask.

The waterproofed map lay folded away in his knapsack. Studying it at their first river campsite, trying to decide if this bend or that ridge was represented by this blue or that brown line, had proved useless. As they continued, everything began to look like everything else in the undifferentiated landscape, and nothing looked like anything on the map. A vestige of hope that cartographic information and visible landscape might still fall together to tell him where they were made him pull out the map and study it again from time to time. But the farther they went, the more pointless this exercise became; he couldn't tell where they started on the river each day or how far they went. He ended up looking at the map in the evening and morning mostly for Gwen's benefit, putting it away again with a confident nod he hoped would tell her he was satisfied with what he saw. But all day long, from the stern of their canoe, he stared at the uncooperative landscape.

In the bow, Gwen took for granted that they were on the Blackstone. Ralph was the self-appointed keeper of the map, and she was glad to leave all questions of navigation to him. His occasional checking between map and countryside confirmed her trust. But she never asked him where they were. The countryside itself, unblurred by feelings like Ralph's, had begun to engage her full and curious attention.

For one thing, the sunlight that lit it nearly twenty-four hours a day with a translucent brightness had a puzzling effect. She couldn't tell how far away anything was. Or how large or small. A hill that looked to be a little way down the river would remain stubbornly unapproachable and the same apparent size all day long, despite their steady paddling toward it. And when, the following day, they'd round a bend and it was suddenly there, it would prove to be farther away from the river and much taller than she'd thought. On the other hand, what appeared to be a distant rock-crested ridge would suddenly jump into the foreground and turn out to be a row of stones just beyond the riverbank. These tricks disconcerted but did not dismay her. They were like a game the country was playing, and Gwen joined it. She was happy when her estimate of scale or perspective proved correct, and when she was wrong, she was amused by her mistake and only provoked by it into looking harder. Gradually her eyes adjusted to the true dimensions of the Arctic landscape.

One morning she invited Ralph to join the game.

"How far away do you think that is?" she said, laying her paddle across her knees and pointing.

"What?"

"That flat-topped hill."

Ralph's eyes found the hill, and he too laid his paddle across his knees.

"Couple of miles maybe."

"Not farther? I bet it's more like five."

"Could be."

"What does the map say?"

"It . . . I'm not sure it would show up."

"Even out there all by itself?"

"Well, wait a minute."

He reached toward his knapsack and then changed his mind. Gwen had her back to him. "Here it is," he said, hands still on his paddle. "It looks like about . . . you're right. About five miles."

"And how about that one over there?"

Again she pointed.

"That's harder to tell. Does it matter?"

"No. I just think it's fun to guess."

By way of reply Ralph picked up his paddle and starting stroking.

Gwen felt the canoe move forward. Still leaning on her paddle, she looked ahead. If Ralph wasn't interested in playing the countryside guessing game, that was all right. Maybe from the stern it wasn't so much fun.

But how lucky *she* was to be in the bow of the canoe! From where she sat, nothing came between her and this uncanny land. She knew it was called "barren," but to her it looked anything but desolate or infertile. There were wildflowers everywhere on the riverbanks and in the fields beyond, and in sheltered gullys there were little spiky trees. Coloured lichens — orange, grey, blue-black, green — grew on almost every boulder and stone, and mosses and heathers and all kinds of grasses and sedges and bracken filled the meadows and slopes. The low hills on both sides of the river embraced it with long green arms.

As Gwen reached stroke after stroke into the smooth water, the landscape around her folded her slowly and steadily into itself.

Behind her, Ralph was not happy. Between strokes he glanced at the knapsack pocket where the useless map was tucked away. He hadn't liked deceiving Gwen, but he felt he had to protect her from the possibility that they were lost. He had to pretend he knew where they were. But lying to her just now about the distance to the hill had made him feel something other than noble and protective, as he usually did when he considered how he was keeping his fears to himself. It made him feel angry.

They paddled on in silence.

At night the sun edged slowly around the horizon behind them — they'd learned to pitch their tent so the sunlight while they slept would not be in their eyes — till finally it disappeared briefly, leaving behind, more often than not, a spectacular sunset. The sunset would then fade into twilight that lasted only a short while before the sky lightened again into dawn and the sun reappeared. It was never really dark.

Gwen slept as if drugged. As a young girl, she'd loved daytime naps, and now, while the sun dipped below the horizon and came up again behind her head, her breathing deepened and shallowed and deepened again with a rhythm as natural and easy as an animal's.

Ralph slept less. No matter how quickly they scrambled into the tent and zipped up the mosquito netting, blackflies and mosquitoes always followed them in. His first job, while Gwen was undressing and getting into the sleeping bag, was to kill the bugs. He'd watch the tiny blackflies crawl along the taut tent wall to a stitched seam or a puckered corner. There, if he was patient enough to let them pile up, he could squash a lot of them with a single swipe of his thumb. Mosquitoes were another matter. Each one seemed to enjoy taking its own maddening time circling invisibly somewhere in the tent and whining in and out of his hearing until, having landed, it suddenly went silent. If he then felt a bite, he could slap and kill it. But he had to spot in flight and snatch out of the air those that refused to land where he could feel them . Every night it took Ralph a long time to kill the bugs. But that was only the beginning of his wakefulness.

As Gwen fell asleep and he finally undressed and lay in the sleeping bag beside her, the events of the day would pass before him in review. Each day ended was a day survived, he told himself, and at first this sensible thought brought him ease. But after a week on the river, with each day's travel taking them deeper into mapless wilderness, some malign quirk of recall began to rob the day's events of their reassurance and infused them instead with risk. An artful paddle stroke that had brought the canoe gliding perfectly into an eddy at their lunch stop lost its artfulness and seemed only lucky. A fractional change in the stroke, he now saw, would have flipped them. A manoeuvre around a rock in midstream during the afternoon, executed in real time with unthinking skill, in retrospect looked ill-advised, even clumsy.

When these distortions first invaded his nightly reviews, Ralph tried to shake them off. He'd turn to Gwen and, taking her sleeping body in his arms, nestle his face against her hair and breathe its familiar, calming scent. But once begun, the malevolent recapitulation wouldn't stop. He couldn't control it. Helplessly, behind closed eyes, he'd watch the day's successes turn themselves into narrowly missed failures or dangerous judgement calls. A day ended might be a day survived, but by what a slim, uncertain margin! Then Ralph would begin to sweat and, releasing Gwen, turn on his side away from her to face his torment.

Every night now, Ralph hoped the ordeal would not begin again, and sometimes, after he'd killed the bugs and settled into the sleeping bag, sleep would blessedly seize him. But usually, before long, fragments of the day would begin to flicker behind his closed eyes and slowly cohere until, as he came wide awake, the malevolent process began again. He'd lie helpless and mesmerized in the sleeping bag until at last exhaustion and some darkening of the sky would allow him to fall into a fitful doze.

But in the morning, Ralph would rinse these disturbing memories from his mind and attack the new day with determination. He'd concentrate on executing with exacting skill every task the day presented, willing this effort to earn him insurance against the night's distortions. But when evening came and he lay again a prisoner in the sun-filled tent, treacherous recall would again subvert the day's accomplishments. Soon his mind began to reach beyond the actual happenings of the day just ended and invent imaginary ones for the day coming up. Onto a river and landscape he now considered dangerous and even hostile, his imagination projected reel after reel of plausible disasters.

In these nightly movies, Gwen played a major role. Whatever the mishap — the canoe swamping was the most frequent, but there were others — he'd try heroically to save her. He'd swim desperately after her as icy water numbed his limbs, or he'd frantically try to distract the charging grizzly bear. But he always failed. Sometimes Gwen died so horribly he'd groan and squirm inside their sleeping bag until the terrible scene played itself out to its awful end — and another began.

Night after night, longing for sleep's release but grimly sleepless, Ralph watched with his mind's fixed eye these projections of death, his own and Gwen's, in the Arctic wilderness that surrounded them.

Beside him, Gwen slept.

By day, they paddled largely in silence. For Gwen, absorbed in the landscape and sensing Ralph behind her watching it too, the silence built between them a daily arc of love that she was happy to leave unexpressed. Ralph kept silent for other reasons.

So passed the first twelve days of the Morrisseys' wilderness canoe trip. The weather held fair; light but steady breezes blew blackflies and mosquitoes away from their heads and hands while they paddled; the banks of the river provided comfortable campsites; trout and grayling struck his spinner every time Ralph fished for supper; clumps of dried willow and dwarf spruce supplied fuel for their morning and evening fires; and overhead, all day long, boisterous clouds moved through a placid sky like images of heaven.

Sedna frowned. No angakuq had swum down from the world above with a comb in his hand to tell her what the terrible wind had done and plead with her to stop

*it. Perhaps Narsuq had not obeyed her. But no, even at
the depth of her stone house, the ocean had been disturbed,
causing seals and other mammals hovering overhead to
ride and sway on unfamiliar currents.*

*Stubborn Inuit! If a wind alone didn't move them,
she'd send them something that would. Sedna searched
her mind . . . A storm! She'd send them a storm like the
one she'd dreamed, so terrible it couldn't fail to frighten
them.*

*Only one spirit could make a storm like that — Sila,
Narsuq's superior and her equal in his control of all the
weather between the earth and the moon. Unlike Narsuq,
invisible but recognizable by his caribou clothing, Sila had
no shape at all. He was everywhere and nowhere, he was
the sky itself, he was all the elements of weather — rain,
lightning, thunder, snow, hail, wind, sleet, fog, clouds, and
cloudless air as well — and he was nothing. He was as large
as the world he enveloped and smaller than a drop of dew.
He existed only in manifestations of himself. But he had
one habit that revealed his presence: when Sila was
preparing big weather, he whistled.*

*Sedna composed her mind for the effort of sending a
request to this remote and powerful spirit.*

*Presently, a sound developed high above the earth that
was inaudible to human ears. But scientists who could see
its sound waves on their instruments sometimes called it
atmospheric whistle.*

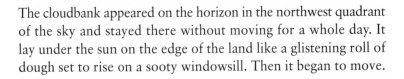

The cloudbank appeared on the horizon in the northwest quadrant
of the sky and stayed there without moving for a whole day. It
lay under the sun on the edge of the land like a glistening roll of
dough set to rise on a sooty windowsill. Then it began to move.

From their campfire, Ralph and Gwen watched it spread through the sky, dark clouds slowly billowing toward them. A wind ran ahead of the clouds and reached their campsite while the sky above was still clear. Sparks flew from the fire, and an empty cook pot went rolling across the tundra. Gwen chased it. By the time they'd put out the fire, picked up their gear and stuffed it into knapsacks, rinsed and nested the cook pots, thrown knapsacks and pots into the tent, found rocks to pile on the tent pegs, pulled the canoe well up from shore, leaving it right side up and weighted with the food pack, and zipped themselves into the tent, the tent fly over their heads was flapping and snapping like a snare drum.

Soon the storm clouds reached the sky above them. The pale light filtering into the tent abruptly darkened. Gwen reached for Ralph's hand.

"It'll be okay," he said. "Let's just get into the bag. But better keep our clothes on. We might have to go outside to check the pegs."

Gwen removed her boots and slid into the sleeping bag. When Ralph joined her, she snuggled against him. Lately, even on nights when he got into the sleeping bag at the same time she did, she had usually felt that he was still awake as she drifted off to sleep. And he was always awake when she woke up. Now she felt the warmth of his body spread to hers through their clothes. He was her protector.

Gwen listened to the wind. It moaned and wailed around the tent. A gust made the cords holding down the tent fly thrum. The wind sounded dangerous, but the sleeping bag's familiar wrapping and Ralph's body made the danger seem unthreatening, even pleasurable. They were snug in their tent, two lovers in a pocket of safety listening to the storm's commotion, riding it out side by side in each other's arms. She snuggled closer.

Ralph too was listening to the wind. It rose to a shriek, and the tent fly gave another drum snap. Now he could also see the wind. Under its force, the tent wall bulged inward over his head. Staring at the bulge, he heard a new sound: rain lashed the taut nylon. Then the sound changed to swishing. Ralph guessed that was snow. The wind rose even higher. It could be a blizzard. It could kill them.

As the minutes lengthened, the swish turned back to splattering rain and then, with a sky-cracking thunderclap, to a rattle of hail and back again to rain and again to what he heard as snow. And the wind never let up. Now it snapped the tent fly like a whip and bellied in the thin wall like a sail. It raged around them, tugging at the tent pegs, making the cords scream.

In all his scenarios of death, Ralph had never projected one like this. But now he saw how it would be. A final gust would tear the tent from its pegs, rip it to shreds, and send its tattered remains streaming through a tunnel of snow, taking everything with it that could sustain their lives, leaving the two of them huddled pitifully together in an icing sleeping bag. If they didn't die quickly of hypothermia, they'd die slowly of starvation.

Tears sprang to Ralph's eyes. It didn't matter now if they were on the Blackstone River or not. It didn't matter now if his incompetence had led them into a mapless wilderness. It was too late for all that.

He turned to Gwen. She was sleeping. The tears trickled out of his eyes. He kissed Gwen's forehead and held her tight. She murmured in her sleep. At the wild centre of the storm, Ralph watched the wall of the tent billow and buckle toward him. He got ready to die.

By morning, the storm was gone. The silence woke Gwen. She yawned and turned toward Ralph. Inches away, his half-open mouth sent warm puffs of air into her face. His breathing was regular and slow. Smelling his breath's familiar morning odour, slightly sour, sending her own back, she studied his face. It looked gaunt, its two-week stubble of reddish beard on hollow cheeks darkened by the blue-grey light coming through the tent. She frowned. It occurred to her that he might have stayed awake all night to make sure their tent held out against the storm. It would be like him to do that. She decided to let him sleep till she had breakfast ready. Sliding carefully out of the sleeping bag, she pulled on her boots, put on her down jacket, and crawled outside.

A dusting of snow covered the ground; frost furred every stalk of grass. Grey clouds scudded overhead, hustling the last of the storm away.

Gwen beat her jacketed arms across her chest and stamped her feet to get her circulation going. Taking a deep breath, she felt the cold air sting her nostrils, and when, having reached back into the tent for a cook pot, she went down to the river and scooped up water, she noticed a fringe of lacy ice clinging to rocks along the shore. She straightened up and looked across the river at a winter landscape stretching all the way to the horizon under daylight the colour of steel.

It had been easy till now, she thought, travelling day after day through a land warmed by sunlight under a bright blue sky. But now they'd have to count on untested strengths to make their way against the grey hostility of this new world. Already her hands ached with the cold, and the handle of the pot cut into her fingers. She hurried back to the tent.

Oatmeal ready and set aside under its lid, coffee water heating in another pot over a hissing propane flame, and bowls, cups, and spoons laid out, Gwen moved carefully away from the stove and laid her hand on Ralph's shoulder. He came awake slowly.

"Breakfast, darling."

"What?"

"Breakfast."

Ralph rolled into a sitting position.

"There's oatmeal. Water's on for coffee. I can even make eggs if you want."

"What happened to the storm?"

"Gone. But there's snow on the ground outside. And you can see your breath."

"Hah."

"You want coffee now?"

"Sure."

Gwen fixed a cup and handed it to him.

"Mmm. That tastes really good."

He put the cup down carefully and rubbed his hands together. "So we made it through the storm. Wow . . . oatmeal. And, yeah, let's have eggs too. I'll make them."

"No, me. You stay there."

The stove was beginning to warm the tent. Gwen unzipped her jacket and spooned oatmeal into their bowls, adding powdered milk and sugar from the commissary pack. She handed Ralph his.

"Snow in July," he said. "How about that. Is there a lot of it?"

"Not a lot. But there's frost, and some ice in the river. And I think the level of the river's come up some."

"Sounds like our easy days are over." He grinned at her. "You ready for that?"

Gwen grinned back.

Sedna was furious. Sila must have honoured her wish, for the seabed around her house had suddenly erupted in clouds of sand, and swirling currents had sent panicky fish, seals, walruses, and even whales helplessly spinning and colliding.

The currents had subsided, but still no angakuq had appeared. Awake at last from long sleeps, she was in no mood for such defiance. If Narsuq's wind and Sila's storm had not made the Inuit send her an angakuq, there was only one thing to do. She began to hum. She'd never brought down an angakuq herself — she hadn't had to — but now she must.

Sedna closed her eyes and concentrated on sending a summons into the upper world. As her thoughts gathered strength, the humming in her throat changed to a high-pitched, warbling song.

The sound spread rapidly through the Polar Sea. Feeling its invisible waves, the fish and mammals scattered by the

storm hung uneasily still for a moment and then began
swimming toward the roofless stone house at the centre
of the basin on the ocean floor.

When the song touched land, it broke into fragments
on beaches and against cliffs. But where river mouths
opened to the sea, it continued up the rivers, reaching in-
land like the long fingers of an exploring hand.

They heard the rapids before they reached a bend in the river, a far-off rushing sound. Ralph reached for the map. In the two days since the storm, the ceiling of clouds had broken up enough to let sun in to melt the snow, and he'd started looking back and forth between the countryside and the map again. Now he saw that there was only one major rapid on the Blackstone, where the river ran through a narrow gorge. Since early this morning he'd been noticing how the hills on either side were closing in, outcrops of black rock appearing on the slopes and slanting toward the water. Now the outcrops had consolidated into low cliffs.

"I think we better stop and take a look at what's ahead," he said.

"Are those rapids?"

"Sounds like it. Keep an eye out for a place to land."

As they paddled on, the sound grew louder and the cliffs rose higher. Just before the bend, the cliff on the right retreated a short distance from the shore, leaving a small beach. They landed there. Gwen pulled up the canoe and held it steady while Ralph climbed out. Small waves slapped stones along the shore that had fallen from the cliff. With Ralph carrying the map, they crossed the beach to a split in the cliff face, scrambled up the loose rock filling it, and walked along the clifftop to the bend.

There they stopped. Below them, the black cliffs closed in tighter on the river, squeezing it into a narrow gorge that continued downstream for several hundred yards and then veered to the left around another bend. Waves danced impatiently back and forth across the water's surface as it hurried toward a pile of boulders that blocked the river halfway to the left bend. The water divided and rushed around the first boulder, joined hands with itself again on the other side and then, as it ran with abandon into more and more boulders, divided and rejoined and let go and rushed on, giving right hands and left hands to itself faster and faster until at last it danced demonically out of sight around the second bend, waving whitecaps as it went. It roared all the way.

"I think," Ralph said, fighting to keep the excitement out of his voice, "I think this is the canyon. The canyon that's on the map. Look."

He held the map so Gwen could see it.

"Here's where I think we are, and here's where the canyon begins." His finger was on a bend in the thick blue line with *Blackstone River* printed beside it. "And here's what we're looking at." His finger pointed to brown topographical lines that moved toward the blue line from both sides, coming together till they touched. "And here's that next bend. Right where it should be." They looked ahead to where the rapids disappeared around the left turn.

"This is it, Gwen, it has to be! We're right here looking at the Blackstone canyon. And all that" — he waved at the cliffs and the boulders — "all that is the famous black stone of the Blackstone River!"

His laugh floated through the billows of noise rising around them.

"Is there more of this ahead?"

"No. This is it. Look. We're about two-thirds down the river. Only about another week to go, and these are the only real rapids. Do you mind if I run them solo? I'll take some gear in the canoe for ballast, and you can hike along here with your pack — looks like a nice flat walk along the cliff — and we'll meet at the end where I can get to shore again. Somewhere around that bend. Okay? That okay? . . . It looks a little risky, but I can tell you, I'm really, really ready to run these rapids!"

He stared at the rushing river, threading with his mind's eye a way through the field of boulders.

"All right, if you really want to," Gwen said. "But you're sure you'll be okay? It's not a little too rough, even for you?"

"Piece of cake. Well, no, not a piece of cake, but . . . challenging. Yes, I can do it."

Through there, there, there, and there, he was thinking as his eye ran over the water again, stopping where the river disappeared around the bend. After that, I'll improvise.

"But be careful, Ralph."

"I will. I will."

Back at the small beach, Gwen lifted her knapsack out of the canoe and leaned it against the cliff. The roar of the rapids was fainter here but still audible.

They divided up the gear.

"I'll take the food pack and my own pack and, yeah, the tent. That should give me the ballast I need. That leaves you with just your pack and the sleeping bag. Can you manage those all right?"

"Easy."

She lashed the waterproof sack that held their sleeping bag to the top of her knapsack frame with a bungee cord. Ralph pulled the canoe further up the beach and began tying in the food pack, his own knapsack, and the tent, using a length of rope. He wedged the spare paddle between his knapsack and the hull, where, kneeling just behind the centre thwart, he could reach it if he needed it. On the beach, Gwen crouched, slung her pack onto her back, straightened up, jounced it till its weight felt right, then cinched the hipband and picked up her own paddle. She stood watching Ralph as he finished his tying in.

"Don't forget your life jacket."

"Don't worry. Give me a hug."

They embraced.

"That's it, I guess," he said.

She kissed him.

"Have a great run."

"I will."

"Wait'll I get to the top of the cliff where I can watch you. I'll wave my paddle so you can see when I'm there."

Ralph nodded.

Gwen turned and crunched across the beach to the break in the cliff face and, using her paddle as a staff, slowly climbed. Ralph watched till she got to the top and then turned back to the canoe. He gave a couple of knots a final tug, twanged a bungee cord, snapped himself into his life jacket, and stood looking at the slick fast-moving water as it sped toward the bend where the rapids began. He felt a familiar twinge of fear and a compensating rush of adrenaline. Running these rapids was going to be pure joy.

But that wasn't the only thing making him happy: they were in the clear. No more worrying, no more pretending. All they had to do till the end of the trip was enjoy it. One more great week. Christ, how he loved being on this river now!

Ralph looked up at the edge of the cliff where it made its turn and presently saw a waving paddle blade. He pushed the canoe into the water, leaped in, and knelt behind the centre thwart. He picked up his paddle, shoved off, and headed diagonally upstream against the current toward the middle of the river. When he got there, he spun the canoe around and paddled hard toward the bend.

As he entered the choppy waves at the beginning of the rapid, he threw back his head and let out a full-throated, joyous howl. Then, stroking furiously, he sped toward the boulders. He passed the first, pried hard against the current to line himself up with a tongue of smooth-running water between the next two boulders, stroked hard again, and shot between them. Stroking, prying, drawing, back-paddling, he twisted and turned his way through the massive rock field, strength and skill and happiness propelling him. When he reached a short stretch of fast flat water, he turned in his seat and waved toward the top of the cliff. As he turned back, the canoe struck a half-submerged rock, rode up it, pivoted, rolled sideways, and threw Ralph into the river.

At the top of the cliff, where the noise of the rapid prevented her from hearing Ralph's howl, Gwen saw him wave and then saw the canoe strike the rock and throw him out. She sucked in her breath. He went under and bobbed up. His life jacket holding his head out of water, he spun around another rock, went over a drop, disappeared again. He came up spluttering and flailing but was immediately pulled down again. Under and up, rolled one way, then another, flailing and gasping, bouncing from rock to rock, Ralph went down the rapid.

"No!" Gwen cried.

And throwing off her pack, she ran after him.

But faster than she could run, the river's current swept Ralph between more rocks, down chutes, into standing waves, up and over them and on until, still struggling, he was whisked out of sight around the bend to the left. Gwen ran harder.

When she reached the bend, she stopped. A tributary stream, now dry, cut a deep arroyo through the cliff face. Across it, the flat clifftop continued for a mile or two, as did the cliff on the other side of the river. Eventually they both gentled down until at last the harsh black rock slid back under soft green meadows spreading away from the river's banks. Till the black rock disappeared, chaotic rubble filled the gorge, impeding, diverting, funnelling, roiling the fast-running river.

Gwen could see Ralph in his life jacket again, a tumbling red dot in the current.

She hopped from one foot to the other on the lip of the arroyo. It was too wide to jump, but to her right its dry bed cut a deep V inland. Ralph was almost out of the gorge now. She started running inland along the edge of the arroyo.

Before the Blackstone River left its high black walls to flow placidly again through open countryside, it had one more surprise in store for its squeezed, rioting water. Near the end of the gorge, a ledge ran across the riverbed from one cliff to the other. Its drop was more than ten feet, and when the current, free at last of inhibiting boulders, reached the ledge and went over it, it smacked the bottom of the river with an astonishing roar and threw back on itself across the whole width of the river a standing wave rising in final exuberance out of a deep, churning trough. Ralph, now barely conscious, slid over the ledge. Tossed up to the crest of the standing wave and sucked down to the riverbed, he spun and spun in the trough.

Back at the top of the cliff, Gwen couldn't find him. She swept the river, hoping to see him swimming to shore someplace, hoping to see him sitting on shore someplace, willing him to have reached the shore. Running around the arroyo had seemed to take a long time. But he was nowhere in sight. Her eyes went to the ledge.

She saw him.

Bright red life jacket still on him like a halter, he rode swiftly up the face of the wave and dropped off its crest back into the trough, his body limp.

"Oh, no, no, no, no."

The words came out in a hoarse whisper, and she started to run again.

Where the clifftop finally reached the riverbank, she turned to go back upsteam toward the ledge. Along the shore, fallen rocks and boulders blocked her way. She scrambled over and around them, jumping from one to another, slipping once and cracking an elbow, skinning her shins, scraping her palms, breaking a fingernail. By her side the river ran fast and smooth.

Gwen stopped and, breathing hard, stared at the slick wall of water dropping over the ledge, at the trench it dug into its own flow, and at the standing wave that rose back out of the trench, towering above her head where she stood on the shore, its frothy crest tossing spray into the air across the whole river. She'd never seen anything like it.

Ralph's in there, she thought.

She had to get him out. She had to rescue him. But the waterfall's roar and the height of the wave and the depth of the trough defeated her. How could she get him out? How could she rescue him?

Gwen's legs gave way. She sat down hard.

Suddenly Ralph's life jacket bobbed to the surface beyond the standing wave. Ralph was not in it. Gwen stared at the red bundle as it bounced down the rest of the gorge, floating on smaller and smaller waves till it disappeared. The sound of the waterfall filled her head. She returned her attention to it.

A lick of current racing along the bottom of the trough grabbed Ralph and whipped him along the riverbed until he bobbed to the surface at the same place his life jacket had. Gwen gasped. Ralph began to float away. She leapt up and started after him over the fallen rocks and boulders.

For the rest of the day, Gwen chased Ralph's body down the river. It went head first, feet first, spread-eagled, in a ball, sideways, upside down, right side up, rolling and turning, snagging on nothing, held fast by the current in the middle of the river whose level had risen drastically after the storm they'd survived. She never caught up with it.

Overhead the sky slowly emptied of the last grey clouds that had moved in with the storm. Summer sunlight once again fell on of the Arctic barren lands.

"What you mean, get land back?" Old Piuyuk said. "Nobody never take it away. Who could take land anywheres anyhow? Go look outside. Land ain't going nowheres. Not now and never did. How come you guys think you can get back something nobody never take away firstways. Don't make sense."

Nate sat on the floor of his great-uncle's summer tent out by the airstrip. He was having a hard time getting ABRA's land-rights policy across to Old Piuyuk.

"Legally, land belongs to government now, Uncle. But ABRA agreement will give us legal ownership. That means we make the rules about it. Means nobody can hunt or fish or trap there without we say so. Means no big company can come in there and dig around for minerals to get rich without they get our permission first and share with us after."

"Who want to hunt there besides us? Indians? We take care of them guys long ago. And what you mean minerals? I been out there all my life and I never see no minerals."

Nate gave up on the minerals.

"But you know how you been setting traps up in them hills like you say all your life. Well, if you show me on this map where you had trapline, then we can claim that land and it gets to be legally ours."

Nate spread the large-scale Canadian Geological Survey map of the Poniktuk area on the floor between them.

"What you trying on me, boy? You want me to show you where I trap? You figger to steal my traplines? Better watch your boots, boy."

"No, no, Uncle. I don't figger to steal nothing. But look. Look where my dad draw all his traplines and his dad's too. And here's Obie's and Zeb's and here's Eddie Qarlik's and his dad's too. We put them all together, we can tell them Feds we have rights to that land, and then they have to let us own it."

Old Piuyuk gave the map and the squiggled lines on it a disdainful glance.

"Them other traplines never produce fur like mine. Not any of 'em. I never show you nothing, boy. My traplines, they stay right here."

He tapped his temple with a bony finger.

Nate gave up on the traplines too. It was hot inside the tent; he was getting nowhere.

Folding the map and putting it back in its case, Nate thanked his great-uncle for listening to him, rose to his feet, and pushing aside the tent flap, ducked outside. Standing there, he placed the map case between his legs and, lacing his fingers in front of him, turned them inside-out and stretched his arms over his head. Through the cloth of his shirt he felt sunlight reach his skin, and he rolled his shoulders under the warm material. It was too good a day for any more work. Beyond the airstrip, hilltops shimmered in the heat.

"Okay I leave my map case, Uncle?" he said, and slipped it back through the tent flap. "I'll pick it up after."

Old Piuyuk grunted.

An hour later Nate stood on the top of a hill looking back at the sea. Beads of sweat prickled his scalp. The distant houses of Poniktuk were tiny cubes strung along the bay that bit into the coastal plain. All around him other hills rose and fell in the rhythms of ancient upheavals; valleys wound among them, deep and shallow. His own hilltop was the highest and must have served Inuit hunters in former times, as it still did, for spotting caribou, because a large stone tent ring was there. Nate had visited this lookout before.

He turned from the view and studied the ring.

The stones would have held down edges of a tent made of caribou skins, and there would have been a stone hearth someplace inside. Over hundreds of years, the stones had sunk into the ground, some in grass and some in gravel, so that now he could only guess at their true sizes. But they had to have been large. Their surfaces were covered with orange, black, and pale green lichens that grew at infinitesimal rates. Gaps in the circle indicated stones that had altogether disappeared.

But today he could see more of the exposed ones than the last time he climbed the hill. Since then, the violent wind that had whipped through Poniktuk had also scoured this hilltop. And a short time later, the torrential rains of the storm that had seemed to come from everywhere at once, bringing lightning, thunder, hail, and even snow with it, had washed away much gravel and dirt.

Something caught Nate's eye. He stepped inside the circle and knelt down.

Between his knees a fragment of some dark substance not the colour of stone showed in the short grass. He touched it. It was smooth. With a cautious finger he poked at the dirt along one edge. There was more of the object underground. Using both hands, he gently pushed away tufts of grass and dug his fingers into the soft earth. Brushing dirt aside, he saw more of the object. It was not large. Continuing to work around it, he little by little exposed a comb. Nate sat back on his heels.

The surface of the comb was as dark as the soil around it. Five rounded teeth, each the length and fatness of an infant's finger, extended straight from a square handle the size of an infant's palm. The comb was carved from a single piece of bone. It had to be very, very old.

Nate picked it up and cradled it in his hand. He brushed dirt from its surface. He noticed how the earth's stains followed the grain of the bone, streaking some parts tobacco brown and others a tawny yellow. He turned the comb over and brushed off its other side. His fingertips felt scratches in the surface.

Nate brought the comb closer to his face. An image jumped at him. Though its lines were faint and the image small, he thought he saw a woman's face. No, an animal's. No, something that was both.

The ground between his knees blurred and tilted. What the fuck? He was flat on his back. Sun stabbed his eyes. He closed them. After a moment, he took a deep breath and sat up. Sweat trickled out of his hair. He blinked against a fuzzy brightness rimming the edges of everything.

Should've worn my shades. Better get home.

Nate rose slowly to his feet and staggered when the blood rushed from his head. Squinting, he focused on the open sea beyond the string of tiny houses by the bay. Mirages danced like long-legged devils on the sea's horizon.

Too fuckin' hot out here, he thought, and took a step.

He saw the comb. For a long moment Nate stared at it, then

picked it up and dropped it into his shirt pocket. He couldn't leave it lying on the ground for someone else to find or a caribou hoof to crush. But he didn't want to look at that scratched face again. Just thinking about it made his fingertips tingle.

Leaving the circle of stones, he started down the hillside. As he walked, his legs found their stride and his head cleared. But along the way, Nate's mind showed him, on and off, a young girl sitting on a rock, combing her hair in the sun. Sometimes she looked like his cousin Della, and sometimes she didn't.

<

The morning after Ralph drowned, Gwen was back on the cliff-top where she'd left her knapsack. When her legs had been able to carry her no farther the previous afternoon, she'd dropped to the ground and given up trying to catch up with Ralph.

The enormity of what had happened hit her then, and a sound came out of her throat that shattered the silence of the tundra air like an animal's cry. She hugged her knees and rocked herself. Eyes shut tight, she sobbed and moaned and snivelled and gasped until her grief exhausted her. Then she sat still. Dry-eyed, she stared at the river and hated it.

When the sun eventually set and the half-light of the Arctic summer night spread across the landscape, Gwen had begun to shiver. When she stood up and beat her arms against her chest, she still shivered. Teeth chattering, legs shaking, she had started walking back along the riverbank, her mind focused solely on reaching the sleeping bag tied to her knapsack where she'd dropped it. She walked all night.

Now, in the warmth of the morning sun, the knapsack beside her, she sat looking down into the Blackstone gorge. The water rioting through it, in which Ralph had so rejoiced, looked heartless and evil. And she saw the canoe. Half submerged, it lay wrapped backwards around one of the boulders that interrupted the river's flow, its bent aluminum gunwales pinned wide open by the current like glistening metal lips of a frothy grin. The same force holding it against the rock kept the packs tied to the thwarts inside it. In time they might rot and spill their contents.

Gwen turned from the sight and loosened the bungee cord that bound the sleeping bag to her knapsack. She pulled the bag from its waterproof sack, shook it out, took off her boots and jacket, got in, and from inside zipped it closed over her head. She took a deep breath. The bag smelled of Ralph. In seconds she was asleep.

When she woke, she wondered what she was doing all the way inside the sleeping bag and automatically reached for Ralph. When she didn't find him and before she remembered, she thought he must be making breakfast and poked her head out of the bag to find herself looking at blue sky, not the ceiling of the tent. Then she remembered. She pulled her head back into the bag and curled into a ball inside its soft folds, hands palm to palm between her thighs.

Panic nibbled at her, and she tried to make her mind go blank, but the pictures cycling through it wouldn't go away. She saw Ralph paddling joyfully through the rapids. Ralph waving. Ralph falling out of the canoe. Ralph trying to swim. Ralph thrown into the air by the standing wave and dropped back into the trough. Ralph floating dead in the river. She saw herself running along the riverbank, scrambling over rocks, never catching up with him. Tears stung her eyes. The finality of Ralph's absence took hold.

But after a while her body, no longer numbed by fatigue, became aware of the ground beneath it, hard, cold, and lumpy. She drew a shaky breath and knew she had to get up.

When Gwen went through her knapsack, she was appalled at how little it contained.

A change of clothes.
Toilet kit.
Sneakers.
Camera and film.
Gloves.

Striped wool cap.
Bottle of bug repellent.
Four chocolate bars.
A bag of nuts-and-raisins trail mix.
That was all. And the sleeping bag.

Gwen felt her knees weaken, and she wanted to fall down. But she told herself not to. What she had to do now was get away from here.

She pushed the sleeping bag back into its sack and retied it to the frame of her pack. Then, lifting it by the shoulder straps, she crouched and swung the pack onto a bent knee as Ralph had taught her and then onto her back, thrusting her arms through the loops. She gave her shoulders a jounce to settle the straps on her collarbones, tightened the hipband, and, leaving her paddle lying on the ground, started walking along the clifftop. She kept her eyes deliberately away from the river, which sent billows of rushing and splashing sounds ricocheting between its high black walls and into the air around her. She couldn't bear to look at the river, but she'd have to stay near it. At its mouth was the Inuit village where they'd planned to end their trip. Ralph had said they were only a week away. She had to get there.

Five days after starting to walk, Gwen stood on the top of a hill a short distance from the river, knapsack at her feet, looking ahead. The land stretched away like a vast carpet without design — green meadows and slopes covered by moss and bracken and grasses and, rising from them, hills a paler green with thinner cover. Higher and more distant hills were coloured brown or tan by windblown dirt or sandy gravel. Outcrops of black rock sliced at random through the mild disorder of the rolling countryside. Among the hills, glints of blue shimmered in ponds. The whole land lay before her, crumpled and heaved and smoothed by forces that had formed and abandoned it long ago. The sky above the land was enormous.

Gwen could see that the river made a long curve to the left, then turned right again against the buttress of a ridge and disappeared. Tracing the river's imagined course from there, she caught a glimpse of it again between two of the more distant hills. The country between here and there would be harder walking than along the riverbank. But it was a shortcut. This morning she'd eaten the last handful of trail mix, there was half a chocolate bar in her shirt pocket she was trying to save for later, and there was still some toothpaste left. But nothing else. She knew she had to follow the river to reach the safety of the Inuit village. Ralph had said they were only a week away, but now she realized he'd meant on the river. Walking took longer.

Gwen glanced back at the river and looked away again. How she hated it for its smooth, complacent flow, as if it had no memory or interest in having killed Ralph. Leaving it to take a shortcut seemed only sensible. With her mind's eye she made a straight line from her hilltop to that distant glint of water and then modified the line to skirt the hills along the way and take advantage of valleys. Once off the hilltop, she'd almost certainly stray from the route, but if she just kept going in the right direction, she'd strike the river again.

She reached into her shirt pocket and took out the remains of the chocolate bar. She broke it in half and bit off a piece. It was amazing how saliva squirted into her mouth as soon as her tongue touched the chocolate. She bit off another piece and let it melt to nothing on her tongue. She ate the rest, tiny bite by bite. When it was finished, her stomach growled for more, but she forced herself to rewrap the quarter of a bar and return it to her pocket.

The discipline made her feel good.

Stooping, Gwen picked up her knapsack, swung it onto her back, looked ahead, and fixed her course once more in her mind's eye. Then she stepped off the hilltop, leaving behind the murderous river.

Many hours later, when she reached the top of a rise and looked down at the water she'd glimpsed, she saw, not the river again, but a narrow lake without inlet or outlet. She stared at it and then descended to its shore. There she dropped to her knees and slipped off her knapsack. It was no use trying to find her way back to the river the way she'd come. It was too far, too complicated, and she was exhausted. Looking over her shoulder, she couldn't even tell where she'd just come down the slope behind her.

Gwen unhooked the bungee cord attaching the stuff sack to her knapsack and pulled out the sleeping bag little by little like a scarf from a sleeve. Next she opened her knapsack and took out her toilet kit. Inside, she found the toothpaste. Holding the tube between her teeth, she crawled to the shore of the lake, squeezed an inch of paste onto her tongue, and swallowed it. Then she scooped up a handful of water, rinsed her mouth, spat, and crawled back to the sleeping bag. There she stared for a while at her feet, wondering if it was worth the effort to take off her boots before she got into the bag. Of course it was, she told herself, coming to with a start. She unlaced and took off her boots. A thought came to her: she'd put the quarter of a chocolate bar she was going to eat in the morning in one of the boots. That way it wouldn't melt in her shirt pocket in the bag. She dropped the bar into the boot, slid into the sleeping bag, and zipped it up. Tomorrow she'd go looking for the river. Now she needed sleep.

As the sun touched the horizon and slowly dropped below it for its brief nightly disappearance, the air grew cooler, and cold and damp from the ground underneath her seeped through Gwen's sleeping bag. She groaned. Every night she hoped it wouldn't be like this, and every night it was — first wonderful, comforting warmth, then creeping cold and damp. She began to shiver.

Between fits of shivering, Gwen got some sleep. But not much.

More days later than she'd been able to keep track of, Gwen sat on the top of another hill. It had taken her a long time to get up it, and she'd had reason along the way to be glad she wasn't carrying her knapsack anymore. She'd dropped it someplace, she didn't know where. The shoulder straps had begun to chafe her collarbones, changing into the clean clothes inside it had seemed like too much trouble, there was nothing left in it to eat anyway, and the thought of taking pictures with the camera was silly.

She hadn't found the river again.

Nor had she eaten anything for quite a while. After the toothpaste was gone, she'd had stomach cramps that made her fall down and double over while wave after wave of pain convulsed her. But they'd stopped. And she wasn't hungry any longer, only thirsty. It wasn't always easy to find water where she'd been walking, but if she could get just enough to wet her lips and wash out her mouth, that was enough. If too much time went by between wettings, her lips cracked and the inside of her mouth went dry and gummy and tasted terrible. But just now, on her way up the hill, she'd found a little deposit of snow in the shadow of a rock, and she'd rubbed some on her lips and let more melt in her mouth, and she was fine.

More troublesome, she seemed to have left her sleeping bag someplace too. She'd felt dizzy and had to stop several times coming up the hill, but when she reached the top, she realized she didn't have the bag with her, and when she looked back down the hill, she didn't see it anywhere. She'd have to look for it later. Because she liked to wrapped herself in it, even if it didn't really keep her warm. But for now, with the sun overhead, her hair tucked under her wool tuque, her jacket open, and her legs stretched out, she was both warm and comfortable.

Lately there had seemed to be more uphill than down, and her legs weren't as sturdy as they had been. She staggered and couldn't always see very clearly where she was going. But her difficulties didn't get her down, her spirits were still strong, and she knew she was going to reach the village. Because Ralph was with her now. And so was her funny twin sister Trish. When she first became aware of them hovering just at the edge of her vision, she turned her head to say hello, and they weren't there anymore. Then she understand they preferred to let her catch sight of them only out of the corner of her eye. They were playing a game.

Now-you-see-us-now-you-don't. She went along with the game. It was fun.

They were also talking to her. Trish had told her how she was going to take her out for lunch every day for a week when she got home, and she listed all the different kinds of food they'd eat in restaurants all over Ottawa where they'd eaten before. She also told her what she was stocking in her shop on Bank Street. Some of the items were kind of weird — gumdrops and hand lotion, socks and fresh vegetables, kittens and hairbrushes — and sometimes she went on too long. But then Ralph would interrupt her, and he never went on too long. He was telling her the whole story of their life together, every detail and every minute of it, from when they met on the Outing Club weekend to falling in love to their wedding to having children and how many and what they were like and how they grew up. Everything that had happened and everything that hadn't yet happened. Sometimes he forgot he'd told her something already and told her again, but those were often the parts she liked best, so she didn't mind.

Right now both Ralph and Trish were silent. Like her they were resting, one on each side of her, just out of sight. In a while they'd all three have to start walking again, but she wanted to stay here a little longer. Her eyes were bothering her again; the small valley below her hill and the slope on the other side were jumping around. They'd be better after she had a nap. There was a grassy hollow on the sunny hillside not far from her feet that looked perfect. She told Ralph she was going to nap for a while and slid down to the hollow and curled up in it and went to sleep.

Sometime later, she woke up, rolled onto her back, and stared at a long cloud filling the sky overhead. She could see it quite clearly. Trish said it looked like the skeleton of a big fish, a lake trout maybe, like the ones Ralph caught in the river. Ralph said she didn't know one fish from another. Gwen smiled and closed her eyes again.

When a chill came into the air, she woke up and, zipping her jacket closed, watched row after row of small cottonball clouds move slowly up from the horizon like a giant tufted quilt. Then her vision got blurry again, and she turned on her side, curled into a ball, and went back to sleep while Ralph hummed a tune in her ear.

That night it snowed.

<

When she didn't get a call from Poniktuk on the day Gwen said she and Ralph would arrive there, Gwen's mother called Trish. She was worried.

"When were they supposed to call you?" Trish asked.

"Today."

"Oh, give them another couple of days, Mother. They could've had bad weather or something. They're fine. Ralph knows how to do what they're doing."

So Edwina waited two more days, and on the third Trish called from her shop.

"Did you hear from them?"

"No. And now I'm really worried."

Trish thought for a moment. "Weren't they supposed to spend a night in a hotel in that town they were catching the flight home from? Maybe they went straight there. Would you like me to call the hotel?"

"Oh, would you, Tricia? I've got the name of the hotel here someplace, uh, the Igloo Inn, Inuvik, Northwest Territories."

"I'll call you right back."

The Igloo Inn said they had a reservation for the Morrisseys for two days ago, but they hadn't checked in.

"Just hold the room," Trish said. "They'll be there."

Then she called Edwina.

"I don't like it, Tricia. I don't like it one bit. It's already four days."

"Three."

"Well, even three is too long. Something could have happened, and we're just sitting here."

"What do you want to do?"

Edwina thought a moment. "I'm going to call Ralph's uncle in Vermont. He taught Ralph all this wilderness stuff. He'll know what to do. But I have to say I never did like the idea of their going up there all alone like that. Why couldn't they just have gone to Bermuda for their honeymoon or, I don't know, some other place, like everybody else?"

"Cuba, Mother. People don't go to Bermuda for honeymoons anymore. They go to Cuba."

"Wherever."

"Let me know what the uncle says. But, Mother, please don't get yourself all worked up about this. It *is* only three days. I'm sure there's all kinds of good reasons for them to be a little late."

Rather huffily, Ralph's uncle said Ralph was highly competent in all the necessary skills for wilderness travel and survival, and a short delay like this on a wilderness canoe trip was almost to be expected. He asked Edwina to give him a call when she heard from them.

But she didn't hear from them. And when another day had gone by, she decided she had to do something. Without telling Trish, she called the Royal Canadian Mounted Police. An Ottawa headquarters constable referred her to the RCMP in Yellowknife. There a constable referred her to an inspector. Telling her story three times made the alarm she heard in her own voice seem more and more justified. The inspector said he'd check their records; she should call back tomorrow.

After a sleepless night and a delay in getting through to the inspector, Edwina lost her temper when he said they had no record of a group of paddlers on the Blackstone River that summer.

"But they're there! They are there! And it's not a group, it's just the two of them!"

The inspector asked her to remain calm. If she was sure the

Blackstone was where her daughter and son-in-law had planned to canoe ("Of course I am!" Edwina snapped), there were procedures to be followed for initiating a search, although he had to say that, in the RCMP's experience, they shouldn't take that step yet. In ninety-nine out of a hundred cases people just turned up late.

"I'm not talking about ninety-nine out of a hundred. I'm talking about my daughter."

In that case, said the inspector, although it was still his opinion that the timing was premature, he'd initiate procedures for an aerial survey of the Blackstone River, as long as she understood that such surveys were costly and the costs would have to be borne, after a certain amount, by her, not the government. He was talking possibly several thousand dollars.

"Just do it!" she said.

Where had they started from?

"Some big lake."

And how long had they planned to be on the river?

"Three weeks."

Finishing at Poniktuk?

"Yes!"

He would call as soon as he had any results.

When Edwina told Trish what she'd done, Trish said she'd done the right thing and offered to kick in something for the costs. But privately she thought Edwina was overreacting. Gwen and Ralph would only be embarrassed when they finally got to Poniktuk or Inuvik and heard about all the fuss over their being a few days late.

Visitations

"Boy, it getting nice out now," said Obie, looking out the window of the Poniktuk Hunters and Trappers Association office.

It was midday, and flies buzzed against the inside of the glass. Seated on a bench under the window, eyes level with Obie's waist, were Nate's older brother Wayne and Harry Ingasuk, Poniktuk's only middle-aged bachelor. They ducked whenever a fly buzzed near their heads, but they didn't move. The bench was the only place to sit in the office besides the chair behind HTA chairman Zebediah's desk. Harry and Wayne had drifted to the office for coffee and a smoke and weren't going to let a few flies dislodge them. In his chairman's chair, Zebediah studied Obie's back.

"Might go caribou hunting after," Obie said.

"Which way?" Zeb asked.

"Just up in them hills."

He stared at the hills.

"Might get lucky first thing," he said, and chuckled.

"You figger?" said Zeb.

And they all laughed.

The hills rising inland shimmered under the July sun. Although there'd been a flurry of snow during the night, the cloud cover had lifted a while ago and the snow had melted, leaving vegetation on the hillsides looking even greener than before. Snowfall in late July was unusual, but the sun in the sky for over twenty hours every day quickly got rid of it. Under that enduring sunlight, some people in Poniktuk slept all day and stayed up all night, some slept in the afternoon and went to bed again at two in the morning, some went to bed at dawn and got up at noon, others never went to bed at all for days on end, and still others slept and rose and rose and slept with such irregularity that they hardly ever knew if it was day or night or afternoon or morning.

Everyone in Poniktuk got a little crazy in the summer.

Obie left the window and crossed to the coffee urn on the table by the door. He had to tip it forward to fill his Styrofoam cup half full.

"Better make more coffee," he said, adding sugar and Coffee Mate and stirring with a plastic spoon.

"Yup," said Zeb, and tipped back his chair, making its springs squeak.

Grins appeared on Wayne and Harry's faces. It was well known in Poniktuk that ever since they were boys, Obediah and Zebediah had been telling each other what they should do. Neither ever did it, of course, or at least not right away; that was also well known. They were each other's best friend.

Obie nodded sagely and sat down next to Harry Ingasuk, who inched sideways.

The green mosquito coil burning next to the coffee urn sent a wisp of smoke curling into the air, where it vanished, leaving behind an acrid smell. For a while, the only sound in the office was the buzzing of the flies.

"You hear about them boys shooting up a whole bunch of caribou and not taking no meat?" Harry asked the room at large.

Wayne and Obie raised their eyebrows to say yes, and Zeb nodded.

"I forget where," he said. Of course it wasn't Poniktuk; all the boys here knew he'd fix their boots if he caught them wasting caribou.

"Over east."

"Kuggies," Wayne said.

The Inuit who lived east of Poniktuk rarely behaved as real Inuit should, or so the Poniktungmiut believed, because they were descended from a different ancestry, or so they also believed, although few had actually met any Kuggies.

"I wonder if they leave the horns on," Zeb said.

"Dunno," said Harry and, ducking a fly, waved a hand over his head.

Zeb touched the edge of his desk.

In its middle drawer was a letter addressed to "Chairman, Hunters and Trappers Association, Poniktuk, NWT," from an import-export firm in Vancouver called Huong Limited. It looked like a form letter, and now Zeb wondered if those Kuggies had got one too. For it offered to pay ten dollars a pound for caribou antlers in the velvet. For five hundred pounds or more, the firm would charter a float plane to pick up the horns at a "conveniently located lake." That meant close to the kill but well away from any settlement, Zeb figured. It was strictly against the law to kill caribou for their antlers only. Payment would be in cash, the letter said. It offered prices even more fantastic for the penis bones of bearded seals and grizzly bears' gall bladders. Zeb had heard Asian people used all that stuff for medicines.

He was thinking of burning the letter. He didn't want it around, even out of sight inside his desk, because caribou bulls would soon start appearing in the hills around Poniktuk, their huge racks still in the velvet. Doing a calculation he'd done several times since the letter arrived, he figured it would take only fifteen or twenty bulls to make five hundred pounds of antlers. That would add up to five thousand dollars. A hell of a lot of money in Poniktuk. If people heard about it, they'd be tempted. So he should burn the letter.

But maybe, he told himself, if he just told hunters when they went out hunting not to forget to bring back antlers as well as meat, they could pile up enough right here in Poniktuk to get a plane in, and that would be legal, wouldn't it? The only question was what he'd tell people. If they knew what was going to happen to the antlers, they'd think selling them to be ground up for medicine was an insult to the caribou. Inuit deeply respected the animals they killed, and it was his job as chairman of the HTA to preserve and promote that respect. So how could he explain to someone like, well, Obie that chopping off caribou antlers to make money was all right?

But ten dollars a pound. Zeb thought of the hundreds, maybe thousands, of pounds of racks in the velvet he and other hunters of Poniktuk had left out on the land over the years after they'd field dressed a caribou carcass and brought home only meat.

So the letter stayed in his desk. Bothering him.

Nate came in. His brother Wayne and Harry Ingasuk nodded to him, and Zeb held his glance for a second. But after noting who'd come in, Obie avoided his nephew's eyes.

"What figger?" Nate asked.

"Not much," Zeb said.

"How's your coffee?"

Nate turned toward the urn and pulled a Styrofoam cup off the top of the stack.

"Finished," said Harry.

"Oh?"

Nate set the cup down and nodded at the can of Players tobacco on a corner of Zeb's desk.

"I could roll one?" he asked.

"Go ahead."

Four pairs of eyes watched Nate reach for the can, twist off its top, put the can back on the desk, open the plastic wrapping inside, pull a cigarette paper from the package nestled on the tobacco, hold the paper in one hand while sprinkling tobacco on it with the other, roll the paper back and forth between fingers and thumbs of both hands till he had a firm, round cigarette, lick the edge to seal it, pinch off shreds hanging from the ends, and strike a match to light it. Then he twisted the top back onto the can.

It wasn't that Nate rolled a cigarette better or differently from everyone else in town. It was just that people paid close attention to everything he did these days. Now the four men watched him inhale and blow smoke out through his nose.

Then Wayne looked down at his foot and started jiggling it, and Harry stared at a map of the land around Poniktuk pinned to the wall behind Zeb's desk. Zeb picked up his pen and started bouncing its clip against the edge of his desk in a soft rat-a-tat-tat. Obie stood up and, turning his back, looked out the window.

"Going out after?"

Obie knew his nephew was addressing him.

"Maybe," he said.

"Might be caribou real close," Nate said.

In fact, he knew there were caribou in a valley just beyond the first range of hills. He'd seen them in his mind. But after discovering during geese hunt that he could always see where animals, waterfowl, and even fish were, he'd learned not to come right out and tell people. Because at first they'd laughed at him. But when it turned out again and again that he was right, they'd stopped laughing and began to look at him funny. So now he either went hunting and fishing by himself, went out with others and led them, as if by chance, to where game was, or concealed his knowledge in a vague remark as he just had to his Uncle Obie. But everyone by now knew that Nate always knew where there was game, and, either grateful that he hid his uncanny knowledge or fearful of him for having it, they concealed their own knowledge of his knowledge as he tried to conceal his knowledge in the first place. They casually tagged along when they saw him go out or picked up his hints when he dropped them or did nothing if they didn't need meat or fish or stayed away from him altogether if the whole thing scared them. Nate sensed people's wariness and was afraid it was jeopardizing his work for ABRA.

They didn't refuse to give him information; for instance, all four men in the office had described their traplines to him. But when he tried to persuade people to accept the land-rights organization's goals and to vote Yes for ABRA's Agreement in Principle with the

Federal government in next month's referendum, he encountered wariness. People would listen, but he could tell they were bothered by a suspicion that there was something more to his explaining and persuading than they understood, as if his power to locate game was a sign of other, more dangerous powers, and all his talk about voting for land rights was really about something else, something secret and harmful. So they listened and gave information but remained noncommittal.

Obie was among the most suspicious. Standing at the window, he was thinking how, as a child, he'd been sent by his parents to a mission school in Inuvik. He'd survived the twin terrors of loneliness and punishment by overzealous Anglican nuns by clinging with all his heart to a belief in Gentle Jesus. And the belief had stayed with him. For many years he'd been a deacon of Poniktuk's Anglican congregation, and when Father Evans had left and not been replaced, he'd switched to the churchless Evangelicals, at whose home meetings he now often prayed out loud, feeling the power of the Lord inspire his tongue. But as a very young child in the years before his parents' conversion, he'd listened to his Great-uncle Iku — Nate's great-grandfather — tell stories in which strange and terrible things happened. His parents had told him Iku was a great magician with powers to see and do what others could not. Then he'd been introduced to Gentle Jesus, and his belief in his great-uncle's fearful magic gave way to belief in Him about whom all the stories were of kindness and goodness and whose magic was nonetheless strong enough to relieve the terrors of residential school. His Great-uncle Iku died while he was still at the mission school, and when he finally came home to Poniktuk, he didn't miss him.

But recently he'd been thinking about him. Even during the period of Father Evans's mission to Poniktuk, when all infants were routinely baptized with Christian first names, parents had given every newborn a private Inuit name chosen from among living or dead relatives whose qualities they hoped the child would emulate. Nate's private name was Iku.

Obie turned to face him now.

"You figger caribou real close? I figger caribou where the good Lord put them."

Nate smiled. Uncle and nephew locked eyes. Wayne, Harry, and Zeb looked anywhere but at anyone. Briefly, the flies in the window only crawled.

"I'll be out to the tank after," Wayne said, breaking the silence, referring to the tank farm at the edge of town where fuel was stored. "Case anybody needs to gas up."

Still affirming with a scowl the Lord's sole right to distribute game animals around Poniktuk and intending his stare to challenge his nephew to refute it, Obie felt a tremor of doubt undermine his certainty. How could he *know* that his nephew *hadn't* inherited his great-grandfather Iku's powers? Grateful for Wayne's interruption, he started toward the door. But as his eyes slid away from Nate's, he caught in them a flicker of amusement. On his way out of the room, he threw his empty Styrofoam cup at the wastebasket under the table that held the coffee urn — and missed. As he crossed the vestibule between inside and outside doors that in winter protected the office from blasts of cold air and stepped into a blaze of summer sunlight, he had the uneasy feeling he wasn't yet beyond the range of his nephew's mockery. He was right.

"Uncle," Nate called after him. "God bless you!"

Feeling the words as a curse, Obie hurried away.

Back in the office, no one moved. Nate had never before invoked the name of the Lord in their hearing. The Nate they knew would not do that. But Zeb and Harry and Wayne had recently come to accept, as had others in Poniktuk, that Nate was no longer the Nate they thought they knew. He'd become unpredictable. And in Poniktuk even the youngest child knew that in the presence of unpredictability the wisest thing to do was nothing. So Zeb in his chair and Harry and Wayne on the bench sat and did nothing.

Smoke curled upward from the mosquito coil and from Nate's cigarette.

For over three months now, Aningan had been living in the

young Inuk like a pulse within his pulse, systole to the young man's diastole. Coursing through Nate's bloodstream on the April morning of his arrival from the moon, his spirit had quickly concluded that he'd made a happy choice. The young man's mind was badly unfocused, but his instincts, such as his love for hunting, were excellent. Having immediately given him the gift of his own extraordinary sight, Aningan had continuously prodded and teased and stimulated Nate in ways that often made his young host surprise himself and, even more often, surprise others. Aningan regretted only one thing: there had been no repeat of the night's lovemaking during the land-rights workshop. Tiny Poniktuk, where everyone was somehow related to everyone else and everyone knew what everyone else was doing almost all the time, was not licentious, anonymous Inuvik. But for the most part, Aningan was having fun.

Nate stubbed out his cigarette in the ashtray on Zeb's desk.

"Thanks for the smoke," he said, and went out the door.

ᕐ

Obie was riding his threewheeler along the airstrip. His .270 was slung across his back, and in a canvas bag strapped with bungee cords to the rack behind his seat were his skinning knife, a box of shells, skinning gloves, and windpants and a down jacket rolled up together. Although the sun would stay in the sky all the time he was hunting, the air would get cold. For now, he could feel the sun warming his scalp through his baseball cap; his windbreaker was enough. Dust rose into the still air behind him and hung above the airstrip in a low horizontal cloud. It lingered for several minutes after Obie had dropped onto the flatlands leading to the hills and then, as a puff of wind caught it, vanished.

Going slow now, down to second gear, and rocking in his seat as the threewheeler's fat tires rolled over hummocks and through puddles, Obie told himself he felt good. Since leaving the HTA office, he'd had a meal, slept for a while, and now he was going hunting. What more did a man need to make him happy? But uneasy thoughts about his nephew had survived his nap, and he now had to make a conscious effort to push them aside. He concentrated on plotting a route to the crest of the ridge ahead of him. Once there, he'd stop and sweep the horizon with the binoculars hanging around his neck under his windbreaker. What he saw would determine where he'd go.

Scoops of green valley, gravelly hilltops strewn with boulders, sweeps of rising meadow, highroads of flat-topped eskers, lakes like sparkling shields — images of the landscape ahead of him as familiar to Obie as the backs of his hands — floated through his mind. Somewhere among them there might be caribou. Or might not. Did he want Nate's prediction to come true, or did he want Nate to be wrong? He wanted caribou all right, but he couldn't escape the thought that in looking for them, even hoping for them, he was somehow doing Nate's bidding. That bothered him, but he wouldn't let it stop him. On any other day he'd have asked the Lord's help with his endeavours, but today, with his nephew's mock blessing still ringing in his ears . . .

Obie drove on.

Standing on a chair, Akpa was brushing her grandniece Sarah's hair. As she stood on her own chair and gripped the back of it, the child was only a little shorter than her great-aunt. They'd moved the chairs to the window of Akpa's living room so they could watch people go by on the road. So far there hadn't been many, but a short while ago Obie had ridden past on his three-wheeler.

"Obie just about up in them hills now, should be," Akpa said. "Maybe he get caribou today. Might be lots of it up there. Honestly, I really feel to have fresh meat. Ribs, even."

Sarah squirmed under the brush.

"Hold still, you. You can't look pretty without I brush your hair. The way you wiggle, I might think you might be fish."

Sarah shook her head vigorously.

"You not a fish?"

The head shook again.

"What are you, then?"

Sarah didn't answer.

"A stone! That's what. How many weeks now you never say nothing to nobody? Just like a stone."

Akpa's small gnarled hands paused in their steady brushing of the soft hair. She stared at the back of Sarah's head; then she sighed. She couldn't remember when her grandniece had stopped talking. Weeks ago, certainly. Maybe even months. Sarah's mother, Young Helen, had been the first to notice her daughter's silence and had failed to make her speak. Then the rest of the family got involved, but no one could provoke any answer from Sarah other than a shake of her head, not even her favourite uncle, Nate. In fact, his attempt had caused the only outbreak from Sarah in the early weeks of her silence — a violent screaming fit and a dash to a hiding place. This only deepened the mystery because Nate had never done anything to frighten her; on the contrary, he'd always spoiled and coddled her. So eventually everyone gave up trying to understand and became used to the nods and head-shakings and pointings that became her only way to communicate. Everyone hoped she'd finally tire of making herself so difficult. Akpa had recently taken her in for a while to see if she could speed up this process, but Sarah was proving the most stubborn child she'd ever dealt with. Now her left hand again lifted hair from the girl's neck while the brush in her right stroked it firmly down from scalp to tips.

"Honestly, you don't smarten up, we going to send you to nursing station when Nurse McGarr get back from holidays. She look down your throat with big pipe to see where your voice get to."

Sarah's features puckered, and her grip tightened on the chair back.

"One time, long ago, little girl just like you stop talking, never say nothing to nobody. She so stubborn, pretty soon nobody pay no attention to her. Nobody feed her, nobody put her to bed, nobody brush her hair, nobody even see her. You know what happen to that little girl? She so all alone all the time, one day she get really scared. *Then* she start hollering, but nobody can hear her no more. Her voice gone for good. Nobody even miss her. You keep on so stubborn, maybe you end up like that-there little girl. You want to end up all alone like that, without even Auntie to brush your hair? What you say to that?"

But it wasn't words that came in reply. Sarah's small body shook with sobs.

"What now?" Akpa said, and put down the brush. "You could cry anyways. That's something. But don't cry. Auntie just tell a story. That's all. Don't cry."

She gripped the child's shoulders to turn her around, but Sarah clung to the chair.

"Auntie just tell story. Baby, look! Look! Here come Uncle Nate! Don't make him see you cry!"

But at this Sarah let out a wail that ended in a choked gurgle, and she climbed quickly backward off her chair and ran gulping, squeaking, and shrilling out of the living room, down the corridor to Akpa's bedroom, and through it to the dark safety of a closet.

"Good grief!" Akpa said to the empty room, and climbed down from her own chair, but not before rapping on the window and motioning Nate to come in. He shook his head and pointed in the direction he was walking: he had to keep going.

Rocking from side to side on her bandy legs, Akpa headed for the bedroom. What on earth were they going to do with this child?

"Sarah?" she called out. "Where you get to now?"

Inhaling the musty odour of Akpa's clothing, Sarah hugged her knees and drew a shallow breath. Seeing Nate through the window had only reinforced the awfulness of the secret she'd been keeping against all efforts to pull it out of her ever since the April morning when the scary thing had happened in their house, when, in the next room, her uncle had turned into somebody or some thing that only looked like him. If she told the secret, he'd kill her. Nobody could help. Not Auntie, not Dadduk, not Mammaluk. The only thing to do was never say anything and hope the bad thing would someday go away — and, for now, hide.

Sitting at his kitchen table, Eli watched Nate come along the road.

"Iku coming," he said in his hoarse voice.

"Mmm," said Ruth, her mouth full of pins.

She was sitting on the kitchen floor with a length of Grenfell cloth in front of her and paper patterns for the parts of a winter parka in a pile beside her. In a corner of the kitchen stood two blue Canada Post bags filled with goose down that she'd plucked. Nate had shot more geese than any other hunter in Poniktuk during spring geese hunt. The parka was for him.

Bending from the waist, she smoothed the pattern for a sleeve onto the cloth and started pinning it. Eli had lately taken to calling their youngest son by his private name, the name of his great-grandfather, the angakuq. She wondered if that meant he believed the rumours going around town.

Ruth finished pinning the paper pattern to the cloth and picked up the pattern for the front. In his own good time, Eli would let her know his thoughts. For herself, whenever she thought of the possibility that her son had somehow become an angakuq, she felt a prickle of pride that she hurriedly stifled under remembered scoldings from Father Evans about the bad old religion. But the prickles persisted.

"Helen!" she called toward her daughter's bedroom. "Iku coming. Make soup!"

Obie reached a crest among the first hills above Poniktuk and, turning off the motor of his threewheeler, sat listening to the silence of the land. The one bad thing about threewheelers was the noise they made. He climbed off and, unzipping his jacket and taking out his binoculars, leaned against the threewheeler. He slowly swept the valley, hillside, and skyline before him in search of the small brown shapes of caribou.

Moving the binoculars up a slope of meadow beyond a low

intervening ridge, he saw something and stopped. Pressing the lenses against his brow to hold them steadier, he sharpened the focus. Then his hands began to shake. The binoculars jiggled. He lowered them.

Sweet Jesus, what that doing there?

He stared at the distant spot, and under his baseball cap his scalp began to sweat.

He lifted the binoculars again. This time he held them steady long enough to establish without a doubt that what he was looking at was a curled-up body. It had its back to him and was wearing a blue jacket. The binoculars began to shake again, and he lowered them to the end of their strap. Although the body had on trousers, its wide hips told him it was a woman.

How come a woman lying there like that? Can't be one of us-kind womens. Must be some other kind. But what kind?

Obie made himself look at the slope again and, this time, found with his naked eye the blue dot. Was she even alive? His stomach heaved. He knew he had to find out.

Obie forced his eyes away from the dot and plotted a route to it. He noted signs along the way — a boulder bright with orange lichen, a willow bush trembling in the breeze. The whole landscape between here and there began to vibrate. He looked away and, undoing a bungee cord, stuffed his binoculars into the bag on the rack of his threewheeler. He wouldn't be looking for caribou any more today.

Obie climbed onto the seat, started the engine, and put it in gear. As he steered carefully down the slope from his hilltop, dropping abruptly out of sight of his destination, a voice inside his head started talking.

"Long time ago there been woman her husband beat her so much she know he finally kill her someday," it said. "So one day she been running away while he out hunting. It summertime and sun been shining all day and all night too."

Obie knew the voice: Great-uncle Iku. He couldn't stop him.

"There be ripe berries and roots everyplace that time of year so that woman she could be eating them when she run away. But at first she don't hardly eat nothing cause she just running, running, running to get far away from husband. But finally she get far away enough she feel safe from him, and then she been spending all the time all day picking berries, digging roots. She find lots of it, but even lots of it turn out too little to keep her living good, and slowly, slowly that woman starve. How long she been starving, that poor woman! After a long time, one day she can't walk no more. She so weak she can't pick even one berry, can't pull even one root, so she lie down to die. But in last thoughts while she been lying there like dead already, she curse that husband real strong for beating her so bad she have to run away from him and end up dying anyways out on that-there hillside.

"But she not die. Without she know it, she been lying down on top of house dug into that-there piece of ground. And when she close she eyes to die, she fall right through ground onto sleeping platform in that house. Now, one man and one wife they been living there. They look like man and wife, but they really be brown bears. They been taking pity on that-there woman, and when she come awake again they been feeding her soup and little bits of meat and sweet marrow from caribou bones till at last she begin to get good again. But them last thoughts about husband, them curses, they been staying in her head whole time she been getting better. And them thoughts get so strong now because of that food them bears been giving her that all of a sudden that-there woman been getting special powers. She been getting power to make self into brown bear too, anytime she want, just by thinking to be bear. And now she want revenge. So one day she say goodbye to them bear people, she been thanking them for taking care of her, and then she start walking back to where she know that-there husband have tent in summertime when he go hunting caribou. And all the time she walking but never sleeping, she been changing into bear, out of bear, into woman, out of woman, practising like, and all the time eating good like bears eat but same time never sleeping neither.

"Finally one day she come to place she know her husband allus head for when he leave tent to hunt, and she lie down to wait. It not long before he come that way. From far off he suddenly see woman lying on ground, and he get curious and come closer. And when he see it a nice fat woman, he begin to have bad thoughts about doing something to her. But when he see it his own wife, sleeping there maybe, maybe even dead, his heart get full to bursting cause he been missing her real bad since she run away. So he creep up to her like, and when he see she still breathing and look real good too, he get real excited. And he just reaching out his hand to touch her so maybe he could begin to do what he been thinking about, fuck her maybe, when all of a sudden, she eyes pop open, and same time he see in them black eyes no bottom to hating him and see too they be animal eyes not woman eyes. And then she just explode into big, growling, mad-as-hell brown bear. And this-here bear it tear his arm right off, and then it grab his neck between it jaws and it just chew that-there husband head off too. After that, Bear Woman eat about half of him real slow and easy like, and then she make self into woman again, and then she go off a little distance and lie down on that-there ground and sleep real good.

"From that day up to right now, Obie, Bear Woman been walking all over Inuit land, sometimes like woman, sometimes like bear, and they's lots of hunters been never coming home from hunting cause they been sneaking up on she like husband did with them-there same ideas, wanting to do something. Seems like sometimes she even been letting them do that thing with her. Leastwise so some hunters say, some of them hunters that been meeting up with she out on the land and been coming home after. Boasting like. But sometimes next time them-there same guys, they the ones never come home."

The voice went silent.

In a quiet broken only by the drone of his threewheeler, Obie felt a pressing need of courage. He started forming words in his mind for a prayer, a petition of the strengthening kind that had always made him feel his Redeemer was at his side. But before the words fell into place, they scattered. Frowning, he started over. The same thing happened.

Obie groaned. Famous among Evangelicals for improvised prayer, he'd never before failed to fit words together into a fluent plea.

"Jesus, Jesus!" he called out loud.

But nothing happened. His Redeemer wasn't there.

Head bent, knees embracing the threewheeler, Obie fought down panic and forced himself to keep a steady pressure on the accelerator under his thumb. If he waited, he told himself, Jesus would come.

But as the threewheeler, engine whining, reached a final ridge before dropping into the narrow valley that rose again to the meadowy slope where the blue-jacketed figure lay, Obie's only companion was the hovering presence of his great-uncle. He reached for his childhood faith. Gentle Jesus, come to me, he pleaded, and imagined the sweet figure rushing to his side across the tundra and, chasing from the land his great-uncle's evil spirit with a devastating sweep of His sword, turning the familiar hills and valleys all around him back into the blessed fields of the Lord. But nothing happened.

Fat wheels squelched through mossy puddles as Obie crossed the valley. Soon he reached dry ground. He hunched forward and took a tighter grip on the handlebars. The ground began to rise.

At last he stopped and raised his head.

She was right there — and Jesus still was not.

Heart pounding, Obie stared. Bear Woman was turned away from him with her knees drawn up. As he'd seen through his binoculars, she wasn't wearing traditional Inuit clothing, but that didn't mean anything. These days she'd wear the clothes she took off the hunters she ate, store-bought like he was wearing.

Obie stood on the pedals and teetered a moment before steadying himself with his fingertips. Now he could see one side of her face. It was tanned dark but not dark skinned. The profile of her nose was sharp, not flat. Most startling of all were the strands of hair escaping from her tuque — they were yellow.

A giggle burst from Obie's lips. This wasn't Bear Woman, it was a white lady! He sat down abruptly. A white lady. Laughter bubbled in his chest. Great-uncle Iku was only telling an old-time story. Jesus hadn't come to his side because He hadn't needed to.

Then Obie saw the blue jacket rise and fall. At once all energy, he switched off the motor, dismounted, and hurried over to the still figure. He stepped around it and squatted. Even with its legs drawn up, it was tall for a woman. He studied her face. Although the sun had damaged it, cracking the lips and scarring the nose with blisters, her cheek, though hollow, looked remarkably smooth and would, he thought, be soft to the touch of his finger. Even damaged, the face filled him with wonder. His eyes moved down the woman's body. Thin sun-tanned wrists disappeared between her thighs. The knees under the taut cloth of her trousers were bony. At the ankle of one leg, the trouser cuff was tucked into the sock above her boot. But the other trouser leg had pulled loose. Between its cuff and the boot, Obie saw a band of skin as white as a cloud. He quickly looked away. He'd never seen a white woman's flesh before.

When he looked back, he kept his eyes on her upper body. The jacket rose and fell again. The lady was alive all right, but she was starved.

Obie grunted. Looking across the body at nothing in par-ticular, he slid his right arm under its shoulders, his left arm under its knees, and stood up. Light as a child's, the body flopped onto its back and hung limp. He tipped it toward him. It fell against his chest. Hugging the body, his mind studiously blank, he stepped to his threewheeler and climbed on. The white lady's legs dangled over his right arm as he reached for the handlebar. He cradled her head against his left shoulder.

Before he started the engine, he looked back at the flattened grass where she'd lain. From just such a bed, Iku had said, Bear Woman had fallen through the ground. But it wasn't Bear Woman he now held in his arms, he told himself, only a poor starving white lady. But he memorized the spot before starting the engine and shifting into gear.

The white lady's hips settled snugly into his lap. As the three-wheeler's wheels bounced over the ground, Obie got an erection. Some time later, when his baseball cap fell off, he didn't stop to pick it up.

Reaching the airstrip on the outskirts of town, Obie coasted to a stop and, the white lady still in his arms, swung a leg over the side of the threewheeler, stood, and then squatted to lay her carefully on the gravel. He unhooked the bungee cords holding his hunting bag to the rack, took his down jacket and windpants from it, and spread them on the rack. Then he lifted the lady onto the rack, folded her legs, put her arms by her sides, and tucked the down clothing around her. He restretched the bungee cords firmly across her body.

It was one thing to carry a white lady in his arms this far, but he couldn't let people in the village see him hugging her.

Obie got back on his threewheeler and drove along the airstrip toward the road to town. His arms felt curiously light. His erection subsided. Presently the white lady's tuque, already loosened by rubbing against his shoulder, jiggled off her head, and her long yellow hair fell down behind the threewheeler. It fluttered in the dust raised from the airstrip.

Obie had missed the half-dozen caribou bulls grazing at the head of the valley he'd crossed on his way to where the lady had lain. And all the way back to town, he hadn't had a single thought about Jesus.

Akpa was on the phone to her sister.

"Obie kill someone! I see it! I see body on threewheeler!"

"Don't talk foolish," said Big Helen.

"I'm not talking foolish. Look out your window. He come by real soon."

"Maybe he get caribou."

"Caribou! You think I don't know caribou? You think caribou wear blue jacket? You think caribou have yellow hair?"

"I don't see nothing . . . Jeepers sakes, I see it! That's a body all right. What we do now?"

"Call Simon," said Akpa.

Simon answered the phone in the settlement office.

"Obie kill somebody," Helen said.

"What you mean, kill somebody?"

"I mean I see body on his threewheeler. It have yellow hair."

"Where you see that?"

"Out the window."

"Yellow hair?"

"It what I'm seeing, Simon. That body have real long yellow-coloured hair."

"Who's at nursing station?"

"Nobody. Ethel McGarr on holiday, and that other nurse give up. What you gonna do, Simon?"

"Where's Obie at?"

"He just going past store toward freezer."

"Okay. I got him now," said Simon and, watching from his window, hung up.

Big Helen's daughter Della slipped out of the house and went looking for her best friend Selma.

"Obie kill some lady have yellow hair," she told her in a whisper when she found her.

"How sick!" said Selma.

"He putting her in freezer."

"Craaazy!"

"Selma . . . you think he eat her after?"

Selma only rolled her eyes.

Obie was at the door to the nursing station. Its windows were dark; no one answered the bell. He got back on his threewheeler and headed toward the other end of town. As he went, he had the road all to himself.

"He coming now," said Lawrence's mother Irene, who was also Obie's sister, to the room behind her. She'd had a call from Akpa and now was leaning against a corner of the living-room window, three inches of curtain held open for a view of the road. Husband and children watched her from behind.

"Alii," she said. "That one white lady all right. Obie in big trouble now."

Lawrence swung away from the kitchen counter and headed toward the front door.

"Where you think you going?" Irene didn't take her eyes off the threewheeler and its awesome burden.

"Out."

"Sit down, boy. Don't you suffer me."

Lawrence stopped, considered, and came up behind his mother.

Together they watched Obie's progress along the road. A large white dog crawled from under Harry Ingasuk's house and trotted after the threewheeler. Patches of its winter coat dangled from its flanks. Obie stopped at the back of Eli and Ruth's house.

"How come he's going there?" Lawrence asked.

"Ruth take nursing course one time."

They watched as Obie got off the threewheeler and, climbing the steps to the back porch, disappeared inside.

The dog, Harry's year-old crossbreed, cautiously approached the bundle on the threewheeler's rack. Neck stretched out, forelegs tensed to spring away, it sniffed the woman's head and sneezed. The sneeze made strands of her yellow hair jump. The dog froze. Then, inviting the hair to play, it dropped to its elbows, hindquarters high, and ferociously wagged its tail. The hair didn't want to play. The dog crept forward and bit into a mouthful of hair. He shook it vigorously. The woman's head waggled on the rack. Irene drew a sharp breath.

At the same moment Obie and Eli appeared on the porch. With a cry that was silent to those watching, Obie jumped down the steps and kicked at the dog. But the dog had already sprung away. Tail between its legs, it ran in a crouch back to the safety of the crawl space under Harry Ingasuk's house.

While Eli and Obie unhooked the bungee cords that held the body on the rack, a figure appeared in the shadows of the storage room beyond the open back door. Lawrence recognized Nate. As the two older men lifted the woman from the threewheeler and carried her up the porch steps, Lawrence kept his eyes on his cousin. But if he was looking for Nate to do something interesting, he was disappointed. When the others had passed him carrying their burden, all Nate did was close the door.

Ruth, Eli, Obie, and Simon were sitting at the kitchen table. No one had spoken for a while.

The woman lay in Nate's bed. Ruth and her daughter Young Helen had first combed her hair, then undressed her, gingerly unbuttoning and unzipping her clothes, turning her on one side, then the other. They were astonished by the whiteness of her skin but neither mentioned it. Nor did they speak as they paused when their undressing revealed a mound of golden pubic hair. With an almost religious care, they'd sponged the woman's body clean. Ruth shook her head at the sight of its protruding bones. Then they covered her with an eiderdown.

Helen now sat on a chair by the bed. Sarah, brought home from Akpa's when finally coaxed out of the bedroom closet, stood next to her, one bare foot hooked behind the other and a fold of her mother's skirt bunched in her fist. She too watched the lady.

In the living room, Nate had his ABRA papers spread before him on the coffee table. He'd volunteered his bedroom for the lady and would sleep on the couch. As his elders in the kitchen discussed what to do with her, their voices drifted in and out of his awareness. He was studying a summary of the section in the ABRA Agreement in Principle that dealt with natural-resource development. But as he read the terms that would apply to industries' extracting gas, oil, and minerals from lands belonging to the Inuit, an excitement that had nothing to do with economic benefits or subsurface royalties distracted him. Standing in the doorway to his room, he'd watched his mother and his sister untangle the unconscious woman's extraordinary hair. When they'd finished, Helen had closed the door as his mother unzipped the woman's jacket, but in his mind's eye Nate now saw the woman's body lying white and clean, naked and golden in his bed.

In the kitchen, Simon stood up.

"So we leave it like that," he said. "Ruth take care of her till Nurse McGarr get back. If she seem like getting worse, we call for medevac. But no use getting all excited when we don't know nothing yet. We look after her good, maybe something good come out of it."

"What if she die?" Obie said, staring at his cup.

"She not going to die," Eli said, in a scratchy whisper. "That one strong lady, never mind she look so bad. Iku protect her."

If anyone was surprised by Eli's putting the woman under Nate's protection or his calling his son by his private name, no one showed it. But hearing his father's words in the living room, Nate smiled and returned his concentration to the equitable distribution among the indigenous population of profits from subsurface mineral rights.

Walking home, Simon wondered why he'd been so determined to keep the white woman, for the moment at least, in Poniktuk. He knew the proper procedure would have been to call in a plane and have her medevaced to the hospital in Inuvik. But he'd decided not to do that. He wasn't yet sure why or what good might come of his decision, but with Ruth looking after the woman, there was no urgency. In the meantime, the mysterious lady was Poniktuk's secret. And Poniktuk's secrets were his business.

In her kitchen Ruth decided she'd leave a note for Ethel McGarr on the nursing station door to say she had a patient in her home. She was going to enjoy taking care of the white lady till Nurse McGarr returned.

As the long afternoon stretched into a sunlit evening, the telephone lines in Poniktuk were busy.

"He find her up in them hills. By that-there little lake."

"Which one?"

"That little one this side Whitefish Lake."

"Oh that one."

"That one."

"How come Obie shoot her?"

"He never shoot her. She already dead."

"She not dead, she just resting."

"How come that white lady lying down up there anyways? What kind lady she is?"

"Dunno . . . tourist maybe?"

"Doctor coming right away. They going to medevac her."

"They going to arrest Obie?"

"RCMP not even know about it."

"Akpa say Ruth tell her white lady not dead."

"Ohh?"

"Not yet leastways."

"Ohh? What they do with her?"

"Put her into bed."

"Whose bed?"

"Never mind that!"

"Harry Ingasuk say he see her out his window sitting up at Eli's table drinking coffee."

"Ohh?"

"She come alive again, like resurrected."

"Jeepers!"

"She float right down out of sky, that lady. Like snow. She put spell on Obie."

"What kind spell?"

"Real bad. Obie can't talk no more. She take his tongue."

"Holy!"

"White lady tell Obie she come from heaven with special message for Poniktuk. She an angel. She in there right now telling

Eli. He going to make announcement. Maybe go on CBC. Maybe even talk to bishop."

"That dog of Harry's been chewing all the hair from off that lady's head."

"No shit!"

"Simon talking to Commissioner."

"RCMP talking to Obie."

"Eli talking to bishop."

"Nate talking to white lady. He say she talk real funny."

"How come you know that?"

"He tell me."

"Ohh? . . . When he tell you?"

"I lie!"

"Obie say he see little peoples carrying her up them hills. When they see him, they just drop her and run away."

"Goodness sakes!"

"She have so white skin you see right through it. You see all her insides clear as anything."

"Alii!"

"White lady dead."

"White lady making love with all them mens in Eli's house."

"Never mind that!"

"White lady sitting up now."

"White lady can't stop talking."

"White lady breathing real slow."

"White lady singing now."

"White lady going back to heaven."

"White lady have ussuk just like man. She lady on top, man down below."

"Jeepers sakes," said Akpa, hearing this last and not knowing if she should believe it.

9

As she lay in Nate's bed, no sensations, thoughts, or even dreams invaded the white lady's sleep. Her mind was an emptiness as clean, unshadowed, and impressionless as the snow that had briefly covered her during the pale hours of the previous night.

But when daylight struck Poniktuk in the early morning, many people stirred uneasily in their sleep. Others, smoking cigarettes or drinking coffee at their kitchen tables, hadn't gone to bed at all. Nothing so strange as the white lady's arrival had ever happened in Poniktuk.

Now, at midday, most of the village was still thinking about her. But except for a gathering of children around Eli's back porch — none of them yet bold enough to climb the steps and walk in to demand a look at her — there was little outward sign of this village-wide preoccupation. Most people knew by now that the lady was still alive, and they went about their usual business in their usual ways. The store was just opening; the second urn of coffee was perking in the HTA office; the town mechanic was under the town front-end loader loosening the petcock on the oil pan; several threewheelers were lined up at the gasoline pump at the tank farm, where Wayne filled one five-gallon container after another; and at the settlement office, Simon was going through mail.

But behind the studied maintenance of these routines, something was happening. Speculation about the white lady, now mostly kept to themselves after last night's telephoning orgy, was beginning to loosen Poniktungmiut minds from their usual moorings, setting them adrift.

Unable to concentrate on filling out a government form for ordering office supplies, Simon swung his chair from his desk and looked out his window. It was a shining day of the kind that came only once or twice a summer. Sun glinted on the rippling water of the bay; the sand bar across the bay shimmered in a heat haze; the lawn in front of the mission building, an Arctic rarity planted long ago by the first Anglican missionary, looked as green as that man who'd longed for his English homeland could ever have hoped it would. Even the dust on the road that ran through the middle of town between brightly coloured houses looked golden. Simon automatically took in these details of the weather, as had his ancestors for the thousands of years that weather had governed their lives, but this morning he took no pleasure in them.

Last night Ruby had turned away from him when he'd wanted to mount her to get rid of a bad dream. So the dream had stayed, and it made him, rolling onto his back and only half awake, connect her refusal to the vague but disgusting crimes of which the dream accused him. As he came more fully awake, it disintegrated, but he had a hard time getting back to sleep and had waked this morning feeling severely disgruntled. He'd been trying to shake the mood ever since. Frowning as the brilliant sunlight bouncing off the rooftops of Poniktuk hurt his eyes, he began to feel that Nate was to blame for his discomfort.

His appointment of his nephew as ABRA's fieldworker in Poniktuk had not turned out as he'd expected. Almost every day for many weeks now, Nate had been going from house to house with papers in his hands to preach the ABRA gospel. And people listened. Simon himself had listened, having insisted that Nate report all the organization's plans to him. The more he understood them, the less he liked them, but he didn't yet know, hadn't yet figured out, how to stymie them. He couldn't guess how many Poniktungmiut Nate's presentations had convinced — maybe many, maybe not — but his nephew certainly had people's attention.

And that wasn't the only thing. All over town, there were whispers that Nate had acquired special powers, old-time angakuq powers. As ridiculous as the notion was, Simon had to admit his nephew had had uncanny luck at hunting lately. And come to think of it, he reflected, wouldn't new powers also explain the startling change in Nate's behaviour? Where was the lazy high-school dropout whose only apparent ambitions had been to listen to rock-and-roll and run around town with his pals? The boy he'd chosen for the ABRA job three months ago, the boy he'd been so sure he could control? Nowhere. That Nate was not today's Nate. Looked the same, but wasn't. Special powers?

Simon sighed. Today his window's sovereign view offered him no reassurances. On the contrary, things were happening out there that he didn't understand. There was the white lady.

Yesterday evening, using only his usual powers of amiable coercion, he had made the others around Eli's kitchen table agree that the woman should for now remain Poniktuk's secret. Recalling his success, Simon's spirits revived, then slumped. Why had he done that? He still didn't know. Was it another bad decision, like appointing Nate? His instincts had told him to make it, but what was he going to do with the lady? He could be as wrong about keeping her in Poniktuk as he'd been about appointing Nate. He couldn't tell. How come he couldn't tell?

Angrily Simon told himself it wasn't like him — long-time settlement council chairman, decision maker for the village — to suddenly be so uncertain, to feel so cranky, so frustrated. With a grunt, he swung his chair back to his desk and tried again to concentrate on the stationery order. How many damn housing-supply forms did he really need? He went down the checklist.

Beyond his window, the day remained brilliant.

Visitors had finally entered Eli's house. The children who'd been standing around the back porch were now standing in the kitchen, sucked there in the wake of Della and Selma, who'd shown the boldness of their thirteen years by marching briskly up the porch steps into the house and demanding to see the white lady. But Ruth's mild refusal, which seemed to acknowledge the naturalness of their curiosity while rebuking it, had taken the wind out of their sails. Thirteen years old or not, they now stood among their juniors as tongue-tied as any of them, jostling each other as they darted glances down the corridor toward the bedroom where they guessed the lady was. Unconcerned, Ruth sat on the kitchen floor cutting small chunks from a caribou shoulder with her ulu. A piece of cardboard under the meat kept the blood off her linoleum. She was going to make soup for when the lady woke up.

Eli sat at the kitchen table, hands around a coffee cup. It was netting time at the mouth of the Blackstone River, and his hands were chapped and roughened from immersion in the river's icy water. But at the moment his mind was not on fish. He'd glanced only once, when they came in, at the children bunched near the door to his storage room, now shuffling, squirming, or merely gaping at him, his wife, the kitchen walls, and the bedroom corridor. He was looking out the window at the same shining day that Simon had seen from the settlement office. But for Eli its elements — the breeze, the sunlight, the glistening water — seemed alive with an energy beyond their appearance. It was said his grandfather Iku had been able, through helping spirits, to call up weather like today's. In his son Iku's bed lay a woman who'd appeared on a hillside close to Poniktuk yesterday. Was it only a coincidence that today was this kind of day? Or had his son summoned both woman and weather?

While Eli pondered, Sarah came padding down the bedroom corridor on small bare feet, wearing a flowered cotton dress elasticized at her chubby waist. She stopped at the entrance to the kitchen. It was the farthest she'd come from the white lady's bedside since taking up a vigil there the evening before. Helen had dragged her into her own bedroom around midnight, but in the early morning hours Sarah had slipped away again to watch the golden-haired sleeper.

Round-eyed and solemn, Sarah studied the other children. They studied her. None spoke, but all had seen where Sarah came from.

Ruth glanced at her grandchild, sighed, and went back to cutting meat.

"Mine," Sarah said.

Ruth's knife stopped cutting. She stared at Sarah and then

glanced at Eli, but it seemed he hadn't heard. Hoping this first word the child had spoken in many weeks might be followed by more, Ruth straightened her legs and, elbows resting on her knees, waited for her granddaughter to go on.

The other members of Sarah's audience also waited, except for Selma, who suddenly giggled but quickly stopped under Sarah's reproachful stare. Communication hung suspended in the kitchen air. Then a collective sigh and a ripple of acquiescence passed through the bunched children.

Satisfied, Sarah stomped across the kitchen to her granny.

"Want juice," she said.

Ahh, thought Ruth. Things back to normal.

"After," she said, and pushing a wisp of grey hair off her forehead with the back of the hand that held her ulu, she lowered the knife to make another cut in the caribou shoulder.

"Want juuuuuice!"

Sarah yanked at her granny's sleeve, making the knife swoop dangerously close to her granny's thigh.

Ruth turned her head and came eye to eye with her grandchild. There was no pleading in the girl's expression, only demand, but Ruth decided that a return to speech after so long and inexplicable a silence might after all deserve a reward. She released her sleeve from Sarah's grip and looked at the other children.

"Get Sarah juice," she said.

Seizing the opportunity, Della broke from the others and sped to the refrigerator. She opened the door and pulled out a can of Coca-Cola, popped its top, took a plastic tumbler from the kitchen counter, and poured out the rich, dark, fizzing liquid for Sarah as the others watched. Della rolled her eyes at Selma while Sarah drank. Selma shrugged in rueful agreement: it was certainly odious to curry favour with a younger child, but sometimes it had to be done.

"Want more?"

Della grinned down at Sarah, who was gasping into the empty tumbler. She nodded. Della poured.

When the tumbler was empty again, Sarah handed it back and, without a glance at anyone, recrossed the kitchen linoleum and re-entered the bedroom corridor. Claiming her reward for service, Della started after her. She signalled Selma to follow but cut short with a fierce glare a shuffling movement to join them that started among the other children. Revealing in hung heads and slumped shoulders that they accepted this exclusion as hard but just, they watched while Sarah and her two attendants passed down the corridor toward Nate's bedroom.

Sarah reached up two fat hands and turned the doorknob. Pushing through, she turned back and held the door open just wide enough for Della and Selma to see, but only by craning their necks, Nate's bed. A blanket covered the window, darkening the room except for a thin strip of sunlight that leaked in along an edge and slanted toward the bed like a finger pointing at the lady's head. Her eyes were closed. Her hair lay spread out on the pillow.

Della and Selma stared. The lady's sunburnt face was pitiful, but her hair was an out-and-out wonder. They'd heard hair could be yellow, but neither had ever hoped to see it. A draft from the corridor lifted a corner of the blanket, and the light on the lady's hair suddenly intensified.

Deciding the older girls had seen enough, Sarah pushed the door closed against them. Della and Selma craned until the latch clicked. In the corridor they exchanged wild looks and then retreated to the kitchen, where, too full of emotion to speak or even to glance at Ruth or Eli, they gathered up the other children and herded them through the storage room and out the back door once more into the light of the blazing day.

But they soon found their tongues. Running first to her Auntie Akpa's, where her mother was visiting, and then for the rest of the day to selected houses all over town, Della told — and Selma backed her up — how just before Sarah closed the door, there had appeared around the motionless head on the pillow a glow that was unmistakably a halo.

As with the story about the lady's sexual parts, Akpa didn't know whether to believe that or not.

"Honest," she said to her sister after Della had left with her co-visionary to spread the news. "Too bad Father Evans get sick so long before that lady get here. He be able to tell one halo for sure. Or maybe only them Catholic fathers could tell halos."

"Really!" Big Helen said. "Sometimes I think you got no sense inside your head. You know that Della say anything, even she's my own daughter. That girl tell you 'Sky is turning upside down,' and she believe it and try to make you believe it too. That lady got no halo. She maybe not even going to live, poor lady. If she die and go to Heaven, maybe then she get one halo."

But Akpa wouldn't countenance levity on a subject as serious as halos. It wasn't that she believed Della; she knew as well as her sister that the need to make herself interesting severely compromised Della's attachment to the truth. Girls her age were like that. But Father Evans had always said that the Lord moved in mysterious ways His wonders to perform, and she for one had always been more than willing to believe him. In fact, since being introduced to the notion, Akpa's personal count of cases of heavenly movement in and around Poniktuk, kept strictly to herself to preserve the mystery, had greatly outstripped the Anglican priest's own more conservative lifetime tally. Who was to say, she told herself, that some kind of holy woman hadn't appeared in Poniktuk and that the Lord, as difficult to understand as ever, hadn't chosen Della as His witness?

"Never mind being smarty," Akpa told her sister, who was shocked into momentary silence by this rebuke, commonly used only against children. "The Lord move in mysterious ways. Obie know all about that. I go see Obie."

And she climbed down from her chair and waddled out of the house without another word to Big Helen. Watching her go, Helen thought how much she'd always loved and always would love the small, determined, misshapen creature, now closing the door behind her, who was her sister. Then she lit a cigarette and wondered, in her sister's empty house, what having that white lady in Poniktuk would do to people.

At Obie's, Akpa found him and his wife Bella, another of her sisters, seated stiffly in their kitchen.

"There's coffee," Bella said.

Akpa shook her head. "Obie going to tell me something." And pulling a chair close to his, she climbed up.

But her hope of discussing heavenly wonders — and in particular halos — with Poniktuk's leading Evangelical was quickly disappointed. Obie met her account of Della's visionary experience with silence. The tongue that at prayer meetings so often praised the Lord for happenings no less wondrous than what Della said she saw refused to loosen.

"You find that lady," Akpa reminded him. "What you think when you first see her? What the Lord tell you about her then?"

Obie remained silent.

"Obie, what you got? You trying to be like little Sarah? Devil get your tongue?"

But at this Obie stood and, indeed like little Sarah, turned away and hurried down the bedroom corridor to his room.

"What I say now?" Akpa asked.

Bella sighed.

"He's like that ever since he bring that lady to Eli. Never say nothing to me when he come home, just talk to hisself. Talk about that old man Iku and them nuns at residential school and I don't know what other. I stop listening. He talk all night, Akpa. Honest, what you think I should do?"

Akpa shook her head in sympathy and then turned the shaking into a sagacious nod.

"The good Lord look after His own," she said. "Obie one of them."

Bella fetched another sigh and said, "Amen."

Zebediah was at the HTA office. For once he was alone. Through the office window he could see Harry Ingasuk walking along the road, undoubtedly on his way to someone's house for something to eat. Harry's back was to him, and he found himself wishing that instead of walking away Harry was walking toward him to come and sit on the HTA bench as he often did, confidently waiting to be invited home for lunch. It wasn't Harry's fault that he couldn't cook or that the only woman who'd ever agreed to marry him had hanged herself while on a drunk before he could secure her conjugal services. People had to look after other people, and Zeb didn't mind taking his turn giving Harry a meal. But today Harry was headed elsewhere.

Yesterday afternoon he'd watched Obie's progress along the road with the appalling bundle on the rack of his threewheeler. Wayne, Harry, Old Piuyuk, and Isaac Ivalu had also been there. They'd crowded to the window, and as if he were still looking over their shoulders, he now saw the image on the road again of his old friend sitting grimly astride his threewheeler. It was going so slowly it didn't even raise dust behind the amazing fall of yellow hair hanging from its rack.

Like everyone else who'd seen her, Zeb had assumed the lady was dead. While that terrible belief held him staring out the window, other terrible thoughts had skittered through his mind. Had Obie killed her? Was it an accident or on purpose? Who was she? What was she?

When Obie and his burden had passed from sight and the others in the office had resumed their seats in stunned silence, Zeb had realized, as the silence continued, interrupted only by the buzzing of flies at the window, that they were waiting for him to say something. Old Piuyuk stared into some personal distance, but Harry and Isaac Ivalu kept shooting him sidelong glances. But he was too appalled to say anything until it finally occurred to him to say that he was closing the office. The others had nodded and left, and he'd left with them.

But standing on the office steps, squinting against the glare of mid-afternoon sunlight, he hadn't known what to do. He'd wanted to see where Obie was going — and he hadn't. He wanted to know what had really happened, and he didn't. After standing there undecided until he realized that must look odd to anyone watching him, he'd simply gone home, where he waited for events to take their course and for a decision to come to him about what to do about or for his old friend. Throughout the rest of the day and into the evening, his wife relayed to him the rumours and stories she kept hearing on the telephone until he couldn't stand it anymore and went to bed. No decision had come to him, awake or asleep, but he'd gathered from the telephone reports that the lady was still alive.

He'd slept badly.

As Zeb continued to stare at the sunstruck road beyond his office window, now deserted by both the real Harry and the ghost of Obie, he remembered last night's dream. He was handing over the limp body of a woman with long yellow hair, like the hair he'd seen hanging from Obie's threewheeler, to a Chinese guy standing on the floats of a plane pulled up to the shore of a lake. It was a beautiful summer day. As the guy reached out to take the woman's body, the image dissolved, and Zeb found himself holding instead a sack full of soft, bloody bones in some other place where it was dark. He couldn't see the guy but knew he was standing right beside him. He dropped the sack and held out his hand for the money the guy was going to give him, but instead of money in his hand, he felt a fine powder trickle through his fingers. Outdoors again, in a place that was no special place, the Chinese guy had turned into Obie, and Obie was holding out his hand and thanking him with a big smile.

Zeb considered the dream. He didn't usually remember dreams, but maybe he remembered this one because it had a good ending: whatever he'd done had made Obie happy. But what did the rest mean? The Chinese guy had turned into Obie, and halfway through the dream the lady with yellow hair had turned into something else too — soft bones in a sack.

Antlers in the velvet.

Zeb's hand reached for the middle drawer of his desk. Now if in the dream Obie was really the Chinese guy, he thought, and if the lady Obie'd brought to town turned into the antlers the

Chinese guy wanted to buy, and handing them over made the guy — who was really Obie — made Obie, then, his oldest and best friend, practically his brother, thank him and be happy, wasn't that telling him how he should make up his mind about the letter in his desk drawer?

Zeb smiled. Of course it was.

He opened the drawer and felt around inside. If Obie had got himself into trouble with that lady, his dream had told him what to do to help. As his hand touched the envelope, Zeb didn't think to ask himself how selling antlers in the velvet would get Obie out of trouble, nor did he consider another message embedded in the dream: that money from antlers might turn into something like dust.

Good thing I never burn this letter, Zeb thought, his hand on the envelope.

Back at Ruth and Eli's, Nate was reading about bears, muskox, caribou, wolves, rabbits, foxes, wolverine, migratory water fowl, and fish. After finishing the section in the ABRA agreement on resource development last night, he'd slept on the living-room couch where he was now sitting and from which he'd noted Sarah's procession in and out of the kitchen and her successful claim of sole visiting rights to the white lady in his bedroom. He'd also recognized — and acknowledged — in his niece's sudden return to speech an early and happy consequence of the lady's arrival in his home. But he couldn't know that at this very moment, as Della and Selma made their apostolic rounds, Della was claiming that Sarah's recovery was the lady's first miracle.

Nate's sleep had been as dreamless as the lady's in his bed and as undisturbed as his uncles' had been troubled. But his normal oblivion had been deepened by the nighttime shift of some inner ground, as if a subsurface area of himself, previously unstable, had settled. He'd waked feeling profoundly good about himself and with a sense of purpose that continued to propel him through the ABRA document before him.

"Notwithstanding the Game Laws and addended regulations of the Department of Renewable Resources of the Government of the Northwest Territories enacted heretofore or hereinafter at any time under any duly granted or acquired power of jurisdiction, be it jurisdiction granted by the Federal Government of Canada or acquired through enactment of legislation by the Federal Parliament of Canada or by the Assembly of the Northwest Territories or by their duly empowered successor or successors under law," he read, "the Permanent Joint Committee on Wildlife Management for the Inuvik Settlement Region (the PJCWMISR) shall regulate the management, use, exploitation, protection, harvest, sale, marketing, sport hunting, and scientific or commercial study of all fur-bearing mammals, whether terrestrial or marine, that inhabit the aforementioned Region throughout the duration of their lifetimes seasonally or permanently or in the course of migration or of any other movement into the Region from any direction or from any point of origin inside or outside the Region."

Yes! Nate said out loud, and paused in his reading.

Poniktuk was the last of seven regional communities to be drawn into the land-rights movement, and its participation in a coming referendum on the ABRA Agreement in Principle was, according to the movement's leaders, essential. Andy Kublu had promised Nate a letter explaining the referendum process and had said that Simon Umingmak would give Nate his full support and cooperation to assure a positive outcome. That's what Andy said, but Nate knew better. For Andy, a Yes vote in the referendum would mean Poniktuk joined the other communities in taking control of matters now in the hands of outside officials. For his uncle, it would mean the end to years of one-man rule. There was no way Simon would cooperate, whatever he'd told Andy.

But pausing in his study of future indigenous controls over wildlife populations, Nate felt sure he could beat his uncle. He didn't know exactly how he'd block Simon's manoeuvring to spoil the vote, but ever since he'd opened the ABRA agreement this morning, confidence had coursed through him like a fever in his blood. He turned eagerly back to reading.

Looking in on him later in the morning on his way to the bathroom, Eli noticed his youngest son's concentration.

Iku never study like that before, he thought as his stream of piss hit the inside of the black plastic bag in the family honey bucket. Old-time angakuq make weather out of air. Maybe new-time angakuq make something out of books.

In the settlement office, Simon was reading a letter from Andy Kublu. The name on the envelope had been Nate's, but when he was handing out mail at the store, Simon had noticed the return address was ABRA, and instead of calling for Nate to step up, he'd put the letter with those addressed to himself.

The letter contained the official terms of the referendum on ABRA's Agreement in Principle. There were the usual requirements of a local vote — a list of eligible voters, a supervised polling station, secret ballots — but an unusual condition of this vote had caught Simon's attention. For the referendum to pass and the agreement to take effect, there had to be a majority vote in its favour in each of the seven participating communities, not just a majority vote of the total population in the region. Simon looked up from the letter to consider the implications. He began to smile. The letter said the purpose of the condition was to force the Federal government to recognize support for the measure throughout the region. But it also meant, Simon saw, that if any one community voted against the agreement, that support collapsed and the whole referendum failed. His smile broadened. Andy had added a handwritten note at the end of the letter saying he was happy that "your uncle Simon's full support and co-operation, as expressed to me when I called him recently, guarantees a positive result in Poniktuk."

The doubts that had troubled him earlier in the day evaporated in Simon's mind. He put the letter down and began to consider how he would undermine the referendum. He was himself again.

"So I figger we have a public meeting coupla days before that referendum vote," he said ten minutes later to deputy assistant superintendent of Local Government Jim Fraser in Inuvik.

"Uh-huh."

"And maybe you could come in for it."

"Okay, but, uh, what for?"

Simon made him wait.

"You still pushing that devolution thing?"

"Oh sure. It's on the back burner now, but it's the commissioner's pet project. That I know."

"Seems to me, like how I understand it, that devolution thing not worth a blueberry in a bear's ass if that-there ABRA thing pass that referendum."

Fraser's laugh had no humour in it.

"Could be, Simon, could be. There wouldn't be much left of my department if the ABRA proposals go through. But I don't suppose that would break your heart, now would it?"

His tone was jocular.

"I dunno, Jim."

Simon's tone was serious.

"Oh?"

"I mean, more I been thinking about it, more I like that-there devolution idea."

"Really?"

"Seems like it's better, Jim. Might be something in it for the both of us."

"How you figure that, Simon?"

"Well, if people in Poniktuk go for it, maybe on a trial basis like, seems to me you could get a lot of credit in your department. Make the commissioner happy too."

"And, uh, where would you come in?"

"You know I allus gotta do what's best for my people, Jim."

"Yeah, I know."

"And seems to me, what I'm hearing," Simon said, enjoying Jim's sarcasm but keeping his own tone sober, "them ABRA people want to take away what you and me allus been doing here in Poniktuk, making everything go good for everybody."

"So?"

"So maybe if you come in to public meeting, we could make people like that devolution idea better than ABRA ideas. Couple days before that referendum vote."

Seeing the light, Fraser felt dizzy.

"But, Simon, you know the terms of that referendum?"

"Seems like I hear something. But like I say, Jim, I gotta do what's right for my people. What I figger, ABRA don't understand Poniktuk. But you and me, we been taking care of things in here long time now. Seems like we do something like I'm thinking, Poniktuk get a good deal, commissioner sit up, maybe you get promotion. We both come out ahead. So you think about it and let me know."

"Yeah, I'll . . . uh, sure, I'll think about it."

"So long then, Jim."

And he hung up.

Holy shit! Fraser thought. Simon wants to scuttle the whole goddamn ABRA agreement! Years of negotiations between ABRA and the Feds, hundreds of thousands of Fed dollars already spent, millions promised for the future if the deal goes through, not to mention everything else they're giving away, you name it, the whole nine yards, the best land-rights agreement ever offered native people in Canada, probably in the world. And Simon Umingmak wants to stop it. With my help. Holy shit!

If Fraser go for this, Simon was thinking in the Poniktuk settlement office, ABRA just about finished. He spun his chair to look once more out his office window. This time the brightness of the day didn't bother him. Glancing at the village rooftops, he settled on Eli and Ruth's house. Now he was glad he'd made sure the white lady lying there in Nate's bed had stayed in Poniktuk. She was a rare secret, and his new mood told him he was going to make it work for him. If he could solve one problem, he could solve another.

In Inuvik, Fraser stared at a government-issued Inuit print on the wall opposite his desk, but he wasn't seeing it. He was seeing James Archibald Fraser, author of the Territorial Government's brilliant new devolution strategy, first implemented in the settlement of Poniktuk and then throughout the north, being sworn in as permanent deputy minister of Local Government of the Northwest Territories by the commissioner himself, who was beaming at him. As Fraser's imagination dwelled on details of this happy ceremony, one question had to be answered: dare I? dare I do what Simon wants? As a lifelong bureaucrat, he'd always used caution as his guide. But this could be the opportunity of a lifetime. He knew his career in government would depend on his decision. And his career in government was his life.

Minutes later he called Bill Tremonte into his office.

"I want you to work up a devolution pilot project for Poniktuk," he told his young assistant. "Drop whatever else you're doing and get it to me by the end of the week."

In the Mona Lisa Lounge of the Duke of Clarence Hotel in Edmonton, Ethel McGarr, Health Services nurse for Poniktuk currently on holiday, sat in her booth and stared morosely at the full glass of beer standing precisely in the centre of the round cardboard coaster that the waitress had placed on the black, shiny surface of the table an hour ago before placing on it Ethel's first beer of the afternoon. Outside in the streets of Alberta's capital, sunlight bounced off concrete, facing stone, and window glass with an intensity that would have made Ethel's eyeballs ache if she'd been out there. But in the Mona Lisa Lounge, all was a restful murk.

She reached a steadied hand toward the glass and raised it to her lips.

Those Eskimos, she thought, they really are something. Do everything we can for them — give 'em houses, give 'em schools, give 'em religion, give 'em birth control, prenatal, postnatal, alcohol and drug abuse, everything — and they go right on living their lives like we're not even there. Why do I keep going back? I'll bet right this minute someone's thinking of getting a couple of cases of CC in on the sched — Simon probably — and they're all smacking their lips at the thought of drinking themselves blind for as long as it lasts. All except Akpa and Eli and Ruth and a couple of others. But who'll look after the kids when everyone's drinking? And those kids. I'll bet at least one of the boys in town has knocked up at least one of his own cousins by now with all the running around all night long they do all summer when the sun never sets. Like Della. Well, she's about ready for her first baby, isn't she? Twelve, thirteen years old? And Old Piuyuk out there in his tent by the airstrip. Can't believe that guy. Toughest old bugger ever walked into a nursing station. Hope they got a sub with some kind of northern experience while I'm not there. Those little twitchy-butt graduates fresh out of nursing school with their caps bobby-pinned on their heads don't know shit about Eskimos.

Her glass made another deliberate journey to her lips. She had ten more days of holiday to go.

If she'd known that her substitute had indeed been a graduate like that and hadn't been able to stand the isolation of Poniktuk and had promptly quit so that Territorial Health Services were right now scrambling to find a substitute for her substitute, Ethel would probably have caught the next plane north to Inuvik and made the first connection she could to Poniktuk. If she didn't know why she kept going back, neither did she know why she couldn't stay away. And she probably would not have stayed away even if she'd known that among many adults and all the children of Poniktuk, whose tongues she'd depressed with wooden sticks till they gagged saying aaahhh and whose ears had all felt the cold invasion of her otoscope while she pinched their earlobes, Ethel McGarr was called Awful McGarr.

But the administrative nurse for the Inuvik Region believed that Ethel needed her time off. So nobody called the Duke of Clarence Hotel, and the nursing station in Poniktuk stayed empty.

Sunlight reflected off its windows now, casting silvery rhomboids onto the ground below them. It was late afternoon in Edmonton, but here the sun was still high in the sky. Inside, the small locked building was hot as an oven and smelled more strongly than ever of disinfectant. If Ethel had been in residence, some of its windows would certainly have been open, especially the ones in the two-bed ward where her patient would have been sleeping. But the door to the station had been locked when Obie tried it, forgetting that both she and her substitute were gone, and Gwen slept in Nate's bed instead.

She moaned in her sleep now, and her eyelids fluttered but didn't open. Under the eiderdown her legs twitched. From a bedside chair, Sarah noted the movement. She was no longer frightened of what had got inside her Uncle Nate and made him scary; this lady had come to Poniktuk to fix that. As soon as she was ready, she'd make it get out of her uncle and go away for good. In the meantime, staying close to the lady would keep her safe.

ꟼ

After bobbing up beyond the river-wide trough of churning water that had drowned him, Ralph's body passed out of the rapids in the Blackstone gorge into a stretch of placid water. Swollen by runoff from the recent storm, the river bore the body swiftly downstream, too swiftly, as Gwen had found, for her to catch up with it. Two days later, the current nudged it into an eddy along the riverbank.

But when the river dropped back to its normal level, the eddy disappeared and the current took Ralph out again. Floating sometimes face down, sometimes face up, spinning lazily in and out of other eddies, he went down the river in amiable suspension, his internal organs bloating. But after a while, water filled his body, forcing out the corrupting gases, and it sank below the surface.

As it flowed toward the sea, the river dropped Ralph over ledges, sped him past sandy beaches and black boulders, bore him smoothly around grassy bends. It was his element now. His lungs were bags of water.

At the mouth of the river, Ralph's body slid easily past silver-bellied fish struggling to free themselves from nets. And when the current, mixing with the still waters of the Arctic Ocean, at last let his body go, it sank to the floor of the sea like a stone.

Gwen felt her head lifted up and the tip of a spoon touch her lips. She opened them. The spoon pushed between her teeth and tilted. A trickle of warm liquid entered her mouth. It tasted meaty. She swallowed. The spoon withdrew and the hand supporting her head lowered it to the pillow. After a moment the hand slid under her head again and lifted. The spoon again presented itself. She swallowed more liquid. The spoon tipped upward and withdrew, wiping its bowl on her upper lip. She went back to sleep.

The next time Gwen woke, she lay for a while feeling the bed's soft support and the lightweight warmth of a quilt drawn up to her chin. When she opened her eyes, she saw a ceiling. She turned her head: a window hung with a blanket. Some daylight seeped through the blanket, but most of the light in the room came from around its edges. She let her eyes travel around this fiery fringe, then turned her head the other way.

A plump little girl with brown skin and black eyes was sitting in a chair staring at her. Gwen smiled at the child. The child did not smile back. Instead she climbed down from her chair and left the room. Gwen closed her eyes.

A moment later, she felt a hand slip under her head. She opened her eyes and saw a woman with friendly fat cheeks and grey-streaked black hair bending over her, holding a spoon in her free hand. Gwen opened her mouth. The woman lifted her head, and the hand with the spoon in it tipped more warm liquid into her mouth. Gwen licked her lips. The woman smiled and lowered Gwen's head. Gwen heard the scrape of the spoon in a bowl and this time lifted her head on her own. She swallowed another mouthful of the meaty broth and went back to sleep.

As she began to wake more often, Gwen learned that when the little girl went away it meant the woman would soon arrive with broth. The little girl was always there. The woman kept smiling. Presently there were bits of meat in the broth. She had no idea how much time was passing.

When Gwen wet the bed, she was embarrassed. But the woman seemed to be expecting this. She'd already lifted the quilt and looked down there two or three times when she came into the room to feed her. Now the wetness seemed to please her. She gave a wide grin, shooed the girl out of the room, and came back with a younger woman. While the older one turned her on her side and held her there, the young one changed the sheet. Then together they put a diaper on her made from a towel. Gwen was amused but also relieved.

Waking and sleeping and swallowing broth, it seemed to Gwen to be always daytime in her room — a muted daytime filled with soft shadows and slashed by shafts of sunlight from around the window blanket. Once she thought she heard the sound of feet shuffling into the room and the rustle of clothing, but she didn't open her eyes to see who might be there. For now the important thing was this: she was warm and safe.

The label inside the tuque read:

L.L. Bean
Freeport, Maine
100% Wool

"Must be," said Selma. "I never see no writing like that before."

She and Della had spotted the brightly coloured object in the dirt under Harry Ingasuk's house. Harry's white dog, lying farther back in the darkness, had thumped his tail at Selma when, on Della's instructions, she'd crawled through an opening in the wire-mesh skirting to get the tuque. Della was holding it now. There were holes in its red, yellow, and green bands, and the wool was stiff in places from the dog's saliva, but it was unmistakably a tuque and, on the evidence of the label, belonged to no one in Poniktuk.

"She wear it to cover her halo," Della said in a quiet voice. "When she don't want nobody to see it."

Selma stared at the tuque. Since their visit to the white lady's bedroom, they'd not been allowed back.

"I could feel something," Della said, with a sudden intake of breath.

"What?"

"Some kinda power. Like it moving in my hands. It . . . oh!"

She dropped the tuque.

Harry's dog stuck his head through the skirting. Della snatched the tuque. The dog retreated.

"It sacred," Della said.

Selma nodded.

"We have to make — whatchucallit? — place for keeping it. You remember how Father Evans allus lock up that cup he make people drink from in that little house on altar?"

Selma nodded.

"We have to make place like that."

Selma nodded again.

"Ooh. It make me ticklish just to hold it," Della said.

Selma shook her head admiringly.

"I know," said Della. "Father's shack!"

Selma's eyes widened.

During Father Evans's years in Poniktuk, a small shed attached to the mission building had gained a reputation for mystery and terror among Poniktuk's children. They were strictly forbidden to enter, and neither Della nor Selma had ever violated the restriction. But older boys or girls who dared force the latch and step into its dim interior had reported piles of strange objects lying around and many fearsome wooden crates. The contents of the crates and uses of the objects had become an inexhaustible subject of speculation, most of it gruesome. But since Father Evans's departure, the empty mission building had lost its place of importance in the community, and the mysteries and terrors of its shed had faded.

For Selma they now revived, but she didn't have the courage to stop her friend. Fearfully she nodded agreement.

Closing the door behind them, the girls let their eyes adjust to the gloom. For a moment, Della forgot the tickling powers of the woollen bundle in her hands as she looked around. There were indeed many wooden crates with rusting padlocks on them stacked along the wall common to the mission building and the shed, and piles of other strange things lay scattered on top of them and on the dirt floor. Neither girl could know that the big round object with once-bright painted circles on it, backed by a pad of straw, was an archery target or that the net rolled up with two metal poles, which Della took for a fishnet, was for badminton. Nor could they know that foxed campfire songbooks and manuals for tying knots and doing other useful tasks filled some of the smaller crates, while the larger ones held mildewed Boy Scout and Girl Guide uniforms in several sizes, or indeed that all the objects packed or scattered about the shed were the decaying paraphernalia of the attempt by a young Father Evans to engage the youth of Poniktuk in the practices of athletic Christianity.

"Where you going to put it?" Selma whispered, eager for the job to be done.

Della nodded toward the crates against the wall.

"Over there."

Together they advanced on the crates. Della studied their arrangement.

"We have to make altar."

Reverently she lay the tuque on the floor and took a mouldy, deflated football from the top of a crate. She carried it to the other side of the shed and put it down. Motioning Selma to join her, she started clearing away a stack of football shoulder guards piled on another crate, carrying the first pair herself across the floor to lay it by the football. Selma's shaking hands rattled the protective plates on the pair she was carrying, and she dropped it with a shriek. Della shot her a stern look. Selma drew a shaky breath, picked the dangerous object up again, and put it down next to Della's.

Together they cleared the crates and then, with Della directing, shoved three large ones together. They placed four of the small crates on top of the three and pushed them against the wall to create a narrow shelf running the width of the larger crates. During these efforts Selma stepped on the tuque more than once, but Della didn't notice. She herself, finding it underfoot at one point, kicked it unthinkingly aside. Now she got Selma to help her prop the archery target in the centre of the waist-high shelf. She stood back and surveyed their work.

"It not good enough yet," she muttered.

Selma rolled her eyes.

Looking around the shed, Della noticed a heap of small warped hoops lying like jackstraws close to the door. They had long handles and slack webbing inside their frames. Next to them she saw little cones of stiff white feathers sewn together with the ends of their quills stuck into a small round base. She studied them, looked back at the stacked crates, and decided. Choosing a badminton racquet less warped than the others, she propped it, handle down, against the archery target. Its hoop fit exactly over the bull's eye.

"Good," she said.

Now she looked around again and, spotting the tuque a few feet away, picked it up and pushed her fist into its crown. She brushed off the dirt, rolled the brim and, stepping up to the racquet, pulled the tuque over its hoop and leaned it back against the target. A faded red band at the bottom of the bull's eye showed through the webbing like a smile above the racquet's chin. Prompted by a final inspiration, she went back to the door and, picking up four of the best-preserved shuttlecocks, smoothed their feathers and placed them upside down in a row in front of the racquet.

Selma stood shifting from one foot to the other, rubbing the goose bumps on her arms.

"We could go now?" she whispered.

Della frowned. There was still some last thing to do, but she wasn't sure what it was. Memory came to her rescue. Dropping to one knee as Father Evans did, she crossed herself before the white lady's tuque.

When they emerged from the shed, the sunlight seemed much brighter than when they'd gone in. They blinked and, without a word, went separate ways.

But their furtive entry into Father's shed had been noticed by several pairs of Poniktungmiut eyes, which then kept a watch on the door till the girls came out. For years, no one, adult or child, had entered the missionary shed, and it was noted that the pair spent considerable time inside. This was unusual behaviour. And because unusual behaviour in Poniktuk was a sure sign that something interesting was going on, before long someone else approached the shed and entered, but not furtively.

It was Akpa.

Reaching up to unlatch the door, she pushed it open with both hands and let a narrow carpet of light fall across the earthen floor. Direct sunlight stopped short of the stacked crates, but Akpa's attention went immediately to the wall where the hatted badminton racquet leaned against a faded archery target. A shiver ran down her spine. She knew an altar when she saw one. She approached the crates.

They stood in dimness, and the shelf on which the handle of the racquet and inverted shuttlecocks rested was only just above the level of her eyes. As an adolescent, Akpa had been one of the girls Father Evans had recruited to play badminton while he still believed in the conversion of Inuit youth through sports. Although her short legs and heavily muscled arms had kept her from the quickness necessary to succeed at the game, the priest had singled her out for praise and blessed her efforts. As she now gazed in the dusty gloom at the carefully arranged remnants of that time and recalled the blessings, a warm feeling flooded her small, unwieldy body.

When she left the shed, Akpa closed its door carefully behind her and headed to Big Helen's house. It had taken her only a moment to guess that the striped tuque on the altar was the white lady's. No one in Poniktuk had one like it. Akpa's heavy legs never allowed a spring in her step, but now, as she hurried along Poniktuk's dusty main street, her rolling gait came close to rollicking. She'd heard, considered, and already half-believed Della's claim that, even while lying unconscious in bed, the white lady had performed a miracle by making little Sarah talk. Hadn't Ruth said the child had come directly from the lady's presence into the kitchen, where she'd spoken her first word in weeks? Now Akpa became almost dizzy at the thought that the Lord might indeed have chosen her ecstatic niece to be His witness and, leading Obie to find the lady in the first place, had once more moved in a mysterious way to perform a wonder in Poniktuk. Not since Father Evans had left had she felt such happy proximity to the workings of the Lord.

"Now it start," Big Helen said when Akpa described how the interior of Father's shed had been transformed and expressed her conviction that Della was right, the white lady was a holy messenger. "Now you begin getting peoples all worked up with crazy talk like that, and who know where it going to finish. How come you believe my Della all of a sudden? You even sounding like her now. What get into you, Akpa? You should be ashame, making mischief like that girl."

But Akpa would not be deprived of her excitement.

"Why else you think Sarah start talking? That child never leave that lady now. She know who fix her up. You just wait. Lady going to make more miracles any day now."

"Ruth say she pissing in her bed. That a miracle?"

Akpa stared at her sister.

"*You* should be ashame," she said. "Father allus say holy

people just like us too, only . . . only same time they belong to choir of the blessed. Bite your tongue, big sister. Lord say he come with sword for some peoples. Maybe that mean you."

"Akpa!"

"You just watch. It coming. White lady going to make another miracle. Then maybe you have some Christian goodness inside you too. Maybe *that* going to be the miracle."

And she climbed down from her chair and left her doubting sister's house.

But as Della and Selma's visit to Father's shack had been observed by more than one pair of eyes, so had Akpa's. And when she was then observed going in and coming out of Big Helen's, the phone there rang.

"What she find in that place?" Obie's wife Bella asked.

"I don't know I want to tell you."

"Oohh?"

Bella stretched the interrogative vowel to allow her voice to swoop up at the end, a common inflection in Poniktuk that expressed interest, surprise, and an expectation of scandal. Big Helen couldn't resist.

"Della been finding that white lady's tuque and been making some kind whatchucallit shrine maybe in that shack. Honestly, that girl of mine think up more mischief than anyone else could think with all their heads put together."

"What Akpa think?"

Helen sighed. She'd always protected and defended her sister when others criticized or mocked her, but Akpa had just insulted her.

"I don't know what get into her," she said. "You hear what Della been saying all over the place about that white lady — some kind of saint? Well, jeepers sakes, Akpa been saying that too after she's going into that shed. Been saying white lady going to make miracles."

"Oohh?"

"Honestly, Bella, she keep saying that, could be peoples believe her. Then what?"

"Mmm," was Bella's only answer.

But "Helen say Akpa say white lady going to make miracles" was what Bella said to Simon's young wife Ruby, whose greatest wish, as yet unrealized, was to have a son by him.

"Oohh?" said Ruby.

And when she called Irene, she said, "Big Helen believe white lady some kind of saint now. Come from heaven, like, to fix things by making miracles. It begin in Father's shack."

"Some kind miracle been happening in Father's shack," Irene said to her son Lawrence. "Go look."

"Me?" said Lawrence.

"Never mind backtalk, boy. Go look in Father's shack and come right home again, you hear?"

Lawrence bowed his head and moseyed out the door.

Big Helen was talking to Simon.

"Trouble is, everyone really respect Akpa when it come to religion. Everyone know she was Father's favourite all that time he's in Poniktuk. So when she say something, peoples listen. That lady being here already making lots of people act funny. What you think happen now if everyone get real excited about Father's old shack and all kind miracles from that poor lady's tuque in there? Honestly, I think we got trouble coming, Simon."

"I'll have a look," said Simon.

But word travelled faster through the village than Simon could decide to commit himself to visit Father's shed. From his office window, he saw his nephew Lawrence approach the shed, pause, pull open the door, and disappear inside. Seconds later he came out and hurried away. Next Bella came walking along, continued walking past the shed, but then, as if a sudden thought had struck her, turned around and darted through the door. Simon decided to stay in his office and watch.

"I don't see nothing," Lawrence reported to his mother. "Bunch of junk in there."

Before the afternoon was over, Simon saw Zebediah, Isaac Ivalu, Irene herself, Young Helen, and his own Ruby approach the shed from various directions with various degrees of visible intent, and stop at its door, look around, and step inside. For a moment it looked like Eddie Qarlik, the school janitor, was also going in, but when he noticed Young Helen at the door ahead of him, he smoothly changed direction and kept on walking as if his business had all along been somewhere else. No one stayed inside for long, but Simon's curiosity intensified when he saw both Zeb and Ruby go in a second time.

He made his own visit the next day. When he was standing inside, he waited for his eyes to adjust to the semi-dark. As a boy he was one of those who'd rejected the Anglican priest's inducements to Christian practice through contact sports, and later he'd been among the boldest for breaking into the forbidden space and, on coming out of it, one of the most inventive in making up gruesome stories about uses of the objects stored there. Now, remembering this inventiveness, he regarded the football shoulder guards piled next to the deflated football by his feet and then turned his attention to Della's altar.

Although he'd never been asked to play badminton, he easily recognized the equipment and also recognized the faded target leaning against the wooden crates. He remembered how passionate he'd become about archery in those days, because it was a skill practised by his ancestors. But his present study of Della's altar had nothing to do with nostalgia or ancestral reverence. When he stepped forward to examine the shelf below the badminton racket, he noticed many objects among the inverted shuttlecocks.

There was a baby shoe and a tine from a caribou antler. There was a scrap of wolverine fur, an earring, two shotgun shells, and bullets of several calibres. People were leaving offerings. And everyone who left an offering saw what others had left — Poniktuk's secret hopes and wishes were being exposed on the packing case. Simon smiled. Already he could guess from the objects who some of the offerants were. That was probably Ruby's baby shoe, for instance.

Back at his desk, Simon pondered how he could use these tokens of belief in the white lady, use her potency. In the back of his mind, like a figure darting in and out of shadows, an idea flitted that wouldn't quite take shape. It told him that if his plan to manipulate Jim Fraser into undermining the ABRA referendum failed, there was a way to use this worship of the lady's tuque to accomplish the same end.

Over the next few days he was pleased to see how many more of Poniktuk's normally sober citizens made furtive visits to Father's old shack. Eddie Qarlik finally got there, Obie did too, and Zebediah returned several times.

His own single visit had been widely observed.

ᑫ

In Ottawa, Edwina stared at a row of books in the bookcase along one wall of her study. She'd just finished talking to the RCMP chief inspector in Yellowknife she'd talked to ten days ago. He'd begun by apologizing for taking so long to get back to her, but for several days bad weather had grounded the plane chartered to look for her daughter and son-in-law, and then, of course, it had taken several more days to fly the search. As it turned out, however, the search plane was the same one that had flown the Morrisseys into the unnamed lake at the beginning of their trip, so it was now established as a certainty that paddling the Blackstone River had indeed been their intention. He couldn't explain why his office had no record. Perhaps they'd failed to sign in. The search plane had covered the whole length of the river from source lake to Arctic Ocean, and he regretted to inform her that it had spotted what looked like the remains of an aluminum canoe wrapped around a rock in the Blackstone gorge. Were her daughter and son-in-law using such a canoe? In a whisper, Edwina said she thought so. The chief inspector cleared his throat and continued. Since no other party was registered to canoe the Blackstone this summer and their records showed no accident in the gorge in the past, it was unfortunately more than likely that the sighted canoe was the Morrisseys'. He was very sorry to report this discovery to her, and it was his duty to further report that, flying over the surrounding terrain, the search plane had seen no trace of any persons. At the very least — again he cleared his throat and regretted having to be so plain-spoken — they must be considered, uh, missing. Of course if they'd survived the upset and salvaged any of their gear, they might still be out there somewhere. But he didn't want to raise false hopes. Did she want them to continue the search?

When Edwina didn't answered right away, he added he felt he should tell her that the cost of the search was already considerable, nearly five thousand dollars, which, as he'd mentioned before, had necessarily to be borne — she would understand the government could not afford to foot the bill for every operation incurred by a canoeing party's misfortunes — by the person requesting the search. There was a brusqueness in his voice as he repeated this caution, which Edwina understood to mean that he thought further searching a waste of money. In fact, the chief inspector's tone expressed his abiding anger with recreational canoeists inexperienced in Arctic conditions who attempted to negotiate wilderness rivers beyond their capabilities, rivers that unfortunately lay within his area of supervision. This wasn't the first time he'd had to inform a relative of lives in all probability lost.

Edwina said she'd let him know and with murmured thanks, hung up.

Now she stared at her books. Her eyes picked out two of them side by side that she'd written herself. She knew the titles by heart, but as she tilted her head and read them on the books' spines, they meant nothing to her. Would she ever again find William Congreve witty or amusing or be able to bear John Webster's refined cruelty?

She reached for the phone.

"They're gone," she told Gwen's twin.

"What?"

"They're gone. Lost. Drowned. They're dead, Trish."

"What? What are you saying?"

"I'm saying" — Edwina took a deep breath — "I just finished talking to that RCMP inspector, and he said the search plane found their canoe. The wreck of it. And no . . . no sign of them."

"I don't believe it."

"Do you think he's lying?"

"No, of course not. But . . ."

"But what, my dear? But don't get yourself all worked up, they're just running a little late? Isn't that what you said? Tricia, they're dead."

Trish was silent.

"Why did I listen to you? If I'd done what I wanted to right away, if I'd started a search right away, when I wanted to, they might still . . ."

She didn't finish, but Trish registered the accusation.

"I don't believe it because I just don't believe it," she said. "Are they sure it's their canoe?"

"Reasonably."

"But what do they mean, no signs? From an airplane? What can they see from an airplane?"

"Enough, he seemed to believe."

Again Trish was silent. Then, "I'm going up there."

"My dear," Edwina said.

"I mean it. She's not dead — they're not dead. I know it. I'll find them."

"Trish."

"Mother, I know. *Twins know.* Remember that time when we were kids and Gwen took a walk from our campsite and sprained her ankle? I knew something had happened to her and I made you come with me and we went out and found her. They're still out there somewhere. I know it."

"Patricia."

"I'll close the shop and get a ticket to . . . where did they fly to? Edmonton. And I'll make a reservation at that hotel in . . . in Inuvik. The something Inn. I was wrong, Mother, okay? When you wanted to do something right away, I was wrong. I thought it would embarrass them. But it's not too late. I'll find them."

"The Igloo Inn. It's called the Igloo Inn."

"Will you be all right here? Maybe I should stay with you."

"No, no, go. I can take care of myself. But it's no use, Trish. That inspector made it all very clear. It's over."

"Don't say that!"

"What should I say?" she retorted, and hung up.

An hour later Trish called back to say her travel agent was having trouble making connections to Inuvik, but she'd probably leave the day after tomorrow, overnight in Edmonton, and catch a plane to Inuvik sometime the next day. Edwina told her to come over for dinner. Then she called Ralph's uncle in Vermont.

"No way," he said. "That can't have happened. Ralph wouldn't . . . Ralph knows . . . even if the canoe did dump. What the hell's wrong with them? Have they really *looked?* What's the name of that inspector? And what's his number?"

Edwina told him.

"I'll get right back to you. Don't go away."

But that was more than an hour ago.

Edwina reached into the centre drawer of her desk and pulled out the topographical maps covering the Blackstone River that Ralph had given her. She spread them on the desk, lining up their edges to make one large map, and with a fingertip traced the course of the river from its beginning in the unnamed lake, pausing at pencil checks Ralph had made where he guessed they might camp at a day's end. Her finger stopped when it reached a section where brown elevation lines crowded so close together along both sides of the river that they touched each other. They indicated, Ralph said, steep walls. They indicated a gorge.

When her finger had completed its journey to the sea, Edwina continued to stare at the maps as if their sinuous markings and patches of colour might contain information beyond the topographical. Then she pushed the maps back together and returned them to the drawer. She looked at her phone and decided to continue waiting, as he'd asked, for Ralph's uncle to call back.

For the rest of her life, she thought, she'd sit at her desk like this and the phone would ring and she'd answer it. She'd do that. But it would never again be Gwen.

9

Beyond swallowing broth and moving her limbs, Gwen could do nothing for more than a week, until one day she sat up. Looking into the room to check on her, Ruth disappeared again and reappeared with an extra pillow. She placed it behind Gwen's back.

"Where am I?" Gwen croaked.

Ruth clapped her hands and burst out laughing.

"Poniktuk!" she answered. "It Poniktuk! We taking care of you."

Gwen frowned. The name sounded familiar. Then she remembered: where she and Ralph planned to end their trip.

"Ralph?"

His name came out in another croak.

Ruth smiled.

Gwen cleared her throat.

"Is Ralph here?"

Ruth added nodding to her smiling.

"Is he okay?"

Ruth still nodded.

Gwen sighed, relaxed against her pillows, and drifted off to sleep, happy in the knowledge that Ralph was also being taken care of.

Ruth left the room to spread the news that the white lady had finally spoken. She kept to herself that she'd continued nodding in response to a question from her that she hadn't understood. It had clearly been the response the lady wanted.

Hearing Ruth's news, Della longed to hear Gwen speak. But, taking her nursing duties seriously, Ruth had forbidden visits to Gwen's room by anyone except her daughter and granddaughter.

She refused entry even to Nate, although the room was his. Della found the ban hard to bear. As first to see the lady's halo and chief attendant at her shrine, she believed she had a right to visit. Seeing other Poniktungmiut make pilgrimages every day to Father's transformed shed, she also felt more and more securely and deservedly wrapped in the white lady's holiness. She watched and waited for Ruth to be away from home.

Although no one in the village mentioned visits to the shed to anyone else, everyone knew who was going there and who was not. Those who made one visit and found the improvised altar either sacrilegious or ridiculous silently condemned Della for creating it. But those who left hopeful offerings on the shelf were grateful to her. And as Della went about the village with a self-important step and an air of elevated purpose, frequently entering and leaving the shed to dust the crates and rearrange the offerings, everyone could see her invisible mantle of sanctity.

Ruth's only visit to the shrine had left her with contempt for the whole business. Tending Gwen, she knew better than anyone who she was — a frail white female who'd narrowly escaped death on the tundra. So she particularly forbad the bedroom to Della and watched with alarm as more and more of her relatives and friends made trips to Father's old shed. To half believe that her son had become an angakuq was as much strangeness as she was willing to consider.

On a day that Eli was at the Blackstone River tending his nets and Young Helen out visiting, Ruth left the house in the afternoon to share her worries and seek common cause against galloping superstition with Big Helen. In Gwen's bedroom, Sarah stayed on her watching chair. In the living room, Nate sat with ABRA papers before him on the coffee table.

He'd made his own visit to Father's shack and found to his surprise, among the objects on the shelf in front of the propped and hatted badminton racquet, a penknife he thought he'd lost, one of the things he'd stolen from the Bay during his high-school semester in Inuvik. He pocketed the knife. (Della had stolen it from the kitchen counter in his parents' house and carried it in her jeans like a fetish for months, rubbing it with sticky fingers to draw Nate's attention to her. That strategy failing, she'd placed the knife before the white lady's tuque in hopes of better results.)

The arrangement of crates, archery target, racquet, and shuttlecocks had evoked in Nate no memories of Father Evans's hopes of developing Christian souls in athletes' bodies. He'd been too young to be involved. But in the offerings placed before the racquet he recognized — as Simon had — belief in a power to make wishes come true, and although the longings might be pitiful, lustful, or mundane, they told him the people of Poniktuk were ready to believe in magic, and the magic they were ready to believe in came from the lady lying in his bed. He'd left the shed certain that her magic included him.

He now sensed that someone had entered the living room and, looking up, saw his niece.

"Lady ready for you now," Sarah said.

"Oohh?" he said.

She nodded.

"Right now?" he asked playfully.

And when Sarah nodded again, he said, "Okay."

Sarah retreated quickly into the kitchen and hid behind the table: the scary thing wasn't out of her uncle yet.

Nate stepped quietly into the bedroom. In the soft light from the blanket-covered window he saw the woman lying on her back with an arm bent above her head. She was sleeping. When Obie and his father had carried her into the house, he'd got only a glimpse of a face blistered by the sun and hollowed by starvation. Now, perhaps because of the soft light in the room, her face looked smooth, its skin still taut over her cheekbones but no longer looking burnt. The lips of her wide mouth were pink, and her astonishing yellow hair lay spread on the pillow.

The lady's eyes opened. They found his. She cleared her throat.

"Hi," she said.

"I'm Iku," Nate said.

"Iku," she repeated. "I'm Gwen."

Nate stepped up to the foot of the bed.

"I am the moon," he said.

Gwen's eyes opened wider.

In the kitchen, Sarah approached the refrigerator and, took out a can of Coke. She popped the tab and carried the can to the kitchen table, where she climbed onto a chair. Taking a sip of the sweet fizzy liquid, she waited confidently to hear the bedroom door open and close: the person who came out would not to be scary anymore, just her favourite uncle.

On the back porch beyond the storage room, Della and Selma were having a whispered conference. They'd seen Eli get into his boat and head across the bay and knew he'd be gone for the day. When they also saw Young Helen leave the house and then Ruth, they realized their chance had come.

"Ruth kill us for sure she find out we go in," Selma whispered.

"*She* protect us," Della said.

"You sure?"

"I feel it."

Selma considered this. "What that feel like to feel it?"

"It feel like . . . like blessing."

Selma considered again. "Della, I don't feel nothing like that."

"Then you stay here," Della whispered fiercely. "*I* go in."

And she opened the back door.

But even sure in the belief that no harm could come to her in the house where the object of her veneration lay, Della tiptoed through the storage room and glanced warily around when she reached the kitchen. At the table, Sarah regarded her over the rim of her Coke can. She smiled and stepped forward: there was no longer any need to curry favour with the child. Crossing the linoleum toward the bedroom corridor, she heard the bang of the can on the tabletop, ignored it, but a second later was nearly toppled when two small arms encircled her right leg from behind. She regained her balance and, feeling a plump body pressed against the back of her thigh, looked down to see two small, fat hand clasped together. She twisted and glared at Sarah's upturned face.

"Let go!" she hissed.

Sarah shook her head.

"Let *go!*"

She reached down to pry the fingers apart. The fingers released each other and gripped her jeans.

"Let me go!"

But Sarah let only one hand go and held on tight with the other. Now Della could at least pivot.

"I have to see white lady."

"No," Sarah said.

"Yes," said Della, and took a step backward.

Sarah grabbed the jeans with both hands again.

"She busy now."

Della frowned.

"What you mean busy?"

"Unca Nate."

Della drew a sharp breath.

"*He's* in there?"

Sarah nodded.

"She fixing him."

"What you mean fixing?"

Sarah shrugged.

"She doing something?"

Sarah nodded.

"With him?"

Sarah nodded again.

Della's heart pounded.

"Doing what?"

Sarah shook her head: that was a secret no one could make her tell. But Della understood.

The room spun away from her, and she might have fallen had it not been for the small, tight anchor on her leg.

"You could let go now," she said when the room settled down. "I never go in."

But Sarah held on.

"I leave now," said Della, and, using her free leg, turned around. The other leg stayed put.

"Let go my leg, you little piss."

But Sarah only continued to regard her with dark, untrusting eyes.

Della drew a deep breath, expelled a sigh, and summoning all her strength, pulled her held leg forward. Sarah went with it. Della sighed again. Step by step, they shuffled together across the kitchen floor and into the storage room. When they reached the outside door, Della stopped.

"You could really let go now," she said.

And this time Sarah did.

Della's hand was on the doorknob when a voice called her name.

"Della!"

She saw Nate coming down the bedroom corridor. She yanked the door open, banged into Selma on the porch, grabbed her sleeve, pulled her down the porch stairs, jumped the last three steps, let go of Selma, and ran.

9

Trish inflated the horseshoe pillow and settled it between the nape of her neck and the back of the seat. She held down the button on the armrest, pushed the seat as far back as it would go, and closed her eyes. She'd already changed planes once, in Toronto, and now the flying time would be more than five hours to Edmonton. There she'd spend the night and then take another plane in the morning to Inuvik, with only a touchdown along the way at Yellowknife. Her travel agent hadn't found a schedule of flights from Inuvik to Poniktuk — in fact, she hadn't found Poniktuk at all — but Trish assured her that it did exist and that flights went there because her sister and brother-in-law had

planned to fly out. And what flies out must fly in. The travel agent
agreed but told her she'd have to arrange that for herself when
she got there. Then she made a reservation for her for a week at
the Igloo Inn and added how sorry she was about the reason for
Trish's trip. (She'd found a seven-day Caribbean singles cruise for
Trish the previous winter that had thoroughly satisfied Trish.)
Trish had thanked her but told her not to worry, her trip was
going to have a happy ending.

The TV screen had already showed passengers how to buckle
a seatbelt and how to inflate a life vest in case of emergency, and
it would be a while before lunch. But she was already hungry. And
that was a good sign, she told herself, because as long as she felt
pangs of hunger, Gwen must be feeling them too and was, if
suffering, at least alive. Now, with her seat back and eyes closed,
she could think about what she was going to do.

Up to now she'd rushed around Ottawa making travel plans,
packing her bags, leaving instructions for looking after the shop,
reassuring Edwina that everything was going to be all right, and
had finally caught her plane this morning and then made the
change in Toronto — propelled through everything by the
conviction that what she had to do to find Gwen and Ralph was
get up there fast.

Now on her way, Trish paused and was assailed by an un-
welcome question. Oh Christ, she thought, what am I doing?
How will I find them even if they're still alive? I'm going to fail.

Her stomach lurched. The airplane engines droned. The man
in the seat beside her shook and folded his newspaper.

But no, she told herself — and punched her seat upright again
— they're alive and I know it because if Gwen was dead, I'd know
that. But I've really got to hurry. So what comes first? Okay, see
that inspector in Yellowknife. He'll help me get organized. So
when we get to Edmonton, I'll change my reservations to give me
a couple of days in Yellowknife. Then Inuvik. Then Poniktuk.

Trish pushed her chair back again and, staring at the underside
of the overhead bin, conducted in her head a forceful conver-

sation with the RCMP inspector. The defeatist inspector. What the hell was his name? MacSomething.

But as the imaginary conversation moved briskly toward a positive conclusion, the spectre of failing prowled the back of her mind.

ᑫ

When Della stopped running, she was alone.

She stood squinting against the dazzle of sunlight on waves bobbing in the bay. She didn't know why she was there. She didn't know what she was doing.

Nate and the white lady! Fucking!

It made her feel faint.

Later, her mind still numb, she stood in front of Father's shed. She pushed the door open and approached the altar and stared at the tuque's stripes of coloured wool stretched by her own hands over the hoop that leaned against the circle of solid colour at the centre of rings of other faded colours on the big stuffed disk that leaned against the wall. Her eyes dropped to the shelf and wandered among the objects there. They stopped. Nate's penknife was gone. She stifled a cry.

He give it to *her!* With a swipe of her hand, Della knocked everything off the shelf.

Selma hadn't known why they were running from Eli's house and hadn't been able to keep up, so she'd stopped and watched while her friend disappeared around a corner of the freezer. But when Della tracked her down that evening as she sat on a swing in the school playground, she gaped while Della told her, through gritted teeth, how the lady they'd been thinking all along was a saint was really a devil who'd put a spell on everyone, especially Nate, and made him give her things and even do that thing with her. Sarah had seen them.

This reversal of all that Della had been formerly led her to believe was too astonishing for Selma to take in at once.

"But what about that halo?" she asked.

"Devil make it *look* like halo."

"But what about that miracle too?"

"What miracle?"

"She make baby Sarah talk. That miracle. You say so yourself, Della."

"I take it back."

"But you say she come here from heaven to make . . . to make things happen for peoples."

Living as she did in the shadow of Della's passion for Nate, Selma had recently discovered that she herself was in love with Nate's cousin Lawrence. She'd placed a hopeful token, a pair of his undershorts stolen as they were drying on the clothesline behind his house, on the altar in the shed.

"I lie. I hate that lady. She never ever do nobody no good, ever!"

Selma felt tears tickle the back of her nose.

"And I never ever believe anything you ever say again, ever!" And giving the scuffed ground at her feet a vicious kick, she pushed off on the swing.

Della watched Selma's back arch fiercely into each swoop, her feet pointing first at the ground and then at the pale evening sky.

"You just a big baby," she called as Selma flew past and, turning her back, walked away.

But her friend had reminded her of everything she herself had once invested in the powers and goodness of the lady, not to mention the prestige she'd gained in the village from being the lady's interpreter and acolyte. It would now be very awkward to reverse herself. She regretted knocking those things off the altar.

Stopping at a corner of the schoolhouse, Della struggled with herself. If what Sarah had said Nate and the lady were doing in the bedroom was true, it was horrible. Her imagination had been torturing her ever since with chaotic images of their commerce. But wait. Were those images so bad as to destroy altogether her faith in Nate and the lady? Did they have to? Something Father Evans had once said in a sermon came back to her, something about people of little faith. That it was bad to be one.

Della's faith began to revive. Although the images wouldn't leave her mind, she now saw them in a new light. Couldn't fucking — an activity, after all, that she was able only to imagine, having yet no direct experience of it — be seen as a divine act when it took place between two beings like the lady and her cousin? By embracing him, wasn't she elevating him into her own world of holiness and blessings? And when she left Poniktuk to go back to heaven, as she surely would, maybe even soon, Nate would still be here. Della caught her breath. So wouldn't it be a suitable reward to her for keeping faith in them, for forgiving them even, as both a worshipper and a girl in love, if the lady, when she left, passed Nate on, beautifully transformed by having fucked a saint, to her?

Della found she believed it would. The carnal images still writhing in her mind lost their horror and acquired a better look. She wished to dwell on them to further understand their meaning, but first there was something she had to do. She hurried back to Father's shed.

ꟼ

Trish's meeting with Chief Inspector Iain Andrew MacTavish at the Yellowknife RCMP headquarters had been worse than unsatisfactory. To start things off, the constable at the reception counter wouldn't tell him she was there because she didn't have an appointment. When she gave him Gwen and Ralph's names and said the inspector knew about them already, he disappeared and came back to say the inspector would see her at four o'clock that afternoon.

Trish stalked out of the building and back to the Yellowknife Inn, where she had a sandwich in the coffee shop and went to her room. It was hot as an oven even though the drapes were closed, and when she opened them, the sun shone directly in. The words "midnight sun" came to her mind and suggested that the room would stay this hot all night. She closed the drapes and, stripping to panties and bra, stretched out on the bed. Sweating and dozing in the sticky heat, she went over how she would get the inspector to help her in her search.

But the brisk words she'd imagined speaking to him died on Trish's lips as she listened to MacTavish tell her there was virtually no chance her sister and brother-in-law had survived the accident to their canoe. Too much time had now gone by. He was sorry, but there was nothing more he could advise her to do. The search had been very thorough. As she listened, his authoritative certainty had made her hopes seem childish, her expectations foolish, and her reliance on something as trivial as feeling hungry as proof that Gwen was still alive insane. Trish salvaged a scrap of self-respect by getting from MacTavish the name and number of the pilot who'd flown the search; then she'd fled his office. If she went on to Inuvik, she might call the pilot. But now she even doubted she'd go on.

After dinner in the hotel dining room, she couldn't face returning to her hotbox of a room. So she crossed the lobby and stepped out into sunlight that still reflected off the buildings and pavements of downtown Yellowknife, although it was nearly ten o'clock. Blinking and a little drunk from a half-bottle of wine with her dinner, she wandered along the street looking into bland store windows and noticing without much curiosity the number of native people standing around. Taking a random turn down a side street, she found herself at the entrance to a bar. At least it must be dark in there, she thought, and a huge dripping air conditioner hanging over the sidewalk promised it would also be cool. She went in.

An hour and two vodka Collinses later, Trish was ready to leave. When her eyes had adjusted to the lighting, she'd walked to an empty table along one wall and, after ordering her drink, looked around. The room's ceiling, walls, carpet, vinyl chairs, and Formica tabletops were red. Red lights played on a big mirrored ball spinning slowly above a red linoleum dance floor. Next to the empty bandstand, a jukebox thumped rock-and-roll at a volume that made hearing anything else more than difficult; at tables people shouted to each other.

To Trish the noise and colour and throbbing beat brought relief. She accepted the mindless rowdiness in the bar and watched the men and women there, who like those on the street outside were mostly native. As they shook and jumped on the dance floor, she began to move her own body to the jukebox rhythms. Halfway through her first drink, she became aware that men at nearby tables were eyeing her. She stopped jiving. Sitting still and gazing nowhere in particular, she managed to avoid the eyes when she ordered her second Collins, but now the looks and grins she saw from the corners of her eyes and the unmistakable hand gestures that went with them had become frightening. She was about to get up and leave when a large white woman approached her table.

"Mind if I join you?" the woman shouted, and without waiting for an answer sat down.

Trish shrugged.

The woman hitched her chair closer and lowered her voice to a confidential bellow.

"I been watching you, honey, and I could see the guys were beginning to get to you. Some of these goons are real bad news for a woman all alone in a place like this. Specially at closing time. I could tell you about it."

Trish gave her a perfunctory smile. The woman had large hands and bony wrists at the end of heavy arms; a blotchy complexion covered her coarse features; her dull brown hair was pulled back in an untidy bun. Even at closing time it was probably rare for bad news to come *her* way, Trish thought.

"Ethel McGarr," the woman said.

"Trish."

"New in town?"

She nodded.

"Tourist?"

She shook her head.

In silence Ethel regarded Trish's profile while Trish looked down at her unfinished drink.

"Got troubles, honey?"

Trish didn't remove her gaze from her glass.

"I'm a nurse, see. I could tell you had a problem soon as I spotted you. I mean something besides the hairy apes hanging out in here. You wanta tell me about it?"

Now Trish frowned and faced the woman. Ethel beamed at her. Trish turned away and took a deep, shaky breath to stifle the impulse, swift as a child's, to tell everything to this ugly, inquisitive, presumptuous woman.

"What say we have that slut of a waitress get us a couple more drinks," Ethel said. "Mine's beer. Yours looks like . . . what is it anyway, a double something?"

Oh what the hell, Trish thought, and managed a smile.

"Vodka Collins. Just a single, though. And I think I'll stay with this one."

Ethel waved her arm and shouted, "Hey!" till she got the waitress's attention and ordered a beer for herself and, with a wink, another Collins for Trish. When the drinks arrived, there was an awkward moment before each paid for her own.

"Cheers," Ethel said and took her first swallow. "Well?"

Music blared, dancers gyrated, tiny red dots of light swept around and around the walls and tables and chairs and clothing of everyone in the room, and the looks men sent her were now loaded with a new amusement. For a moment, Trish doubted she could shout her story to Ethel McGarr while watched by these witnesses, who apparently found something funny in their encounter. Then that made her angry.

"I'm looking for my sister," she said, aiming her voice directly at the side of Ethel's head that she'd turned to her.

While she studied the whorls inside Ethel's large ear and picked out grey hairs among the brown that swept into her bun, she heard the uninflected drone of her own voice marshalling events as she remembered them and editing the story into a succinct narrative. Every now and then Ethel nodded and shot her a glance, but she didn't interrupt. When Trish finished, Ethel sat still for a long moment before turning to her.

"Honey," she said, "you sure came to the right place tonight. Do you know, I'm on my way to Poniktuk myself right now. I'm the nurse there. How about that!" She slapped the table. "Let's chugalug and get outta this dump to somewhere we can really talk. Don't you give up hope, honey. I could tell you stories . . ."

She picked up her glass and drained it. Trish took a sip of her Collins.

"Where you staying?"

"Yellowknife Inn."

"Me too. But I'll bet they gave you a room on the sunny side. Am I right?"

Trish nodded.

"Goddamn! They always do that if you don't ask. Me, my room's always just where it should be. Nice and cool. They wouldn't dare put me on the hot side."

She barked a laugh.

"Come on. We can talk there. I got a case of beer under the bed."

There was still daylight when they stepped into the street, but now it had a pale, silvery quality Trish had never seen before. As she walked beside Ethel, listening to stories about patients she'd treated in Poniktuk who'd survived unbelievable ordeals, injuries, and illnesses, Trish sneaked a glance at her lumbering companion. The woman was an odd duck, no doubt, and she might have to watch it in the hotel room when she brought out that case of beer — none for me, thanks, Trish planned to say — but she obviously had a good heart and knew in detail the world that she might soon encounter. For Ethel believed Gwen and Ralph could still be alive. Trish felt a rush of affection for her.

Ethel's room had an armchair in it, and while Ethel used the bathroom, Trish kicked off her shoes and claimed it. That left the bed to Ethel.

By the time she was on her way back to her own room, shoes

in hand — the carpet felt deliciously cool to her bare feet — her head was crowded with names like Zebediah and Obie and Ruth and Helen. ("Don't any of them have Eskimo names?" she'd asked. "Oh, honey, sure they do," Ethel said. "But those are private.") But, more important, she had a plan. Ethel had laid it out for her.

"It'll cost a bundle," Ethel had said.

"I'll put it on my credit card. My business one."

"What business?"

Trish told her about Trish's Treasures.

"Oh, that's cute!" Ethel said.

Then Trish had another idea. "Is there anything in Poniktuk I could buy for the shop? Like handicrafts? If there is, I could write everything off as a business expense."

"There's lots," Ethel promised.

When she got to her room, it was hot and airless and still full of light, but Trish hung the Do Not Disturb sign on the doorknob, undressed, got into bed, and fell instantly asleep, her mind afloat on waves of hope and trust. Trust in the pilot she was going to hire, trust in the people of Poniktuk, trust in her luck, trust in dear Ethel, who hadn't made a pass at her after all. She'd passed out instead. And hope that her search for Gwen would succeed.

Thousands of kilometres away, a sliver of a moon lay on its back high in a starlit sky over Ottawa. Lightning skittered around the edges of the night's black western horizon. Edwina couldn't get to sleep. In the long unmoving darkness, she lay in her bed listening to the mutter of thunder that never came nearer, waiting without hope for the healing sound of rain.

ᑫ

His clothes floating in shreds about his body, his boots rotting on his feet, Ralph lay on the floor of the Arctic Ocean. Small currents moving across the seabed turned

*him gently one way, then another. The flesh on his body
was no longer tense with muscle; here and there bruised
yellow or blue, it covered his bones like soft dough. Above
him, on the wind-stirred surface of the ocean, motorboats
went back and forth between Poniktuk and the fishing
camp at the mouth of the Blackstone River.*

*A small school of Arctic char swam past, flashing silver
sides and pink underbellies, and then turned back. They
approached and surrounded him and pushed at his clothing
with mouths working and tail fins sculling until on a sudden
shared impulse they flashed away again.*

*From deeper in the ocean, two ringed seals appeared,
spinning and bobbing in Ralph's direction. When they
reached his side, they nudged him with their snouts. His
body rolled; a leg rose, an arm floated, his head turned,
dark hair waved above it. The seals pushed harder.*

Ralph opened his eyes.

*Light shimmered above him. He stared for a long time,
watching beams of aqueous sunlight shift and dance. They
reached at him like fingers. At last he lifted his head and
saw two seals hovering by his feet. He dropped his head
again and closed his eyes.*

*Soft muzzles pushed against his thighs, his ribs, his
arms, his neck. Ripples of water slid across his face. He
opened his eyes again and stood up.*

*He swayed in small currents created by his own and
the seals' movements. The seals swam away, and as the
currents around him subsided, Ralph lifted one foot, then
the other. His boots fell off. Bending, he peeled away the
remnants of his socks. Upright again, he plucked at the
rest of his tattered clothing — shirt, trousers, underwear.
Soon scraps of cloth were floating all around him. Ralph
stood still for a moment and then stepped through them.
Water slid heavily past him. Behind him fragments of his
clothing spiralled in an eddy. His bare toes sank
sensuously into sand.*

The seals swam away through curtains of watery light. Ralph slipped easily through the water after them. Gradually the shafts of sunlight became thinner and withdrew higher above his head. In the increasing dimness everything around him — sand, plants, scatterings of pebbles and stones — took on a soft shadowless lustre. Light was leaving this underwater world; illumination was replacing it. He kept his eyes on the ocean floor.

Presently he felt a push of water against his chest and, stopping to look ahead, saw a cloud of sand. Large and dense, it heaved and swirled, hiding what lay inside or beyond it. The turbulence slowly diminished, and the cloud thinned. Through a veil of descending sand he saw two huge stones at rest some distance apart. Suddenly they spun in place and rolled swiftly toward each other. Instantly the cloud of sand was thick again, and Ralph felt again a lunge of water against his chest just before he heard a concussive thump.

Ahead of him the seals sped toward the cloud. Ralph followed.

As he drew nearer, the cloud rose high above his head until, standing at its edge, he stood before a wall of sand. Moments earlier, the seals had shot into it and disappeared. Swirling sand prickled his skin, and the constant spinning, colliding, and withdrawing of the stones, seen dimly inside the cloud, caused the water around him to seethe. But he stood in a small eddy among the currents, a pocket of calm. Ralph watched the stones. There was no pattern to their motions, but they never stayed at rest for long before they drew back and rushed together again.

Ralph blinked and turned to step out of the eddy and around the stones. His feet came out from under him. Recovering his balance, he stepped to the other side. The same thing happened. He paused and took a step back. A wall of water pushed against him. He was trapped.

Ralph reached ahead. Suction teased his fingertips.

He reached farther. His hand was tugged. He pulled it back. Then, closing his eyes, he stepped forward. Lifted off his feet and yanked into the cloud of sand, he felt a rough caress on his shoulder, buttock, calf, and then as the stones collided savagely behind him, he fell to his hands and knees. He rose unsteadily to his feet.

Before him lay a broad, earthlike plain. Winding through it like a riverbed with elevated banks, a ribbon of pebbles, rocks, and boulders swept in from his left, crossed the plain, and in a long curve disappeared again among low hills. Elsewhere on the plain, other hills of gravel and sand rose and fell and folded in on one another. An even aqueous light, brighter than the soft illumination that had lit the ocean floor on the other side of the colliding stones, filled the landscape. Ralph stepped ahead.

Fine sand rose between his toes, but after a dozen steps, mounds of moss cushioned his feet. When he'd gone a distance, he looked back.

Like brown rain, a curtain of sand drifted toward the ocean floor. It swayed, billowed, and slowly settled until only a few grains remained suspended. The stones had vanished.

He continued across the watery plain. As he reached the riverbed and followed it, schools of Arctic char swam up behind him and skimmed above his head, flashing their shiny flanks like birds showing undersides of wings. Once, a fierce-looking fish with spiky spines on its back hung for a moment before him at the level of his shins, a miniature monster blocking his way. Then, with a flip of its tail, it let him pass. And once, behind the hump of a hill, a larger hump that might have been a whale rose and disappeared again. The two ringed seals were nowhere in sight.

Reaching at last the edge of the plain, he climbed a hill. A small current caught him from behind and lifted his testicles.

He stood on the rim of a basin. At his feet the ground dropped away in a sloping cliff. But he couldn't see where it ended, for filling the basin was a huge mass of sea creatures turning, hanging, darting, rising, diving, spinning, rolling, a mass so dense it seemed to form a single pulsing body. Fish and seals of every size and marking, walruses, narwhals, blue whales, white whales, grey whales, mountainous humpbacks all crowded into a thick swarm of pelts, scales, and barnacled skins.

As he stared at this heaving, rippling mass — if he'd knelt he could've touched the edge of it — Ralph detected movement in it: the thousands of swimmers and floaters were languidly circling the basin.

He stepped off the rim.

As he passed under the canopy of sea animals, the light grew dimmer and the water murky, but his ears picked up the faint notes of a high, sweet singing. He stopped to listen. The tune was like a child's song, rising and falling and rising again in easy intervals that reached him through the water like warbling. Spread all around him on the ocean floor were plants that even in the clouded light showed rich colours against the sand — deep greens, ochres, dark reds, purples. Some plants hugged the seabed; others sent out spiky branches or long wavering fronds. But Ralph barely glanced at this vegetal profusion. He was listening to the song. It drew him on.

He soon saw, at the very centre of the basin, a small walled building of black stone. It seemed the song was coming from there.

FOUR

The Meeting

Except among certain adolescents, whose appetites for the bizarre had been whetted by listening to KISS and Tiny Tim, the events at the public meeting before the referendum on the ABRA agreement were seldom mentioned in Poniktuk. Which is not to say these events did not live for many years in the memories of those present and in the region's lore. But in their immediate aftermath, the elders of Poniktuk kept silent out of superstition, the middle generation out of shame, youngsters out of awe, and every man, woman, and child in the village out of shock over what happened to Sarah.

Even the adolescents, who went over the events with each other all night long and leaked the story in excited midnight calls to relatives and friends in other communities, began to feel uneasy the next morning when they heard about Sarah. And when they met again in the following days, most were reluctant to remind themselves of what they believed they'd seen at the meeting. (After many years it was this same group, by then leaders of the community, who denied that anything at all unusual had happened. Some even denied such a meeting had taken place.)

Whatever the reasons for silence in Poniktuk, for a while the people in other communities could talk about nothing else, although they got much of the story wrong. But lack of truth by no means prevented the spread of rumour, which, with a speed unusual even among Inuit communities, had in a matter of days turned scraps of gossip into an accepted body of knowledge. The details of the story might vary from village to village or balloon into grotesque exaggeration in some overstimulated minds, but its general shape was the same.

And although time blurred this shape, the consequences of its having once been well-defined in the minds of almost every adult and child in the region persisted well beyond its decay. The vote on the land-rights agreement took place four days after the meeting, and talk then became all about that. But Poniktuk's reputation was permanently damaged. If children of the children of adults alive in the other communities at the time continued, without knowing why, to look askance at Poniktungmiut, this habit of caution could almost certainly be traced to tales about what had happened at the meeting.

The almost perfect silence in Poniktuk surrounding the meeting did not extend to circumstances preceding it. These were the subject of lively commentary and speculation as soon as the next day, especially among the elders for whom, if the events themselves already lay under a taboo, the signs and portents that should have told them something was about to happen did not. Whether these earlier phenomena were, in fact, true signs or whether they acquired the aura of prediction only in retrospect was not a question anyone raised. Chief among them was, of course, the uncanny presence of Gwen.

b

Several days before the meeting, Gwen lay on Nate's bed in a light sleep. Fed and bathed and her improvised diaper changed by Ruth and Young Helen, Gwen had slept and waked and slept again since regaining consciousness with only a vague awareness of the passing of time or of life beyond her shadowy room.

While she slept, dreams sometimes improvised retellings of her wandering on the tundra. Images of her suffering there made her moan and thrash, but mercifully the images vanished when she woke, although her body often ached. Ralph frequently appeared in these dreams, sometimes trying to relieve her distress but more often sharing it. But neither awake nor asleep did she ever relive Ralph's drowning in the Blackstone gorge. Even her dreaming memory would not go there. And although, when awake, she sometimes puzzled over how she and Ralph, maybe as weak as she was, had come to be in Poniktuk, for now she was content merely to know that he was there, as Ruth had assured her he was, and to leave all explanations to the time that was coming — she hoped soon — when they would see each other.

The older woman and her daughter, whose name Gwen had learned was Helen, came less frequently into her room, and the little girl she'd usually seen sitting on a bedside chair when she woke up was there no longer. Gwen believed she'd once had another visitor, a young man who'd stood at the foot of her bed and told her stories. But he'd never returned, and her memory of one story, about a brother sun and sister moon — or was it the other way around? — was so vague she thought she might be confusing it with a daydream about Ralph coming to see her or some childhood tale.

Gwen's bedroom door was now sometimes left ajar, and when that happened, the sound of voices elsewhere in the house reached her down what she came to think of as a long corridor. She could never make out what the voices were saying or even the language they were speaking, but she found their low mumbling and lengthy silences reassuring. They made her feel like a child tucked up cozily in bed listening to invisible but protective grownups discussing important subjects, possibly herself, but so far away that she was spared having to understand.

This morning she heard voices from time to time through the door but, for once, took no pleasure in the sound. She felt a bowel movement coming on and was distressed by the thought of doing it in the diaper. She waited for a lull in the murmuring and, when it came, called out "Bathroom!" as loud as she could. The murmuring instantly stopped.

"Bathroom!" she called again.

Ruth came into the room. With some embarrassment, Gwen explained her need, but Ruth only smiled, helped her up, wrapped her in the eiderdown, and, with an arm around her waist, walked her out the bedroom door.

The corridor was shorter than Gwen expected. When they reached the end of it, she saw to her surprise nearly a dozen women in the room into which it opened, a kitchen. Some sat at a table, others stood along the walls, and two or three sat on the floor. Gwen smiled at them and, leaning against Ruth, felt their eyes follow her as she shuffled in a continuing silence across the kitchen and to a closed door. Inside, Ruth pointed, said "Honey bucket right there," and left.

Gwen wondered why so many people were gathered in the kitchen but then focused her attention on the toilet. It was not a flush toilet. Her nose had already told her that. She saw a squat column of galvanized tin set on the floor. A toilet seat rested on its rim, and a ventilation pipe, clearly ineffective, came out the back and rose through the ceiling. When she edged closer, she saw a metal bucket inside the galvanized column, lined with a heavy black plastic filled almost to the top with feces, urine, and used toilet paper. She dropped the eiderdown, undid her diaper, and sat down.

In the kitchen Ruth went back to kneading dough.

When Gwen was finished, she cleaned herself and, getting up, couldn't resist inspecting what she'd done. Her bowel movement didn't look much different from the others there. She picked up the eiderdown, wrapped it around her shoulders, and left the diaper on the floor. Now that she knew where the honey bucket was, she wouldn't need it.

The eyes that had watched her cross the kitchen watched her again as she stood in the bathroom door for a moment to gather strength for the walk back to her room. Ruth raised flour-whitened hands from a bowl of punched dough to offer help, but Gwen shook her head. She saw the little girl who'd been her constant watcher and smiled at her, but the child only looked away. After smiling vaguely at all the women, she shuffled across the linoleum, too busy concentrating on her balance to notice that none of them had smiled back.

Steadying herself on the corridor wall with the hand that wasn't holding her eiderdown together at her neck, Gwen moved toward her bedroom and its welcome bed. She had no way of knowing that the minds behind the eyes that watched her cross the kitchen floor held beliefs centred on an altar dedicated to her tuque. So neither could she know that to those minds she was not a human being.

b

Inland from Poniktuk, the hills that rise from the flatlands beyond the airstrip fold over one another like green and brown wrinkles until higher hills with steeper slopes rise up behind them. These too buckle and heave, but the highest eventually flatten as they join together to form a plateau that then stretches south for hundreds of kilometres. The Blackstone River flows across this plateau and on its way to the sea cuts a gorge through the hills. Among the hills lie valleys connected by streams that sometimes widen into lakes or ponds before squeezing back into tributaries of the Blackstone. Other valleys dead-end and fill in summer with pools of stagnant meltwater or mudflats or spongy marshes.

Through this landscape twice a year, the caribou of the Tasiqpaaluk herd migrate. In early spring, when snow still covers the ground but the sun is already strong, they make their way north to calving grounds near Lake Tasiqpaaluk east of Poniktuk, tens of thousands of yearlings, mature bulls, and pregnant cows, all travelling north after wintering below the treeline. Then, in late summer, young and old bulls come wandering back through the same hills and valleys, sometimes alone, sometimes in small companionable groups or pairs, but never in large numbers. The cows and calves go a different way. They all eventually meet again on the plateau and head south toward the woods that will shelter them before they turn north once more in the spring. Millions of trails worn by the hooves of the herd over centuries crisscross the hills and valleys like threads, and although they may vary slightly from year to year, these trails reveal the pattern of spring and summer migrations by the Tasiqpaaluk caribou, on which the people of Poniktuk and their ancestors have always depended for food.

Now that pattern was broken.

Since obeying his niece's summons to visit the white lady, Nate had felt more confident than ever that his work for ABRA would succeed. Standing at the foot of her — his — bed in the darkened room, he'd poured out story after story about all kinds of fantastic things taking place on the moon. He'd had no idea where the stories came from, but they so delighted him as he heard himself telling them and so clearly enthralled the lady that he just kept telling them until suddenly they stopped coming. Then he'd nodded to her and left the room, laughing out loud in the bedroom corridor at having invented such wonderful tales. But before renewing his study of the ABRA papers before him on the coffee table, he wondered if the lady herself, just by looking at him, had inspired the stories. Others in the village believed she had magic in her and had left things for her in Father's shed. Nate thought of something he could leave there to replace the pocket knife he'd removed. If it pleased her, who knew what else she might inspire in him? Maybe how to defeat his Uncle Simon.

Later that afternoon, Nate placed below the hatted badminton racquet the bone comb he'd found in a tent ring in the hills.

While he continued going house to house, inspiration seemed to follow him. As the stories had poured out, arguments for voting Yes in the ABRA referendum rose to his lips with eloquence. People listened spellbound. But today he'd decided to stop; enough was enough. After waking up early, he'd drunk a cup of coffee and left the house for a walk. The morning air was cool and fresh. Except for some children on the beach throwing pebbles at the still surface of the bay — they'd probably been up all night and were now too strung out and too hypnotized by what they were doing to stop — he had the village to himself.

Walking along the road to the airstrip, idly kicking stones, he looked up at the hills beyond the strip, their slopes pale green in the morning sun. Suddenly the feeling of excitement that had led him, months ago, to the stream where he'd shot the year's first geese came back to him. As his mind's eye soared into the cloudless sky and gave him a view of fold after fold of hills that ended in the high plateau, he saw what he was going to see from a hilltop ahead of him. He quickened his pace.

Two hours later, people in Poniktuk saw a figure moving toward the airstrip. No one more than glanced at it until they noticed it was carrying something. ("Not another white lady!" Simon muttered, squinting from his office window.) Binoculars were picked up: the figure was Nate, and he was carrying a caribou calf on his back. This was surprising but not astonishing. In the days before threewheelers, all hunters hunted on foot in the summer and came back to town with their gutted kills across their shoulders, forelegs gripped in one hand, hind legs in the other. Everyone knew Nate didn't own a threewheeler. That he seemed to have gone hunting anyway was unusual, but, given everything else that was rumoured or thought or believed or admired or envied or feared about him lately, there was no reason to be astonished. What was strange was that his burden was a calf. Calves were not supposed to be in the hills this time of year. Equally strange, Nate was not carrying a rifle.

But what people saw next *was* astonishing. Nate knelt on the airstrip and carefully slid the calf off his back onto the gravel. It instantly twitched its spine and, stumbling to its feet, stood for a second with legs splayed, then lifted its head, shook itself, gave a jump, and trotted off the airstrip back toward the hills. Nate continued into town.

He put his head in the door of his cousin's home before going to his own. "Keep an eye on them hills," he told Lawrence.

Irene overheard him, and soon it wasn't only Lawrence's eyes that were fixed on the hills. Presently, fifteen or twenty brown dots that could only be caribou appeared on the hilltops and ambled down the slopes. Binoculars revealed heads with antlers and others, those of cows and calves, with small horns or none at all. Several young men, Lawrence among them, wanted to grab rifles and rush up there, but they were stopped by their elders, who were filled with wonder at the sight of cows and calves among the bulls. They were dumbstruck by what followed. Now even the young men wanted only to watch. For behind the ambling leaders browsing down the hillsides came more caribou that crested the hills and started down the slopes. And behind them came more caribou. And more. And more. And unimaginably more.

Within an hour a mass of caribou covered all the hills behind Poniktuk like a rippling brown blanket. A warm wind blew into town an overwhelming smell of ungulate — pungent, acrid, tantalizingly sweet.

The dogs went crazy. Those tied up strained against their collars, barking and howling, jumping and twisting in the air, risking broken necks. Loose dogs ran helter-skelter through the town, colliding with each other in their frenzy, snapping and snarling, crazed by a scent so pervasive it led them everywhere at once. Parents sent boys to chase the loose dogs and tie them up. As excited as the dogs, the boys caught all except Harry

Ingasuk's big white crossbreed, which crawled too far under Harry's house. Several boys were nipped but none seriously bitten.

As the edge of the herd started slowly across the flatlands between the hills and the airstrip, Zebediah summoned the village's leading hunters to the HTA office. From there they walked out to the strip, Obie, Simon, Eli, Wayne, and Harry Ingasuk among them, and stood on the gravel, waiting. In town, their wives and children and other relatives watched at windows and from porches. At Big Helen's, Della and Selma, best friends again after Della explained to Selma that the carnal connection between Nate and the white lady had been divinely inspired, speculated in whispers about who or what had made the caribou appear. Standing on a chair at her bedroom window, from which she could see a slice of the airstrip, Akpa had her own ideas. Old Piuyuk squatted outside his tent.

The smell of caribou got stronger.

Just short of the strip, the caribou stopped, and after standing for a moment, the leaders lay down. But the pressure of animals still coming over the hills forced the bulk of the herd already on the flats to keep moving. They moved sideways. And as the herd spread around the head of the bay and along the ocean shore in both directions to embrace — and confine — the village, there was eventually nothing as far as any eye could see but thousands and thousands of caribou. The grunting of cows keeping track of their calves rose from the mass in a deep continuous mutter, and the clicking of ankle bones as animals kept moving or, hemmed in, milled in place filled the warm air with a sound like the snapping of millions of twigs. Zeb and the hunters walked back to town.

By late afternoon the hillsides had delivered the last of the herd. By early evening all the caribou had lain down.

Zeb called a meeting in the school gym. With the exception of Gwen, Sarah, Nate (who was asleep), and some young mothers with cranky infants, the whole town showed up. They packed themselves in, adults standing on the shiny hardwood where basketball and floor hockey were the normal activities, children squatting in front of Zeb, who'd placed himself under a basketball hoop at one end of the gym. Young people leaned against the climbing bars along the walls.

"Okay," Zeb said when everyone had settled down. "Them caribou is here. I never see nothing like it, but . . . seems like there's more . . . more caribou . . ."

His voice trailed off. Of the tens of thousands of animals, he'd estimated at least a third had to be bulls with racks in the velvet. Since coming back to town, he'd been trying to calculate the value of those antlers at ten dollars a pound. But he couldn't multiply that high. Now, in the restive silence of the gym, while everyone waited to hear what he would say, thoughts of the white lady lying in Nate's bed mixed with awe at the riches sprouting from the bulls' heads at rest beyond the airstrip. Could one small chip of antler laid on a packing case in Father's old shed have produced such spectacular results?

Zeb was not alone in connecting the presence of the caribou with Gwen's tuque. While waiting for Zeb to speak, many of the hunters in the room who'd paid visits to the shed now wondered if, whatever wish or offering they'd made at the time, they hadn't also been wishing for caribou.

"We could eat good till springtime," Harry Ingasuk said with reverence. Having himself left a scrap of bannock before the tuque, he was now imagining roasts and stews and caribou soups all winter long whenever he dropped into a house for a meal.

Some of the young men along the walls sniggered. Everyone knew Harry's habit.

"How we know there ain't something wrong with them caribou, so many of them coming this way wrong time of year?" said Eddie Qarlik, better known for the polish on his school floors than for a knowledge of animals.

The question brought Zeb back to his responsibilities as chairman of Poniktuk's HTA. But before he said anything, Eli spoke.

"Them caribou is good," he said in his hoarse whisper.

"Mmm," intoned several of the older hunters. Torn between

believing that a miracle of plenty had arrived and fearing that, whatever they'd wished for in the shed, the miracle was tainted by sorcery, they accepted Eli's word gratefully.

But Eli's pronouncement had little to do with the caribou's health. As he walked to the meeting, he'd thought: first, the white lady found on a hillside, next a day of weather like his grandfather had been said to be able to call up, then on the same day, seen with his very own eyes, his youngest son, a failure in school, happily studying books and papers. And now a vast herd of caribou surrounded Poniktuk at the wrong time of year, and the same son had signalled their arrival. Could he any longer doubt that, like the man he was named for, Iku controlled spirits that controlled the workings of the world?

"It no use trying to figger why them caribou come here like that," Zeb said. "But it only make sense, like Harry say, to fill the freezer while we got the chance. But we gotta do it right. They waiting out there now, but we don't know how long they'll stay."

Hums and murmurs of agreement rippled through the gym.

"And what I say is," Zeb went on, "what I say is . . . bulls only. We been seeing how them bulls is good and fat, like Eli say. We don't need no cows nor calves taken. They's plenty of bulls to go around. You all figger?"

His eyes sought the elders and members of the HTA committee. They nodded.

"Bulls is best," said Isaac Ivalu.

Then Obie spoke. He had left no offering on the packing case in Father's shed. On his only visit there, the sight of the tuque that had covered the white lady's head when he found her had caused his cock to swell as it had when her buttocks nestled in his crotch on his threewheeler. Leaving the shed, he'd held the erection with a hand in his pants pocket so people wouldn't notice. But thoughts of the woman lying in Nate's bed kept springing to his mind without warning no matter where he was or what he was doing, and they always had the same effect. It made him angry and ashamed to have to reach suddenly into his pocket to grip his swollen member, and in fact people had noticed the gesture and made much ribald commentary on it behind his back. For Obie, slaughtering caribou was a welcome distraction.

"Maybe each family send just one hunter," he said. "No use lots of us getting in the way. Then maybe everybody shoot at once and just keep shooting till they have what their family need. And stop. That way we don't get no overkill and also them caribou can't run away before we're finished."

As he looked around the gym, some of the young men along the walls frowned and shifted from foot to foot. He knew what they were thinking. Few, if any, would be their family's designated shooter. They'd miss the chance to take part in a caribou kill that was sure to become famous. He sympathized, but not much. Young men had to get used to being frustrated.

"What you think?" he asked Zeb.

"What I think?"

"What you think about one hunter each family?"

"Okay by me. But we talking bulls only, no matter who's shooting."

"You already said that," Obie said.

"When you figger we do it?" Isaac Ivalu asked.

"Sooner the better," Simon broke in, seeing in the slaughter a providential prelude to the meeting he was going to call in three or four days. By the time everyone had skinned and dressed and butchered and carried thousands of pounds of meat to the freezer and cooked some of it fresh at home, they'd be so exhausted and stuffed and happy that they'd accept anything he proposed at the meeting.

"Soon as it light, then," Zeb said.

Again murmurs and nods and hums of agreement rippled through the assembly. Eli hummed along with the rest but privately knew the caribou would stay for as long as it took them to make the gift of themselves his son had summoned them to offer.

"I'll call around when it time," Zeb said. "We meet at HTA and then go out to airstrip."

The meeting was over.

Outside, the sun had set, and darkness had crept into the eastern sky. The temperature had dropped, but in the sunset's afterlight, the cool air was only slightly less pungent with the smell of caribou than the warm air of the afternoon had been. Here and there, dogs still barked.

Akpa sat in triumph on Big Helen's couch.

"It the other miracle!"

"What?"

"I tell you white lady going to make another miracle after she make Sarah talk again. And it here! You going to tell me them caribou not a miracle?"

For once Big Helen had no answer.

Zeb sat at his desk in the HTA office with the letter from the Vancouver import-export firm in his hand. His dream had come true, but he realized he had a problem.

When he'd first considered the offer, he'd seen himself shooting a bunch of bulls up in the hills when they started coming by and then caching the antlers till the Chinese guy could fly in to pick them up and pay him. But it wasn't like that anymore. With all the caribou in plain sight, the whole town would have to be in on the deal. But everyone knew that selling antlers, especially in the velvet, was illegal. And even if he could persuade some to break the law to get rich, how could they get away with it? Air-traffic control in Inuvik would quickly know about lots of planes flying in and out of Poniktuk, and when they discovered what was in them, they'd alert the game officers. Word would leak out, someone would tell, and . . .

But still . . .

Still, what was breaking the game laws against the riches unbelievably spread out as far as the eye could see in every direction from town? Just thinking about the money filled his mind with a Sears catalogue of things he'd heard of but never seen: TVs, microwaves, VCRs, bedroom suites, sharkskin suits, call girls, power tools, inboard motors, barbecues, automatic firearms, caterpillar tractors, executive jets. They could be the richest Inuit in the world!

But it was one thing for chance or luck or even supernatural powers to be offering Poniktuk such riches. It was another to get them without being caught.

Zeb put the letter back in his desk drawer and stared out his fly-specked window. It was already getting light, the pastel-coloured houses he could see were casting shadows, the sun was up. Soon there'd be plenty of daylight for the kill, and he'd have to start calling around.

He closed his eyes and spoke to the woman lying in Nate's bed. If she was indeed responsible for making his wish for antlers come true, maybe she'd also show him how to get away with selling them. Then he reached for his phone.

The sky grew lighter. The band of white above the rising orange globe turned pink and then pale blue. There was not a single cloud to take colours from the sunrise. It was going to be another perfect summer day. In a group, the designated hunters walked out to the airstrip. Nate was among them, Eli having passed his right of seniority to him.

The caribou watched them come. Later, some of the men would say it was the enormous mass of animals behind them that kept the nearest from running away as they approached. Normally the shyest and most watchful of animals, caribou could be stalked only with extraordinary stealth. But those at the fringe of this great herd merely stood up when they saw the men and then stared at them. For other hunters, the stillness of the animals only increased the strangeness of their presence. For them, after the events that later took place at the land-rights meeting, this unnatural stillness became yet another sign to look back on that should have been taken as a warning. But none of the hunters, whatever they thought at the time of the kill or later, ever forgot the look in the caribou's soft, dark, liquid eyes.

Reaching the airstrip, the men fanned out in a single line, stood or knelt or sat to shoot, chose their animals, snugged their guns against their shoulders, and sighted. On a shout from Zeb, they shot. Bulls fell heavily to the ground. Now the spell was broken, and alarm seized the nearest animals. Cows bellowed and tossed their heads, rolling dilated eyes; calves bleated; bulls jumped stiff-legged in the air in preparation for flight. But the caribou behind penned the caribou in front. Aiming, shooting, ejecting shells, aiming and shooting again and again, the hunters of Poniktuk steadily brought down their winter's supply of meat.

From outside his tent near the airstrip, Old Piuyuk watched the slaughter. Yesterday, when the caribou had arrived, the grunting and clicking and smell surrounding his tent had filled him with a rare happiness. Not having heard about the meeting at the school, he'd spent the night on his cot, knowing he could leave it at any moment, step outside, and see caribou. The thought alone had contented him. When dawn broke, he'd dressed and, without a thought for breakfast, squatted in the tent's doorway to observe the animals. Now the volleys of gunfire sent them wheeling and churning around him. They caused him no fear, but he wondered if a killing frenzy would take hold of the shooters. There were stories about that, and none of them had happy endings.

But whether it was Obie's warning against overkill or the sight of Zeb putting down his gun or their count of the carcasses piling up and the thought of skinning and butchering them all or the exercise of instinctive conservation — an impulse as old as hunger — or some altogether other restraining force, all the hunters stopped shooting as abruptly as they'd started. The smell of burnt gunpowder floated around them, mixing with the tang of caribou urine. In the silence of the ceasefire, the grunts of cows and click of ankle bones again became audible. But the surviving animals made no effort to escape. They stood calmly in place or, lowering their heads, scraped hooves on the turf and nibbled grass. The men took out their skinning knives and pulled on their skinning gloves. Before them lay nearly a hundred dead bulls.

Hearing the shooting stop, young men standing at windows or on porches or sitting alone in their rooms knew the kill had ended. When their fathers and uncles and older brothers sent for them to lend a hand in preparing the kill for the freezer, they felt even more ill-used, but they went to the airstrip anyway and set about skinning and butchering with bitter energy.

In her bedroom, Gwen had heard the crackle of gunfire and wondered what it was. Rolling on her side, she'd lifted a corner of the blanket over the window. Except for glances outside on trips to the bathroom, this was her first real look. She saw the wall of a house with pink siding. She knelt on the bed, ducked under the blanket, and got a wider view. A strip of grass lay between her window and the pink house. To the left was the corner of another house, painted blue, and to the right a stretch of bare ground and a road in front of more houses, all painted bright colours. From utility poles along the road, wires ran to all of them. There was not a person in sight. Gwen dropped the blanket and lay back. The distant crackling stopped. She dozed.

At the sound of gunfire, the town's dogs, all still tied up except for Harry Ingasuk's, which remained under Harry's house, had stopped barking. Now they started again.

On through the morning and into the afternoon, the men of Poniktuk skinned, gutted, quartered, cleaned, and carried to the freezer the products of their slaughter. They cut out tongues, livers, and hearts and put them aside for a first meal. They hoisted ribs, hindquarters, and shoulders onto their own shoulders and backs and carried them to lockers and shelves in the freezer, where they tagged them with names scrawled on scraps of cardboard. Some hindquarters weighed nearly eighty kilos. When all the lockers and shelves were full, they stacked meat on the floor. Blood and inedible offal covered the ground where they worked on the carcasses. Only metres away, living caribou cropped grass. At last, carrying wet hides slung over their shoulders for their women to stretch and peg to the ground and scrape and let dry in the sun for sleeping pads or sled rugs, and with tongues, livers, and hearts in their bloody gloved hands for their wives to cook, the men went home.

The herd settled down. Except for dogs that lay exhausted at the end of their tethers, whimpering or chittering their teeth in dream-broken sleep, the town appeared empty. When the sun finally set, a full moon appeared in a cloudless sky still blue.

In an uneven line beyond the airstrip, nearly a hundred severed caribou heads rested on velvety antlers and soft noses, their sightless eyes glazed open. Flies began to buzz around their lips and nostrils, and the bloodied flesh at their necks turned crusty.

b

When the people of Poniktuk looked back privately on the events of the land-rights meeting, many decided they wouldn't have happened without the massing of the caribou. For the herd did not go away. As the days went by before the meeting, tension increased among the young men cheated of taking part in the kill, and their craving to grab guns and dash to the airstrip was barely kept in check by threats and warnings from cranky parents and elders. But even those who felt grateful to the animals for the meat piled high in the freezer began to feel trapped by them. And a spell of unusually hot weather now set in. Day and night the stench of caribou filled the air, while the dogs, throats swollen and raw, never stopped lunging against their ropes and croaking hoarse barks.

On the morning after the meeting, when shame and horror at the behaviour that had swept the grades six, seven, and eight classroom the night before demanded an immediate laying of blame, many told themselves the caribou and dogs had driven them crazy.

But in the surrounding communities the verdict was unanimous: the people of Poniktuk had only themselves to blame. Legend said that the site of Poniktuk was where Sedna had lived as a girl with her father and brothers before she became a great spirit who controlled all sea animals from her home at the bottom of the sea. Support for this belief lay in the claim that the place name came from *panik,* meaning daughter, so Poniktuk might mean "place of the daughter." Although the old religion had long been abandoned by all communities in the region, those holding this opinion suspected that heathen proclivities still lingered in Poniktuk and were not surprised to hear how badly the Poniktungmiut had behaved at the land-rights meeting. Others believed the derivation of the name was more ordinary, coming from *pangniq,* meaning bull caribou; they pointed to the number of those animals that always passed close to the village in late summer.

The truth about the naming of the village was lost in the distant past, where one or the other pronunciation might have settled the matter. More recently, the Canadian Geographical Survey had failed to ratify either source when the village name appeared on its official maps with a spelling incorrect for both derivations. But whether the source of the name was zoological or legendary, the Poniktungmiut were widely considered quirky, dangerous, and far too pleased with the natural richness of their environment — caribou and fish in abundance, for instance — that communities forced to survive on poorer natural resources were quick to point out the Poniktungmiut did nothing to deserve. Reports of the extraordinary slaughter of a whole winter's supply of meat at the town's airstrip shortly before the shameful events of the meeting did not soften this judgement.

But whatever the people in other communities felt, most Poniktungmiut believed themselves stricken by a visitation that night, not visited by a judgement. There was some truth in that view, but not everyone took it.

For the rest of her life, Akpa castigated herself for having been seduced from orthodox Christian practice, however briefly, by the frightening glamour of idolatry, and she became, as time went by, an ever more severe chastiser of other people's morals. Big Helen blamed herself for not speaking up sooner, more often, and louder as a voice of reason in the village before unreason overwhelmed it. And both Obie and Zebediah privately believed that what happened that night in the sweltering schoolroom was the consequence of personal transgressions, their own and perhaps others' too. But neither ever mentioned this aloud, even to his friend. They remained silent sharers of private guilts from the night of the meeting to the day of their deaths several years later when, hunting caribou together along the coast one summer day, they loaded their boat with too many carcasses and were caught in a squall going home. The boat swamped. They both drowned.

But in the end, as time elapsed and the events of the evening receded year by year into the past, slipping away from local memory into local lore, most of the blame for what happened came to rest on Gwen — or, rather, on the two Gwens.

6

The day of the meeting began with a fiery sun rising out of the sea. The sky above it was empty except for a few small clouds hanging precariously close to the horizon. It was going to be another hot day.

Akpa got up early. Wearing only the child's blouse that served as her nightgown, she slid off her bed and, bending her gnarled knees, knelt to say her morning prayer, forehead resting on clenched hands pressed against the mattress. It was always the same prayer, asking the Lord to bless and protect her till she went to bed again and expressing a firm belief in his ability and even his willingness to do so. But this morning the words ran past her lips without her mind paying attention.

If the arrival of the caribou nearly a week ago had justified her faith in the white lady's power to work miracles, their continuing presence puzzled her. Poniktuk had its winter's meat, so why hadn't the lady sent the herd away? Bulls killed and freezer full, the animals still surrounded the town, filling the air with their stink, driving the dogs crazy. Was that what the lady wanted, or were the caribou waiting for something?

Waiting for what? she asked herself as she mouthed her morning prayer. Her nephew Nate had announced their arrival. Were they waiting for him to dismiss them? No. Despite his surprising eloquence about those whatchucallit rights and his recent successes at locating game, she hadn't allowed herself to join the speculation about his having acquired angakuq powers. Nate was Nate, even if his private name was Iku. Well, but Iku . . . wasn't persuading animals to let themselves be killed something her Great-uncle Iku had been able to do? Before Father Evans taught her the true religion, she'd believed fervently that spirits made everything happen and that people like her great-uncle talked to them. Especially — now she remembered the story — since Sedna, the greatest sprit of them all, was said to have started life as a girl right here at Poniktuk before running off to marry a seahawk and end up living at the bottom of the sea, controlling all its creatures — and spirits of the air too, if she remembered right. And of the earth? And caribou?

Akpa stopped mumbling and, with a quick plea to the Lord for forgiveness and an urgent request for provisional protection until evening, when she promised to deliver a better-than-ever bedtime prayer, got to her feet and, pulling the child's blouse over her head, reached for her panties and bra. She had something serious to discuss with her sister. Moments later, as she hurried along the dusty road toward Big Helen's house, not only the heat of the day caused sweat to bead her brow and trickle down her spine.

Akpa wasn't the only one having difficulties. Obie rolled out of bed, leaving Bella's warm and pungent bulk to the pleasures of more sleep, and sat with his elbows on his knees and his head in his hands. Why, he asked himself — as he did every morning when he woke to the absence from his side of Gentle Jesus — was he being made to suffer like this? Since his one visit to Father's shed, he'd often thought of storming back and knocking everything down like a latter-day Samson. That might redeem him and bring Jesus back. But because of what always happened when he thought of the striped tuque, he hadn't done it and knew he never would. It happened now. Like a Biblical affliction, Obie's cock swelled. He groaned and, standing, slapped the devil down. He pulled on his pants and shuffled into the kitchen. While the coffee-pot bubbled and spat, he considered the weather; it was going to be hot again. Bleakly he wondered what new torment the day held for him.

On his living-room couch, Nate stretched and yawned. Though he'd slept late, there was still much time to fill before evening. He let his thoughts run lazily back over his weeks of visiting and explaining and promoting ABRA's Agreement in Principle. He was pleased with his work and ready to challenge his uncle. He had no plan. When the time came, he'd trust himself to be inspired.

Nate swung his legs off the couch and wondered what to do with the rest of the day. Ordinarily he'd take a walk in the hills, but the caribou blocked that direction. He decided to borrow his father's boat, go to the river, and check the nets he knew were full of fish. To spend the hours between now and the meeting away from town would clear his mind.

In his cubicle, area officer Bill Tremonte flipped through a document entitled "Devolution and Population Distribution in Poniktuk: A Proposal." Its pale blue binder identified it as a document of the Government of the Northwest Territories. Bill liked the look and feel of it. Although the title page bore the name of his boss, James Archibald Fraser, and his own name appeared only in footnotes referring to research he'd done at university while getting his degree in Aboriginal Studies, he'd written the whole thing. Bill had expected Fraser himself to present it in Poniktuk, but his boss had declared that although Bill didn't have the ranking for credit as author, he deserved recognition for his work. So he was letting him have the pleasure of personally presenting the proposal to the people it was designed to benefit.

Bill turned to the executive summary. The DPDP proposed to counteract the societal ills that Euro-Canadian culture had, from the beginning of contact and with ever-worsening results, caused in Inuit communities. (Mentally, Bill ticked off alcohol and drug abuse, spousal abuse. Diseases: tuberculosis, cancer, syphilis, the common cold. Loss of self-esteem, joblessness, poverty, despair.) It tied together the NWT policy of devolution (which according to Fraser was a pet project of the commissioner) with a revitalization of traditional Inuit values and lifestyles, but in a contemporary way. Returning people to living on the land in extended-family groups but allowing them to maintain ties to the village through up-to-date technology, the plan would teach skills, create jobs, restore self-confidence, and improve health. It put the present in service to the past and the past in service to the future.

Good phrase, Tremonte thought and, closing the binder, looked at his watch.

He had an hour and a half before he was due at the airport, but he needed to eat and pick up a forty-ouncer for Simon Umingmak at the liquor store. He took a quick look around his cubicle: his desk, filing cabinet, typewriter, Post-it notes to himself, and postcards of Inuit artworks pinned to the partitions might all look different the next time he saw them. Today's trip to Poniktuk was his first solo assignment. He was starting a life-long adventure; he felt a little scared but excited too.

In his corner office, Jim Fraser made a phone call.

"Yup," Simon said.

"Simon, it's Jim Fraser."

"Hello, Jim."

"Simon, I'm sending Bill Tremonte in for that meeting today. He'll be on a charter that's going on to Uugaaqtuk. It'll pick him up on its way back."

"Oohh? You not coming yourself?"

"Uh, no. I've got — I forgot I have a businessmen's dinner tonight. Giving a speech. Can't get out of it."

"We'll miss you, Jim."

"Well, thanks, Simon, but Tremonte's a good man. You won't be disappointed."

"What time he get here?"

"Should be around six-thirty."

"I'll meet him."

"Great. He'll have, uh, he'll have a copy of that plan with him. He can tell you all about it before the meeting."

"Okay."

"Simon, you sure this thing's going to fly?"

"Sure I'm sure."

"I've got a lot riding on it, you know."

"I know you do."

"And you do too, don't forget."

Simon grinned at that absurdity. He might not even use the plan.

"Don't worry, everything sitting good in here. You tell Bill to pick up something for me?"

"I sure did."

"So I'll talk to you after, Jim. Let you know what people here think about that there plan of yours."

When he hung up, Simon chuckled and shook his head. For a government guy, Jim Fraser never did have much balls.

Christ, thought Fraser, staring out his window. I hope I'm not screwing myself. Maybe I should've let Tremonte put his name on that plan after all.

In Poniktuk, the day lengthened passively under the fierce sun. An early breeze had long since died. By midafternoon the blue sky had turned a scalded white, and the small clouds floating there had evaporated. Now no one went outdoors unless they had to, and if they did, they went slowly. Children even played slowly.

Too hot for us Huskimos, Big Helen thought, fanning herself at her window with pages from an outdated Sears catalogue as she watched Akpa waddle away along the heat-stunned road.

"No," she'd told her sister, "them stories about Sedna was only about fishes and seals and like that. Nothing to do with caribou. But how come you getting all worked up about spirits now? It not enough you all worked up about that white lady? The one making miracles? You don't like her caribou miracle no more?"

Akpa's confusion allowed Helen a sweet moment of revenge.

"You forget what Father Evans preach about them old-time spirits coming from devil? You believing in them now, again? You of all peoples? Shame, little sister!"

Akpa had protested, but her sister's mockery only increased her confusion.

Still, Helen thought, as Akpa disappeared around a corner, something wrong about them caribou coming like that, even they bring us lots of meat. And now it feel like some kind big weather coming too, she added, looking at the cloudless sky. It too hot to stay good. And meeting tonight too. Too much happening same time now.

A hundred kilometres inland from Poniktuk, a single-engine float plane circled a small lake, flew away, turned back, and skimming over the tundra, landed on the lake with a soft bump. It taxied toward a sandy beach. Just before it got there, its engine stopped, and the plane slid forward till its pontoons scraped bottom. The pilot stepped onto a pontoon, secured one end of a rope to a cleat, and jumped ashore in his cowboy boots. He tied the other end around a boulder. The passenger door opened, and two women, one after the other, stepped onto the pontoon on their side. They teetered to its front and took the pilot's hand to be helped ashore. The heavy-set woman got her feet wet. The pilot went back into the plane and brought out lunch. It was their third day together.

"Don't be discouraged, honey," Ethel said, lowering herself to the hot sand and stretching out her legs so her boots would dry. "There's still lots of ground we haven't covered. We could spot them yet."

Trish said nothing. She applied herself to covering her face and hands with mosquito repellent. As they had done yesterday and the day before, they'd been flying low over the Blackstone River since midmorning and had just made several passes over a gorge where, the sun being high overhead, all three had spotted a glint of metal and, on another pass, identified the remains of an aluminum canoe bent around a rock.

The pilot, Gary, offered Trish a sandwich wrapped in clingwrap. Trish shook her head.

"There's iced tea," he said, indicating a thermos.

Trish nodded and, accepting the thermos, unscrewed the cap that served as a cup and poured it full.

"Should keep your strength up," Ethel told her, accepting a sandwich.

Trish nodded again and gazed past the plane at the glittering surface of the lake.

Gary and Ethel ate in silence. At the end of the meal, Trish accepted a pear.

"I'll just fuel up," Gary said, "and then we can fly some more of the grid before we drop off Ethel in Poniktuk. Okay with you?"

Trish said that was okay.

In Simon's kitchen, Bill Tremonte put the blue government binder on the table. He also handed Simon the forty-ouncer in a brown paper bag.

"Oho," said Simon. "Looks like you figger to get something outta me."

Bill forced a smile.

"Just a present from Mr. Fraser."

Simon tilted his chair back and with two thick fingers and a thumb picked up drinking glasses from the kitchen counter.

"You taking it straight or watered?" he asked, setting the glasses on the table.

Bill didn't know if the twinkle in Simon's eye was a gleam of friendly invitation or a sly reminder of the other time he'd accepted a drink here and choked on it like a ten-year-old.

"Just a light one with a splash of water, thanks," he said.

Simon nodded.

"Siddown," he said, and after fixing Bill's drink, poured himself a tall one, straight.

He sipped and smacked his lips.

"So what you got in this-here plan of yours?"

Tremonte took a deep breath. He was already sweating, and the heavy animal stench that had made him gag when he stepped off the plane was still strong in Simon's kitchen. He took a sip of his drink. Simon had said nothing about the caribou, and although he'd never seen one before, Bill hadn't wanted to seem a goggle-eyed idiot when he climbed into the truck at the airstrip, so he hadn't said anything about them either. Their presence might be normal, although the pilot's reaction suggested it wasn't. "Holy shit! Look at those caribou!" he'd said, as they circled before landing.

Bill took another sip and put caribou out of his mind. He laid a hand on the binder.

"We think this is a plan that combines the best of traditional values and lifestyles with the best of the new opportunities available through up-to-date technology. It's an experimental plan that would first be carried out in Poniktuk if you and your council and people want it. Then it could be used elsewhere. The main point of the plan is, it gives you, as a community, in a step-by-step process, increasingly greater control of your lives in a number of areas that we, as the government, presently administer. It involves a return to living on the land."

He'd memorized this speech on the plane coming in.

"Tell me about them areas and that-there process," Simon said.

Bill took a deep breath and started in on the details of "Devolution and Population Distribution in Poniktuk: A Proposal." Simon poured himself another drink. Soon, Bill was way beyond anything he'd memorized.

Outdoors, although late afternoon was moving toward evening, the sun still blazed in the cloudless sky.

b

*Excitement loosened Sedna's throat and swelled her
singing. An angakuq was coming, he was almost here.
Soon she would learn what was happening in the world
above. Soon her hair would be combed and braided and
her body cleaned.*

The sea animals overhead swam faster.

Ralph stepped through an opening in the wall.

*Sedna stopped singing. What was this? A man, no
doubt, she could see that. But what a disgusting one:
skin white as caribou fat, hair all over his chest and belly!*

*A belch of anger escaped her lips. Was this two-legged
pile of blubber with its pink, shrivelled sex peeking at her
from a nest of reddish hair the only man who'd heard her
song? Could the song summon only this pale, foreign
grub, this disgusting white slug with bulging fish eyes,
pulpy mouth hanging open, useless hands dangling, not
even holding a comb?*

*Sedna slid off her bench, swam across the room,
grabbed Ralph's jaws with her fingerless palms, and,
giving a kick, rose into the thick canopy of sea animals
overhead, pulling Ralph with her. When she broke through
to the other side, she let Ralph go and, kicking and stroking,
kept rising, drawing after her a great spinning pillar of fish,
seals, walruses, narwhals, and whales.*

*As Ralph's body fell back through the sea animals, flukes
slapped his soft flesh, tusks poked it, spiny fins and flipper
nails scraped and tore it. Pieces of Ralph came loose. And
when the animals had at last all vanished from the wide
sandy basin centred on Sedna's home, and the water there
returned to its timeless calm, what was left of Ralph
settled slowly to the ocean floor.*

In time marine biota picked his bones clean.

227

b

At eight o'clock, Eddie Qarlik unlocked the school door and carried extra folding chairs into the grades six, seven, and eight classroom. He pulled down the wide yellow shade on a window that was letting in too much sun.

People drifted toward the building. Most disliked the prospect of sitting in a hot schoolroom at children's desks, but at least a meeting provided distraction from the caribou. A mild curiosity also drew them. Although in the end they'd heard too much about ABRA from Nate, which made deciding how to vote in the referendum all the more difficult, Simon had not yet told anyone what he thought. They expected to find out at the meeting.

Entering the school's vestibule, they took off boots and shoes and went along the corridor in stocking feet to find seats in the classroom. The room slowly filled. Sunburnt from his trip to the river, Nate came in with Lawrence. He'd found so many whitefish and char in Eli's nets that it had taken all his strength to lift the nets in sections onto the bow of the boat, where he could disentangle them. He considered the catch a good omen and, with Lawrence's help, had stored it in the freezer. Now he leaned against the classroom wall as he'd done at that other meeting months ago where he first spoke out. Covert glances noted his arrival. Clothes rustled, and speculation about what he might say tonight engaged several minds while everyone waited for the meeting to begin.

Simon arrived. With him was the new area officer seen earlier walking around the village. Simon stood a moment inside the door, then fixed his eyes on the teacher's desk, walked to it, sat down in the teacher's chair, and stared out over the rows of heads. Oh-oh, Akpa thought, Simon been drinking. Those damn government guys allus bring booze for Simon, Big Helen thought. What kind meeting we have now?

Bill Tremonte pulled up a folding chair and sat beside the desk, blue government binder in his lap. Sweat ran down behind his ears and oozed from his hairline. His time with Simon in the kitchen had not gone well. As he'd plunged deeper and deeper into details of the DPDP, Simon had regarded him with attention but had made none of the grunts or nods that might indicate agreement or even understanding. Their absence had rattled Bill, and the more rattled he got, the faster he talked, and the faster he talked, the more mixed up he got until, to his alarm, he heard himself babbling and made himself stop. Simon had smiled, poured him more whiskey, and said it was hard to understand but he'd keep trying. Which meant Bill had to keep going. As Simon poured himself more whiskey, Bill went back over main points, rephrased explanations, added examples, and elucidated problems until he couldn't think of anything more to say. Simon still said nothing. Bill had sat till the silence was unbearable, then excused himself, saying he wanted to see the village. But this too had gone badly. Out of doors the caribou stink was overwhelming. He breathed through his mouth to minimize it but closed his mouth again when the few Poniktungmiut also outdoors stared at him. Children also stared, but when he said "Hi," they ran away. And now he sat in a stifling schoolroom, still stared at by what seemed to be the whole village, with no idea how he was going to carry out his boss's orders. If he'd failed to explain the DPDP to Simon, how could he explain it to this audience? Worse still, he had no idea what Simon was going to do. On returning from his tour of the village, he'd noticed the forty-ouncer on the kitchen table was already half empty. More sweat prickled Bill's scalp.

"Look at that!" Gary shouted above the engine noise and jabbed a finger at the ground.

They'd come in over the hills behind Poniktuk and were heading toward the bay. Ethel and Trish looked out their windows.

"Wow!" said Ethel.

Trish leaned across the aisle and tugged her sleeve.

"What are they?" she shouted.

"Caribou! Those are caribou!"

Ethel looked out her window again.

"Jesus," she breathed. "They go all the way along the coast!"

"What are they doing there?" Trish shouted.

"God knows!"

The bay was calm. The plane taxied to the beach.

"Pee-yew!" Ethel said when she'd stepped onto a pontoon. "Those critters stink! Pass me my bags, will you, Trish?"

"I'll get them," Gary said, and after he'd handed Ethel ashore, he carried her suitcases to the beach as Trish pushed them out of the cabin.

"Funny," Ethel said, looking around. "When a plane comes in, there's usually lots of people to meet it. Where is everybody?"

Gary shrugged.

"Let's get your stuff to the nursing station. I don't like the look of those clouds building up. Could be one mother of a thunderstorm coming. We should get out of here as soon as we can."

"I'd like to have a look around the town," Trish said.

"Oh, okay. There's time, I guess. Want one of us with you?"

"No thanks."

"You go ahead, honey," Ethel said. "Take your time. When you're ready to leave, just ask anyone where the nursing station is. Gary and I'll be there."

She patted Trish's arm. Trish climbed the low bank from the beach. Ethel waited till she was out of hearing.

"I think she's given up," she said. "Seeing the canoe did it."

"I guess," said Gary. "How long you say those two have been missing?"

"Almost a month. This is where they were supposed to end up."

"Not a chance in hell of surviving out there that long. I could've told her."

"Me too. But you never know. Miracles happen."

"Costing her a lot."

"Her sister was a twin."

"Ah. Well, let's get these bags to the station. You have air conditioning there?"

"You bet."

"Never seen anything like those caribou. Weird."

"You said it."

"Why we waiting anyways?"

The question from Simon caused a shifting of buttocks and thighs at the desks and on the folding chairs. The meeting was finally starting.

Simon remembered why they were there.

"Nate been telling you about this whatchucallit. Thing we supposed to vote on. Maybe he want to tell some more. You feel to do that, Nate?"

Forcing his eyes to focus, he searched the room for his nephew and, when he found him, raised his eyebrows at him.

But Nate knew better than to do that. First to speak usually lost in a contest with his uncle, even drunk, or maybe especially then. He shook his head and gestured for Simon to begin.

Simon tried again.

"You the one knows all about it. You sure you don't feel to help me out?"

Nate smiled and shook his head again. He knew everyone in the room knew as well as he did that Simon wasn't really asking for help, he was trying to trick him into saying something he could then attack.

As the silence in the room continued, it dawned on Simon that his trick had failed. That annoyed him. He raised his voice.

"You holding out on me, boy?"

His tone sent a ripple of uneasiness through the room. Everyone there had crossed Simon's path when he was angry. Those were bad memories. Memories of Simon angry and drunk were even worse.

The tone caused Nate a twinge of fear. But a quickening in his blood made him realize that he might win this contest simply by letting his uncle lose it. He smiled and shook his head again.

Simon glared.

"You trying to suffer me?" He brought a fist down on the teacher's desk. "You getting smarty?"

Nate continued to regard his uncle with an amiable gaze, but he felt Lawrence tense up and heard more stirring in the crowded classroom. A sure way to lose respect in Poniktuk was to lose your temper in public, and although the standard attitude toward Simon was forbearance when he misbehaved or broke rules, Nate sensed that at this moment, in this hot room, people might be less inclined than usual to indulge their leader. As he and Simon continued to lock eyes, another round of ankle crossing and thigh and buttock shifting told Nate he was right. The bodies squeezed into children's desks or stuck to metal folding chairs had begun to feel impatience with Simon, maybe even disapproval.

Simon sensed the disapproval.

"What you peoples thinking?" He turned to glare at them. "I figger it out. Them land rights? They no good for nobody. 'Cept maybe Nate. Make him feel like Big Man."

The room became quiet.

"This-here reefer . . . riffer . . . whatchucallit. It bullshit. Nate tell you vote Yes and good things happen. That bullshit! Look at all them papers he have. You want papers like that tell you what to do? Government white guys already coming in here all the time, make meetings, messing up things. You want more like that?"

Bill Tremonte, the only government white guy in the room, felt his scrotum contract. How many others here felt the way Simon did? He forced himself to make a quick survey of the heads ranged before him. Some of their dark, impassive eyes were, in fact, studying him. Bill took a tighter grip on his blue binder.

A vision of his village under Nate's authoritative thumb filled Simon's mind. "What wrong with you peoples? You believe him, you believe anything. Don't matter how crazy. Like that white lady."

This swerve away from land rights surprised his listeners and provoked a variety of responses. Mention of the white lady had its usual shameful effect on Obie. Saint or old-time spirit? Akpa's anxieties whispered to her. Saint getting ready to go back to heaven, thought Della. Nice good lady, Sarah thought, snuggling in Ruth's lap. Poor woman almost die of starvation, thought Big Helen. Brought caribou, thought many others.

What white lady? Tremonte thought. He wiped sweat from his forehead and looked carefully around the room in case he'd missed a pale complexion. There was none.

"She nothing," Simon declared. "She just one white lady. Who cares how she get here. But you peoples think she really something. Make secret place for her in Father's shed and ask for things. I know. Give her things too. And thank her, I bet. How many years you been asking *me* for things? How many years I been giving? And who thank *me*? Tell me that. Who thank Simon Umingmak? You peoples want land rights, you vote for it all right. Me, I say bullshit. That's what I say. Simon Umingmak, he say fuck land rights. He say fuck you too."

He folded his arms across his chest and stared over the heads of the people of his village into a future that seethed with disappointment and anger.

Absolute silence fell.

Sarah squirmed in Ruth's lap.

"Baby, don't," Ruth whispered into her hair.

But Sarah twisted and slid off. Her stockinged feet touching the floor, she buried her face in the skirt that clung to Ruth's thigh. The cloth smelled comfortingly of her grandmother's sweat. But even nuzzling there, Sarah knew that everything in the room had gone funny, the way it had that morning when a bad thing got into her uncle Nate. Was that happening again? Sarah gripped her granny's skirt.

I really don't like this, Tremonte told himself. His knowledge of the ABRA agreement was sketchy, but it didn't take a political genius to see that the two plans, the DPDP and ABRA's, wouldn't work together, or to understand which plan increased Simon's hold on Poniktuk and Fraser's reputation in the Territorial bureaucracy and which took power away from them both. So why wasn't Simon helping him out with the DPDP? Because he was drunk, that's why. And now he'd told everyone to get fucked. Maybe, Bill thought, I better get out of here.

Beyond the classroom window, daylight suddenly died. Thunder murmured in the distance, and the classroom darkened. Everyone noticed the change, but their attention was fixed on Simon — brother, uncle, cousin, in-law, friend. Losing his temper had been bad enough, but that word! And saying it twice! In the school! And at them!

In the sweltering room at a meeting none had much wanted to attend but all had loyally come to, on a topic already causing headaches and confusion, to be openly cursed by the man they counted on to lead them not only strained the assembled Poniktungmiut's forbearance, it wiped it out. The disapproval that had earlier made many shift uneasily in their seats became anger.

Nate felt the hostility and realized the meeting was no longer about ABRA. The quickening that had alerted him to stay silent while his uncle taunted him now alerted him to be ready for anything.

As Simon continued to stare belligerently over people's heads, and they stared angrily back, waves of hostility washed toward the front of the room. Although for now directed at Simon, how long might it be, Tremonte wondered, before the anger spilled onto him? Something deep in the dynamics of the village was happening in the room, something explosive, and it made Bill more acutely aware than ever that he was the only outsider present. Get out, he told himself. Get out now. And he looked toward the classroom door.

A woman stood in it. She had skin like his.

"Hi," he croaked.

Several eyes fixed on Simon flickered toward him.

"Hi," said Trish.

Hearing her voice behind them, many turned their heads. What they saw startled them. But the women who'd seen Gwen shuffle through Ruth's kitchen wrapped in an eiderdown now saw another

Gwen standing in the doorway, fully dressed and miraculously changed. Her face was no longer a gaunt mask reddened by the sun or her body the starved skeleton they'd imagined under her eiderdown. Her face was full, and the body under her trousers and long-sleeved blouse was rounded, well-fed, and even, in the eyes of some, Obie most painfully, voluptuous. And her hair wasn't long and yellow, it was short and red.

Standing along the wall not far from Nate, Della, eyes shining, clutched Selma in a fierce hug: another miracle!

Jeepers sakes, Big Helen thought. Is that what that lady look like? I thought they say she has yellow hair. And she don't look like she suffer much to me.

Ruth couldn't believe her eyes. Only an hour ago she'd left Gwen at home in bed. She was getting stronger every day for sure but . . . but that hair. And where did those clothes come from? She tried to stand, but Sarah's grip on her skirt held her down. She looked sideways at Eli, but Eli was watching Nate. Nate stepped away from the wall.

"Hi," Trish repeated, and smiled at the people.

Tremonte got up from his chair but stopped when Obie jumped to his feet. Sweat soaking his armpits, he saw Bear Woman in the doorway, come to him at last, alive and seductive, with her hair in flames.

"You!" he shouted. "You . . . I do it now! This time I really do it!"

His hands fumbled at his belt buckle. His hips began to thrust.

"I fu-fu-fu-fu-fu-fu-fu-fu-fu-fu-fu . . ."

Obie's hands flew up, his eyes rolled back, his knees buckled. He fell.

For a moment no one moved. Then several things happened at once. Ruth felt Sarah bite through her skirt and with a cry slapped her grandchild away. Sarah let out a wail, let go her granny's skirt, and scampered into the forest of chair legs, desk legs, and people's legs toward the schoolroom door. Nate turned his head at the sound of his niece's wail, lost her among people standing to crane for a look at Obie, and when he turned back to the doorway, saw the lady was gone. Old Piuyuk farted. Zebediah tried to catch Simon's eye, but Simon's face was a wall. Nate's brother Wayne caught Harry Ingasuk's eye. Nate started after the woman, but Sarah, almost at the door, saw him coming, squealed, increased her speed, and skidding on stockinged feet, slid out ahead of him, collided with the backs of Trish's legs, spun her around, scrambled past her down the corridor, and escaped through the shoe-filled vestibule into the outdoors. There was another rumble of thunder.

At the top of the schoolhouse steps, Trish was looking to see which way the girl had gone when she was seized from behind and lifted into a pair of arms. When she turned her head, she saw at her shoulder a young man's face.

"I take you home," Nate said, and, careful not to trip on his untied shoelaces, started down the steps.

"What?"

"We go home now."

"What d'you mean, home? I'm . . . I'm going to the nursing station. Put me down."

"Nursing station closed."

"It's not. Now please put me down."

She twisted in his arms. He hugged her tighter. They reached the bottom of the steps.

"Listen, buster," Trish said. "I'm not going anywhere in this town except the nursing station. Now *put me down!*"

Nate put her down. But he could still feel the softness of her body in his arms.

"We going to do it now."

"What?"

He reached for her.

"Get outta here! Christ, don't touch me!"

She turned on her heel and walked rapidly away. Thunder moved closer.

Nate watched her buttocks moving vigorously against her trousers and hurried after her.

"Okay," he said. "I take you to nursing station."

He placed a hand under her elbow.

"Really?"

Nate nodded.

"No funny business?"

"It this way," he said, and steered her down the road.

Trish let him lead her. They left the road, crossed an empty lot, and passed between a pair of houses. When we get to the nursing station, she thought, Ethel and Gary will be there, and I'll say goodbye to Ethel. Then we'll leave before the storm hits. That's all I want. Spending time in the village where Gwen and Ralph had meant to end their trip had been a mistake. Until drawn into the schoolhouse by its open door and the sound of voices inside, she'd not seen a single person, and the bizarre behaviour of the people in the classroom had ended her hope of finding someone who might have seen them somewhere out on the land. Now she finally must accept that, as her mother had said, they were gone. Now she was only tired. So she let the young man guide her between houses and back along the road in the increasing darkness. His grip on her elbow remained gentle. She leaned into it.

Zeb had jumped from his chair, pushed to the front of the room, grabbed Simon by the arm, shouted his name, and pulled him from his chair toward the fallen Obie. Simon allowed himself to be pulled. Wayne gave Harry Ingasuk a nod, and they too pushed forward. Zeb knelt beside his friend. Simon collapsed to the floor.

"Obie!" Zeb called. "Obie! Obediah!"

"Put him up," said Wayne.

Zeb shoved Simon aside, and he and Wayne each gripped one of Obie's arms and hoisted him into a sitting position. His chin dropped. People sitting behind those who'd risen when Obie fell stood up and leaned or ducked or peered around other people's backs to get a better view, and along the wall teenagers stood on their chairs. Closer to Obie, Akpa turned her chair around, climbed it, and gripped its metal back.

Obie raised his head. His eyelids fluttered.

"Aaahh," he sighed.

Zeb held up a hand.

"Aaahh," Obie sighed again.

The room attended.

Obie opened his eyes and stared at the ceiling. His hands groped for and found the hands of the men supporting him.

"Ah Jesus!" he said in a louder voice.

The room held its breath. Obie closed his eyes again.

"I see you," he said.

The room let out its breath. Hope rose in the minds of Obie's fellow Evangelicals that after too long an absence from his tongue some heavenly vision was about to command his speech.

"Hear me," Obie said.

"Hear him!" called two female voices.

"And forgive me!"

"Oh, forgive him!" the voices echoed, joined by a third and fourth.

"Forgive my trespass!"

"His trespass!" several voices cried.

Tensions loosened throughout the room. Minds strained by political controversy, distressed by Simon's anger, outraged by his cursing, minds overtaxed by daylight hours lasting all night long, troubled by strange events (a half-dead white lady, a huge herd of caribou surrounding the village, angakuq powers in a young man previously famous only for shoplifting), minds enthralled by a shrine to the white lady's tuque and, only moments ago, astonished by her appearance in the classroom door, looking totally unlike herself — minds so afflicted, whether Evangelical or not, now welcomed a release.

"What trespass?" a voice unmistakably Bella's called.

"Lusting!" Obie answered.

"Lusting!" more voices called, some masculine.

"Oh Lord!"

"Amen!"

"Lusting in my body!"

"Lord, Lord!"

"Who for?" called the same female voice.

"Bear Woman!"

"Who?"

"Bear Woman! He say Bear Woman!"

"Alii!" Akpa cried.

"Protect me, Jesus!" Obie implored.

His hands tightened on Wayne's and Zeb's. Simon remained slumped beside them.

With soft thuds, grateful Evangelicals slid from their seats to kneel on the schoolroom floor. A scattering of raindrops pattered on its roof.

"Sweet Jesus, protect him!"

"Forgive him!"

"Save him!"

"She tempt me!"

"Alii!"

"Bear Woman tempt him!"

As he crouched behind the teacher's desk, the hair on Bill Tremonte's neck stood up. *Bear woman?* Listening to the wails and cries rising from every corner of the room, some repeating the improbable name, others calling for protection or salvation, he searched among the pitching and rocking bodies for what he dared not think to see.

"I've sinned!" Obie cried, his voice louder than the others.

"*I've* sinned!" cried another voice.

"Oh Lord!"

"Zebediah sin!"

"Tell us!"

"I been coveting!"

"Lord!"

"Coveting what?" Bella called.

"Antlers!"

"What?"

"Antlers! I been coveting antlers!"

"He say antlers!"

"In the velvet!"

"Antlers in the velvet!"

"Lord forgive him!"

A fever of self-reproach ran through the room.

"I steal!" a voice cried. "I steal my cousin's watch!"

"I steal Nate's knife!" cried Della.

"I bust the Herman Nelson and never tell nobody!"

"I steal gas from tank farm!"

"I put my finger up Baby!"

"I steal char from freezer!"

"I fuck with Isaac!"

"I watch Father piss in the honey bucket!"

"I make home brew!"

"I blow-job my dadduk!"

"I cheat at poker!"

"I lie! I lie!"

Voices rose and fell in loud self-censure.

Behind the teacher's desk, Bill Tremonte closed his eyes and pictured where the door was. While others were preoccupied with competitive disclosures of their wrongdoings, he had a chance to escape. Satisfied that he knew his route to the door, he jackknifed to his feet and launched himself. Planting hands on the shoulders of sitting or kneeling figures that swayed and bobbed, he pushed them aside or rose unsteadily into the air between them. He dodged desks, swerved past chairs, jumped over bodies. Always on the balls of his feet, Tremonte bolted through the noisy chaos of the room, into the corridor, through the vestibule, out the open schoolhouse door, and down its steps into an evening of steadily falling rain and rumbling thunder. As he continued to sprint toward the airstrip, he saw only as a vague and irrelevant blur the naked figure standing outside the school.

Sarah too had a brief encounter with the figure. Thinking only of hiding, she'd left the schoolhouse steps as fast as her stocking feet could carry her and started to circle the building toward her destination, an opening in the wire mesh nailed to the structure's skirting. Turning a corner, she'd come face to face with a bare knee. She'd stopped, raised her head long enough to take in a black pubic patch, a round belly, and, dangling next to dirt-covered thighs, hands horribly missing all their fingers, and then rushed on, found the opening, and ducked under the school. There she'd scrambled around wooden pilings until she reached the shallow pit under the floor of the grades six, seven, and eight classroom that every child in Poniktuk knew as a safe haven. It was also a whelping bed used by the town's bitches. Sarah wasn't alone in seeking refuge there.

"Go way," she said to the large white dog that, frightened by thunder, lay curled nose to tail in the sandy hollow.

She gave it a push, lay down herself, and, turning her back on the dog, sucked her thumb. The dog growled.

After losing the strangely dressed child into the ground under the big square igloo, Sedna had walked around the building, stopping from time to time to see if the child would come up at another opening, like a ground squirrel. It did not. Making her circuit of the school, she missed seeing Nate carry Trish down the steps but arrived at the front again in time to see Young Helen walk away.

Following Obie's collapse, Helen had heard Sarah's wail and had stood to watch her dodge between desks and chairs and come briefly into view again before skittering out the door. Passing people getting up from desks who blocked her way, she'd taken longer to cross the room than Nate, and she'd stopped in the vestibule to put on her shoes. At the top of the school steps, she'd been too late to see Nate and Trish disappear around a house and too early to see Sedna. She'd scanned the playground and the road as fat drops of rain struck her face.

"Sarah?" she called. "Bunnik?"

Sarah didn't hear her.

"Bad," she said to the dog and hit it on the nose. It was

pushing her. Overhead the muffled babble of voices grew louder, and thumps sounded on the floorboards. The dog growled deeper in its throat and bared its teeth.

Getting no answer, Helen started toward Akpa's house to see if the child had gone there.

Sedna watched and noted that she, like the child, wore clothing dyed strange colours and made of skins so thin they fluttered around her legs.

Expecting to see at most several tents of caribou hide where her father's tent had stood, the sea spirit had been startled, when she walked out of the ocean, to find herself under the tail of a giant insect standing motionless on the shore, its wings extended, its feet on the beach. She'd backed away and moved around it. Behind her the surface of the bay churned with fish and seals, narwhals and whales. Climbing the low bank from the beach, she'd seen tall, square structures in rows, made of something that didn't even look like skins. They puzzled her. Then she'd smelled caribou, and looking inland at the hills — and noting that they at least were as she remembered them — she'd seen the great herd spread across the flatlands. Why the caribou had gathered to greet her she didn't pause to consider. Although they were not her animals, she acknowledged their hommage.

She approached a house. Running a fingerless palm along its siding, she felt something smoother than anything she'd ever touched. She sniffed and then licked it. Neither experience told her what the substance was; she spat out its bitter taste.

Putting aside this puzzle, Sedna had filled her lungs with great gulps of air that, after breathing water for so long, chilled and caressed her mouth and tongue while her nose filled with the sweet stench of caribou. Whatever the structures were, the hills and bay and ground beneath her feet welcomed her back to the country of her childhood, no longer a foolish girl sitting on a rock, combing her hair and dreaming of a lover, but a great spirit in command of all the creatures of the sea and, so it seemed, caribou too. Even the sky saluted her. Home to Narsuk and Sila, spirits of the weather whom she also controlled, it was filled with black clouds boiling up to welcome her.

For a while, Sedna had walked among Poniktuk's houses looking for someone to question and, finding no one, had arrived at the big square dwelling where the child ran into her. Now, while raindrops spattered the dust at her feet, she stood at the foot of a little hill that rose in narrow, even ledges to an opening in the dwelling's wall and heard, from inside, voices. They answered a question that had begun to trouble her: if the caribou had gathered to welcome her and Narsuk and Sila sent black clouds to swallow the sky in her honor, where were her people?

Although she could not make out single words, Sedna heard pleading in the voices. Reassured, she was about to enter the dwelling when a man bolted out of the opening and down the terraced hill. He was already past her when she realized the skin on his hands and face was the same colour as the disgusting creature's who'd appeared at her underwater home in response to her song. Now she listened more carefully to the voices and could hear some individual words. They were not in her language.

At the foot of the schoolhouse steps, Sedna hesitated.

Inside, the people of Poniktuk continued to raise their voices.

"I pray to tuque!" one called.

"Me too!" called another.

"I make offering!"

"I make offering three times!"

"I offer for earrings!"

"I offer for Walkman!"

"I offer for shotgun!"

"For wolverine!"

"For toaster!"

"I wish for baby!"

"I wish for Lawrence!"

"I wish for threewheeler!"

"For skidoo!"

"I wish for wife!"

"Fee simple absolute!"

"I wish for Nate!"

"For Pampers!"

"For panties!"

"I wish for Tiny Tim!"

As teenagers along the wall competed to name absurd wishes, bursts of laughter greeted their choices.

But others in the room were silent. Obie was deep in a spell of wonder at the return to his side of Gentle Jesus. Next to him Zeb, having confessed to coveting antlers, now found the joking or earnest naming of desired objects uncannily like the list of purchases he'd imagined from the sale of the antlers. Simon was trying to clear his head of fumes so he could understand how the meeting he'd called to demolish land rights had led to his sitting on the floor surrounded by people shouting nonsense. For Akpa the noise was not nonsense. The impulse that had made the confession fly out of her mouth that she'd once spied on Father Evans relieving himself and the laughing, confessing, and shouting in the room told her a terrible truth: the people of Poniktuk, herself included, were possessed.

But it was the laughter that made up Sedna's mind. She climbed the schoolhouse steps, crossed the shoe-filled vestibule, entered the corridor, and, oblivious to the strangeness of these enclosures, stopped at the classroom door. Glancing around and noting that, however strange their dress, their dwellings, or their language, the faces there were faces of her people, she raised her arms and commanded the people of Poniktuk to be silent.

Hearing her, those nearest the door turned their heads and stopped shouting. From them, as a wave of shouts still washed across the room, a counterwave of shock swept row after row. When it reached Akpa on her chair, it took her no time to name the naked body glistening with sea muck in the door, tangled hair falling over shoulders and breasts, raised hands fingerless.

"Sedna-a-a-a-a!" she screamed.

Stepping into the room, the sea spirit answered her call.

Outside, a cold wind rushed through the village, driving hard pellets of rain before it. Lightning flashed, and a thunderclap rattled the classroom windows. Rain pounded the roof, and as the creature in the doorway began to speak in a language none understood, the people of Poniktuk fell as silent as, seconds earlier, they'd been boisterous. Then panic seized them. Those who'd fallen to their knees to pray scrambled to their feet and joined others squeezing out of desks and leaving chairs. All backed rapidly away from Sedna into other desks and chairs. Grunts and curses rose from people blindly shoving and being shoved.

Sedna paused for breath and stepped farther into the room.

Chairs clattered to the floor, desks tipped over. Books and papers spilled. Thighs and groins met edges of upturned desks, shins banged against flanged metal feet, scissoring chair legs pinched stockinged toes.

Akpa fell off her chair. Ruth brought Eli's hand to her mouth and bit down hard on a finger. He let out a bellow and pulled her to her feet. Bella slipped on a notebook, let out a yell as she fell, and grabbed a neighbour, who fell noisily with her. Someone gave Irene a sharp push in the back and sent her flying breasts-first into Old Piuyuk's startled arms. Big Helen jumped to her feet and dropped a cigarette she'd nervously lit. Promptly stepped on, the cigarette burned through the stepper's sock and singed his foot. He yelped and, hopping on the other foot, rammed an elbow into Helen's ribs. Helen elbowed him back. Small children clung to or darted among adults' legs till they were roughly snatched up and lifted overhead, where they rode above the riot like trophies. Poniktuk's teenagers, thrilled by the storm outdoors and enthralled by the indoor spectacle of their parents and relatives cursing and pushing and shoving each other, paid little attention to the figure in the door. Pushing Selma from her side, Della backed into a corner and crouched there. As hailstones rattled on the school roof, the tangled shouts of fear, anger, desperation, and injury ricocheted around the grades six, seven, and eight classroom.

The crashing, stamping, and shouting overhead terrified Harry Ingasuk's dog. He began to claw Sarah. In the classroom, no one heard her screams.

Sedna kept up her harangue. In the language of their ancestors, its vocabulary a rich amalgam of innuendo and accusation, she reminded the Poniktungmiut of her power and their obligations. Rough gutturals and smooth fricatives spun from her mouth in loops forming chains of sentences that recalled her subjects to their duties. Did they not remember that she made rocks groan and stones tell stories? That she could speak through an angakuq's voice like trickling water or rushing wind, waves breaking, a walrus snuffling, a bear growling? That she could send them horrible ideas that drove them crazy? That she could make food dance in their cooking pots or jump out altogether? That all the bounty of the sea was hers to give or refuse?

As Sedna's mind swelled with the telling of her powers, she also remembered her life as a child here, when her father said the air was always full of spirits, good and bad, when animals were the same as people and they spoke one language, when her brothers thanked the animals who died so they could eat, when there was no difference between land and sea.

But the more Sedna boasted and chastised her people, the more they struggled away from her. Understanding nothing, some nonetheless remembered stories about punishments sent their ancestors by a powerful sea spirit. Old fears squeezed their bowels. For those with no such memories, the sight of Sedna's mangled hands and filthy body and the wrath in her voice were enough. The pushing, shoving, pushed, shoved, scrambling, struggling, frightened Poniktungmiut squeezed into a corner of the classroom.

Wayne saw the way out. He and Harry Ingasuk had tried to stay close to each other, and now he signalled Harry with a tip of his head. They worked toward the classroom window whose yellow shade Eddie Qarlik had lowered. Wayne tugged at it, and the shade flew toward the ceiling, where it snapped and spun on its dowel. Turning back to the room, the two men picked up a desk and threw it through the window. They pulled shards of glass from the window frame, stepped into the rain, and tipped the desk aside.

Eli, an angry and flailing Akpa tucked under his arm, was the first to see the opening. With Ruth behind him, he handed Akpa to Harry and Wayne and turned to help Ruth through. Then others saw their chance. If the retreat from Sedna inside the room had been brutal, the rush to get out of it was nearly lethal. Several children fell and came close to being trampled before they were picked up and handed through the window. Clawing hands gripped clothes and tore them, elbows jabbed, fists punched, legs tripped, feet slithered, mouths cursed and grunted. In a vicious gush, the people of Poniktuk spewed through the shattered window. Some landed on their hands and knees and cut themselves on splinters of glass. Others, landing on their feet, felt slivers pierce their socks and, pausing only to pull them out, limped away.

With a final whoosh through the village of ice-cold air, the thunderstorm passed. Its black clouds fled the sky, and melting hailstones sparkled in the returning sun.

Wayne and Harry stayed to the end, offering help to anyone who needed it, catching some before they fell, lifting others bodily across the windowsill. But their efforts went unthanked at the time and later too. At the time, people intent on getting home simply shook off their helping hands. And like any reference to the cuts and bruises and black eyes that appeared on Poniktungmiut the next day (and indeed like any acknowledgement of the confessions, confusions, shouting, praying, laughing, fighting, stampeding, and hysteria that had overtaken the meeting), any reference to the two men's actions was by tacit but universal agreement — except, briefly, among some of Poniktuk's voluble teenagers — suppressed.

In the only action that might be called an implicit recognition of the evening's events, some people returned to the school in following days to retrieve their shoes. But others did not. A number of shoes and boots, lined up neatly below the coathooks used by Poniktuk's children for their outdoor clothing in the winter, joined the single mittens, abandoned caps, and unmatched socks that Eddie Qarlik eventually gathered up and took to the dump. It was also Eddie who, the next day, put desks back on their feet and into rows, picked up books and papers (including, near the teacher's desk, a blue government binder), and stacked and put away the folding chairs. A crew from housing nailed a sheet of plywood across the open window. It remained there for a month, a blind eye in the school's facade, until a new window arrived by air freight and was installed.

When the last person hurried away from the school, Wayne and Harry went home.

But three figures remained in the grades six, seven, and eight room. Sedna had stopped talking when the rush to the window started and had watched the riotous exit in silence before turning to leave. A young man stood in her way. He began to speak. From her corner, Della listened and watched.

"Is this the nursing station?" Trish had asked Nate as they climbed the steps to the back porch of his parents' house. "It looks like just another house."

"This the place," Nate said, and opened the door. The raindrops falling on him and the black clouds overhead told him the worst of the storm was about to strike.

When they entered the kitchen, Trish turned on him.

"This isn't a nursing station! I thought you said you were going to take me to the nursing station!"

Nate shrugged.

"It closed. I already tell you. Nurse on holiday."

"And I'm here to tell you nurse is back from holiday. So you can just point me the way."

Lightning lit the kitchen; thunder followed.

"And be quick about it. I'm wet enough already. Well?"

Nate said nothing.

When he'd seen the woman he took to be Gwen in the classroom door, he'd been as astonished as the women who'd watched her cross his mother's kitchen. But in the seconds before Obie jumped up and collapsed and his niece cried out and people stood and craned to see her, his astonishment had turned to wonder: the frail, damaged woman who'd listened to stories from his bed had turned herself into this beautiful creature. As he pursued her out of the school, images from a certain night in Inuvik urged him on.

But she was resisting him.

"Before you get any more ideas," Trish said, "let me tell you that Ethel is right here in this town waiting for me at the nursing station and Gary is with her. You're only going to get in a lot of trouble if you try something, so just tell me how to get to the nursing station and I'll be on my way."

But as another lightning flash lit the world outside the kitchen window and a crack of thunder thumped the air, the rain on the roof became torrential. For the moment, Trish realized, she wasn't going anywhere.

Nate knew that too. He smiled.

"We wait for storm to pass," he said. "Then I take you to station. Or maybe you feel to call there? Phone on the table. Number is 4276. But storm could be crooking it. You want coffee?"

"I'll try the phone," Trish said. But all she got was a buzz.

As she sat at the kitchen table to wait out the storm, sitting where Eli had sat three months ago looking out the same window at a radiant day, wondering if his youngest son had caused it, Nate was not in her thoughts at all. She was imagining Gwen's body out there somewhere pelted by this storm.

Gwen's thoughts too were on the storm, but less on the one outside her bedroom window than the one she and Ralph had endured in their tent by the river, when they had waked the next morning to a clear, cool day. She wondered if Ralph was remembering that storm too. She swung her legs off the bed. She wanted to see him. She must ask Ruth where he was. Gwen stood up and pulled the eiderdown off her bed.

Movement in a corridor leading from the kitchen caught Trish's eye. She turned to see a figure wrapped in a quilt.

"Jesus!" she said.

"Trish?" Gwen said.

Nate looked back and forth from one to the other.

Now on the back porch, he leaned against the door he'd closed behind him and felt rain wash his face. He couldn't understand what he'd just seen, but his desire to make love had drained out of him as fast as the rainwater gurgling down a nearby pipe.

When the rain lessened and then stopped, Nate saw people hurrying along the road and past neighbouring houses. They were all coming from the direction of the school, and some were running. Others limped, and the way that no one looked at anyone else and everyone hunched over made him wonder what had happened at the meeting after he left and if anyone was still there. Taking the porch steps two at a time, Nate landed on wet, gleaming grass and, under a clearing sky, walked toward the school. No one he passed raised a head toward him.

In the deserted classroom, he came face to face with Sedna. Excitement seized him, and in an easy flow, words came pouring from his mouth. From her corner, Della heard him speak the same language the naked woman had spoken. When they stopped, Nate turned and left the room. Sedna watched him go.

Almost at once she'd heard Aningan speaking in the young Inuk's voice. That her old rival should confront her as soon as she was back among her people did not surprise her. What he said did. Although he'd spoken their common language, there were many words and phrases in it that she didn't understand: expressions that might mean "gripping the land" or "ruling the animals" or "digging up stones from under the ground." He'd thrown them at her mockingly, as if to flaunt his knowledge and to ridicule her ignorance. He told her she didn't know what her people were like now. He told her to go to her home in the sea; no one believed in her anymore.

If true, this was serious. But Sedna smiled.

How could she have forgotten Aningan's love of trickery? If true . . . but course it wasn't. He'd made up all those words she couldn't understand. And as for people no longer believing in her, look how she'd just terrified them. Clearly her powers were as great as ever, and Anigat's attempt to convince her they were not only proved how envious he was. Sedna looked complacently around the wrecked classroom — and saw Della. The girl shrank farther into her corner.

But in Della, Sedna saw her own young self. She began to speak again, but in a softer voice. She told Della how she had once sat by the bay, combing her hair and waiting for a lover, and how the handsome man who'd sung her into his kayak had proved to be a seahawk, not a man, and how her father and brothers, coming to rescue her, had cruelly maimed her — here she lifted her hands — but how falling through the ocean to its floor had changed her into the great spirit she now was. Della listened and, although understanding nothing, heard in Sedna's voice, as it reached her across the silent wreckage of the classroom, something that made her fear evaporate and a warmth spread through her.

While the last black clouds vanished from the eastern sky, Sedna told the girl what she must do to become the angakuq she wished her to be, what enabling ordeals she must endure, and when they were done, what spells to use to visit her in her stone house under the sea, bringing news of her people and a comb. When she was finished, she turned and walked out of the room. Tangled black hair falling onto her shoulders, breasts, and back, she passed through the empty village between its alien structures toward the giant insect still nodding at the shore walking under a cloudless sky fading toward the pallor of an ordinary Arctic summer midnight. Her mind rinsed as clear as the air, she reached the beach of her childhood and walked back into the sea. From behind their windows, some people in Poniktuk saw her go, but none ever said they did. In the bay, fish, seals, and whales followed her into deeper water.

The sisters had finally fallen asleep side by side in Nate's bed. While he lay, still awake, on the living-room couch, marvelling at all that had happened this evening, and Ruth and Eli — but not the other two usual occupants of the house — had retired bewildered to their own bedroom, two figures were still outdoors in Poniktuk under a sky that was lightening once more toward dawn.

One of them, clothes slowly drying, stood at the airstrip, waiting for the plane from Uugaaqtuk. It would carry him away from here on the first leg of a lifelong journey of many flights. He avoided looking at the severed caribou heads lying tilted on their antlers near the strip and gazed instead at the land beyond, where at first a few and then more and more living caribou broke from the fringes of the herd and moved toward the hills. As the whole mass of animals stirred and shifted and slowly withdrew up the hillsides like a rippling brown tide, the clicking of their ankle bones and the grunting of cows filled the morning air. Behind him, a float plane took off from the bay.

The other solitary figure, one of the two usual occupants still missing from Eli and Ruth's house, stood looking down at what Harry Ingasuk's dog had left at the edge of the schoolhouse berm. It was the other still absent member of the household. Young Helen stooped and picked up her daughter's body.

FIVE

Village, Moon, Sea

"Will you take me to Ralph?" Gwen asked Trish first thing the next morning.

"But we don't know where he is."

"Ask Ruth."

"All right. And if the phones are working, I'll call mother from the nursing station. God, I can't believe I found you!"

She hugged her sister and left her. In the kitchen she found four people seated by the window. They turned their heads as she came in.

"I'm Gwen's sister Trish," she said, smiling. "Or maybe you've told them already." She looked at Nate, the smile frozen. He shook his head. "Anyway, she's told me how you've looked after her. I don't know how to thank you. You saved her life. But now we're looking for Ralph. Are you Ruth?"

Ruth nodded.

"Can you tell me where he is?"

Ruth shrugged.

"Do *you* know?" Again to Nate. Again he shook his head.

"Oh. Well, I'll find out from Ethel. She came back last night, you know."

Only Eli acknowledged this piece of news. He lifted a hand.

"So where is the nursing station?"

Nate pointed.

"Big blue building that way."

"Thanks." No one moved or spoke. "And thanks again for taking care of my sister."

After wondering for an awkward moment why they were all so quiet — she'd ask Ethel — Trish crossed the kitchen and the storage room and stepped onto the back porch into bright sunlight. She squinted and took a deep breath. She'd found them, and they were all right. Thank God.

"I was frantic," Ethel said, as they drank coffee in her apartment above the nursing station. "We didn't know what had become of you. Then that storm hit and the phones went out, and when it was over Gary said he had to leave. I didn't know what to do."

"I'm sorry. I tried to call you."

"That's okay, honey. I figured somebody would take you in. But when the rain stopped and you still didn't turn up, I got worried again. But I told myself I know the people in this town, and there's no one going to do you any harm. Except now you tell me that randy young Nate tried to put some moves on you, the little bastard. I guess you took care of *him*. Anyway, I got some sleep and had breakfast and went looking for you, and there you were looking for me. But I can't believe it. Both your sister and her husband right here in Poniktuk. I told you not to give up."

Trish smiled.

"Still, there's something funny going on. The whole town's deserted. But that's not it. Everyone sleeps late all the time. But something's happened. And now that you tell me Ruth and Eli didn't say anything about your brother-in-law, and Young Helen too, not even hello. But we'll find out. Meantime, we'll just fix up the beds in my ward for your sister and him, and what'll you bet, before we're finished, someone'll come running to tell me what's going on. Della, maybe. Then we'll go back to Eli's and find out where that guy is."

But no one came running to tell Ethel anything. And after finishing their coffee and making the beds, and after Trish had tried without success to use Ethel's phone to call Edwina — it sometimes took three or four days to fix the phones, Ethel said — they left the nursing station.

In the kitchen at Ruth and Eli's, they learned that today was not, after all, a day for celebration.

"Dog kill our Sarah," Eli told Ethel. "We wrap her up good and put her in bedroom. Maybe you could take her to nursing station till we dig grave?"

"Dear Father in Heaven!" Ethel said.

But that wasn't all.

"No," said Ruth, shaking her head. "I never say nothing about husband, about white fella. We never find nobody like that. We just taking care of lady."

Trish went into the bedroom and told Gwen. While she sat holding her sister, speaking words Gwen didn't hear, an angry voice exploded in the next room: Young Helen, refusing to let Ethel take Sarah's body.

Later, when Ruth brought Gwen her clothes, washed and neatly folded, the sight of them evoked what her memory had suppressed.

"He drowned," she whispered. "He drowned in the river. I saw him."

And she collapsed.

Around noon, she and Trish moved into the nursing station's two-bed ward. Ethel had roused the town mechanic from sleeping off the six-pack he'd drunk the night before and got him to drive them in the water truck. Too hung over to more than glance at his passengers, even the two unfamiliar females, though he made a mental note to find out who they were later, he let them squeeze into the cab, Ethel beside him, Gwen on the outside. During the ride, Gwen paid no attention to the village.

From their windows some Poniktungmiut watched the truck

go by, but all day long no one, except a few children, ventured out of doors.

C

Four days later was voting day in the land-rights referendum. Normally the school served as the town polling place, but Nate put up notices naming the fire hall instead.

He set up a table and chair inside the hall door and put the voter registration ledger, the ballots he'd received from ABRA, and the ballot box on the table. He sat down behind it and waited for people to come and vote. But although many had by now resumed at least an appearance of normality in their lives, visiting from house to house or riding threewheelers to the store or just walking around town, no one except Lawrence stopped to sign the ledger and mark a ballot. At lunchtime Nate went home and, after lunch, asked Lawrence to mind the table for the rest of the afternoon while he joined Wayne in tending a small fire on the outskirts of town in the cemetery. It had been started three days ago to melt the permafrost.

At six in the evening, the close of polling hours, Nate returned to the fire station, and noting that no one besides himself and Lawrence had signed the ledger, he picked it up along with the ballot box and the unused ballots and carried them all upstairs to the settlement council office. Simon was waiting for him and, producing a key, unlocked the box.

Inside they found eleven ballots. Poniktuk had a voter registration of one hundred and seven. Of the eleven ballots, five were marked in favour of the ABRA agreement (two were Lawrence's and Nate's), four were marked opposed (one was Simon's, who'd voted while Nate was having lunch), and two were spoiled. A crude drawing of a female body with breasts hanging off a stick torso below a balloon head covered one of the spoiled ballots. The face was distorted in a grimace of terror or rage, its eyes huge and surrounded by heavy lines like rays and its mouth full of pointed teeth. The body had no arms. Simon and Nate studied the drawing in silence. There was writing in symbols on the other spoiled ballot that, after a moment's study, Simon said must be Old Piuyuk's because he was the only person in Poniktuk who'd ever learned syllabics. Neither he nor Nate could read them.

The question was what to do with these results. The ballots for and against the agreement and the spoiled ones lay in three little piles on Simon's desk.

"No use reporting," he said. "It too pitiful."

"If we don't report, they'll ask us."

"We tell 'em Poniktuk forget to vote."

"But we voted."

"So little vote don't count for nothing!"

"But it's how we voted."

"It so pitiful everyone make fun of us if they know. 'Poniktuk vote eleven, two spoiled.' You want whole region to know that?"

"If that's the vote, that's the vote," Nate said.

They both knew the rule about a majority needed in each community for the whole referendum to pass, but the rules said nothing about how many people in a community had to vote.

"Maybe I just tear up them ballots," Simon said.

Nate's eyes went to the piles on the desk. He suppressed an impulse to lay his hand on them.

"What if whole region hear about *that?*"

"You tell, I kill you."

But even as he spoke the words, they both heard the threat ring false. Simon had disgraced himself at the land-rights meeting, and he knew it. And he knew Nate knew it. And he knew everyone else who'd been there knew it too. In that one display of anger, he'd compromised his years of power.

"It don't bother me what you do with them goddamn ballots," he said, sweeping them off his desk. The ballots fluttered to the floor as he left the room.

Nate watched his uncle go and knelt to pick up the pieces of paper. His face showed no emotion while he re-sorted and stacked them, sat in Simon's chair, and reached for the phone to report Poniktuk's results to headquarters in Inuvik. But his heart was high: if things had gone well in the other communities, his village was about to join them in a great future.

At headquarters Andy Kublu accepted Nate's report without comment. Later, as Andy had told him to do, he called him back and learned that the region had voted overwhelmingly Yes.

But when word of Poniktuk's five-to-four majority spread to the other communities, the village did not escape the ridicule Simon had feared, although that was nothing compared to the censure and shock over the reports of mayhem at the pre-vote meeting, rumours of spirit worship and even of the sacrifice of a child. The other ABRA villages began to feel uneasy about Poniktuk joining them in anything. But awareness of this uneasiness reached Poniktuk only slowly, and when it did, the Poniktungmiut ignored it. They had other things on their minds.

First was the matter of the two Gwens, or the single Gwen split in two. Almost everyone who'd been at the meeting remembered it was the red-haired, full-bodied Gwen in the classroom door who started all the trouble. And although an explanation of how one white lady had apparently made herself into two circulated through the village after Ruth sent Nate to the nursing station to find out how Gwen was doing and Ethel told him about twins, persistent superstition about her arrival in Poniktuk and tenacious longings associated with her tuque left many unconvinced. Most people were familiar with the biology of twins, twin caribou calves being sometimes seen, but the need to blame someone for their actions at the meeting, coupled with the fact that no one had seen the women, separately or together, come out of the nursing station since they went in, kept suspicion and uncertainty alive.

And then there was Sarah. After Young Helen had refused to let Ethel take her body to the nursing station, Eli had made it clear he'd not allow it to remain in Helen's bedroom long. Isaac Ivalu suggested the community freezer, but that was already packed to the ceiling with caribou carcasses, and Helen objected fiercely to her child's being treated like meat. So when Obie, newly restored to grace, offered to lead a graveside service as soon as a grave was ready, everyone agreed, and Nate and Wayne and others started the small rectangular fire at the cemetery.

Now the grave was dug.

In the meantime, there had been another kind of digging. Waking at midmorning after the meeting, Zebediah had lain in bed in a sweat recalling what had happened. When he turned on his side, the pain from a bruise on his ribs reminded him of an elbow jab he'd received while trying to reach the classroom window, and that reminded him of his own pushing and jabbing. The memory shamed him, and blotting out the sight that had caused his and everyone else's panic, he heard again the babble of voices that had earlier filled the room and his own voice among them confessing about antlers. As the whole improbable scheme to saw off antlers in the velvet from more than a hundred caribou heads, call in the Chinese guy with a float plane to take them away and give him thousands of dollars, and then to flood Poniktuk with exotic products, when the whole village knew that the sale was illegal and just one loose or boastful tongue would land him and who knew how many others in jail — as the scheme came back to him in excruciating detail, he realized how crazy it had been from the very beginning. What had got into him? But now he must do something. He rolled out of bed and dressed.

Zeb stopped at the HTA office only long enough to remove a letter from his desk and put it in a pocket of his jeans. Then he went to the town garage and, pushing aside the town mechanic, climbed into the seat of the town's front-end loader. Driving out the airstrip road, he continued across the meadow beyond the strip till he reached a ravine at the base of a hill. There he'd dug a large pit. When he judged it deep enough, he climbed off the loader and threw the letter in. He watched it flutter down. Then he drove back to the strip.

He'd not been home since then. Using the front-end loader

to carry two or three heads at a time, he'd gone back and forth between the caribou killing ground and the pit. At the beginning of each trip, he stopped the rig alongside the airstrip, climbed down, and, gripping a head by its antlers, heaved it into the scoop. The heads were heavy and awkward, and often when he swung one, the velvet on the antlers came off in his hands. They soon became sticky with scraps of velvet and blood from under the velvet. He wiped his hands on his jeans. When he reached the pit, he dumped the heads in.

Once, the town mechanic came out and shouted at him to bring the rig back to the garage so he could change the oil, but Zeb ignored him. The mechanic went to Simon and asked him to intervene. But Simon had finished the forty-ouncer of CC that Tremonte had brought him and, despite Ruby's loud objections, had started on another bottle taken from a remembered hiding place. He said he didn't give a flying fuck what happened to the front-end loader. The mechanic gave up and went home, put his feet on the coffee table, and popped a can of beer. It bothered him to hear the distant groan and whine of the front-end loader's gears and the rattle of its treads as Zeb drove back and forth to the burial pit, but, like Simon, he kept on drinking.

Now Zeb was moving the last two heads. The rig moved slowly along the tracks it had made in the fragile topsoil. They would be visible for many years to remind the Poniktungmiut, whether they liked it or not, of the time when a huge herd of caribou had arrived out of season and stayed for days and of the many strange things that had happened then. When Zeb had unloaded the last heads, he sat looking at the pile. The pit he'd dug wasn't deep enough. Soft unblinking eyes stared up at him, and antlers pointed in every direction. Zeb made a last swift calculation of the money he was burying: a fortune. Then he backed up the rig, turned it toward the earth he'd dug out of the pit, and, scooping a load, emptied it over the heads.

When the last staring eye had disappeared, he drove the rig onto the mound, backed off, and then drove on and off, back and forth across the mound to pack it down. The roar of the loader's engine muffled the sound of snapping antlers. When he was finished, he turned back toward town but abandoned the loader halfway there when its engine seized. He walked home.

Stretching out fully clothed on his bed, Zeb fell asleep. Although his dreams were filled with images of caribou eyes and Obie and a Chinese guy and hands with no fingers, this time he didn't remember them when he woke. For two days he stayed in bed, getting up only to eat and go to the bathroom. So he missed Sarah's funeral.

But the rest of the village was there. Under a sky whose infinite blue bowl of the day after the meeting had been gradually filling with flat grey clouds that brought with them cold air in a first hint of winter, the people of Poniktuk walked out to the cemetery. They stood with bowed heads among wooden crosses around a small mound of fresh earth.

"The Lord bless us and save us," Obie said.

They said, "Amen."

"Lord been taking little Sarah to him," he went on, looking at the sky. "We never know why he do that kind of thing, but this time I been feeling to really trust his wisdom in it because it seem like maybe it not time yet for her to go." He stopped, and his audience waited apprehensively to hear if this line of thought would lead to laying blame on anyone for her early going. "But the Lord know best even we don't understand," he continued, lowering his eyes to regard his audience, which breathed easier. "And we trust him. Oh yes, Lord, we trust you even they's lots of things been happening these days we find hard to figger. Some peoples been doing things these days make it seem like maybe they been forgetting you. Been, like Bible say, worshipping false images. Golden calf. But worse. Some peoples, much worse. But we asking you right here, Lord, please forgive us. And please take away right now them things, even maybe them persons, that been causing us to be forgetting you, causing us to fall into all kinds evil ways. You send them things maybe just to test us, but we fail you this time, Lord. We fail you bad. And maybe you been taking little Sarah from us so we see just how bad we fail." Again he stopped, and there wasn't a listener whose conscience neglected to present him or her with an example of recent failed behaviour. "Little Sarah an angel now," Obie concluded. "She happy now up there in Heaven playing with all them other angels. She been suffering terrible while on earth, but now she happy and blessed. We ask you, Lord, help us get that way too. Amen."

After murmuring their own Amens, people lift their heads and, one by one, left the cemetery. Few met others' eyes, but most had a feeling of being cleansed that might have come from having admitted failures to themselves but more likely came from feeling absolved from blame because it had been laid elsewhere. Now, many thought, if only them womens would go away.

Among Obie's fellow Evangelicals there had been some disappointment when his graveside service had not included speaking in tongues. Only as time went by did it become clear that he would never speak that way again, although, out of their hearing, for the rest of his life he held long silent conversations with a not-so-Gentle Jesus.

C

In Ottawa, Edwina was on the phone to Ralph's uncle in Vermont.

"I'm so sorry," she said for the third time.

"I just can't understand it. He knew how to run rapids. I taught him myself."

"Yes."

"And you say they haven't found a body?"

"No."

"Just the canoe? Or what they think is the canoe? What's left of it?"

"That's what Tricia said. And that's what . . . Isn't that what the inspector said too, when you talked to him?"

"Yes. Yes, that's right."

There was a silence.

"I expect we'll have some kind of service here when Gwen feels up to it," said Edwina. "You'll come up for it, I hope."

"Of course."

There was another silence.

"I just can't believe it. I just can't."

"I know."

"But I'm so relieved Gwen's all right. I really am. He'd have wanted that."

"Yes."

"When she's feeling ready, whenever that might be, do you suppose she could tell me what happened out there? Only if she wants to, of course."

"Of course. I don't know yet myself."

There was more silence.

"Thanks for calling, Edwina," Ralph's uncle said.

"I'm glad I did."

"We'll talk."

And they hung up.

Edwina considered the bookshelves lining the wall of her study. There was something she hadn't mentioned, something she was almost ashamed to be thinking. But the thought persisted. Was it too much, was it crass of her, to be wondering — and, she had to admit, hoping — there was a chance that Gwen was going to have a baby? Or would her ordeal have made that impossible, even if she'd started a pregnancy early in the trip. It had been, after all, a honeymoon.

No, really, I mustn't think about that, she told herself. It's too soon. Where was I? Oh yes. She turned to her computer.

Before a year had passed, Edwina would have her wish, but which daughter granted it would surprise her.

C

Gwen was feeling stronger, but Ethel said she wasn't strong enough to travel. The weather had remained cool and skies overcast, and from the windows of Ethel's apartment on the second floor of the nursing station, Gwen and Trish saw nothing to tempt them out of doors. They stayed inside and talked. In answer to her sister's questioning, Trish described their mother's worry when she didn't get the expected phone call and her own determination to come north. She left out her losing hope and Chief Inspector MacTavish's grim conclusions, dwelling instead on her lucky meeting with Ethel in Yellowknife and praising the nurse's unfailing encouragement. In turn, Gwen little by little told her what she remembered of wandering on the tundra and then, one afternoon as they sat side by side on Ethel's couch, described Ralph's drowning. When she finished and tearfully expressed again her belief that Ruth had told her Ralph was also being taken care of in the village, Trish hugged her and said nothing, but she privately believed Gwen had made that up. They spent time cooking, browsing through Ethel's collection of romance and detective novels, sleeping long hours in the two-bed ward, and, when the phones worked, calling Ottawa. They also made reservations on the next sched out of Poniktuk.

Making her rounds of the village, Ethel picked up gossip and repeated it when she thought the sisters would be amused, but she kept to herself the hints she heard that they were responsible for Sarah's death. The allegation shocked but didn't surprise her. People in Poniktuk needed scapegoats when something bad happened, and as strangers Gwen and Trish were an obvious choice. But no one dropped any hints to Ethel about the disastrous meeting on the evening of her return or about the goings-on in Father's old shed while she was away.

Della had missed her. As the only representative of the outside world residing in Poniktuk — Della discounted the town mechanic — Ethel had become a dispenser of wisdom to Big Helen's adolescent daughter and, as a nurse, a source of awesome information about the human body and its diseases. But now Della stayed away from the nursing station. She'd seen the water truck go by and had heard the explanation given to Nate about identical twins. That it came from Ethel carried great weight, and its description of the two white ladies as ordinary human beings, one even having been on a canoe trip, caused Della's belief in that person's miracle-making to seriously deteriorate. But this loss of faith hardly concerned her now; her thoughts were filled to the brim with reviewing her experiences in the classroom after everyone else had fled. The arrival in its doorway of the mutilated naked figure seemed to her now, just by itself, more miraculous than Obie's discovering a lady on a hillside. But that wasn't all. Nate's encounter with the figure, his speaking her language, and finally the figure's speech to her that, by its tone alone, had been kind and even loving — all this convinced Della that she'd moved far beyond attending an improvised shrine to a lost tuque. She was now the guardian of greater mysteries. But she hesitated to share her knowledge, even with Nurse McGarr and certainly not with Selma, although she'd taken pains to make it clear to her friend that she now possessed a powerful new secret. Selma's pleading to hear it and her threat that she'd never speak to Della again if she didn't tell provoked only smug, tight-lipped grimaces and dismissive, heavenward eye rolling. But there *was* a person who stood beside her in the aura of those mysteries: Nate. To hold that thought and imagine the moment, which was sure to come, when she and her cousin would consecrate their sharing in acts like the ones she'd once imagined him and the lady in his bed performing thrilled Della. She clung to that vision of a future union and never returned to Father's old shed. Nor did any Poniktungmiut except, on one occasion, Nate.

As years passed, the straw in the archery target rotted and sagged, the upside-down shuttlecocks and offerings on the shelf in front of it gathered layers of dust, the badminton raquet fell on its face, and the striped woollen tuque stretched over it, like the Boy Scout and Girl Guide uniforms lying folded in the crate below it, mouldered.

Poniktuk having chosen, by however small a margin, a future of shared self-government, Nate now had time on his hands: no more fieldwork to do because the next steps, Andy Kublu said, were debate, passage, and proclamation of the Agreement in Principle by the Federal Parliament, and that would take a while. He'd call him when his help was needed for implementation.

But Nate was not enjoying being idle. Although his old occupations of walking in the hills, checking his father's nets, and listening to tapes with Lawrence and other fans of Tiny Tim and KISS still attracted him, their practice left him restless and dissatisfied. Sarah's ghost haunted the rooms of his parents' house, and he returned there only to eat and sleep. But sleep did not come easily as he lay in his own bed again; the eiderdown under his chin and the pillow under his head smelled of the woman who'd been lying there. He tossed and turned, trying to escape her scent and also relishing it. During sleepless nights and idle days, images of making love to her or to her sister or to both of them obsessed him. He took to dawdling at vantage points in the village from which he could watch the nursing station. Every now and then visions of the women moving inside the building, dressing or undressing, cooking, reading, talking, came into his mind and tantalized him. Then he'd rub the object in his jacket pocket that he'd taken back from Father's shed; perhaps its magic had already worked to turn one woman into two.

"I think I'll go for a walk," Gwen said, standing at a window of Ethel's apartment on the afternoon of the day before she and Trish were due to leave Poniktuk.

Billowy folds of cloud filled the sky, but under them a soft, grey light fell on the distant hills.

"Want me to come with you?"

"No. I'd just like to go up there and look around."

"Up where?"

"Those hills."

Remembering her own refusal of Ethel's company when their plane had landed in Poniktuk and she'd accepted at last that both Gwen and Ralph must be dead, Trish didn't press her sister.

"You sure you feel strong enough?"

"I feel fine."

"I might have a nap," Trish said.

When Gwen had picked up her jacket from the ward, Trish said, "Don't overdo it," and watched her sister start down the station's corridor. Ethel stepped out of the dispensary.

"Where you going, honey?"

"Just for a walk."

"Sure you feel strong enough?"

"Yes, yes. Thanks. I'm fine."

"I'll walk you as far as Big Helen's. Gotta talk to her about something."

They went out the door. Nate saw them.

He wasn't the only one to watch Gwen walk along the village road. For those familiar with her tuque in its shadowy sanctuary, it was a chance to examine Gwen herself in daylight. And although the yellow hair falling onto her shoulders looked as remarkable as Della had once said it was, the lady herself in the light of day looked almost ordinary, a woman much like other women in the village, if thinner and with skin a colour that confirmed that she was white. (This walk through the village marked the beginning for many people of the separation of Gwen's actual self from the imagined being who'd lain so long out of sight in Ruth and Eli's house, had been the subject of so much awe and superstition, who now was being blamed for the recent shameful happenings, and who would haunt their collective memory for years to come.)

But Nate was the only one observing Gwen whose thoughts were on her twin. Waiting till Gwen was out of sight, he stepped away from where he'd been pretending to study the sky for weather and sauntered toward the nursing station. He tightened his grip on the object in his pocket.

269

Inhaling the sharp smells of disinfectant and mopping fluid in the pale green corridor, Nate paused. He heard nothing. Proceeding past the dispensary to the ward, he held his breath, lifted the latch, released it, pushed the door open, and stepped through. In the soft light filtering into the room through half-closed venetian blinds, he saw Trish lying on a bed. She was asleep. Nate closed the door as quietly as he'd opened it and began to take off his clothes.

Halfway across the spongy meadowland leading to the hills, Gwen's legs were already tired from adjusting every step to the uneven ground, sometimes soft, sometimes firm. Hoofprints everywhere had also broken up the soil, but she'd made up her mind to reach the top of at least the nearest hill.

Half an hour later, sitting and resting her back against a boulder on the gravelly hilltop, she looked inland. As far as her eye could see, more hills and ridges rose and twisted and veered and fell away down cliffs and slopes into gullys and valleys. With no wind stirring, the stillness around her was so deep it seemed physical, as if the hills stored silence in them like a mineral. Only bird calls floated by her in the motionless air. There had to be several birds in places hidden from her sight, for the calls, always sounding the same single, rising note, came to her from different distances and directions. As she listened to the wistful, questioning calls pass back and forth, she imagined that if all the birds were asking one question but none was answering it, they might at least take comfort in all having the same question to ask.

Some clouds had moved away, and sunlight splotched many of the surfaces in her view, brightening the tan of sand or gravel and the green of shrubs and grasses. Out there somewhere was the place where she'd been found. It didn't matter where. But studying the broken landscape as the sun advanced across it toward her, she realized that she knew intimately all its textures — gravel's graininess, grasses' slickness, bushes' prickly twigs, hard rocks. But in the quiet of this soft afternoon, the awareness stirred no memories of pain. Rather, it recalled her first views of this so-called barren countryside as it stretched away from the shores of the lake where she and Ralph had begun their trip and how, under other skies, she'd studied other hills and ridges and meadows and slopes while they travelled down the river. Ralph's death, her wandering, her wakening in a strange bed, her sister's miraculous appearance — all these events seemed to lie before her, spread over the hills like a story told by landscape.

Gwen took a deep breath and sighed it out. For a moment Ralph's love and her love for him had a clarity that seemed to owe as much to the brightness of the sun on the hills before her as to her sudden understanding that her life with him was now conclusively over.

The sunlight reached her hilltop. Feeling its warmth penetrate her clothing, hearing the bird calls, letting her eyes drift across the landscape she knew she'd never see again but would always carry with her, she felt a lulling contentment. Soon she found it difficult to form well-ordered thoughts. Then having any thoughts at all seemed not only difficult but unnecessary. Gwen closed her eyes. She let her mind go blank. In the silence of the afternoon, birdcalls and whispers of wind brushed past her.

Trish felt a hand on her left breast and squirmed pleasurably. The hand went away. She whimpered. A hand unzipped her trousers. She came wide awake.

Leaning over her was a face propped on an elbow. It belonged to the young man who'd taken her in his arms on the schoolhouse steps. Trish lay still. The young man smiled and moved his hand to the top button on her shirt. From hand to shoulder and as far down his chest as she could see, he was naked. Call Ethel, Trish thought. No. She went out with Gwen. She met his eyes firmly with her own. He kept smiling and returned her look. His large black eyes between lids that came together at their outer corners in a decided slant were really quite beautiful. And, now that she studied it, so was the rest of his face: smooth, dark skin, high forehead, wide cheekbones, full lips. Wondering how long she'd been asleep, Trish hoped that Gwen wouldn't come back from her walk soon.

Nate finished unbuttoning her shirt and, releasing his left arm from propping up his head, used both hands to slip the shirt off her shoulders. Trish unbuttoned the cuffs herself. She wasn't wearing a bra. When her shirt was off, Nate rose to his knees, straddled her legs, and grasped her trousers at the waist and pulled. Trish raised and wiggled her hips. When her trousers and panties were at her ankles, she kicked them off. Now he stretched out beside her, head again propped on an elbow, lips still smiling. But this time his free hand rested for a moment on a hipbone and then brushed gently across the dip of her abdomen to her ribcage and over her ribs to a breast and, lifting, cupped it in a warm, dry palm. Trish closed her eyes. A thumb rubbed her nipple. The nipple became hard. She lifted a hand of her own to his wrist and moved her fingertips slowly over a sinewy forearm, around the corner of an elbow, and up over biceps to a muscular shoulder.

Trish felt him press full length against her while the arm that had been holding up his head went around her shoulders. She smelled his hair.

Presently Nate's hand left her breast and, trailing fingertips, moved lightly back over her hip and down her leg to a knee, where it paused while a finger traced her kneecap. Then the hand reversed, drawing slightly scratchy fingertips up the soft inside of her thigh. Trish opened her legs. Nate's hand stopped. She shifted tighter against him and, moving the arm trapped between them under his waist, let her hand feel the bottom of his spine. Her other hand left his shoulder and, moving down, traced the bony ripple of his ribcage, felt the fold of muscle at his waist, and pushing his hip away moved across his abdomen to a patch of silky hair. His hand kneaded her thigh. Her fingers entered the hair and circled the stiffness they found there. She heard him catch his breath, and his own hand stopped moving. Her fingertips moved upward, following a swollen vein, and delicately peeled back the foreskin.

A musky odour reached her nostrils. She gripped the slippery, jumping glans. Nate gasped. Then his own hand moved swiftly to her mound, and, forefinger and thumb parting wet lips, plunged a thick possessing finger into her. Trish cried out.

When he moved his body onto hers and put a hand under her buttocks, she bent her knees and, rolling back on her hips, guided him into her.

"I am the moon," a soft voice whispered in her ear.

"Whatever," Trish murmured and, gripping his buttocks, let her mind go blank.

Old Piuyuk saw Gwen coming. He was sitting in front of his tent on a sled he used as a bench in the summer; in the winter it was for trapping. He watched Gwen approach across the flatlands leading to the hills. Soon, he figured, she'd see him. She saw him. He motioned her over.

Gwen hesitated and then changed direction. She hesitated again when she stood in front of him because he didn't look up. She sat down beside him.

They both stared at the hills.

"Bygone days," Piuyuk said, "us Huskimos see lotsa things. That time, old-time stories say animals and peoples not different. Animals could be peoples any time they feel to be. Other way too. Birds even. Animals and peoples, them days they play games together. All kinds games. How many years now we never play them games. White peoples come. Them games finished. Them times gone. Nowadays we living all the time whiteman time. Huskimo time been finished.

"Only sometimes maybe it not always like that . . .

"Obie bring you down from them hills one day. I see it. Where you come from? How come you get there, lying out on that-there hill? Like caribou maybe. Maybe like bear . . ."

He paused and tipped his head as if listening for something.

"I see you going up to them hills today," Piuyuk went on. "I think maybe you don't come back. I think maybe you on your way to where you come from first time. But you come back all right. I see you. But what you look like when you get up there? In them hills. What you do? Me, that's what I been asking. I figger maybe that-there first time in them hills, sleeping like, you been putting on one white skin just to fool us Huskimos. Play games with us, like old times. I figger maybe you not white lady even right now, sitting here by me on sled. Maybe not animal too. Maybe . . . maybe something else. But that don't scare me. Like some other peoples.

"Some other peoples, they see you at big meeting, they get all funny. You have red hair that time. They holler like crazy. They see other things too. Lady with no clothes on, no fingers on hands neither. They jump out window. Me too, I jump out window. Me too, I feel to be crazy. Then I calm down."

Again he paused, and the warm air stirred around them.

"Then I get to thinking maybe whiteman time never finish Huskimo time like I been believing. Maybe Huskimo time been going on all the time same time whiteman time been going on. Only we just never see it. We been forgetting. Maybe that's why you been lying down on that-there hill, putting on whitelady skin, letting Obie find you. So we could stop forgetting.

"Huskimo time been going long, long time. Whiteman time real short. Maybe they be going on together all the time and us not know it. Maybe we still playing them games . . .

"I finish talking to you now."

Gwen sat still. She'd tried to follow what the old man said: something about different times mixed up together and her being someone else out there on the hills — a caribou or a bear? — and maybe even now, sitting next to him. That was absurd. But just before, on the top of one of the hills she was looking at — but she couldn't tell which — she'd certainly drifted away from herself. Who had she been then? Was it so absurd to be someone you didn't know you were at the same time you were who you thought you were?

I've changed, Gwen thought. I know that. So I'm not who I used to think I was. But I'm still myself. So who is that?

The green interfolding hills in the distance showed tan on their sunstruck summits.

She and Old Piuyuk sat side by side in companionable silence till he got up and went into his tent. Gwen sat a while longer and then walked into town. In the nursing station's two-bed ward, she saw that her sister had taken off her clothes and got under the covers for a real nap. She was still sleeping.

The next day Gwen and Trish caught the sched. At the bottom of Trish's purse lay a small bone comb with some scratchings on one surface. She'd found it in a shirt pocket when she got dressed again yesterday. I'll put it up for sale in the shop, she thought. Or maybe I'll keep it for myself. One of Trish's private treasures.

All the Poniktungmiut who'd gone to the airstrip to meet the sched followed Simon's truck back to town to get their mail. Only Ethel stayed to watch the plane take off. As it rose and dipped a wing to turn toward Inuvik, she waved, hoping to see a face in a window and a hand wave back. But she didn't. She watched till the plane was swallowed by a cloud.

After handing out mail in the store, not stopping to make jokes, Simon sat in his office for the first time since the land-rights meeting. He was hung over. There was a lot of unopened mail on his desk. From his window, he could see people going home, some with packages he'd handed them, others with groceries. Distributing the mail was his first public appearance since the land-rights meeting. Fragmentary memories of his behaviour there had cropped up, enraged and embarrassed him while he was drinking, and he had wondered how people would treat him. He needn't have worried. If anyone had missed his jokes at the store, no one showed it. Everyone listened patiently while he read out names on packages and letters. Some went home rewarded, others empty-handed. Like always.

Nate had posted the results of the referendum at the fire hall, but it wasn't clear that anyone had bothered to read them. Although the outcome had not pleased him, Simon had concluded, when he finally sobered up, that if changes came to

Poniktuk, as they would, there was no reason he shouldn't control them. New government, new problems, new challenges, new strategies. He was up to the job, and people's behaviour in the store proved that the village population was still firmly under his thumb.

Certainly the view from his window was the same as ever. Beyond Poniktuk's brightly coloured houses, the bay sparkled in afternoon sunlight, and the dunes across the bay shimmered in a heat haze. For the moment at least, it was summer again. Simon turned back to his desk. A letter with the return address of RCMP headquarters in Yellowknife caught his eye. He opened it. It was dated several days ago. He read:

> TO: Simon Umingmak, Chairman
> Poniktuk Settlement Council
> Poniktuk, NWT
> FROM: Ch. Insp. Andrew Iain MacTavish,
> RCMP HQ, YK

> Sir:
> It has recently come to my attention as the result
> of a telephone call from RN Ethel McGarr, Poniktuk
> Nursing hall, that a certain Mrs. Ralph Morrissey,
> for whom a massive Search and Rescue operation
> was recently undertaken — at great expense to the
> Government and others — and subsequently aban-
> doned in the belief both she and her husband had
> perished while descending the Blackstone River,
> has in fact been alive in Poniktuk for some time.
> The Morrisseys were the subject of YKHQ Com-
> muniqué No. XPF52983, dated 82.08.02, which
> requested you, as Poniktuk Settlement Council
> Chairman and senior public official responsible
> for government operations in that community, to
> cooperate fully with said Search and Rescue oper-

ation. I am writing to inform you that your failure
to comply with the terms of this communiqué is
considered by RCMP Headquarters to be of the
utmost seriousness. Whether or not it resulted from
deliberate dereliction of duty is only one of many
questions for which an investigation now being
initiated will seek to find answers.

You are to consider yourself the principal subject of this investigation and are to hold yourself
unconditionally available in the settlement of
Poniktuk for interview by RCMP personnel.

I must further inform you that a memo has
been forwarded to the Minister of Local Government this day requesting that you be suspended
from all functions and authority as Poniktuk
Settlement Council Chairman pending completion
of the aforementioned investigation and the
determination of any consequent proceedings.

(signed) Iain Andrew MacTavish, Ch. Insp.
 cc: Dept. Local Government, Inuvik

Simon read the letter twice and then the last paragraph again.

That goddamn woman! What the hell she end up here for
anyways? Shit, I never even see no communiqué. He glanced at
the unopened mail on his desk.

But cursing Gwen, he also remembered how he'd sat here on
the day after Obie brought her to town and how he'd decided to
keep her presence in Poniktuk a secret: he thought he could use
her.

As Simon cursed himself, he skimmed through the letter again
— "dereliction of duty," "interview by RCMP," "suspended,"
"aforementioned investigation," "consequent proceedings." They
were big words in long sentences, but there was no doubt what
they meant: Government was mad at him and RCMP was coming

after him. Simon's years of manipulating Government and being Government had taught him what Government could do when it got mad. Not to mention the RCMP. A queasiness squeezed the settlement council chairman's bowels.

He poked at the pile of unopened mail with a fat forefinger. Under several other envelopes was one from the Office of the Minister of Local Government with IMMEDIATE AND OFFICIAL stamped on it in big red letters. He didn't pick it up. Simon swung his chair back to the window. The sun was still bright on the bay, on the houses, on the dunes. The view hadn't changed, but his life had.

Simon's mouth watered for the taste of CC.

Nate was also thinking about change. A few moments ago, in the middle of the night, he'd come violently awake when he felt all his breath being suddenly sucked out of him. He'd sat up and gulped air.

Now his lungs had filled again, and he reached to lift aside the blanket over his window. Moonlight fell on the outside world. There was night now, summer was ending. Soon geese would start flying back south, strong and fat from their summer feeding. Beating the air with wings newly layered with feathers and flying too high to shoot, they'd ignore any cries, however skilful, to call them down. Now would also be the normal time for bull caribou to appear in the Poniktuk hills, coats glossy and thick and underlaid with fat. But this year, Nate thought, that probably won't happen.

He dropped the blanket and lay back. Pulling the eiderdown to his chin, he considered the goodness of life in Poniktuk. There was a whole winter's supply of meat in the freezer, char were still running at the river, he'd earned enough money from ABRA fieldwork to make a down payment on a snowmobile for trapping, and even if the town's vote in the referendum had been ridiculous, changes were on the way.

Nate went over in his mind section headings in the Agreement in Principle: Game Management, Job Training, Land Management, Cultural Preservation, Economic Development, Education, Self-Government. These magical words created visions of a whole new way of life in Poniktuk, visions as clear and detailed as any he'd ever had of flying geese or migrating caribou or a giant suit of skin clothing high in the sky. But, unlike those, these visions were populated by his friends and relatives.

Nate visioned himself to sleep. And if his sleep was deepened by a sense of certainty about the future of Poniktuk, it may also have been sweetened by memories of making love to a red-haired lady who'd kept deliciously changing back and forth beneath him into one whose hair was yellow.

At the graveyard, the remaining ashes of the fire that had thawed a small rectangle of earth lifted into the air in a gust of wind and blew away in darkness toward the Poniktuk hills. Mounds with crosses at their heads surrounded the small mound covering the rectangle. In the moonlight it did not yet have a cross.

At the town dump, Harry Ingasuk's dog lay on a pile of black plastic garbage bags and oozing honey-bucket bags. Dried blood stiffened the hairs under his jaw and stained his forepaws. Around the bullet hole in his head and the trickle of congealed blood at the corner of his mouth, flies crawled.

And on top of the same hill above Poniktuk where Gwen had sat listening to invisible birds call back and forth across a sunlit silence, moonlight glowed on rocks and gravel. A streak touched the hilltop and lifted off. Anyone watching might have seen a wisp of cloud rise higher and higher into the sky toward a luminous full moon.

C

In the Department of Local Government in Inuvik, Area Officer Bill Tremonte was cleaning out his desk. Since he'd had the job for only three months, there wasn't much to clean out. It was now two weeks since he'd fled the land-rights meeting in

Poniktuk, and not once had he regretted handing his boss a letter of resignation the next morning. Today was his last day.

He'd already taken down from his cubicle walls the postcards of Inuit sculpture and the calendar of Inuit prints with which he'd personalized his workspace. They were now in the wastebasket. The only thing on his desk was a blue government binder. Swivelling in his chair, he opened it to the title page and read "Devolution and Population Distribution in Poniktuk: A Proposal." The upper right-hand corner was stamped "Draft Only." This was his last copy. He turned to the Executive Summary.

". . . research indicating serious dissatisfaction among contemporary Inuit with settlement life . . . originally for humanitarian reasons, but perhaps too sudden and drastic a change from centuries of nomadic existence . . . burden of welfare payments on the Territorial budget . . . phased project . . . family units . . ."

It all sounded great, and it was all bullshit. And he'd written every word himself.

How eager he'd been to please his boss. And how naïve, jumping at the chance to show off his university degree. He'd used all his thesis-writing skills to make the plan seem plausible. He'd even believed what he was writing. But the only purpose of the DPDP had been to get the people of Poniktuk to reject ABRA's land-rights agreement so Simon Umingmak would stay in power and Fraser would look good to the commissioner.

He'd been used.

Tremonte sighed. His resignation letter had been a good one, studiously avoiding any reference to what had happened at the meeting, making its case entirely in terms of "seeking elsewhere, perhaps in the private sector, alternative opportunities for putting to use my academic training." By now, he almost believed that really was why he was quitting.

So that was that. And he was out of here. But he hated that he'd been used. His hand hefted the government binder, and he had an idea.

Tremonte mailed the envelope on his lunch hour. Fraser

hadn't even invited him to lunch on his last day. At the end of the afternoon, however, the deputy assistant supervisor stepped into his cubicle.

"Well, Bill, all set?"

Bill stood up.

"Yessir."

"Desk all shipshape and ready for the next guy?"

"Yup."

"Personally, I'm sorry to see you go," Fraser said, "but you're doing the right thing. Some people just aren't cut out for the north. And there's no use hanging around if you're one of them."

"Yessir."

"I've looked through your final report and everything seems in order. But I wanted to stop by and wish you luck in your next . . . uh, position."

"Thank you."

Fraser shook his hand.

"By the way," he said, "now that the ABRA agreement will be taking effect, that Poniktuk plan is completely obsolete. You don't have a copy of it around here anywhere, do you? Simon's got himself into some trouble with the RCMP. Something to do with a woman canoeist, don't ask me what. But there's an investigation. I wouldn't want the boys in striped pants to get their hands on that proposal. It might make matters worse for Simon. It still around here somewhere?"

"I destroyed all the copies."

"Good man," said Fraser, and went back to his corner office, where late afternoon sunlight streamed through the window and across his desk.

Several weeks later and many thousand kilometres away, Bill Tremonte, pursuing an alternative opportunity for putting to use his academic training as a waiter in a vegetarian restaurant in Halifax, had made sure that he'd properly set all the tables with silverware, glassware, placemats, salt and pepper, candles, and napkins, and stood in the kitchen memorizing the evening's specials. It was only a temporary job, he'd told himself. When he got his shit together, he'd know what to do with the rest of his life.

At almost the same moment, given time-zone differences, Jim Fraser was on his way to the commissioner's office in Yellowknife to have his transfer cancelled. What kind of public works could there be in Grise Fjord, the most isolated northern settlement in Canada, pop. 80? PW wasn't even his speciality. There was some mistake, some bureaucratic fuck-up that a word from the Commish would straighten out. Fraser had made an appointment as soon as he got the transfer notice; going straight to the top was always the smartest thing to do.

Following a panelled corridor on the building's executive floor and anticipating watching the commissioner make a phone call or dictate a memo, Fraser turned a corner and saw the man himself.

"Ah, Jim, just the person I was hoping to run into," the commissioner boomed, raising a hand the size of a bear paw in a way that some might have found more threatening than friendly. "No need for us to meet in my office. I've just forwarded your transfer documents, and I'm already late for my next appointment. My secretary will give you everything you need."

Fraser wondered how the commissioner could be late for his next appointment when he hadn't even started the appointment with him. Then what he'd said sank in. He stopped in his tracks. The commissioner towered over him. Not for nothing was he nicknamed "Aklak" — grizzly bear — among the Inuit.

"You'll love it in Grise, Jim. Give you a chance to get away from all the administrative hassles you've had to put up with in Inuvik. Get back to working with the people. I know how much you've been wanting to do that. Your proposal for Poniktuk was really interesting. Thanks for sending it. Impractical there, but Grise might be just the ticket. Lifestyle's really traditional, almost nobody speaks English. Not much in the way of public works, so you'll have plenty of time to learn the language and try out your ideas. Walrus and seal in the waters around there too, I hear. Damn good thing, probably. Supply barge sometimes has a hard time getting in. No more pork chops on the back porch barbecue, eh Jim? I expect you'll acquire quite a taste for seal flippers."

The commissioner smiled good-naturedly. "We'll be expecting great things of you in Grise, Jim. We'll be keeping an eye on ya, fella."

The commissioner clapped him on the shoulder and passed by. But halfway down the corridor he stopped and spoke over his shoulder.

"You probably won't need to know this in Grise, Jimbo. But just for your personal information, it was always Territorial Government policy, my policy, to be a hundred percent behind the ABRA land-rights agreement. Anything getting in the way of that would be a real no-no."

Then, unlocking the door to keep his next appointment, he stepped into the executive men's room.

C

*Aningan tethered **his dogs** and looked around. His own soft moonlight fell on the hills of the land in the sky. On the shores of silvery lakes and rivers stood many caribou-skin tents. Everyone inside them was asleep.*

He was happy to be home.

Hurrying to the double house he shared with his sister Siqiniq, he wished he could tell her the many things he'd learned while visiting the world below. But the events during winter dancing time that had sent them rising into the sky while they changed from adolescent boy and girl to ruling spirits of the upper air had separated them forever. While he slept in his half of their house, she stayed awake filling the sky with light, and while she slept, he sent his pale reflection of her radiance into the darkness. Although she never left their double home, he kept himself busy, while he could, with looking after the Inuit dead who'd come to the land in the sky to be with him.

To them, he now thought, he'd tell his adventures in the world below, where they too had once lived.

But when Aningan told these listeners about land ownership in fee simple absolute and royalties from subsurface mineral rights and economic development strategies and game management and about refrigerators and garbage trucks and snowmobiles and telephones and radios and airplanes and schoolbooks and toasters and chairs and tables and KISS and Tiny Tim, their eyes widened, and they sucked their breath in between their teeth. If they didn't actually disbelieve him, he realized, neither did they understand him. To hunt, fish, eat, sleep, and play games — these were their activities. His stories about living Inuit evoked in these Inuit dead only the shy respect they always paid him. Aningan gave up detailing the wonders of the modern world.

But if he couldn't share his experiences, he didn't abandon his memories. For his sojourn in Poniktuk in the body of the young Inuk had revealed to him new ways to perform his old role of benefactor. He'd quickly understood that helping Inuit was no longer a matter of providing men with hunting dreams and women with impregnating rays of moonlight. It had even embarrassed him to discover how out of date such ideas of benevolence were. But in the Aboriginal Rights Alliance's goals of Inuit self-determination, Aningan had recognized new ways to perform his traditional activities. It had taken some prodding and the bestowing of a magical gift or two to make the young man see things the way he wanted him to, but he'd appreciated Nate's excitement when he began to understand the purposes of their combined exertions.

One of the most vivid exertions had been the hour they shared, on a warm afternoon in a darkened room, with a woman whose surprising hair kept changing colour and whose skin was soft and white as a cloud. He'd always relish that memory.

As he'd also always relish the brief meeting he'd had with his old rival Sedna, who must have heard he'd returned to earth and had risen from her home at the bottom of the sea to challenge him. He'd trounced her.

These and many other memories stayed with Aningan as he lived on the moon, where days and nights came and went but never added up to any measure of human time. There was only the endless changing of darkness into daylight and daylight back to darkness and darkness to daylight again.

But now that he'd lived once more in the world below, the moon spirit often knelt before the opening in the floor of his home and, having pushed aside the bleached caribou shoulderbone that covered it, looked down at that world while winds of the upper atmosphere sighed and whistled past. In particular he studied the village of Poniktuk. And as human time there added up to weeks and months and years, he observed — sometimes with exasperation, sometimes with pleasure — how life there endlessly went on.

C

In her home on the floor of the Polar Sea, Sedna sat on her stone bench. Her father Isarrataitsuq lay on his bench across the room. Seals and whales, narwhal, walruses, and fish swam languidly overhead. She was waiting.

Her visit to the world above had been everything she'd wanted it to be. Her people might speak a new language and they were certainly living in strange new igloos and wearing strange clothes, but her power over them was indisputable. Even now she could hear their frenzied babble inside the big square igloo, imploring her to enter, and could see in her mind's eye their terror when she did appear and how they fled from her through a shattered panel of clear ice in the wall. These were satisfying memories. So was the memory of how quickly she'd understood the moon spirit Aningan's attempt to trick her into believing her power over her people was gone.

Now she was waiting for the girl.

A tremor rippled the surface of Sedna's mind. Would that girl, so like herself when she was young, who alone had stayed behind in the big meeting place when all the others fled, do as she had told her? To become an angakuq was a difficult task, often painful, especially for a girl.

Sedna raised an arm to her forehead as if to brush away doubt. A wash of water caressed her face.

She'll be here, she told herself. The girl will come.

Her fingerless hand stroked the hair floating around her shoulders.

The girl will come, Sedna thought, and when she does, she'll comb and braid my hair and clean my body. For I am Sedna.

Great Sedna.

The thought swayed in her mind like sea grass. Then she slept.